"YOU WOULD MARRY ME TO ACQUIRE LANDI"

Megan's green eyes flashed as she continued, "Am I supposed to be flattered?"

"What a little romantic you are, Megan!" Kurt laughed scornfully. "I'm offering you my name and my fortune, and you want tender declarations. So—will you marry me if I tell you I love you?"

Megan winced. "To get that land you'd do or say anything, wouldn't you, Kurt? Even sell yourself to me like a gigolo—"

There was a deadly stillness, and Megan knew she'd gone too far. Suddenly she was aware of her sheer nightgown, how her body must be outlined against the moonlight.

With steely hands he grasped her shoulders and forced her to him. "You may question my motives," Kurt declared in a voice hoarse with fury, "but you will never question this." And his mouth came down on hers.

AND NOW...

 HARLEQUIN SUPERROMANCES

As the world's No. 1 publisher of best-selling romance fiction, we are proud to present a sensational new series of modern love stories— HARLEQUIN SUPERROMANCES.

Written by masters of the genre, these longer, sensual and dramatic novels are truly in keeping with today's changing life-styles. Full of intriguing conflicts, the heartaches and delights of true love, HARLEQUIN SUPERROMANCES are absorbing stories—satisfying and sophisticated reading that lovers of romance fiction have long been waiting for.

HARLEQUIN SUPERROMANCES
Contemporary love stories for the woman of today!

THE MUSIC OF PASSION

LYNDA WARD

Harlequin Books

TORONTO • LONDON • LOS ANGELES • AMSTERDAM
SYDNEY • HAMBURG • PARIS • STOCKHOLM • ATHENS • TOKYO

Harlequin first edition, May 1981

ISBN 0-373-70003-2

Copyright © 1981 by Lynda Ward. All rights reserved.
Philippine copyright 1981. Australian copyright 1981.
Except for use in any review, the reproduction or utilization of
this work in whole or in part in any form by any electronic,
mechanical or other means, now known or hereafter invented,
including xerography, photocopying and recording, or in any
information storage or retrieval system, is forbidden without
the permission of the publisher, Harlequin Enterprises Limited,
225 Duncan Mill Road, Don Mills, Ontario, Canada M3B 3K9.

All the characters in this book have no existence outside the
imagination of the author and have no relation whatsoever to
anyone bearing the same name or names. They are not even
distantly inspired by any individual known or unknown to the
author, and all the incidents are pure invention.

The Harlequin trademark, consisting of the words
HARLEQUIN SUPERROMANCE and the portrayal of a Harlequin,
is registered in the United States Patent Office and in the
Canada Trade Marks Office.

Printed in U.S.A.

CHAPTER ONE

KURT VON KLEIST yanked back the maroon velvet draperies and stared out at the trees. Across the sweeping lawn from his study window a stand of tall birches shivered and bowed restlessly under the onslaught of the hot foehn wind. Beyond the slender, silver-barked birch trees massive oaks and beeches covered the hillside, their thick foliage virid, almost luminous under the July sun. Kurt could see one arm of the lake glinting through the forest at the foot of the hill, its usually serene surface agitated and troubled, a reflection of his own mood. Little whitecaps contrasted sharply with the water that was even bluer than the Austrian sky, but for once the breathtaking beauty of the scene failed to soothe him. It had all been familiar and beloved by him since birth, but now as he looked at it he repressed a frisson of foreboding. Countless von Kleists before him had stood where he stood, admiring the same view, accepting it as their birthright—but would those who came after him be able to do the same?

As Kurt gazed out the window he reached automatically for his cigarette case, fumbling at a pocket until he remembered that the container was in his suit jacket, slung across the back of the swivel chair in which until a few minutes earlier he had been trying fitfully to work. With jerky nervous movements unusual to him he extracted the flat gold box and opened it. He grimaced. The case was empty, although he had refilled it only that morning. He coughed derisively as he looked at the overflowing ashtray on his desk. When he crossed the room in long strides to get more cigarettes, he thought wryly that if the smoking didn't kill him, his doctor just might. He was under orders to cut down.

From a cabinet behind the bar he took out a pack of strong filterless cigarettes. With practiced ease he tore off the tape with the thumb and little finger of his left hand. He stopped and stared at his injured hand. Ordinarily he was no more conscious of it than he was of the long graceful fingers of his right hand, but now, with a visitor coming, he regarded it anew. After twenty-five years the scar was only a ragged hairline running across the tanned skin just below the knuckles. It was almost invisible, except for those times when it whitened with his efforts to bend the stiff middle fingers. A doctor had once told him that his ability to move those fingers at all suggested that the severed nerves could be restored through microsurgery, but Kurt had said he couldn't be bothered. Had the technology been available when the accident happened, when he was a boy of thirteen, his whole life might have been quite different; but now, a quarter of a century later, there seemed no point in pursuing the matter. He managed very well with his minor handicap: it was simply the way he was, and as far as he was concerned, anyone who didn't like it could be damned.

But what would the American woman think? Would she even notice? If she did, would she be so ill-bred as to comment? It seemed unlikely, and yet Kurt was all too aware that some people had an underlying prejudice against any physical imperfection. If she was one of them, he might have trouble persuading her to do what he wanted. He took a deep drag from his cigarette. He wished he knew more about her.

Kurt looked at his watch. It was a few minutes until one. Anytime now Karl should be picking her up in the town square. Once again Kurt regretted the travel arrangements he had approved so thoughtlessly while he was still in Vienna. He hadn't been thinking clearly at all. It would not have been difficult—in fact, it would have seemed the obvious course of action—to meet her at the airport in Salzburg and drive the remaining fifty kilometers in the limousine. But the word had come unexpectedly from his American agent, almost a shock after all the months of silence, and when it came he was heavily involved in negotiations for a small but choice private collection of works by Braque and Matisse. He had delegated the travel plans to Gabrielle.

Only after telegrams and tickets had been dispatched did it dawn on Kurt that the American woman might resent having to take the bus to Kleisthof-im-Tirol; that she might consider it rather arrogant treatment of a poor relation. Her airline tickets from Los Angeles to Salzburg had been first-class, his one stipulation. Gabrielle had snorted that tourist class would have been more than adequate for an "American fortune hunter"; but then, that was exactly the sort of remark Gabrielle would make. The actions of the unknown American woman since Erich's death had been unusual, but they seemed to indicate she was anything but mercenary.

What was she like, Erich's widow? What kind of woman had his troubled younger brother fallen in love with? Kurt took no pride in the knowledge that the marriage had lasted almost two years and he still didn't even know what his sister-in-law looked like. If that one rather delirious letter of Erich's was to be taken literally, she was a statuesque brunette a little older than her husband, which would make her now in her early thirties.

Kurt's eyes darkened. Erich had been intoxicated with his wife, and she had repaid his devotion by running away with another man. Yet curiously enough she had performed her duties as Erich's widow in exemplary fashion. True, the brief letter she had written to Kurt to inform him of her husband's death was stilted and formal, but perhaps that was to be expected under the circumstances. She had not asked for money, and Kurt, unaware of her defection and presuming

Erich had provided for her, had offered none. It wasn't until he discovered that she had used Erich's precious violin to settle his debts that he had wondered if she had any resources of her own. While it was always possible that her paramour was supporting her, a genuine Guarneri was not the sort of asset one parted with lightly....

Kurt had made some tentative efforts to locate the American, but they had failed, and he'd concluded that she had settled somewhere with her lover. Later, when the Bachmann business had made it imperative that he find her, he'd hired a New York detective agency recommended by a business associate. After months of searching, the agency had found her in Los Angeles, working as a pianist in a cocktail lounge, using the name Megan Halliday. She had not remarried but had resumed her maiden name. Kurt wondered bitterly if it was guilt or an odd sort of pride that kept her from using the von Kleist name she had dishonored. Whatever the reason, it was ironic that she had rejected the von Kleist name, considering how Erich had struggled for the right to use it.

Kurt sat down at his desk and began flipping through the stack of auction catalogs. He really should be getting some work done instead of wasting his time brooding. After he had read the first page three times without absorbing a single word, he pushed the books aside.

He leaned far back in his chair, his long legs stretched negligently in front of him, and the springs creaked as he rocked absently. Through a haze of cigarette smoke he stared at the portrait of his father that hung over the fireplace. Graf Friedrich Johannes Horst von Kleist, the thirteenth man to bear the title of "count." He had been in his late fifties when that rather mediocre portrait was painted, but even the artist's indifferent skills had not been able to disguise the fact that Horst was still a very handsome man, tall, slim, with piercing blue eyes and classic von Kleist features accentuated by his years, the patrician bone structure he had passed on to two of his three sons. The first time Elisabeth had seen that painting she'd hugged Kurt and teased, "Well, darling, now I know what you'll be like in thirty years. I look forward to our old age with renewed confidence."

Kurt suppressed the pang he always felt when he thought of his late wife, and he regarded the picture wryly. No one who had met his father ever doubted that he was anything but what he looked: confident, arrogant, an aristocrat to his fingertips. Only the most intimate members of the family had realized that Horst was bewildered and depressed by the world he lived in. He was a man out of his time, born to a position of wealth and unshakable privilege in a social structure that had begun to crumble even before he was a teenager, with the onset of the First World War. The old man had clung to his outdated values and tried with varying degrees of success to inculcate them in his children. Now ironically the task of preserving the von Kleist heritage fell to Kurt, the son most ambivalent about its monetary worth. He loved his heritage, he loved the Schloss von Kleist, the ancestral home and yet he was the one who had left its museumlike ambience to make a life of his own in the commercial world of Common Market Europe. Now he was back again, cast in the unlikely role of defender of the von Kleist faith, but he was motivated more by love for his dead parents and responsibility to his daughter and the few remaining members of his family than by any abiding conviction in the justice of his cause.

He lounged farther down in his chair and stared up at the ceiling that was ornamented with a trompe-l'oeil painting of gods and goddesses in vaguely military attire. Local tradition attributed the ceiling frescoes throughout the schloss to Tiepolo, but in Kurt's opinion the dates were against it. He blew smoke rings and recalled the family history that had been drummed into him since birth. It was a stirring saga; Wagner should have turned it into an opera. In 1683 the Holy Roman emperor granted the vast Tirolean estate to Otto Kleist, a crony of Prince Eugene of Savoy, as a reward for his part in helping drive the Turks from Vienna. One of his grandsons became archbishop of Salzburg. Later, during the Napoleonic era, Graf Leopold von Kleist retired there to recover from wounds suffered at the Battle of Leipzig. Throughout the centuries the von Kleists had been proud leaders, both military and religious, and despite the vagaries of politics and national fortune they always clung tenaciously to the estate in the Tirol, drawing nourishment from it the way the giant Antaeus drew his from the earth until he was slain by Hercules. Now the von Kleists were threatened, not by some mythical hero but by a very real American woman, and Kurt wondered if he, a slightly crippled art dealer, was strong enough to defeat her.

"FRAU VON KLEIST," the bus driver said gently, "we are in Kleisthof-im-Tirol now."

Megan awoke with a start. Her smoky green eyes, the shape and color of rose leaves, were wide with alarm until she remembered where she was. *"Danke,"* she stammered, her soft girlish voice thick with sleep, "I—I'm sorry, I didn't mean to doze off." She stood up, smoothing the pale gray cotton of her pantsuit where it had stuck to her damp skin in the heat, and brushed away the errant tendrils of her long red hair that had come loose from the wide gold barrette she wore at the nape of her neck. "I didn't mean to delay you," she said diffidently, stumbling over the harsh German vowels. "I'm sorry. *Es—es tut mir leid.*"

The bus driver smiled at her nervous attempt to speak his language. Years of conveying tourists between Salzburg and Innsbruck had given him a fair knowledge of American English, and he assessed her accent—or rather, lack of accent—as pure Californian, the smooth monotone that indicated a life spent within a Frisbee's throw of the

Pacific. She obviously spoke very little German, and while they journeyed southward along the autobahn he had found himself wondering how she had managed to marry into the local aristocracy. She seemed much too young to be *Frau* anybody, much less one of the illustrious von Kleists. Was there a stateside branch of the family he was unaware of?

He had been able to conduct a leisurely study of the American woman's reflection in his rearview mirror as he drove the near-empty coach higher into the mountains. *Ja*, he knew he was a happily married man with four grown children and a grandchild on the way, but he still enjoyed looking at a pretty girl, and this one was very pretty, even exhausted as she obviously was. Her clear ivory complexion was innocent of makeup or freckles, which was unusual, because she had the reddest hair he'd ever seen. He knew from the way the light played on her curls, reflecting gleams of amber and dark gold, that no dye bottle had produced that color. He was too familiar with the outrageous shades of red affected by many middle-aged tourists to be mistaken.

Now, as he unloaded Megan's suitcase from the luggage compartment, he watched appreciatively as the wind molded her Calcutta-cloth pantsuit to her body. She was not tall, but her legs were long for her height, and while she was a little too thin for his taste, her breasts were full and round. On second thought, the driver decided judiciously, it was not surprising that a von Kleist had married the girl. She would have been a prize catch for anyone.

As she stood at the edge of the neat little village square, Megan squinted into the wind and pulled out of her handbag a pair of wraparound mirror sunglasses. Her eyes blinked with relief behind the dark lenses. "Is it always this warm?" she asked. "I expected the weather to be rather cool at this altitude."

"We are not yet so high up," the driver said. "Besides, it is the foehn, the wind. It comes down the side of the mountain and gets heated by—what's the word—compression. It's good for the farmers, but in snowy areas it sometimes causes avalanches."

Megan said noncommittally, "In the fall we have winds like that in Southern California. We call them Santa Anas." She glanced around as she talked, noting the trim, flat-fronted buildings of three and four stories that faced the square. The area was deserted except for her and the bus driver. A long-haired youth in jeans had disembarked just ahead of her, but a blond girl wearing a dirndl met him, and the pair of them had already disappeared somewhere. Megan shivered with apprehension.

The driver noticed her agitation. He looked down at her luggage and then at the empty street. "Do you know where you go from here?"

"Yes, of course. Schloss von Kleist."

He raised his eyebrows and nodded, clearly impressed. "That is several kilometers farther," he said. "Do you need a taxi? I'm not sure that there is one available around here."

"Oh, no, someone is going to meet me. I'm certain they'll be here any moment now."

"Well—" The driver was interrupted by a rude shout from the interior of the coach. Two men in Tirolean hats were gesturing impatiently to him. "I must leave," he said reluctantly, assailed by paternal compunction. "Are you certain you will be okay?"

"I'll be fine," Megan answered bravely. "You've been very kind. *Vielen Dank.*"

"Goodbye," the man called as he reboarded the bus. "Enjoy your say in Austria."

"Thank you," Megan responded. *"Auf wiedersehen."*

She watched the big red-and-white bus disappear around a corner, and the self-assurance she had affected for the driver vanished in a puff as if blown away by the wind. She was all alone. She shuddered, hugging her thin arms to herself. Someone was supposed to meet her. The telegram had been quite specific: someone would be waiting for her. But here she was in a deserted town in a strange country, and she wondered for the first time if she had made a ghastly mistake in coming. Ever since leaving Los Angeles nearly twenty-four hours earlier, she had been too excited to question what she might be getting herself into. Except for a one-day excursion into Tijuana when she was eleven, Megan had never been out of the United States before. She had flown between New York and Los Angeles a number of times, but the trip to Munich and then on to Salzburg had seemed the height of adventure.

Austria! Land of Mozart and waltzes and operettas and all the music that was ingrained so deeply in her soul. She ought to be dancing around the square from the sheer joy of being here. But now she was exhausted and full of an odd foreboding that had first hit her early that morning when she watched the sun climb over the battlements of Festung Hohensalzburg, the huge twelfth-century fortress looming over the city of Mozart's birth. As the shuttle bus from the airport crept through the deserted streets of the awakening city, crossing and recrossing the Salzach River, Megan had stared high upward over the thickly forested hillside to the shining crenellated towers of that awesome structure, gray walls gilded in the rising light. She had gasped in dismay. She belonged to a world of beaches and neon lights and franchise taco stands. What was she doing in the shadow of an honest-to-God medieval castle?

Megan took off her sunglasses and rubbed her aching eyes. She looked at her watch. One o'clock. Doing a quick mental calculation she discovered that in Los Angeles it was four in the morning, the time she usually fell into bed, exhausted from work. No wonder she was tired! At that very moment Dorothy, her co-worker and next-door neighbor, was probably massaging her feet, swollen from eight hours in spike heels, while she slipped out of her Hollywood-style sarong and vowed as usual to give up being a cocktail waitress and become a typist.

Megan remembered the look of amazement on Dorothy's face as she'd watched Megan pack up her sheet music. "What do you mean, you're going to Austria to meet your husband's family? I didn't even know you'd been married!" Megan had muttered that her husband had been dead for more than a year. Dorothy's mascara-smudged eyes had blinked as she said remorsefully, "Oh, Meg, I'm sorry. When you had the—when you were sick, I thought.... God, that's awful." She stared at her young friend as if she'd never seen her before. "You couldn't have been married very long."

"I was nineteen when we married," Megan had said roughly, knowing full well what Dorothy, what everyone, had thought. "We were together about two years, then he got killed in a car wreck. I—I don't like to talk about it."

Dorothy had scowled at the bitter undertone in Megan's light voice, but obviously trying to respect her friend's feelings she'd chattered brightly, "A European adventure, that's terrific! Lucky girl, I'll be doing well if I get to Catalina this summer. How long do you think you'll be away?"

"I don't know. There's some family business that's so important that the von Kleists—"

"Von Kleist?" Dorothy had queried.

"That's their name," Megan explained with a shrug. "Mine, too, I guess, though I haven't used it for a long time. They want me there badly enough that they're paying for my plane tickets, and I don't know how long the business will take. I'm not worried about it. I have some money saved, and I figured I might do some sightseeing on my own before I come back, if there's time. The boss said he'd keep my job open for a month."

Dorothy had observed cynically, "I'll just bet he did! In all the years I've worked in this dump there's never been another piano player who's anywhere as talented or as pretty as you are, and he knows he'll never replace you, not for the lousy money he pays."

Megan had chuckled in agreement. The manager of the Polynesian Paradise was not noted for his generosity. "Well," she sighed, "the tips are good."

Dorothy had drawled, "Yeah, but the big tippers seem to want an awful lot for their money! Tonight we had a pincher, did you see him? That creep with the toupee, the one who—"

Now, thousands of miles away in Austria, Megan smiled at the memory, her first smile of that long weary day. Dorothy was a good friend, one who never made demands or asked questions, one who never seemed to be shocked at anything. When Megan had found the job as pianist at the bar, her mind was still raw and bewildered by Erich's death and the events just preceding it. But then she'd met Dorothy Butler, a breezy woman in her late thirties who had come to Hollywood to be a star and instead had married three times and become a very good cocktail waitress. Sometimes Megan thought that Dorothy's unfailing good humor was the only thing that had kept her from cracking up. Certainly, without the older woman's support Megan's illness would have been far more serious. She'd have to send lots of postcards: Dorothy would enjoy them, even if Megan got back to Los Angeles before the cards did.

She looked at the functional but hideous mirror sunglasses her friend had pressed upon her at the airport, a last-minute going-away present. "You'll need them to protect yourself from the glare of all that snow in the Alps," Dorothy had said, apparently thinking of the Matterhorn or the Eiger. Thus far Megan hadn't seen any snow or any mountains that looked higher than the Sierra she had grown up with. The bus driver had told her they were still in the lower ranges; that the high Alps were farther west.

Megan surveyed the closed-up shops facing the cobbled street around the square once more, and she came to the chilling conclusion that Austrians, like their Italian neighbors, must take a siesta in the early afternoon. She couldn't read the signs to tell when the shops would reopen, and the knowledge made her increasingly aware of her isolation. If no one came for her, would she even be able to make a telephone call? She doubted that she could translate an Austrian directory, and if she needed an operator, her conversational vocabulary was extremely limited. It hadn't mattered at the airports, where everyone had seemed to speak

English, and even on the bus the driver had been delighted to display his linguistic talents. But here in a small town her limitations were going to cause difficulties. Oh, damn Erich, anyway! He could have helped her when she tried to learn his language, instead of laughing scornfully at her accent. Megan decided resolutely that she would wait another fifteen minutes and then she would find a phone. She'd manage somehow. If worse came to worst, she could build a fire and send up smoke signals.

She leaned against the low stone wall enclosing the square and drowsed. She was very tired. Nearly twenty-four hours of sitting in one plane or another had left her aching and stiff. She was used to perching for hours on a piano bench, but that was different from confinement in the cramped seats of the airliners. What she needed to do now was jog around the block a time or two to loosen her knotted muscles. She stretched languidly, drooping her head so far back that her long red hair brushed the wall she leaned against, then extending her arms high and to the side. The motion pulled her tunic taut across her breasts. For a long moment she remained arched backward, conscious only of the sweet pain of tense muscles gradually relaxing, then she straightened up.

Suddenly she realized she was being watched. Someone—a man, she thought, but the glare of the sunlight on the glass made it difficult to tell—was standing at the second-story window of the corner house, staring down at her. Megan quickly hunched her shoulders. She flushed as she thought how provocative she must have looked. She glanced surreptitiously toward the window again. The watcher was gone.

A voice said, "*Entschuldigung. Sind Sie* Frau von Kleist?"

Megan jumped. A rosy-cheeked man with gray hair was standing beside her. Was he the man at the window, she wondered wildly before she noticed the long silvery Mercedes-Benz limousine parked at the curb. Deep in her reverie she hadn't heard it pull up. The man was wearing a severely cut brown suit that was not quite a uniform, and Megan noticed that his otherwise immaculate trousers were stained with grass and mud at the knees.

"*Sind Sie—*" he began again.

"*Ja, ich bin* Megan von Kleist," she said awkwardly, fearful she could not even tell him her own name without mispronouncing it. Her tongue, which could handle a mellifluous language like Spanish easily, seemed incapable of coping with German gutturals. But apparently her accent was sufficiently accurate that the Austrian assumed she spoke more of his language than she did, for he began rattling off long sentences she could not follow, although she did glean the fact that he was explaining why he was late.

"*Bitte,*" she interrupted again in her best one-semester-of-German tones, "*ich spreche weniger Deutsche*. Do you speak English?"

"*Nein,*" he replied regretfully, and for a few

seconds they stared helplessly at each other. Megan frowned as it occurred to her that she didn't know who this man was, that he might be a relative, perhaps the mysterious Kurt von Kleist who had signed the terse note that had accompanied her plane tickets—although he did seem rather old to be Erich's brother. Besides, the note had been in English. Maybe someone had translated it for him? She asked painstakingly in German, "Excuse me, but what is your name? Are you Kurt von Kleist?"

The man stared, astonished and obviously a little horrified. He sputtered, "*Nein, nein, ich bin* Karl Weber, *der*—" Megan felt herself losing the thread of the conversation again. The man was the chauffeur, and he was aghast that she had mistaken him for her brother-in-law. He kicked at one of the tires and motioned as if using a jack, and to their mutual relief Megan finally comprehended that he was late because the car had had a flat. Hence the stains on his suit, she realized, though who'd believe such an aristocratic automobile would have anything so plebeian as a punctured tire?

More relaxed now, Megan told Karl as best she could that she did not mind the delay, and if it was all right with him she would like to go to the von Kleist house now. From his momentarily puzzled expression she gathered she had messed up the verb order in her sentence, a serious offense in German, but he shrugged it off in good humor, and after he had placed her two suitcases in the trunk they drove away. As the car pulled out of the square Megan impulsively looked back over her shoulder. At the entrance to the corner house she saw a young man staring after the retreating limousine.

MEGAN SANK BACK WITH A SIGH onto the luxurious dove-colored suede upholstery. She glanced around her at the interior of the elegant automobile, vastly different from the delapidated Pinto she kept in Los Angeles. She had never been inside such an expensive vehicle before. She had seen limousines occasionally, unloading equally sleek people in front of the concert halls where Erich was performing. That, of course, was after she had quit being Erich's accompanist, when she was forced to spend the frantic moments before the concerts wandering outside the stage door or lingering to one side in the wings like the useless hanger-on she had become. In the beginning, when her name still appeared after his in the program—always, of course, in much smaller type—those last few minutes before the curtain were far too hectic to worry about the audience or their automobiles. She would be scurrying around, smoothing her long black dress, asking the stage manager for the fourteenth time whether the D-flat on the piano had been retuned, checking on the position of the music stand, doing the hundred little things she did to spare Erich the worry, so that nothing might intrude on his concentration.

Erich.... When she thought of him nowadays, for the sake of her sanity Megan always tried to remember him as he had looked onstage, alone in a circle of white light, tall and imposing, his silver blond hair gleaming in sharp contrast to the elegant but severe black dress clothes he wore when he performed. He would stand motionless for a few seconds while the audience waited breathlessly, an almost electric tension building between them and him. Seated at the piano, Megan always heard a few feminine gasps when Erich surveyed the house, his gray eyes murky with a passion only she understood. She doubted he ever heard those women who exclaimed over his beauty, for by that point he was already enrapt with the one true love of his life, his music. Slowly he would raise the precious Guarneri violin to his shoulder, the long fingers of his left hand caressing the slender neck like a lover. Then the bow arm, alive with erotic tension, would come up, and by the faintest of nods Erich would signal Megan to begin the introduction to the sonata or concerto or whatever piece he had chosen to open the recital. Megan, responding to his passion even when it was not directed at her, would strike the opening notes on the piano, and together the two of them would weave a musical fabric as sensual and seductive as satin sheets. For the fleeting interval of a musical composition they were one.

Those were the good times—and looking back Megan realized she could count on her fingertips the times during the two years of their marriage that they had actually achieved rapport. Oh, she had tried. A desperate, confused nineteen-year-old, she had tried to reach him, first as a woman, then as a musician; but she had failed on both counts. After a disastrous honeymoon when even to someone of Megan's inexperience it was obvious that Erich touched her with total indifference, she had demanded to know why he had bothered to marry her. He had shrugged her aside as if she were a petulant child, and stung and humiliated she hurled at him the unforgivable accusation. She regretted the words the moment they were uttered, but then it was too late. She could still feel the cold fury with which Erich had turned on her. "Well, *Liebling*," he had gritted, the German endearment like a slap in the face, "if that is what you think of me, then rest assured I will not distress you by sharing your bed any longer, doubtful pleasure though that is. I married you because you are an adequate accompanist and are handy to have around. In return you get to continue your music lessons and you have the honor of being Frau Erich von Kleist. If that is not enough for you, you are free to leave whenever you like."

She hadn't believed him. She had thought that if she apologized abjectly enough he would forgive her her rash words and together they would rekindle the love that had flared so suddenly between them. Only after a series of humiliating rejections did Megan realize that Erich had spoken the simple truth when he said he would never touch her again. Only then did she realize that the love had all been on her side.

Yet she had not left him. Her mother was dead, her father had dropped out of her life a dozen years earlier, and she hád no one at all to turn to—a situation Erich must have considered when he proposed, she figured out too late. At nineteen even a sterile life with Erich seemed preferable to a solitary existence teaching piano to unwilling children, so she had continued as his accompanist and general factotum, living for the moments when they responded to each other musically, and hoping, always hoping. No one knew that their physical intimacy had ended almost before it started, and in time Megan began to regard those few nights with her husband as only a bewildering and disturbing dream. Events later proved to her that she had been wrong to question his manhood, but by then she was past caring.

Their musical life hadn't lasted, either. After a year it had become obvious that Erich's virtuosity was far beyond Megan's capacity to accompany him. During a recital at a small college in Pennsylvania she had botched her part of the Halstead sonata so badly that only Erich's consummate skill managed to salvage the piece. After the set ended he had stormed offstage without looking at her. She stumbled to their dressing room to face his fury, only to find that he had locked her out. When Herschel Evans, Erich's manager and patron, had come looking for her, he found her whimpering quietly in a dark corner of the greenroom.

Herschel had patted her shoulder and said, "Don't take it so hard, dear; it's not the end of the world. We've all seen it coming for some time now. You're a very good pianist, extremely good for someone your age, but Erich is a genius, and we both know you just can't keep up with him anymore. That's not a disgrace." The old man had sighed. "So far Erich has been playing at universities and in the smaller cities. Now he's getting ready for the big time...New York, Boston, San Francisco, the places every musician dreams of performing. The tour that's coming up in a few months is going to be the most important of his life, the one that will turn him into one of the top violinists in the country. I don't have to tell you how much time and money I've invested in Erich's career so far—and now, well, it's time I started getting some return on my investment."

Megan had sniffed, "And you think I'll spoil it for you, is that it?"

"Don't make me sound so crass! I care about Erich, and I care about you, too. You're just not cut out for concert work, Megan, not at this level. The pressure is getting to you. When Erich brought you to meet Lavinia and me, I thought you were one of the prettiest girls I'd ever seen. I still think so, but now you're pale and thin and you have circles under your eyes. I know it's the strain of all this traveling and work. You ought to settle down, relax. Maybe have a baby." He had looked at her quizzically. "You'd be a good mother, Megan, and a baby would be a wonderful way to celebrate Erich's triumphal tour. Maybe Lavinia and I could be godparents?" Megan had looked up into the man's warm brown eyes and felt a stab of pain in her heart. If only he knew! She'd thrown her arms around his neck and moaned, while Herschel patted her shoulder helplessly.

Megan looked down at her hands. Her fingers were curved into claws, and her short, carefully trimmed nails were raking deep scratches into the suede upholstery. She hadn't realized what she was doing. She glanced up at the lush green countryside through which the Mercedes was passing. Austria was a gorgeous country, and it was hard to imagine why Erich had chosen to give it up in favor of the frenetic urbanized jungle of the United States. Megan sighed deeply. There was no point in brooding about Erich. He was dead. Some of his music lived on in the two recordings he had made, but the arrogance and cruelty that had caused her so much heartbreak were finished, wiped out instantly in a flaming car crash. The police had told her he was dead before the car exploded. At least she had that much consolation.

The limousine was passing through a wooded area where the dappled light made chiaroscuro patterns on the rich grass under the waving trees. Megan tried to concentrate on the scenery, but her mind was playing tricks on her, wandering off on uneasy tangents, and she felt almost as if she had been drugged. It was jet lag, of course. Her wristwatch showed the time as early afternoon, but to her body it was still the middle of the night. She didn't know how far they had driven from Kleisthof-im-Tirol, but she was vaguely aware that the Mercedes-Benz was no longer on the highway. Karl was maneuvering the long automobile skillfully around the twists and turns of what appeared to be a private road. Soon the von Kleist house would have to be in sight.

Megan closed her eyes and tried to recall what she knew of Erich's family. Her knowledge of her in-laws was absurdly inadequate. Erich had never talked about them, and as far as she knew he had not been in regular contact with them. Just before their first anniversary—their only anniversary, as it turned out—he'd received a letter postmarked Osterreich, and had seemed as surprised as Megan when he said, "It's from my brother Kurt." Megan had watched across the breakfast table while Erich pored over the pages densely covered with a tight Germanic script, which of course she couldn't read. When Erich had finished it he gazed into space with an inscrutable expression.

"Is that bad news?" she'd ventured timidly.

Erich had stared at her blankly, a thin smile playing over his hard mouth. "I suppose that depends on one's point of view. Kurt says that our father and oldest brother, Wilhelm, were killed in a skiing accident at Innsbruck."

"Oh, my God!" Megan had cried in horror.

Erich had brushed aside her sympathy impatiently. "Spare me your condolences, Megan. Wilhelm never gave a damn about me, and my father—his affection was too little, too late."

Gasping at his callousness, Megan had asked, "Do you want to go back for the funeral?"

Erich had shrugged. "The funeral will be long over by now. It was something else Kurt wanted me to know about, something...surprising." He had dropped the pages of stationery one by one, and they drifted like autumn leaves onto the polished surface of the table. "Too bad," he'd mused. "I had always thought that one day I would go back and show that old man— Oh, well, now I will never go back." As it happened, he never did.

After Erich's funeral Megan had sifted through his possessions—the most intimate contact she had had with him since she met him, she realized bitterly—until she found the letter from his brother. She'd copied the return address in Vienna and written an awkward note explaining briefly the circumstances of Erich's death. She knew as she wrote—in English, praying Kurt could read it—that she sounded cold and unfeeling. But how could she tell a total stranger that his last surviving brother was dead? After that she'd given all of Erich's valuables to Herschel Evans, as partial repayment for the time and money he had invested in Erich's career. Then she'd fled to Los Angeles to begin her life again.

Months later she'd received a tattered letter that had followed her across the country. Markings on the envelope indicated it had been misdirected more than once, partly because it was addressed to Mrs. Erich von Kleist, and by that time she had resumed her maiden name, Megan Halliday. When she read the letter she was stunned. It was from a lawyer in New York who said he was acting as agent for Kurt von Kleist, her late husband's closest relative. A matter of some urgency regarding Erich's estate—what estate, she asked herself—required Mrs. von Kleist's presence in Austria. The von Kleist family was generously prepared to pay all expenses.

Megan couldn't imagine what kind of business was so important that Erich's people were willing to send all the way to California for her, especially since they had heretofore ignored her existence. But she was bored with her job at the cocktail lounge, and a free trip to Europe was an offer too attractive to refuse.

Now she was riding in style in a chauffeur-driven limousine toward... what? A tremor of fear shook her. She had embarked on this trip as blindly as she embarked on her marriage to Erich: would the results be as disastrous? Erich had said, "I wish you to be my wife," and Megan naively assumed he was also saying, "I love you." His family had said, "Here are tickets to Austria." Did it follow that she would be glad she had come? Megan shivered. Suddenly she wished she were back in her cramped apartment in Los Angeles, with the friendly sound of Dorothy's snoring filtering through the thin walls from next door.

"Frau von Kleist," the chauffeur said again. Megan realized with a start that he had been speaking to her and she hadn't heard him.

She stammered in German, "What did you say?"

"I said, we are almost to the house now. You will be able to see it as soon as we cross the hill," he replied in the same language.

"*Danke*, Karl." Megan sat forward in her seat, straining to catch her first glimpse of the place to which fate had brought her. The silver Mercedes hummed powerfully as it broke out of the forest and surged up a hill covered with clover and wild flowers. At the crest of the hill Megan could see a stone arch with a big wrought-iron *K* embedded in it—like the opening shot of *Citizen Kane*, she thought wildly. The gates were pulled back and the long car slipped through. Eagerly Megan looked down at the house. She gaped.

The mansion nestled against the lush hillside like a jewel in a green velvet case. From her vantage point at the top of the rise Megan could see that the house was a wide shallow horseshoe that pointed away from the gate, the back wings extending like arms to embrace the lawn that swept down the hill to a lake that shone in the distance. The front facade was of creamy white stone, with three stories of tall mullioned windows trimmed with ornate brownish gold masonry. Megan could make out a fourth bank of much smaller windows high up under the beveled verdigris roof.

Karl beeped the horn twice and started the limousine down the sloping driveway, past elaborately trimmed topiaries in vast urns, past the classic fountain where Nereids cavorted with a spouting dolphin, down to the columned portal out of which servants spilled onto the wide stone steps. As he pulled the car smoothly to a halt, Megan's eyes were drawn upward to the entablature over the entry. The *K* of the gate was carved into the arch, this time as a heraldic device, on a shield borne by griffons rampant.

Megan shrank back into her seat, utterly bewildered. This...this castle had been Erich's home, and she'd never suspected.

Karl appeared at her door, swinging it open with a dignified air at odds with his stained suit. He was obviously pleased at how impressed she was. He bowed with a wide gesture toward the house. "Schloss von Kleist," he said proudly.

CHAPTER TWO

"Frau von Kleist wishes to see you, Frau von Kleist," the little maid in a light brown shirtwaist dress said in German. Megan nodded mutely, too bemused by her surroundings to note the awkward repetition of names. Numbly she followed the maid through a series of long passageways, turning and returning until she was disoriented. She passed tall leaded windows that overlooked a vista of manicured lawns and waving trees. She walked down corridors lined with dark, obviously valuable paintings in massive gilded frames. She glimpsed a van Eyck portrait she was sure she had seen in an art book somewhere. The wooden heels of her sandals clomped and echoed embarrassingly in the hushed coolness, disturbing her thoughts as she tried to reconcile what she was seeing with what she had expected.

She had always been more or less aware that Erich's people were well-off. His violin, for example, was an antique from the workshop of an Italian master craftsman who was an artist in his own right. Erich had told her the instrument was a gift from his father. Occasionally Megan had wondered why, if they could afford such a munificent gift, the von Kleists did not finance Erich's rising career. Instead they had let him go deeper into debt to Herschel Evans, who although a kindly patron was still an outsider. Of course she had never dared ask Erich. Drawing on her personal knowledge of Austria—derived from telecasts of the Innsbruck Olympics and a student production of *The Sound of Music*—Megan had conjured up a picture of the von Kleists as prosperous burghers dressed in lederhosen and dirndls, who lived in a snowbound chalet ornamented with hearts and flowers and staghorns.

This opulent mansion represented wealth on a scale vastly beyond anything Megan could have imagined, and the realization made her even more uneasy than she had been before.

She followed the maid through the hall, trying not to gawk at the Italianate splendor of the rooms she passed, glancing through scrolled doorways into chambers lush with gold-leafed carving and richly flocked wallpapers. In some rooms sensual cherubs simpered down from highly colored ceilings, reminding Megan irresistibly of the figures on Capo di Monte porcelain. Not until much later did it dawn on her that many of the rooms weren't furnished.

"Frau von Kleist asked that you be brought to the morning room at once," the maid said, and Megan, recalling herself with a jerk, wondered apprehensively who this Frau von Kleist might be. Erich's mother? No, she had died when he was born, Megan was sure of that. A sister-in-law or cousin? She had no way of knowing. Fear swelled inside her like an expanding balloon. Who was this woman, the first of Erich's family she was to meet, and what was her relationship to the dead musician? What were her feelings toward him? Had she loved him? Could she look into Megan's heart and see that she, his wife, had long since grown to despise him?

The maid halted in front of a festooned door and tapped lightly. She opened the door and murmured, "*Hier ist* Frau Erich von Kleist, Frau von Kleist." Megan hesitated, marveling at the servant's ability to make such a redundant introduction with a straight face. Then she took a deep breath and stepped into the room.

After the dim hallway, the morning room at first glance seemed lambent and inviting, a symphony of white and gold. Gold silk walls shimmered above creamy painted dadoes outlined with gilt scrollwork. The long windows overlooking the flower garden were draped with gold velvet, and the fabric was repeated in the upholstery of the delicate rococo armchairs clustered around the white Louis Quinze escritoire. But when Megan's first spasm of pleasure subsided, she frowned, struck by the somberness of the meticulously coordinated furnishings. The room was just too perfect. She wished the decorator had had the imagination to introduce something of another hue—perhaps a jade statuette or a vase of scarlet roses—to take away the stultifying harmony of the color scheme. Even the gown of the woman in the Winterhalter portrait over the mantel was gold.

Then Megan's eyes were directed toward her hostess.

The woman had been pointedly looking out the window when Megan entered the room, and only after a carefully calculated interval long enough to be intimidating without being blatantly rude did she turn around. Megan took one look at her and knew that here she would find none of the inviting *Gemütlichkeit* she had heard was characteristic of Austrians. The woman was tall, at least six inches taller than Megan's five foot two, and she had the angular, hollow-cheeked good looks Megan associated with models for the most haute of couture. She might have been a beauty in her youth, but now, somewhere around forty, while she was still certainly attractive, her face had taken on the look of a carefully painted mask, and Megan had the feeling that she would react to inevitable expression lines with the same distaste that she must feel for a gum wrapper discarded on the floor of that glossily perfect room. Her hazel eyes were as hard and unyielding as the heavily lacquered brown hair that was teased into an elaborate coiffure, and coldly they raked over Megan.

Megan suddenly felt very young and schoolgirlish. She admired the perfectly tailored natural linen suit the woman was wearing, and by comparison her own lightweight Calcutta-cloth slacks and tunic, badly rumpled from the hours of travel, seemed cheap, even shoddy. The woman's eyes flickered up to Megan's windblown hair, and the girl became aware of the tendrils that had pulled loose from her barrette and were dangling over her eyes like rusty metal shavings. Self-consciously she brushed them aside, and she saw the older woman's eyes light up in triumph.

"You are Erich's widow?" the woman asked rapidly in German.

Oh, God, here we go again, Megan thought wearily. *"Ja,"* she answered, *"ich bin* Megan Halli—Megan von Kleist. Do you speak any English?"

The woman switched effortlessly to English—beautiful English with only the faintest trace of an accent, Megan admitted grudgingly—and said smoothly, if pedantically, "Since your husband was Austrian, I should have thought you would speak his language. But perhaps you lack the gift for languages?" The derision in her voice was unmistakable.

Megan bridled. She loathed sarcasm. "Because we lived in the United States," she said stiffly, "Erich never felt it necessary for me to learn German. His English was excellent, as I expect you know."

The woman nodded. "Of course. Because of their position, the von Kleists have always considered it their duty to learn the significant foreign languages."

Megan choked. She had the feeling she should be honored that the von Kleists considered English "significant." After she caught her breath she said, "As for my capacity for languages, I speak fluent Spanish, and I know some French."

The woman smiled condescendingly, and Megan realized at once that, being Austrian, her French would be at least as good as her English. *Round one to her,* Megan thought—*and why in God's name am I carrying on like a schoolgirl bragging about my grades when I ought to be finding out why I'm here in the first place?* She straightened her tired shoulders and asked aloud, "May I know your name, please? I'm afraid I don't know who you are."

The woman lifted one penciled eyebrow. "Why, I am Gabrielle von Kleist, Erich's sister-in-law. I thought you knew."

Megan shook her head. "Erich and I never bothered to discuss relatives," she said inadequately. "Our interests lay in other directions."

Gabrielle blinked. She surveyed Megan once again, evaluating her petite figure and cosmetic-free face. "You are very young," she said as if it were an accusation.

"I'm twenty-three."

"Indeed? You look younger. Erich was almost thirty when he died. Didn't the difference in your ages bother you?"

Megan felt herself grow cold. She had only just arrived and already someone was questioning her about the quality of her marriage, a subject she was obviously reluctant to discuss, especially with the von Kleists. They had no right! What she had gone through with Erich she had suffered privately, and no one was going to force her to talk about it. She lifted her head and declared, "My relationship with my husband is none of your business."

Gabrielle's hazel eyes narrowed. "On the contrary," she said menacingly, "your relationship with Erich is the only reason you are here. It is most certainly our business; it is von Kleist business!" Megan noticed with a thrill that Gabrielle was clenching her fists so hard that the long blood-colored fingernails were making crimson crescents in her palms. "I told Kurt to leave it alone, not to go looking for you. I said we would manage somehow, that there was no reason at all to drag some American fortune hunter into what was purely a family concern. But he said no, Erich's wife is part of the family now, and we must act with honor." She laughed bitterly. "Honor, *mein Gott*! As if there is honor in letting a mere girl, a foreigner at that, blithely waltz in and destroy all that the von Kleists have represented for three hundred—" She broke off abruptly, her face white and pinched under the makeup. Glaring at a point behind Megan she demanded in German, "What do you want now?"

Megan turned and saw that the little maid in the tan dress had returned and was addressing her mistress timidly. After an exchange too rapid for Megan to follow, the servant left the room, and Gabrielle looked icily at Megan once more. The fury in her eyes made the younger woman want to retreat in confusion. Only the certainty that Gabrielle would like to see her run away made Megan stand her ground. "I have no idea what you are talking about," she said more calmly than she felt. "I am here at the invitation of—"

"Yes, I know why you are here," Gabrielle said, and as Megan watched, the woman seemed to withdraw into herself. The eyes that had burned with anger and even hatred—Megan shuddered—lost their feverish glow and went dark. Gabrielle said evenly—and somehow the deadly quiet of her voice frightened Megan more than her open hostility—"Yes, it is probably true that you do not know why you are a threat to us. You may not wish us any harm at all. But you are like a carrier of some dread disease, and ignorance of your power only makes you more dangerous. If I had my way you would be banished from here at once, before you do any damage. I would even destroy you if it became necessary. Fortunately for you, Kurt does not see it that way. He insists on being civilized." She shook her head in wonder. "That is Kurt's greatest fault, his insistence on civilized behavior in a barbaric world.

"Go now. He wishes to see you. Greta will show you to his office. After that she can take you to your suite. I am sure you will want to rest awhile following your journey, and you may need refreshment. I will have something sent up. We have cocktails at eight-thirty, dinner at nine. We dress for it." She glanced at Megan's disheveled pantsuit. "I realize that all this—" she paused, making a casual gesture that took in the opulent glory of the mansion "—I realize that all this is rather different from what you are used to. If you feel that your clothes are not suitable, my cousin Adelaide may be able to help you. She is close to you in age, and she might have something appropriate, although she is of course much taller than you."

"I have clothes," Megan gritted.

Gabrielle's eyebrows lifted in polite disbelief. "Very well," she said blandly, "then I expect we will meet again at dinner. *Guten Tag.*" Abruptly she turned away, toward the window.

Megan backed out of the golden room, unable to tear her eyes away from the shocking woman who had threatened her and then in the same breath wished her a good day. The instant the ornate door closed, she leaned weakly against the wall and gasped for air, her heart pounding.

The waiting maid touched her shoulder gently. Megan looked up and saw that the Austrian girl's face was pale with concern. "Frau von Kleist," she said anxiously, "are you ill?"

Megan stood upright. *"N-nein,"* she stammered, "I am only tired." *Yes,* she thought, *I'm just tired. The whole encounter has been a surrealistic fantasy brought on by my fatigue; it can't be anything else....* In the real world that Megan inhabited, people did not threaten to "banish" or "destroy" other people. The very words had had an archaic ring that made them more suited to the days of feudal barons than to modern Europe. Honestly, what power could she possibly possess that could "wipe out all the von Kleists stood for"? The whole idea was idiotic, melodramatic, the product of an overwrought imagination. Gabrielle was clearly a woman with emotional problems.

Megan longed to sit down, but Greta forestalled her request by saying, "Please, may we go now? Herr von Kleist was most disturbed when he discovered you had not been taken to him as soon as you arrived."

"Then let's go," Megan agreed wearily with some irritation. Apparently it was asking too much to expect the von Kleists to come to her.

"This way, please," the maid murmured, leading Megan through double doors into a spacious salon with an ornamented ceiling that reflected darkly on the gleaming parquet floor. Scrolled cabinets were built into the walls, and Megan spotted what appeared to be speakers for a stereo system, but the room was otherwise bare except for a mismatched chair and love seat and the biggest piano she had ever seen. It was a huge concert grand of inlaid rosewood, obviously an antique built by a master, and she approached it reverently. The veneer was unlike any she had ever seen before, cut carefully from heartwood so that the grain made distinct stripes of light and dark. Megan gaped almost lustfully at the piano. Her fingers itched to touch it, to stroke the silky wood, to press the ivory keys that were yellow with the patina of great age. She tried to estimate how old it was. It wasn't one of the original furnishings of the schloss, she knew: under the raised lid she could see that the wires were cross-strung in layers, a development of the early nineteenth century. It was so beautiful! She wondered if the tone lived up to the example of the cabinet. It would be blasphemous for such an instrument to be tinny or out of tune.

There was sheet music facedown on the stand, and heedless of the maid Megan flipped it over to see what pieces were being played on the magnificent piano. Liszt, she thought, or Chopin or Mozart, surely. With considerable disappointment she discovered that the music was something called "Das Mädchen und Sein Hung," and the large notes and fingering numbers marked it as an elementary piece for a very young child. Not a particularly good piece, either, Megan noted ruefully, scanning and playing it mentally; it was the sort of insipid tune that made young pupils anxious to do anything but practice. She wondered who the child was who had to perform scales and finger exercises on this beautiful instrument. Erich had never mentioned any children. Megan recalled the twangy upright on which she had learned to play. Compared to this, her first piano had been about as musical as a kazoo. The little spinet she now kept in her apartment in Los Angeles would pale next to this. Did the child appreciate what he had? Most likely not....

"Frau von Kleist, we must go," Greta pleaded. "Herr von Kleist is waiting!" Her tone made it clear that Herr von Kleist was not a man used to waiting for anything.

Let him wait, Megan thought defiantly, reluctant to tear herself away from the piano. *He's been ordering me around ever since I got that letter, and I haven't even met him yet!* But a glance at Greta's nervous eyes made Megan reconsider. Her dallying might get the maid into trouble, and that wouldn't be fair. Megan would wait until she faced Kurt von Kleist directly before she asserted her independence. She followed Greta out of the music room, looking back with longing as she did. At least once before she left this place, she promised herself, she was going to get her hands on that piano.

Megan followed Greta through a series of large rooms as opulent as the ones she had already seen. The furnishings varied from room to room, she noted, as if a decorator had quit halfway through the job, but the rococo elegance of the structure itself was almost oppressive. The building was as perfect as a museum—and as cold. After the heat outside, the coolness contributed to the sense of unreality. When Megan stepped into a draft of refrigerated air, she realized with surprise that the building was air-conditioned; the ducts were cleverly concealed behind wall decorations. She supposed the air conditioning was necessary to preserve the elaborate furnishings, but the resultant dry, chill atmosphere gave the building the feel of a mausoleum. It was like a stage set for *Der Rosenkavalier*, left behind when the theater closed permanently, inanimate now and without substance. Phantom dancers in velvets and powdered wigs could gavotte through the rooms, their slippered feet leaving no mark on those polished floors. A woman in a flowing gown might pose coquettishly on that sweeping staircase while she sang a ghostly aria, but no one could *live* there. And yet people did indeed carry on their daily activities among the gilt and the cherubs. Kurt von Kleist lived here, Megan knew, as well as Gabrielle, who was presumably his wife; and somewhere there was even a child.

As if in answer to her thoughts, Megan heard a sound and glanced up. From halfway up the grand staircase a little girl was gawking down at her. Megan stared back, waiting for her to speak. The child was about nine years old, with wide blue eyes in a rather severe face, and her long straight hair looked like corn silk. Her slight body was clothed in blue jeans and a T-shirt, and Megan might have mistaken her for an American were it not for the German motto on the shirt. Some kind of greeting seemed in order, so when the little girl descended to the foot of the stairs, Megan said tentatively, *"Guten Tag."*

"Guten Tag," the child replied. She eyed Megan blankly.

Megan tried again, in her faulty German. "I'm Megan von Kleist. What's your name?"

Suddenly the girl grinned broadly at Megan's clumsy pronunciation, and her smiling features revealed the promise of great beauty. "I'm

Elisabeth von Kleist, but everyone calls me Liesl," she said in English. "Are you really Tante Megan from America? I thought you'd be an old lady."

Megan smiled back, wondering what a nine-year-old would consider to be an old lady. Before she could make an appropriate reply, Greta said impatiently, "Fräulein Liesl, *sein Vater*—"

Liesl's face fell. "You have to go see my father now," she told Megan, "and Karl is waiting to take me to the stables so that I may ride my horse, so I won't see you for a while. But I would like to talk to you, please. I want to hear all about the film stars you know."

"But I don't know any," Megan answered in surprise.

Liesl's eyes narrowed and regarded Megan with suspicion. "I thought you were from California," she accused. "Adelaide says everyone in California knows film stars. Adelaide is going to go to Hollywood someday and be a star herself."

Megan made a face at the unknown Adelaide. She thought with wry amusement of the thousands of girls who arrived in Southern California every year with that very ambition, one that Megan, fortunately, had never had. But when she noticed the doubtful frown marring Liesl's small features, Megan thought quickly. She could tell she was in imminent danger of falling from grace in the child's eyes unless she claimed friendship with someone famous. "Once I saw Burt Reynolds at Disneyland," she said lamely, neglecting to mention that the man in question had been fifty feet away, wearing dark glasses, and she had supposed it was Burt Reynolds only because her date insisted it was.

"Disneyland!" Liesl squealed. "You've been to Disneyland?"

"Oh, yes, many times."

Greta touched Megan's arm and muttered desperately, "Frau von Kleist, please!"

Megan nodded absently. To Liesl she said, "I have to go now. We'll talk later." The little girl waved and ran off in the direction from which Megan had come, calling a goodbye over her shoulder. Megan watched her disappear around a corner, her long, almost colorless hair streaming behind her.

Megan turned and said, "I'm sorry, Greta. We'll go at once." She fell into step behind the maid, and as she walked she thought about the pretty child, the first friendly person she had met at Schloss von Kleist. The presence of an ally, even if she was only a little girl, made Megan feel less isolated. With difficulty she tried to connect the smiling Liesl with the imposing and frightening woman she had met earlier. Somehow it was very disturbing to think of Gabrielle as Liesl's mother.

The maid tapped at a door not unlike the one to Gabrielle's morning room. "Don't they get tired of all that gilt?" Megan grumbled inaudibly as Greta opened the door. She heard the maid plead forgiveness for taking so long to get her there, and Megan forgot her fatigue temporarily as a wave of anger washed over her. She squared her shoulders.

She was an American and nominally a relative of Kurt von Kleist, and she could defy him, even if the maid could not. She strode resolutely into the room. "If you have a complaint about the speed with which I was brought here," she declared, "I suggest you take it up with me. I caused the delay." She noticed the maid retreat from the room.

Megan posed stiffly, filled with an embarrassing sense of anticlimax. She had marched into the room, banners flying, ready to do battle for the downtrodden servants of the world, and instead of bowing under her onslaught the man seemed unaware of her presence. She wondered if, like Gabrielle, he was putting her in her place, reminding her that she was only a poor relation. His dark head was bent over a pamphlet of some kind, and he was penciling notes in the margin.

Nervously Megan glanced around her. Although the walls and ceiling of this room were as richly decorated as those of Gabrielle's morning room—here the predominant color seemed to be maroon—this was obviously an office, the appointments chosen for function rather than design. The long contemporary walnut desk clashed uncompromisingly with the lavish fireplace. An overstuffed leather armchair had nothing in common with the spindly Louis Seize table at its side or the Chinese cloisonné bowl half-full of cigarette butts. On the far side of the room a portable wet bar was pushed against the wall, and facing the desk a student's easel held a large painting in a brushed chrome frame. When Megan tilted her head slightly forward so that she could see the painting, she was astonished to find that it was not a gloomy old master as she might have expected, but rather a rainbow-colored abstract by Jackson Pollock. She backed away, puzzled. The eclectic arrangement of the room was utterly at odds with the rigid formality she had seen elsewhere in the building.

Her eyes wandered idly once more to the marble fireplace, and then her gaze was riveted to the portrait over the mantel. At first startled glance she thought the tall slim man posed before that very fireplace was Erich. Then she saw that the man's deep-set eyes were blue, not gray, his face was lined, and his hair had been silvered by the passing years. Was it Erich's father, she wondered. It had to be. The resemblance was uncanny. Megan knew the planes, the bone structure, of that face as well as she knew her own. She had fallen victim to its devastating attraction the first time she ever saw it.

A movement in front of her drew her attention back to the man at the desk. With a murmur of apology he pushed aside the books he had been working with and looked up at her. His sea-blue eyes met hers, and Megan caught her breath. As he stared at her, one thick eyebrow shot up until it almost met the lock of dark brown hair that drooped in a comma over his forehead, marking an oblique line across his tanned skin. After a second Megan lowered her lashes, deliberately obscuring her expression to disguise the thrill of—something—surging through her. Erich's brother. What she felt *must* be merely a pang of recognition, a response to the remarkable resemblance between the men. To see Erich's features mirrored in a portrait had been shock enough, but now to confront that same face living, moving.... Did all the von Kleist men look alike? Did they all wear as on an escutcheon those same identifying traits, the narrow face with high cheekbones and long aristocractic nose, the strong chin? If Megan had first encountered Kurt von Kleist in a crowd somewhere, anywhere, she would have known him at once for who he was.

Oh, the coloring was different, of course. Erich's eyes had been gray, his hair platinum white. His older brother had dark brown hair with the subdued highlights of Danish walnut, and his eyes were the color of the ocean Megan had watched for hours from the airplane. His straight eyebrows came together as he frowned at her thoughtfully. When he reached up absently with his left hand to brush aside that errant lock of hair, Megan saw that his fingers were long and spatulate, as Erich's had been. She was puzzled. It was a musician's hand, and yet he moved it with a certain rigidity she could not pinpoint.

When Megan realized that her professional interest in his hand could be interpreted as insensitive curiosity, she quickly averted her gaze, but not before he had noticed. Slowly he stood up to a height of well over six feet, a couple of inches taller than Erich had been, and with an air of nonchalance Megan could only admire he pulled on his ash-gray suit coat and adjusted his blue-and-gray-striped tie with his injured hand. Megan could see the pallid scar now. She understood instinctively that this lean, self-assured man was not trying to prove anything to her. He was far beyond the stage of having to prove anything to anyone. She wondered what had happened to him, how he had been hurt. It was another thing that as Erich's wife, she should have known, and her ignorance filled her with impotent anger at her dead husband. He had no right to have put her in such a position, no matter how much he'd despised her....

Megan drew on her innate courage to stand her ground as Kurt began to survey her silently. His eyes lingered a moment on her coppery hair before they stroked across her face. He noted the breasts that were just a little too full for her small stature, the trim waist and coltish legs. He appraised her body as if she were an indifferent painting, reserving judgment until he had analyzed her point by point. Megan tried not to tremble. During the long months of working in the cocktail lounge she had become inured to the glances of customers who mistakenly assumed she was part of the menu, but Kurt's impersonal evaluation disturbed and confused her—mostly, she admitted honestly, because she could not tell whether he liked what he saw.

To hide her confusion, Megan in turn began to

study him. She knew after the most cursory of examinations that she definitely did like what she saw. He was tall and lean and lithe, and his body seemed vibrant with restrained power. He had the controlled movements of an athlete—a fencer, she concluded. Yes, she thought, he would be a swordsman. He had that aristocratic panache that made it easy to imagine him wielding a saber. Megan could see him move with sinuous grace, pressing forward, never retreating, as he vanquished anyone who dared to impugn the honor of his lady. She could almost hear the ring of crossed blades reverberating in the polished corridors of the schloss—

Suddenly he broke into her fantasy. "I understand you do not speak German," he said. Megan blinked. His baritone voice was surprisingly soft for a man of his size, rather gravelly, and the accent, oddly enough, seemed to be British.

"I speak a little German," Megan replied for at least the fourth time that day. She deliberately enunciated with more variety than was normal for her California monotone as she added, "But I'm afraid I don't know enough to carry on much of a conversation. I can't tell you how glad I am that you and your wife speak English."

"My wife?" Kurt repeated blankly, his eyes darkening.

Megan stammered, "Yes, isn't the woman I met—Gabrielle—isn't she your . . . wife?"

Kurt scowled. "My wife has been dead for seven years," he said tersely. "Gabrielle is my sister-in-law, the widow of my late brother Wilhelm. I am surprised that you didn't know."

Megan said lamely, "I knew there was another brother, but I didn't know about his wife."

"There were three brothers," Kurt said, and unconsciously he began to tick them off with the fingers of his good hand. "Wilhelm was the eldest. He died along with my father when the cable snapped on the ski lift they were riding at Innsbruck. He and Gabrielle had no children, although just a few years ago they did informally adopt Gabrielle's young cousin Adelaide. Erich, of course, was the youngest. He, too, died without issue." Megan flushed at the injustice of the unspoken accusation. Kurt continued implacably, "Of all the von Kleists who ever were, there remain only me and my daughter, Liesl."

Megan, eager to change the subject, said brightly, "I met Liesl as I passed the stairs. She seems to be a delightful little girl."

"I think so," Kurt agreed, smiling. Megan caught her breath at the change that came over his face when his daughter was mentioned. The harsh lines around his mouth softened, and suddenly he seemed years younger. He couldn't be more than thirty-seven or thirty-eight, she calculated quickly, but he looked as if he had stored up enough bitterness for a life twice that long.

Megan was sure she was never going to be offered a chair, although she was uncertain whether the von Kleists were just inherently rude or whether it was part of some insidious plan to put her in her place, for heaven only knew what reason. She fidgeted and glanced restlessly around the room, and she noticed with surprise that the booklets on Kurt's desk were catalogs for some of the most famous auction houses in the world. She recognized Christie's in London, Sotheby Parke Bernet in New York, and there were others from Paris, Milan and Frankfurt that she expected would be equally well-known to people more knowledgeable about art than she was.

She looked up through her lashes to see Kurt lounging against a side table, his long legs extended languidly in front of him, the gray wool of his narrow slacks stretched tight over his powerful thighs. He appeared relaxed, but Megan had the curious feeling that he was tense and alert to every move she made. "Y-you're an art collector?" she stammered inanely, recalling the scores of paintings she had seen displayed around the mansion.

Kurt scowled. He reached inside his coat and pulled out a flat gold case. When Megan refused a cigarette, he took one for himself and lit it with a wafer-thin lighter. He inhaled deeply and blew the smoke out through his nose. "I am by profession an art dealer," he said quietly. "I have a gallery in Vienna. I don't suppose you knew that, either."

"No," Megan said miserably, "no, I didn't."

"Do you know about art?"

Megan shook her head. "You mean paintings— A little. As the cliché goes, I know what I like. My field is music."

"*Natürlich,*" Kurt murmured, and Megan

thought she caught an ominous undertone in his voice. He asked, "You are a pianist, aren't you?"

"Yes. I was Erich's accompanist."

He looked at her sharply. "I saw Erich perform in Boston, and I did not see you." His eyes swept over her. "Red hair, green eyes...you are rather—distinctive. I hardly think I would have forgotten you."

Megan felt her heart jump unexpectedly. She wondered why, since she wasn't even sure his remark had been a compliment. "When was this? Erich never mentioned your attending his concert." *Not that he would have bothered to tell me,* she added silently.

Kurt inhaled again. "Erich did not know. I was in Boston on business, and he happened to be performing. I dropped in, that's all."

But it couldn't have been as casual as all that, Megan protested inwardly. The concert at the Boston Symphony Hall had been the most successful Erich ever had, sold out weeks in advance to a public eager to hear the young man rumored to surpass Menuhin or Stern. The program had been a good one, starting with a few incidental pieces, and then Beethoven's Concerto for Violin and Orchestra in D Minor. Erich had been magnificent. The critics raved. Aloud Megan said, "I didn't perform with Erich in Boston. He—that is, we—thought I...needed a rest. But for heaven's sake why didn't you get in touch with us? To be so close and not...."

Megan's voice trailed off. The glower on Kurt's

face told her she was somehow saying the wrong thing again, that there was something here she was ignorant of. Not that that was anything new. Her whole life with Erich had been founded on deceit and subterfuge, most of which she discovered only when his contempt for her became so great that he didn't even bother to lie anymore. When Erich died Megan had thought she was at last free of his treachery. She had settled his affairs as honorably as she could and then told herself, none too convincingly, that her husband was no longer an influence in her life. But now she was facing his brother, a man who struck her as infinitely more dangerous than Erich had ever been, and she had the uneasy feeling that once again she was going to be the scapegoat. As if she hadn't paid for Erich's misdeeds a thousand times each day while he lived, and in her nightmares since his death. She had not seen the automobile accident that took his life, but the survivor had related it to her in excruciating, sadistic detail, an agonizing narrative that had ended with the woman screaming, "It's all your fault! You accepted the arrangement and then you refused to live up to your part. You goaded him into it, you did, *you did*!"

In her fugue Megan did not realize that her face had gone pinched and gray, her smoky green eyes glowing in feverish contrast. The man watching her closely could tell she was in acute mental distress, but he misinterpreted the reason. After savagely crushing out his cigarette, he took one long stride that brought him directly in front of Megan so that her eyes, which had been staring blindly at the side of the desk, were now focused on the tiny cabochon sapphire he wore as a tie tack. When she did not shift her gaze, he put his hand under her chin and jerked her head up roughly. She blinked in astonishment at the hard blue eyes that glared down at her so chillingly. She couldn't breathe. His mesmeric gaze probed her pitilessly, searching for...something. Her heart began to pound, and each beat was a small shock wave. Then she realized with a shiver that the electricity that seemed to pulse through her body was in reality ripples of pain cause by his fingers still tightly gripping her throat.

"You're hurting me," she choked, and without a word Kurt released her. As she looked entranced into his eyes, Megan touched her fingertips gingerly to her aching jaw. Her tender skin was going to be bruised, she was sure. They were standing so close together that when she lowered her hand it brushed across the front of his jacket, and she retreated hastily.

Kurt did not miss the quick withdrawal. One eyebrow quirked sardonically. Abruptly he backed away so that he leaned against the front of his desk. He busied himself with yet another cigarette. After he slipped the case back inside his coat he said calmly, "All right, I was curious to see just how far you were willing to go with this charade, but it's obvious your nerves are not up to it. Since I don't enjoy watching people fall to pieces, let's get this over with. Who are you, *Fräulein*, and who sent you here? What is the purpose of this masquerade? Why are you trying to pass yourself off as my brother's widow?"

Megan gaped at him. He watched her with the deceptive languor of a panther ready to pounce, his long lean body tensed for the attack, and she knew he would be as merciless as one of the big cats if she did not quickly establish her credentials. "Of—of course you don't know me," she stammered, confused and more than a little frightened. She struggled to get control of her voice. "I—I'm just some...strange American to you. It's natural that you should want identification. I have my passport with me here, but the—the marriage license and birth certificate your agent requested are in my luggage."

Kurt's face was grim as he snorted impatiently, "Documents can be forged. Let's not play games, shall we? We both know you are not who you claim to be. If we may skip the—"

Megan stared. The sheer absurdity of the charge made her want to laugh hysterically. "Forged documents?" she sputtered. "My God, what do you think this is, a James Bond movie? I'm Megan Halliday von Kleist. Why should you think I'm not?"

Kurt eyed her with open contempt. "You accomplish nothing by underestimating my intelligence, *Fräulein*. You come here claiming to be the woman who was married to my brother for two years, but that is impossible. You are little more than a child."

"I'm twenty-three," Megan retorted, her hysteria turning to anger. "I was almost twenty when we married."

Kurt ignored her. "You know nothing of Erich's background or his family. You say you were his accompanist, but I have seen with my own eyes that his pianist was a man. Most damaging of all, you do not in the least resemble the description Erich himself wrote me of his wife!"

Megan gasped, "Erich wrote to you about me? Why?"

"Why, indeed? Is it unnatural for a man to wish to tell his brother about his wife?"

"Not ordinarily," Megan cried, "but he—we...." She caught herself. She couldn't bring herself to tell Kurt what a farce the marriage had been from the very beginning. Unless absolutely necessary she would not sacrifice the little self-respect she had retained so painfully through her silence.

Kurt said, "I still remember Erich's words, partly because his letter was the only communication I had from him after he left Austria, and also because it seemed so out of character for him to rhapsodize in that fashion. My brother was not a man who expressed his emotions with words. 'I have met the woman of my dreams,' he wrote, 'the only woman in the world for me. She is tall and voluptuous, with eyes like the night, a dark Valkyrie—'" Kurt raked his eyes insolently over Megan's petite figure. "You are a very attractive girl," he observed with biting sarcasm, "but you must admit you are not in any way 'a dark Valkyrie.'"

Megan went hot, then icy cold. Damn, she ought to have known. Another of Eric's lies that had long outlived him. She glanced resentfully at the man who watched her so suspiciously. If this had happened in the United States she would have thrown his idiotic charges back in his handsome sneering face and walked away. But here, whether she liked it or not she was at his mercy. She had sworn she would never be at a man's mercy again.

She took a deep, rasping breath before she spoke. She tried to sound very sophisticated, very matter-of-fact as she said, "No, I admit those words don't fit me at all, but they *are* rather a poetic description of the wife of Erich's manager, Lavinia Evans, who was Erich's mistress even before I met him."

Megan stared down at the intricate arabesques on the Oriental carpet, unable to face Kurt as she remembered Lavinia, the pampered wife of a doting, elderly, gullible husband. Herschel Evans had been Megan's friend, but he believed the hysterical lies his wife told him after the car crash; how Megan was supposedly running away with another man and Lavinia and Erich had followed to bring her back. The fact that Megan was alone when Herschel found her at the airport had never registered on him.

And Erich.... Megan was certain it was Lavinia who gave Erich the idea of finding a naive and tractable girl to marry, someone who wouldn't have the guts to fight back when she discovered her marriage was only a blind to cover the fact that Erich was cuckolding the one man most responsible for establishing his career. Megan had filled the requirements perfectly: nineteen, halfway through music school, penniless, with no family to support her when the going got rough. She was resigned to dropping out of school when suddenly Erich appeared—handsome, dashing, brilliantly talented. She fell in love with him on sight. After the most frantic of whirlwind courtships they were married. Erich wedded and, briefly, bedded her, then she found out the truth. Megan gave herself to her husband timidly, with shining innocence, and he used her as impersonally as he would use a tissue to wipe his nose. Megan knew that the humiliation of Erich's abuse would rankle in her heart until the day she died. It was tragically ironic that Lavinia had accused her of betraying Erich, for after the way he had treated her, Megan could barely tolerate the thought of a man touching her.

Kurt watched the expressions play over Megan's face, the haunted, stricken look in her smoky eyes. He said thoughtfully, "I have met Herschel Evans, but not his wife. What was she like?"

Megan looked up at him and smiled sardonically. "You really expect an unbiased opinion from me?" She shrugged. "Lavinia was—still is, as far as I know—young, beautiful, utterly selfish. Seductive. Sort of a brunette Circe—or at any rate, all her men seem to turn into swine."

"Did you know about her when you married Erich?"

Megan shook her head. "No, not at first. But soon." She bit her lip, wishing she had never mentioned the other woman. Her pride hurt too much for the knowledge that only on the last night of Erich's life, after the ultimate humiliation, had she found the guts to fight back. She would rather be considered an adventuress than a doormat. It was less degrading. Megan said, "We had what Erich liked to call a 'civilized' marriage."

Kurt looked at her oddly. "I am familiar with civilized marriages. In most cases they develop between middle-aged couples who no longer love each other but find it inconvenient to divorce. You and Erich were rather young for that sort of thing." For a moment he studied the ash on the end of his cigarette while he seemed to debate how to frame his next question. He said, "Since Erich had a mistress, I suppose you had a lover? That's usually the way it works."

Megan smiled thinly. "Somehow I don't think Erich would have liked that at all. He preferred me to be—abject in my devotion."

"That's not what I heard," Kurt said mildly. "It is my understanding that you were in the process of leaving him the night he was killed."

"How did you find that out?" Megan gasped. "Did Herschel tell you?"

Kurt's eyes narrowed. "Then it is true?"

"It's true I was leaving him, but not with another man." She met his gaze. "Look, Herr von Kleist, I don't know exactly what you've heard, just as I still don't know why you found it necessary to drag me all the way to Austria—but no matter what is going on, I refuse to answer questions about Erich. I don't owe you any explanations."

Something that might have been respect flared in Kurt's blue eyes, but before he could speak again the telephone rang. Megan was startled by the familiar dissonant sound of the bell, so like that of the phone in her apartment in Los Angeles. She thought wildly that Austrian telephones should be more musical, perhaps pealing out a phrase from Haydn.... She rubbed her temples. Her thoughts were getting out of hand, a sure sign that she was on the verge of a migraine. If only she could get to her medication, buried deep inside one of her suitcases.

Kurt picked up the receiver. "Von Kleist *hier*," he announced irritably. "Oh, it's you, Swanson. *Was wollen Sie jetzt?* No, there is no point in further discussions. I thought I had made my position clear. *Warum*—" Megan listened with half an ear, fascinated by the way Kurt shifted effortlessly between German and English. He was obviously displeased. With his pen he scratched angry little designs on the blotter as he talked. "*Nein*, Swanson, I have told you before that you are not welcome on my property, *verstehen Sie*? Look, I have a guest, and I request that you trouble me no further. *Auf wiederhören!*"

He slammed down the receiver, then glanced up at Megan, a little abashed at his display of emotion. "One of your countrymen," he said. "An otherwise agreeable young man who believes that persistence will succeed where reason does not."

Kurt flashed Megan a disarming smile, but she did not see it. Her eyes were shut tight against the onslaught of her headache, the one symptom of her emotional turmoil she had never been able to control. During the fifteen months of her widowhood Megan had taught herself with difficulty not to dwell on the past, not to cringe when a chance word or a passage of classical music rubbed on an old wound. She was proud of the way she was rebuilding her life, the unsuspected resources she had discovered within herself. Then just when she was doing so well in her solitary life in Los Angeles, the summons had come to fly to Austria. She had been a fool to come, more than a fool to think she could have a pleasant European holiday and yet not suffer from contact with the von Kleists. She was unbearably tired. It was all starting again, and she was too weary to fight it—

Megan cried out in astonishment as Kurt's hands slid under her and swung her off the floor. "Put me down!" she squealed, trying vainly to squirm from him as he carried her across the room.

"Be still," he commanded as he settled her into the leather armchair. "You were about to faint."

The moment she sat down, Megan began to shake with fatigue. Her bright head lolled forward like some tropical flower on a broken stem. Kurt knelt before her and with gentle fingertips stroked back the flaming tendrils that had fallen across her eyes. His hand was warm and comforting on her skin; she had to force herself not to rest her cheek against it. She peered up through her lashes into his concerned eyes, then she looked down again, too drained and aching to hold his gaze. He asked quietly, "Are you all right?"

"I am very tired."

"Of course you are," he said. He rose from his knees so that he towered over her. "You have just completed an exhausting journey. I should have realized. I am truly sorry. This whole business has turned me not only into a suspicious fool but into a boor, as well." He muttered something in German that sounded like curses. "Is there anything I can do for you—Frau von Kleist?" Megan noticed the hesitation before he addressed her by name, the first time he had done so since she arrived. A faint line appeared between his eyes. He regarded her quizzically. "I understand you were no longer using Erich's name when my agent located you."

"That's right." Megan wondered if he was affronted. "I feel more comfortable with my maiden name now. However, the passport still says von Kleist." She paused, longing to retire but knowing that she had to ask one last question. "Herr von Kleist, why am I here? What is this urgent business you need me for?"

He shrugged dismissively. "It has to do with some property you inherit as Erich's widow, but that's not important now. You've only just arrived, and you need to rest. We'll discuss it later."

Megan nodded wearily. "Very well. May I go to my room now?"

"Of course. Are you sure you can make it?"

"I'll have to, won't it?" she answered without thinking.

Kurt took her hands and helped her to her feet. Her legs were trembling weakly. "I suppose I could carry you—"

Megan drew away hastily. "No—no, I—" she stammered before she saw the teasing glint in his eye. She grinned back reluctantly. A moment later Kurt summoned the maid, and Megan turned to say goodbye to him.

"Rest well, then, Frau von Kleist," he said. "Or should I call you Fräulein Halliday?"

"Why not call me Megan?"

As he looked down at her, his hard mouth widened into a warm smile that made him seem almost boyish. "Then, good afternoon, Megan," he repeated. He paused as if tasting the name. "Megan. I like that. Rather unusual, isn't it?"

"Not unusual, really, just not too common. It's a Welsh name. I come from a long line of Celts."

His eyes flicked over her face. "With that coloring, I'm not surprised," he murmured. "Of course, you must call me Kurt."

"Kurt."

He frowned. "No, that's not quite right. Don't make it rhyme with 'hurt.' It's more of a long *u*."

She tried again. "Kurt."

"*Sehr gut.* Soon you'll be speaking German like a native."

"I doubt that," she said. "I've tried before and I just can't seem to...." Her voice died away in a husky whisper as her green eyes met his blue ones. She gazed entranced into his dark face, and she began to quiver with a sensation she was afraid to define, the same trembly hollow feeling she had experienced three years before when Erich stormed into her practice room and demanded that she play the piano for him because his regular accompanist had been taken ill.

That lock of hair was straying over Kurt's forehead again, and Megan had to dig her fingernails into her palms to keep from reaching up and brushing it back. Kurt watched her, and his smile became complacent, almost a smirk. Megan blushed and tore her eyes away from him. *It couldn't be happening like this,* she thought indignantly. *Not again, not with Erich's brother....*

Kurt touched her arm and motioned in the direction of the door. "The maid is here, Megan," he said softly, an undertone of laughter in his gravelly voice. "She will take you to your room now. Get some rest, and I'll see you again at dinner."

Megan nodded. She was afraid to speak lest her voice betray her. After one last flash of bewildered green eyes, she fled from the study to follow the girl through the corridors to the wide curving staircase. As she mounted the steps she noticed that her fingers were stroking her arm where Kurt had touched her.

CHAPTER THREE

THE WESTERING SUNLIGHT was slanting obliquely across her room when Megan awoke. Its fading beams were tinted pink by the sheer curtains that masked the exit to the balcony connecting the suites in the guest wing. She had been asleep almost five hours. After the maid had showed her to her room, Megan had paused just long enough to gulp down a couple of her headache tablets before she kicked off her sandals and collapsed across the bed. She still felt groggy as she looked around now, and she noticed that while she slept, utterly exhausted, someone had quietly unpacked her luggage and laid out her bathrobe and toilet articles. On the table at the foot of the massive bed was a tray with a little pot of coffee, stone-cold, and a covered plate revealed a rather flaccid sandwich of some kind. Obviously it had sat there for hours while the lettuce wilted and the juices in the meat congealed, and now despite her hunger the offering looked singularly unappetizing. She shrugged. If meals were served on time here—and she suspected Gabrielle demanded military precision in the running of the household—then she had little more than an hour to wait before dinner.

Megan studied her surroundings with pleasure. The suite was spacious and thoroughly feminine. The large canopy bed was carved from mahogany, and its deep ruddy luster bespoke years of conscientious care. It was obviously an antique, but of a later period than the ornate French furniture in Gabrielle's morning room. The soft rose color of the bed curtains was repeated in the lovely old carpet, its flower pattern mellowed and muted with the passage of time. Megan thought the room the most appealing she had seen so far in the schloss.

When she went into the adjoining bath, she discovered that it had contemporary fixtures of dusty pink, including a shower and bidet and a tub large enough to swim in. She turned on the water as hot as she could stand it and scooped in a handful of fragrant pink bath salts. Soon the room was full of perfumed steam. Megan stepped gingerly into the scalding water, gritting her teeth as her aching body stung with the heat. She luxuriated blissfully, mindlessly, and her weariness seemed to leach out into the water, so that when she emerged reluctantly from the tub her fair skin glowed and she felt relaxed for the first time since leaving Los Angeles.

She wrapped her terry-cloth robe around her damp body and padded barefoot to the wardrobe, where she pondered what to wear for dinner. Gabrielle had said they dressed for the meal, a practice Megan was unused to. In Southern California "dressing" could mean anything more formal than a bikini! But after the older woman's catty remarks Megan was determined to be impeccably correct in her attire. She rejected the rather flashy gowns she wore for work and finally settled on one of her favorite dresses, a silky off-the-shoulder print in tones of emerald, sapphire and amethyst. It had a flowing skirt that molded her legs as she walked, and there was a wide ruffle at the hem. She piled her thick hair into an Edwardian pompadour, leaving two long curls to dangle loose in front of her ears. She applied a little eye makeup and darkened the gold tips of her long lashes with mascara. She slipped into high-heeled sandals and fastened a narrow velvet ribbon around her neck with a jade cameo that had once been her grandmother's.

Preening in front of the cheval glass as she put jade studs into her pierced ears, Megan approved her reflection. She looked rather like a provocative Gibson girl. Slowly she ran her hands down her body, enjoying the feel of the cool smooth fabric as it clung to her skin under her caressing fingertips. She had forgotten how much pleasure there could be in simple things like the texture of a piece of material or the blending of bright colors. For more than a year she had lived like a robot, with all senses turned off—except for the sense of hearing, perhaps—but now she was coming alive again. Now she could remember with amazement and no little impatience that she had quit wearing the jewel-toned colors she loved because once Erich had told her cuttingly, if not very originally, that green made her look like a Christmas candle.

After glancing at her wristwatch, Megan scurried from the bedroom. Her heels clicked lightly on the polished floor, reverberating in the empty corridor. When she reached the top of the staircase she paused. The steps sweeping down before her were steep and strangely intimidating, almost frightening. She had to fight back an unusual sensation of vertigo. After a moment she timidly lifted her skirt and began the descent, clutching the banister with her free hand. It was hardly the grand entrance the staircase demanded, and she chuckled self-consciously as she decided that the only way to come down those stairs properly would be in a high powdered wig and farthingale, with a flourish of trumpets and a lackey to announce her to the assembled multitude below. Marie Antoinette probably could have carried it off, but never Megan Halliday! But no one was near to watch her as she alighted, and the rooms she passed through were deserted, their beauty somehow repellent in the chilling, lifeless atmosphere she had noticed before.

In the salon Kurt stood alone at the far side of the room, mixing a drink. At first he did not notice Megan's arrival, and in those few seconds she gazed at him intently. She wanted to know, to understand this enigmatic man. He was tall and suave and elegant in the midnight-blue dinner jacket that must have been tailored especially to fit his broad shoulders. The dull sheen of the rich fabric contrasted sharply with his snowy ruffled shirt, the frills of which seemed to emphasize his dark masculinity. Megan shivered as she watched him. In profile Kurt was astonishingly like Erich, but she recognized that his long lean body possessed a strength and raw power his brother had lacked. She had always considered her husband the handsomest man she ever knew, but she saw now that although Erich had been more beautiful in a conventional sense, there was something compelling about Kurt's face, the hard, uncompromising features, the vivid blue eyes under that errant lock of brown hair. By contrast Erich seemed almost effete. If she had met them together, she wondered suddenly, would she even have noticed Erich?

Megan caught her breath sharply, bewildered at the direction of her thoughts. At the sound Kurt turned to face her, and for a long moment she found herself scrutinized as closely as she had studied him. His eyes swept from her hair and face down her body, lingering over her full breasts and small waist and noting the way the bias-cut skirt clung to her hips before it flared into the wide ruffle. Megan quivered as if he had touched her, and she did not miss the hot light that flamed momentarily in his blue eyes. She thought wistfully, *if only once Erich had looked at me like that....*

Kurt asked in his deep quiet voice, "Are you feeling better now, Megan?"

"Yes," she murmured huskily.

He said, "You look—quite charming." Their

eyes met, then he gestured toward the bar. "May I fix you a drink? Do you have a preference?"

She shrugged. "Oh, anything will do as long as it's not rum." Kurt tilted his head interrogatively, and she explained, "I work at a cocktail lounge called the Polynesian Paradise, and everything they serve contains rum and pineapple juice. It gets—tiresome."

"I can imagine," he said dryly as he handed her a whiskey sour. When she nodded her approval he asked, "But don't you find your job rather tiresome, as well? With your background in the classics I should think playing nothing but popular music would be unbearably tedious."

Megan grinned. "Well, I have been known to break into the *Ritual Fire Dance* when things get too slow." She shook her head and the smile vanished. She sighed, "No, Kurt, I accept my job for what it is: a stopgap until I go on to other things."

"What sort of things?"

"Teaching, perhaps. I think I could be a good music teacher. It's an idea that seems increasingly appealing, now that I'm older."

"Older?" Kurt laughed. "A child like you?"

Megan said harshly, "I'm old enough to have found through bitter experience that I have neither the talent nor the temperament to become a first-class concert pianist. I tried very hard for years, and the effort nearly destroyed me."

"The effort?" Kurt's voice was free of mockery. "Don't you mean Erich?"

Megan turned away without answering. She wandered over to a window. The sun had finally gone down, and she could see a single point of light gleaming on a hillside on the opposite side of the valley. She sipped her drink, already noting the fuzzy feeling behind her eyes. She was uncomfortably aware that she was going to become light-headed if she didn't eat soon. She asked, "Will your daughter be joining us for dinner?"

"Yes. Liesl and Gabrielle should be here any moment now. Adelaide, too, if she gets back in time from wherever she's run off to."

Megan frowned involuntarily. She had forgotten the older woman she found so disturbing. She looked at Kurt again. "Well, since we seem to have a few minutes free, will you tell me about this property that belonged to Erich? I never heard him mention it, and naturally I'm curious."

Kurt drained his glass and reached for the decanter to refill it. Megan watched him, and she noticed again the inflexible fingers of his left hand. Kurt said, "This is your first night in my country, Megan, and I want it to be a memorable one. We mustn't spend it talking business."

Megan's green eyes narrowed at his rather patronizing air. "Suit yourself," she said ungraciously. "It's just that I thought Austrians were supposed to be very efficient and businesslike."

Kurt laughed shortly. "You're thinking of Germans. We are different, you know. There is an aphorism—not overly complimentary, I suspect—

that states that when a German first meets you, he asks your name and occupation. An Austrian, on the other hand, will ask your name and what books you've read lately."

Megan shrugged and smiled. She was beginning to feel warm and relaxed. She savored the smooth bite of her whiskey before she asked archly, "Well, aren't you?"

"Am I what?"

"Going to ask me what books I've—" She stopped abruptly and shook her head, then glanced around for a place to set down her glass. "When I start getting all kittenish," she muttered, "I know I've had enough." She peeked through her lashes at Kurt, who was watching her with some amusement. She said defensively, "I haven't eaten since this morning, and I'm not used to this altitude."

He chuckled softly, taking a step closer, "Oh, yes, undoubtedly it's the altitude."

Megan blushed. She never flirted, and she couldn't imagine why she was doing so now. There was more to it than just the drink, and more than the normal response to admiration from a handsome man. A fair percentage of the men who tried vainly to pick her up at the cocktail lounge were good-looking and well mannered, but she had never felt attracted to any of them and rejected their advances firmly. Now Kurt was simply looking at her, and her breathless response puzzled and frightened her.

Kurt observed with interest the wildly fluctuating rose tint in her cheeks, and Megan thought resentfully that the greatest disadvantage to being a fair-skinned redhead was that there was no way to disguise the remarkable spectrum of color her emotions could produce. She could not hide the heat his caressing gaze generated, and she was astounded by the violence of her reactions. *God,* she thought as hot prickles of awareness began to burn under the skin, *that drink hit me harder than I realized!*

The expression in Kurt's heavy-lidded blue eyes darkened, and his nostrils flared when he noticed Megan's taut nipples pressing against the clingy fabric of the jewel-toned dress. He took a step toward her, and quickly she turned away, mortified. When he touched her bare shoulder, she shook her head fiercely, the long curls bobbing against her flushed cheeks. *I won't let it happen like this,* she vowed silently. *I won't put myself through that hell again!*

Kurt's fingers pressed into her pale silky flesh. "Megan—" he grated, his voice low and urgent.

From the door to the music room Liesl called, "*Vati*—daddy! Look, Tante Gaby let me wear my new dress!" The little girl bounced into the salon, very pretty in a long shell-pink voile dress that made her fair skin glow.

Instantly Kurt dropped his hand from Megan's shoulder, and his eyes were unreadable as he watched his daughter approach him. She threw her arms around his waist, and he stroked her corn-silk hair with his scarred hand, gently brushing back the strands from her face. "You look very beautiful, *Liebling*," he said with great tenderness, "but I thought you were saving that dress for your name-day party."

"I'll wear it then, too," Liesl said innocently, "but Tante Gaby said I should wear it tonight because we have company. She said we must show Tante Megan that real von Kleists know how to dress suitably."

Megan blanched. Damn that woman, how dare she talk about her in front of the child! Momentarily blind with anger, Megan turned smartly on her heel, and she immediately stumbled into a fragile-looking table. Before she could catch herself she had upset an ornament, a delicate porcelain cupid, and it shattered on the strip of gleaming floor between the carpet and the wall.

Sick with embarrassment, she stared stupidly at the fragments. Then she dropped to her knees and tried to scoop up the shards as she moaned incoherent apologies for her clumsiness. But before she could gather up even the largest piece, Kurt swooped down and caught her by the wrist, pulling her roughly to her feet. "Good Lord, Megan," he exclaimed, "what do you think you're doing? You'll cut yourself!"

"But the—the figurine. I'm so sorry, I didn't mean to—"

"Forget the damned thing," he said harshly. "Let a maid clean it up." He glanced at Liesl, who was watching them wide-eyed. "Go find Greta or one of the other girls and tell her there's been a slight accident." When the child reached for the bell rope he repeated sternly, "I said, go *find* one of them!" Liesl stared at her father and retreated from the room.

The door slammed behind the little girl, and Megan was left alone with Kurt, who was still gripping her wrist. She tried to pull away from him, but his hold was too powerful. With a twist of his arm he forced her up against him, so that only their two hands were between them. When Megan pushed at his shoulder, he caught her other wrist easily and pinned it behind her. She could not move without wrenching her whole arm, and she was acutely aware of the pressure of his knuckles against her breast, the heat of their bodies together. She glared up at him indignantly for a few seconds before she tried again to loosen her hand. Her fingernails snagged on the ruffles of his shirt, and she squirmed with impotent rage as he jeered softly, "Are you always so clumsy?"

"I'm sorry about the porcelain," she retorted irritably. "It was an accident, but I was upset."

Kurt's eyes narrowed. "I apologize for my daughter. She didn't realize what she was saying."

"I know that!" Megan stared at him, then she lowered her lashes. Glancing down she saw that while Kurt still held her wrist in his strong fingers, the pressure had changed, and instead of gripping her arm painfully he was delicately rubbing her breast with the back of his hand. Megan shivered and whispered huskily, "Please don't do that."

He smiled silkily. "Why not?"

Megan gulped, "Because—because I don't want you to, that's why not."

He shook his head. "*Mein Schatz*, I don't think I believe you."

She choked, "Kurt, *please*!"

With surprise he heard the undertone of genuine panic in her girlish voice, and he released her instantly. He stared down into green eyes that were wide and dark with fear. "Megan?" he murmured uncertainly.

From the doorway Gabrielle said, "Kurt."

Megan jerked her head in the direction of the voice. Gabrielle was lingering at the entrance to the salon, tall and predictably soigné in oyster-colored satin, but her face was twisted with some fierce emotion Megan couldn't define. Kurt swore under his breath. He nodded to his other sister-in-law, who glared at the younger woman before launching into a torrent of angry German. Kurt answered her in kind. The exchange was sharp and brief, and Megan, burning with embarrassment, was glad for once that she could not understand what was said. She watched Gabrielle shudder and turn pale before finally nodding in reluctant acquiescence.

When Kurt handed Gabrielle a drink, she sipped it silently. Her hazel eyes flickered suspiciously as she peered at the other two over the rim of her glass. Megan wondered suddenly if Kurt and Gabrielle were or ever had been lovers. It wasn't inconceivable. After all, her husband had been dead more than two years, and she wasn't so very much older than Kurt.

That uncomfortable line of thought halted when Liesl returned with a maid. Gabrielle noticed for the first time the shattered ornament, and she cried out in horror, "Oh, no, not my Sevres—"

"Forget it, Gaby," Kurt muttered.

"But, Kurt, that was a wedding present from—"

"I said, forget it!"

Gabrielle shrugged and turned away, but just for an instant she glared venomously at Megan.

Kurt glanced at his watch. "It's time for dinner. Where the hell is Adelaide?"

Gabrielle frowned. "I let her drive over to St. Johann today to visit one of her school friends. I expected her home long before this. Do you suppose she could have had an accident?"

Kurt said irritably, "If anything were wrong, we would have heard by now. Adelaide probably just decided to stay over and as usual forgot to tell you. She's a good driver. It's her manners that need improving." Abruptly he offered Megan his arm. "Dinner is waiting," he said.

Dinner did not begin well. When Kurt escorted Megan into the huge dining room, he jerked to a halt at the sight of the lengthy table, which was shrouded with embroidered linen of frosty whiteness. A massive ornate silver epergne at least ten feet long gleamed with candles and flowers in the center, and the five place settings were crowded with sterling flatware, crystal goblets and gold-rimmed bone china. Still holding Megan's arm, Kurt glanced sidelong at Gabrielle and asked,

"Isn't this rather—elaborate for a family dinner?"

Gabrielle said, "But, Kurt, you told me to make your guest feel welcome."

"Welcome, yes," he snorted, "but *mein Gott*, Gaby, that centerpiece has been in storage since Franz Josef was emperor!"

"I was only following your instructions, Kurt."

His jaw tightened, but he was silent as he led Megan to the far end of the table, where he seated her at his right. Liesl scurried to Megan's side, while Gabrielle sat across from her and studied her as if she were some new species of insect. Acutely uncomfortable, Megan trained her gaze on the intertwined dragons and mermaids of the florid epergne. Liesl touched her hand and whispered, "Isn't it pretty? It took two days to polish off all the tarnish. I helped."

Megan smiled down at the child. "You did a good job, dear," she said, and Liesl beamed.

At a signal from Gabrielle servants trooped in bearing trays of food, beginning with cold smoked trout, followed by fried veal rolled with ham and cheese, and a bewildering succession of creamy noodle-and-vegetable dishes that should have tempted Megan's appetite but didn't. Although she was hungry, she only toyed with her food, oppressed by the outrageously elaborate meal. Kurt tried to keep the conversation going, but voices tended to die out in the room that should have seated sixty rather than just four. When Megan spoke, her replies were terse, and Gabrielle said almost nothing. Even Liesl became subdued, obviously puzzled by the adults' behavior.

Megan was just beginning to pick at her dessert, an incredibly rich chocolate pecan torte she might have enjoyed were it not flavored with rum, when the door flew open and into the room burst a tall teenage girl dressed in tight jeans and a skimpy scarlet halter top. "Sorry I'm late," she laughed carelessly in German before she halted abruptly and stared at Megan. Megan stared back. The girl was younger than she, eighteen or nineteen, leggy and angular, and she had hazel eyes and very straight chestnut hair that was cropped short into a smooth helmet on her well-shaped head. Light freckles powdered the creamy skin across the bridge of her retroussé nose, and her mobile features twisted into an exaggerated grimace of bewilderment as she puzzled over Megan's identity. Finally she grinned. "Hi! Who are you, Kurt's latest lady friend?"

Megan choked. Kurt muttered repressively, "Mind your manners, Adelaide." To Megan, who was sipping her wine in an effort to clear her throat, he said, "May I introduce Adelaide Steuben. She's Gabrielle's foster daughter, and a pleasant enough child when she isn't trying to be witty." He turned back to the girl. "Adelaide, this is Megan, my brother Erich's wife. We told you she would be visiting from the United States."

Adelaide shook her head as she flopped into the chair next to Gabrielle. When she switched to English, Megan noticed that her accent was harsher than that of the other von Kleists. "I must have misunderstood. I thought you were expecting some old family retainer whom you planned to pension off. Gaby said—"

Gabrielle said severely, "Adelaide, surely you don't intend to eat dressed as you are."

The girl shrugged her tan shoulders. "Oh, don't be archaic. If I go upstairs to change, dinner will be cold by the time I come back."

"You might have returned home sooner," Kurt suggested mildly.

Adelaide beamed flirtatiously. "I did try. But the traffic was unbelievable. You know what it's like in Salzburg during the festival—"

Gabrielle accused, "You told me you wanted to go to St. Johann to see your friend from the university."

"Well, I did. And Barbel's brother had one of his friends visiting from Naples, and the four of us decided to drive down to Salzburg to see that new Al Pacino film."

Kurt sighed, "And I suppose it didn't occur to you to advise us of your change of plans?"

"No. Why should it?"

Gabrielle said, "If I'd known you were going to Salzburg, you could have seen about those roses I've ordered for the dance. I want them chosen personally this time. Last year the flowers they sent were impossible; I might as well have used the ones in the garden here."

Kurt added, "Had I known your itinerary, I could have arranged for you to pick up Megan from the airport and thus save her a long and tiring bus ride."

Adelaide stared down at her fish. "All right, I'm sorry I didn't tell you! Now I suppose—"

Megan pushed crumbs of cake and whipped cream around her plate with the tines of her fork. She hated being forced to listen to a family squabble. She and her mother had never argued. Their relationship had been close and affectionate, and Megan supposed that the intense loneliness she experienced after her mother's death had been one reason she fell in love with Erich as quickly as she did.

Adelaide's voice pierced Megan's reverie. "But Franco's uncle works for di Giulio in Rome, and he said he can get me a job there as an extra anytime I want it! Please, can't I go just for the rest of the summer?"

Gabrielle murmured, "Adelaide, you know I need you here to help me with the ball, and after that I plan for us to begin refurnishing the music room."

"But if I already have some film work to my credit, think how it will help me when I go to Hollywood."

"Oh, Adelaide!" Gabrielle sighed impatiently. "How many times must I—"

Kurt said, "Adelaide, perhaps you ought to talk to Megan about Hollywood. After all, she is from Los Angeles, and she has been in the entertainment field."

The teenager stared incredulously at Megan. "I didn't know that. Are you an actress?"

"Goodness, no!" Megan laughed uncomfortably, acutely embarrassed by the girl's avid gaze. "I've never thought of myself as being in show business, and I don't think my experience would have much bearing on what you are interested in, even if I do live in L.A. now. I met Erich in New York, and that's where we stayed when we were not on tour."

Gabrielle seemed intent in turning the subject away from Adelaide's movie talk. She asked, "How did you meet Erich? You seem such an... unlikely couple."

"I met him at the Halstead Conservatory, where I was studying piano. He was giving an impromptu recital one day, and he needed someone to accompany him." Megan closed her eyes, quivering slightly at the memory of her first sight of Erich. For a few seconds she relived those moments in the practice room, the totally unexpected, gut-wrenching impact when she saw him and knew he was the man she wanted. Nothing that happened later ever quite canceled out the ecstasy of that first instant. One smile and she had been lost forever, seduced by his looks, inspired by his talent....

Megan blinked. The four von Kleists were staring at her. Gabrielle said, "I'm afraid I've never heard of the Halstead Conservatory, but then, I'm not really familiar with American music schools. There's Juilliard, of course."

Megan snapped, "Halstead may be a small school, without the reputation of Juilliard, but the teachers are excellent and I was honored to be a student there."

"Yes," Gabrielle said sweetly, "and I'm sure you're a credit to the school. You play in a bar now, don't you?"

Adelaide sniggered. Megan gritted her teeth. She said with as much dignity as she could muster, sounding unbearably pompous even to herself, "Yes, Frau von Kleist, it's true that the work I do now is not in keeping with my training, but I'm sure you'll agree that few things in life turn out exactly as we plan them." Out of the corner of her eye Megan saw Kurt's mouth curl up in the faintest hint of a grin, and she thought, *damn him, he's enjoying this!*

She turned angrily to him, but before she could speak he said blandly, "Liesl is studying the piano now. I think she shows promise."

Megan forgot her anger as she looked down at the little girl, who was surprised to find herself suddenly the center of attention. Megan asked, "Do you enjoy music, Liesl? How long have you taken lessons?"

"I started when I was seven, and I like playing the piano very much, almost as much as riding my horse." She added wistfully, "I just wish I could take lessons during the summer."

"But why can't you?"

Gabrielle snorted, "Surely you don't expect to find good teachers here in Kleisthof!"

Megan looked helplessly at Kurt. "I'm sorry, but I don't understand. Where does Liesl study, if not here?"

"In Vienna," Kurt said. "Liesl and I live in Vienna most of the year. It's only during her school holidays that we are able to spend much time in the Tirol, and even then I must commute frequently because of my business."

Megan nodded. "Yes, you did say your gallery is in Vienna." Delighted and relieved that the conversation was on neutral ground again, she commented, "I realize it would be difficult to run a successful art dealership from here in the mountains, but I'm surprised you didn't establish it closer to home—say, in Salzburg."

Kurt said quietly, "Vienna is my home, Megan. You must remember, I did not expect to inherit the estate."

Megan colored. She had forgotten about Wilhelm, the oldest brother, Gabrielle's late husband. She glanced at the other woman, who was staring bleakly into her wineglass, and a wave of compassion washed over her. *What must it be like,* she wondered, *to live in such splendor, expecting that someday it would belong to you, and then have a freak accident deprive you not only of your husband but also of all rights to the estate?* The frustration didn't bear contemplating. No wonder Gabrielle seemed neurotic at times. Megan said simply, "I'm sorry, Frau von Kleist. I meant no offense."

Gabrielle turned on Megan, her voice harsh and

scornful. "When I want your pity I'll ask for it. You have less right here than any of us. Even Adelaide is my cousin. You're just a—a fortune hunter!"

"Gabrielle!" Kurt roared. "You will apologize to our guest at once!"

Gabrielle turned to Kurt, her face haggard. "But Kurt," she pleaded, "how can you take her side against me? I am a von Kleist by blood as well as marriage. She's just the discarded wife of an illegitimate upstart!"

"Gabrielle—" Kurt warned.

Megan stared blankly at them. "Illegitimate? I don't understand. What are you talking about?"

Gabrielle snorted, "Didn't your precious husband tell you? For all his fine airs, he was still just a shopgirl's bastard." She stood up, waving her arms rather wildly. "Did you think he grew up here? Why, he was fourteen years old before he ever set foot inside this house, and if Willi had had his—"

Kurt jumped to his feet, and his voice, chilling and implacable, cut through the woman's raving. He said firmly, "Gabrielle, you are not yourself tonight. Please make your excuses and retire."

Megan shivered. Kurt's voice was like dry ice, burning cold, and she fervently prayed she would never be on the receiving end of his anger. She almost pitied the older woman, who seemed to crumble visibly as she stood there trembling, incapable of movement. The carefully painted mask had cracked, and Gabrielle looked much older than her years.

Kurt snapped, "Adelaide, help her upstairs."

Adelaide protested, "But, Kurt, I haven't finished my—"

"Adelaide!" Kurt took a deep breath. In a normal tone of voice he said, "I'll have the rest of your meal sent to your room, but for God's sake don't argue with me now."

For a moment the girl glared at him, then slowly she set down her fork and rose to her feet, tall and proud even in her skimpy casual clothes. "Of course, Kurt," she said in a voice devoid of expression. "When a true von Kleist orders me to do something, who am I to disobey?" She went to Gabrielle and put an arm around her sagging shoulders. "Come on, Gaby," she murmured as the older woman stumbled from the dining room, a pathetic figure in her designer gown and elaborate hairdo. Megan sighed with relief when the door closed behind the pair. She had no way of really understanding Gabrielle's mental state, but she ought to realize better than most that appearances were deceptive.

Kurt sank back into his chair, and as Megan turned to him she caught sight of Liesl sitting rigid and bewildered beside her, frightened by the interchange among the adults. Megan suddenly felt guilty that the child had been exposed to such an ugly scene. When the little girl hesitantly asked her father a question in German, he rubbed his temple and mumbled something Megan translated as

"Please, dear, not now!" Liesl's lips quivered, and she leaped up and fled from the room.

Megan started to push aside her own chair, but Kurt signaled her to remain seated. "Please," he said, "don't go yet. I know this has been an unfortunate beginning for your visit, and I apologize sincerely. Won't you stay and talk, perhaps help me finish the wine?" Megan nodded, and Kurt refilled her glass. She picked up the fragile crystal goblet and swirled the straw-colored liquid around, watching the way it reflected the flickering candlelight. The fruity bouquet wafted upward and tickled her nose. When Kurt lifted his own glass he said wryly, "I know that toasts are supposed to come at the beginning of the meal, but I think it might be appropriate to drink to—a better day tomorrow."

"Yes," Megan agreed fervently.

They drank in silence, then Megan set down her glass and asked, "Was Gabrielle telling the truth?"

Kurt scowled. "You mean about Erich's being illegitimate? Yes. I gather you didn't know."

Megan shook her head. "I knew so little about Erich's background, a point you've already observed. I never had any reason to think he was anything but the cherished child of a normal family."

Kurt nodded his dark head. "It would be like him to encourage such a fantasy." He drained his glass and put it aside, then pulled out his cigarette case and offered Megan one. When she refused, he lighted his own and muttered, "I make no excuses for my father. I suspect, although of course I have no way of knowing, that my parents never resumed their conjugal relationship after I was born. My mother was not well, and there were other...difficulties between them. Whatever the reason, eventually my father began an affair with a girl named Eva Müller, who worked in a dress shop in Kleisthof-im-Tirol. She was, I understand, very beautiful, with the same remarkable white blond hair that Erich had."

Kurt paused, frowning as he smoked. He said, "You realize, of course, that much of what I tell you is simply hearsay. I was only about eight years old at the time." When Megan nodded, he continued, "I don't know if the girl was in love with my father or if she was just flattered that the Graf von Kleist paid court to her. Either is possible. My father was an attractive and virile man until his death. Eva may have thought that he would divorce my mother, although personally I doubt it, since the von Kleists have always been at least nominally Roman Catholics. But the question became academic...because Eva Müller died when her son was born."

A spasm of pain creased Kurt's face, a glimpse of some anguish that Megan recognized instinctively did not come from his pity for the doomed shopgirl. He ground out his cigarette on the bone-china dessert plate, then glanced down with disgust at what he had just done. He dropped the butt into an ashtray and said roughly, "Until recently, good emergency medical care was difficult to come by here in the mountains." He shook his head angrily, then smiled as though to apologize for his display of emotion. "Eva was dead," he continued, "and the child was left to be raised by his maternal grandparents, a God-fearing couple who were always a little embarrassed by their daughter's...lapse. As far as I know, my father provided some financial support all along, but he did not acknowledge Erich formally until after my mother died, when Erich was fourteen."

Megan's green eyes met Kurt's, and she asked quietly, "When he was a child, living with his grandparents, did Erich know who his father was?"

Kurt's mouth twisted into a bitter line. He sighed, "There are always people who delight in passing along information like that."

Megan stared at her empty wineglass and thought about her dead husband. She had never known him, not at all. That incredible arrogance, that delight in hurting her—apparently these were ways he repaid the pain and humiliation he had suffered as a child, taunted for his birth. What must he have felt down there in the village, looking up with longing at the castle on the hill, knowing he ought to be there himself? What did he think when he saw the man he knew to be his father? True, he had been recognized—but fourteen years too late. Megan shook her head sadly as she absently tapped her nails on the goblet, appreciating its bell-like tone. "Poor Erich," she said.

Megan was trudging along the corridor to her room when she heard a muffled sound coming through a half-open door, a sound she puzzled over until she realized it was a child crying. Surreptitiously she pushed the door farther open until she could see the interior of the room, a lace-and-organdy confection that Megan assumed was some decorator's mistaken idea of the perfect setting for a little girl. A small lamp beside the heavily draped angel bed threw amorphous shadows on the walls papered with moiré silk, and she could just make out huddled on the darkened window seat a slight figure in a long pink dress—Liesl, clutching a rather bald teddy bear.

Megan winced as she repressed an almost sickening sensation of déjà vu. Thus she used to sit. She had been younger than Liesl then, with riotous carroty curls instead of hair like corn silk, but she would crouch in that same position, hunched over a rag doll, trying to shut out the sounds of the adults arguing downstairs. Megan had long ago resigned herself to the failure of her parents' marriage, but she could still remember the fear and guilt she had felt when they quarreled, the childish certainty that she was somehow responsible.

She took a hesitant step toward the child. "Liesl," she called gently. When the girl looked up, Megan repeated, "Liesl, is there any way I can help?"

Liesl shook her head mutely and turned back toward the window.

Megan sighed and sat down beside her, wondering as she did if she was overstepping her duties as a guest. She said tentatively, "Liesl, this afternoon when we met, you said you'd like to have a chance to talk to me. Well, I'm here now, and sometimes it helps a lot to talk to someone."

Liesl still didn't speak, but she watched Megan thoughtfully with her dark blue eyes—Kurt's eyes, Megan recognized now. Megan went on, "Sometimes adults can be very stupid. They yell and call each other names and carry on in a way that would get a child spanked in short order—but there's no one to spank them, so grown-ups just keep getting louder and crankier. That's what happened tonight. People said and did a lot of stupid things, but tomorrow it will all be better. Do you understand?"

Liesl made a little jerky movement that could have been a shrug. She sniffed, "But it's always like that around here."

"What do you mean?"

"Whenever we come to the schloss there are arguments. *Vati* and Tante Gaby make each other angry, and sometimes Tante Gaby shouts at Adelaide or even me, like when I wanted to hang up the posters that came with my new record album."

Megan stifled a chuckle as she glanced around the lush room. "Liesl, you must admit that posters would be a little out of place here."

"Adelaide has old movie posters in her room," Liesl said. "Tante Gaby told her not to put them up, but she did anyway. But I can't do that because my father told me that this is *Tante*'s home and I must mind her whenever we're here." After a pause she continued fiercely, "I hate it here. I wish we didn't have to come every summer. I wish we could stay home in Vienna."

"Perhaps your father thinks you're better off to get out of the city for a while. Many parents like their children to spend their summers in the country. And this is a very beautiful place."

Liesl sat up, pouting indignantly. "But except for the horses there's nothing to do here! *Tante* tells me I should spend my time learning how to be a von Kleist, but that's dumb; I've been a von Kleist all my life. At home there are places to go, and I have friends, and I can take my piano lessons."

"Don't you have friends here? I seem to recall your father saying something about a party for you."

Liesl gave Megan that sidelong look of disgust that children use when they think adults are being particularly stupid. "The party isn't for me," she snorted. "They just say that because it happens to be on my name day, and that's just because my name is the same as my mother's was. The party is a big charity ball they hold every year to raise money for the clinic my father and grandfather started after my mother died." Suddenly Liesl's eyes were bleak. "She died here, you know," she said in a tiny voice.

Megan shook her head. "No, I didn't know."

The little girl tightened her grip on the teddy

bear. "I can still remember it," she said. "Nobody believes I can remember that far back, but I remember people running around, shouting at each other, and later there were lots of candles, and *Vati* was crying."

Megan shivered. She could not for the life of her imagine Kurt von Kleist crying about anything. *He must have loved his wife very much,* she thought, and wondered what kind of woman it would take to inspire Kurt's love. She asked, hating herself for pumping the child, "Do you remember your mother?"

Liesl puckered her forehead. "I'm not sure. Sometimes I think I do, then I wonder whether I can really remember her or if I'm just thinking about pictures or things people have told me. *Vati* has a picture of her on his dresser at home. She was English before she married him, and she had blond hair like me. He says I look a lot like her."

Megan smiled tenderly. "Then I think your mother must have been very beautiful." Liesl's face lighted up, losing that pinched look, and she scooted closer to Megan. Megan put her arm around the little girl's thin shoulders and hugged her. She said, "About your piano lessons: I won't be here very long, but if you like I might be able to give you a few pointers, perhaps show you something new you could work on until you return to Vienna. Would you enjoy that?"

Liesl squealed with delight. "I'd love it!"

Megan said, "Maybe we could help each other. You can give me German lessons." When Liesl grinned, she continued, "Why don't you tell me the kinds of things you've been doing, and we'll see what we can come up with."

Liesl set her teddy bear down on the floor and held her hands in the air as if curved over an imaginary keyboard. She moved her fingers with great concentration. "Fräulein Brecht, my teacher, was trying to show me how to form chords, especially the—the...." For once her English failed her. She described the chord, and Megan prompted her, "The dominant seventh chord. Some people call it the V^7."

"Dom-i-nant," Liesl repeated.

"Das ist sehr gut," Megan approved.

Liesl wrinkled her nose and snickered, "Your pronunciation is terrible."

"I told you I needed help. Why are you having trouble with the dominant? You seem to understand it well enough."

Liesl looked bashful, as if she were about to reveal a shameful secret. "I can't make my fingers stretch that far. My hands are too small."

Megan caught Liesl's hands in her own and examined them. "Don't worry, sweetheart," she said indulgently, "your hands will grow. I can tell just by looking at them that you could be a very good pianist. See, your fingers are already almost as long as mine. I'll bet when you are all grown up you'll be able to stretch a tenth easily. Now, my hands really are too small; I can barely reach an octave. That's one reason I couldn't keep up with—" Megan stopped abruptly. She shook her head slightly as she said, "Let me show you a good stretching exercise. It would be easier to explain at the keyboard, but this is what you do...."

Slowly, patiently, Megan talked to the little girl about music, answering Liesl's eager questions in simple terms, illustrating her points with rhymes and jokes, and Liesl opened up to her the way a flower opens to the sun. Then Liesl began correcting Megan's German pronunciation, and her mock-serious demeanor soon had them both giggling so hard that they never even noticed Kurt pause in the corridor to light a cigarette. He watched them through the open door for a long time, his face inscrutable, before he silently walked away.

CHAPTER FOUR

MEGAN SAT UP in the big canopy bed, hunched over her knees. She pushed aside the rose-colored hangings and peered into the morning gloom. During the night the wind had died down and clouds rolled in. Now soft rain spattered the balcony on the other side of the French windows. She had slept long—overslept, in fact—but she was not rested. Her fatigue had been too intense to let her relax, her thoughts too disturbing. While she tossed and turned, her nightmare had come again, the succession of sound images—her training had made Megan a very audile dreamer—that still had the power to leave her sweating and shaking.

It began as always with a simple phrase of piano music, a light theme soon picked up sequentially by the violin and turned into an elaborate counterpoint. But just as the two musical lines began to twine together like disembodied lovers, her dream was ripped apart by a woman's raucous laughter and a faintly accented male voice that declared, "You are my wife. You will never leave me!" Then came another voice, her own, girlish, frightened, pleading incoherently. All the sounds—the music, the laughter, the distressed cries—were repeated louder and louder until the cacophony was somehow the squeal of tires on wet pavement, grinding metal and shattered glass, a deafening explosion—

Megan buried her face in her arms. In the first days after Erich's death she had been literally afraid to sleep, afraid of the recurrent dreams, and her fears had left her exhausted and totally incapable of rebuilding her life. It was at this point that she had met Dorothy Butler. The older woman with the enchanting Southern drawl had taken one look at the wraithlike girl who moved into the cramped apartment next to her own and quietly adopted her, feeding her when she forgot to eat, guiding her to the job as pianist at the cocktail lounge where she herself worked. The night Megan collapsed with a miscarriage, unaware until then that she had been pregnant, it was Dorothy who rushed her to the U.C.L.A. Medical Center; Dorothy who told the admitting nurse that as far as she knew Megan Halliday had no husband, no next of kin. She did not tell the nurse that almost every night through the pasteboard walls separating their two apartments she had heard Megan whimpering in her sleep, calling for someone named Harry or Errol or something like that.

In time the nightmares had become less frequent, less vivid. Megan regained her strength and even teased Dorothy about fattening her up. When Dorothy contemplated—and ultimately decided against it—getting married a fourth time, Megan listened sympathetically and offered advice when asked for it. But she never talked about the years when she had lived away from Los Angeles, and eventually only the persistent violet shadows under her eyes remained as a legacy of the past.

And now after one night in Austria the nightmare had returned and she was falling for an arrogant stranger who happened to remind her of her dead husband.

What was it about that combination of features and mannerisms that she found so irresistible? Why did a certain arrangement of muscles and bones stir her to instant response? With Erich, one look was all it had taken to bind her to him for life, and even at the nadir of their relationship she had been drawn to him physically. Now the prospect of repeating the experience with Kurt was almost more than Megan could bear. The man had been barely civil to her when they first met, and yet by nightfall she had responded to his not-very-subtle advances with the hungry intensity of a schoolgirl just released from a convent.

But perhaps it was simply a matter of hunger, of physical need. She was twenty-three years old and had never known sexual satisfaction. Erich had been indifferent to her needs, and later when she was approached by men where she worked she still had been too traumatized to consider accepting what they offered. Now, however, her health was restored, her mind more or less at peace, and her body stirring in ways she had repressed for a very long time.

She needed a lover, she reflected. It was as simple as that. And someday soon she would find one, probably some reasonably intelligent, attractive man she would meet at the cocktail lounge. She had no particular requirements for the man she would invite to share her bed, except that he wouldn't drink ropy mixtures of rum and pineapple juice, and he wouldn't ask her to play whatever movie theme song happened to be currently popular.

And he wouldn't be a von Kleist.

MEGAN DRESSED in shocking-pink slacks and a matching long-sleeved cheesecloth shirt. She tied her hair at the nape of her neck with a scarf of the same color, startling but surprisingly effective against her red hair. Liesl was waiting in the formal dining room when she came downstairs, and she led Megan into a smaller, more intimate "family" dining room, where breakfast waited on heated trays on a sideboard. Once again the child wore jeans and a T-shirt, but this time the shirt bore a picture of a pop group.

In one long breath Liesl rattled off the message she was supposed to deliver. "*Vati* asked would you please excuse him because he has a painting he must crate up before he goes back to Vienna tomorrow and Tante Gaby and Adelaide are in the morning room working on plans for the party." Then the little girl picked up the heavy silver coffeepot with the aplomb of a society hostess and asked, "How do you like your coffee? *Melange?*"

"I beg your pardon?" Megan said blankly.

Liesl said, "Oh, *Melange* means half coffee and half milk. That's the way we usually drink it in the morning. If you want just a little milk, it's a *Brauner,* or if you want more milk, it's *Milch gespritzt.* If you—"

Megan interrupted hastily, "Thank you, but why don't I just fix it myself?"

Liesl snatched a bun from the sideboard and plopped back down at her place at the table while Megan filled her plate. Megan sat beside her and said, "I'm sorry I overslept. It was kind of you to wait for me. I hope I'm not keeping you from anything."

Liesl muttered, "Well, I did want to take out my horse, but it's raining." She sounded as if the rain had fallen especially to keep her from her ride. She munched in silence for a moment, then her pale face brightened. "Instead of the ride, could we have that piano lesson you promised me?"

"Of course, dear, if no one minds." Megan realized suddenly that she had no idea what was required of her as a guest of the von Kleists. If she was expected to amuse herself, the music room was the place she would much prefer to spend her time. As soon as she had finished her coffee and rolls, she followed Liesl through the salon to the room where the antique piano waited in solitary splendor. As Megan pulled the spindly side chair into a position next to the piano bench, she said lightly, "All right, Liesl, will you play something for me?"

After a great deal of squirming and adjusting of sheet music Liesl took a deep breath and began playing "Das Mädchen und Sein Hund"—badly. Even the exquisite tone of the piano could not compensate for her poor performance. She flinched with every wrong note and glanced furtively at Megan.

Recognizing the child's nervousness, Megan said quietly, "You may begin again if you like." She leaned back in her chair so that she could study the ornamented ceiling. The painting here was of a chorus of buxom angels clad only in wisps of revealing drapery, who floated among billowy white clouds in an impossible blue sky and plucked at improbable stringed instruments. As Megan wondered what song was causing the decidedly sensual smirks on those angelic faces, Liesl pounded her fists on the keyboard in frustrated discord.

"Don't do that," Megan reproved her automatically. "You might shake the piano out of tune."

"I hate this piece," Liesl declared. "It's boring."

"Yes, it is," Megan agreed equably. "Don't you have any other music?"

"Only my exercise book. I forgot to pack the rest before we left home."

Megan glanced around the near-empty room.

"There ought to be some music somewhere. I've never yet been in a house with a piano that didn't have a pile of old sheet music somewhere close at hand."

"We could look in the cupboards," Liesl suggested. She hopped down from the piano bench to riffle through the contents of the cabinets hidden behind the scrolled paneling. "Nothing here. Or here. No, that's the stereo console. Maybe—no, I can't get this one open, Tante Megan. Can you?"

Megan pulled lightly on the handle. "I think this cabinet is locked, Liesl."

A footstep behind her alerted Megan to Kurt's presence just before he asked, "May I help you?"

Megan turned quickly. Kurt, dark and devastating in black cords and a deep red shirt unbuttoned at the throat, was peering down at them with a faint frown, and Megan's color rose. "I wasn't snooping," she said uncomfortably. "We were just looking for some more music, since Liesl forgot to bring hers with her."

Kurt glanced at his daughter. "You forgot it, *Liebchen*? Why didn't you tell me? I could pick it up for you while I'm in Vienna."

"I didn't think of that," Liesl said, scuffing her sneakered toes together.

Kurt was looking at Megan. "What sort of music do you want?"

"I was hoping we could find a collection of some of the easier classics—'The Happy Farmer,' that sort of thing. The piece Liesl is working on is hardly inspiring."

Kurt nodded sagely. "I think I may have what you want." He pulled out a set of keys from the pocket of his tight slacks and inserted one into a lock hidden in a gilt curlicue. He jerked open the doors, and Megan noticed the dank musty smell of old paper. On the bottom shelf of the cupboard a stack of exercise books and sheet music lay yellowed and crumbling. Liesl squealed with delight and grabbed at them, but the top sheet disintegrated under her avid fingers.

"Weichlich, mein Kind," Kurt warned. Then he said to Megan, "Some of those books are more than thirty years old, but I'm sure you can find—"

But Megan was not listening. She was gasping with shock at the black leather violin case on the third shelf. She would have known it anywhere. She had seen it daily for two years, touched it a thousand times, tended it with the loving care usually reserved for newborn infants. "Is it—" she choked.

"Yes," Kurt said.

"But how did you get it? I gave it to—"

Liesl looked up from her treasures and asked, "What's that, *Vati*? May I see?"

Kurt carried the violin case over to the piano bench. "It's the violin that used to belong to your Uncle Erich, Aunt Megan's husband." He unfastened the case, and Megan watched breathlessly as he pulled back the white silk scarf that swaddled the instrument. From Erich she had learned to treat the Guarneri as if it were a holy relic, and she cringed at the thought of anyone scratching it. But Kurt touched the violin sensitively, carefully, and after Liesl lost interest and returned to the pile of old music, he handed the instrument to Megan.

She looked it over, assuring herself that it was the same as it always had been, perfect except for the long abrasion that had marred the bridge for literally centuries. Just a few scraps of wood and varnish, yet in the right hands capable of producing sounds of incredible beauty and sonority. "Does no one play it now?" she asked Kurt as she reverently returned it to the case.

"No one," he sighed, shaking his head. "Such a waste." He put the case back into the cupboard and closed the door.

After reassuring herself that Liesl was ignoring them, Megan said quietly, "I gave the violin to Herschel Evans. How did you get it?"

"Evans sold it to me. He knew it was a von Kleist heirloom and that I would want it back. Why didn't you contact me, Megan? If you needed money...."

"I didn't sell it to Herschel," Megan snapped. "I gave it to him. I didn't realize it was an heirloom. Erich always said it had been a gift from his—your father. I didn't know you would expect to have it back. Erich died owing Herschel a tremendous amount of money, and the violin was the only thing I had that could settle the debt."

"But surely you must have realized that a genuine Guarneri in near-mint condition would fetch at least twice what Erich owed his manager?"

Megan scowled. "You and Herschel must know each other well for you to have found out exactly how much money Erich owed him."

Kurt made a dismissive gesture. "I don't know Evans at all. We arranged to meet the last time he was in Europe. He was very fair about the violin. He asked only enough money to reimburse the actual expenses of Erich's career. He said there was no way to pay him back the time and love he devoted to his protégé."

"Love," Megan snorted.

"I think Evans loved Erich," Kurt said mildly. "He spoke of him with affection. But I'm afraid he was very bitter about you."

Megan gritted, "Yes, I know. Thanks to darling Lavinia, Herschel blamed me for Erich's death." She turned away to hide the hurt twisting her face.

"What exactly happened that night?" Kurt asked from just behind her. His warm breath made the pink scarf flutter against her neck. She shivered. He said, "Evans was rather vague, and that stiff little note you sent me at the time said only that my brother had died in an automobile accident."

"I'm sorry the note seemed cold," Megan said. "But I didn't know you then. I didn't even know if you could read English."

"I'm not blaming you, child. I simply would like to hear your side of the story."

Not the whole story, Megan thought grimly; never the *whole* story! She took a deep breath that came out almost as a sob. Although she saw that

Liesl was still absorbed in the old sheet music, she moved away from the child to the far end of the room, where she stood before the tall mullioned window and stared at the dripping beech tree just outside. Kurt joined her. Together they watched the rain.

Megan observed quietly, "It was raining the night Erich died. I was on my way to Kennedy International to catch a plane for Los Angeles. I was leaving Erich because he—because the situation had become intolerable. Erich and Lavinia came after me in Lavinia's car. Erich was driving. The roads were slick, and he had been drinking—did you know that?"

Kurt grimaced. "Evans never mentioned it."

"Maybe Herschel didn't know. Erich rarely drank. He usually preferred to get high on music. Unfortunately, this was one time when he used alcohol." Megan shuddered. "The car skidded into a utility pole and exploded. Knocked out the power in a twelve-square-mile area, and left Erich dead and Lavinia seriously injured. She could hardly explain to her husband that she and Erich had been trying to catch me because they feared that once I was out of Erich's reach I'd tell Herschel about their affair, so she concocted a wild story about my leaving Erich for another man. Herschel believed her." Megan's green eyes clouded. "Herschel had been my friend, but at the funeral he wouldn't even speak to me."

Kurt watched her intently. "So you were left with no husband, no friends, no money?"

Megan bridled. "You make me sound like the little match girl! It wasn't as pathetic as all that. I managed. People usually do, you know. And even if Erich had lived, I wouldn't have taken anything from him, unless—" She stopped abruptly and pretended great interest in the beech tree.

"Unless?" Kurt prompted.

Megan looked up at him. She winced with remembered pain. "I had a miscarriage a couple of months after Erich died," she murmured. "If I hadn't lost the baby I might have needed help."

Kurt's face was pale, and his blue eyes bored into her. He choked, "Erich's child?"

"Yes, of course."

Kurt brushed back his hair with the palm of his hand. "I'm sorry," he said hoarsely, "I didn't realize. I assumed from what you told me—I didn't know you and he had that kind of relationship."

Megan sighed. "There are a lot of things you don't know."

BY LUNCHTIME THE RAIN HAD STOPPED and the clouds were beginning to break up. As Kurt escorted Megan and Liesl to the dining room he offered to take them for a drive later in the afternoon. He included Gabrielle and Adelaide in the invitation, but Gabrielle declined with the explanation that she was expecting a telephone call from Salzburg, some last-minute difficulty with the orchestra she had hired for the party. When Adelaide said she wouldn't mind going with the others, Gabrielle reminded her that she had to supervise the cleaning crew in the ballroom.

Megan had dreaded seeing Gabrielle again, but to her amazement the older woman was courteous to her, even charming, totally different from the wild-eyed virago she had been the night before. After lunch when Kurt returned to his office for a while, Gabrielle showed Megan around the mansion, with Adelaide tagging along behind. Gabrielle was extremely knowledgeable about the building, and when they passed through some of the empty rooms she explained that she was slowly redecorating, trying to refurnish with antiques similar to those that had been sold during the depression following the First World War. She sighed, "It's heart-rending to think of von Kleists being reduced to selling their furniture—but that is all in the past. I am determined to restore the schloss to its former glory."

Megan said, "That must be a tremendous undertaking for one person."

Gabrielle shrugged. "Oh, I am not alone in my work. Kurt advises me on the art treasures, and Adelaide is a great help. She is studying interior design at the university, you know, as well as Austrian history, so that she can better understand the task before us."

Megan glanced back at the girl, who walked with her chestnut head bent. *Where does Hollywood come into these lofty plans,* Megan wondered. When Adelaide looked up suddenly and her hazel eyes met Megan's, the teenager's face was blank.

As they strolled through the hallways, Gabrielle pointed out details of the exquisite architecture and decoration, and every now and then she pressed Adelaide for clarification of some point. Adelaide's replies were precise and mechanical, like those of a well-trained tour guide. Gabrielle, on the other hand, grew animated and enthusiastic as she gave thumbnail sketches of the generations of von Kleists who had lived there. She said, "Schloss von Kleist is relatively new, not quite three hundred years old." When Megan blinked, Gabrielle laughed. "I know that to an American that seems ancient, but you must realize that a number of structures in this part of Austria go back as far as the twelfth century. The foundations were laid in 1690, and construction went on for more than fifty years. What is remarkable about Schloss von Kleist, apart from its great beauty, is that the estate has remained intact and in the hands of one family clear up to the present." Gabrielle's voice grew strident. "Not one hectare of the original grant has ever passed out of the family!"

But am I part of the family, Megan asked herself, finally getting a hint of why she had been summoned to Austria. Aloud she only commented, "That's an incredible heritage."

"Yes, it is," Gabrielle agreed. "And believe me, no one is more aware of that heritage than Kurt." She turned a corner and now they were in a gallery lined with dark portraits, dimmed and crackled with age. Gabrielle was gesturing to the first painting when suddenly Adelaide excused herself, muttering something about the ballroom.

Megan watched Gabrielle smile affectionately as the girl disappeared up the stairs. "Dear Adelaide," she murmured in a faraway voice. "She has been such a joy since she came to Willi and me. I longed to give him a son, you know, an heir—but in her own way Adelaide helped ease the pain. Of course it was not easy at first, taking on the care of a teenager—so many unsuitable notions, silly dreams—but I think she is settling down now. She does well in her studies. She is not a von Kleist, and yet—and yet I truly believe she has the calling."

Megan stared at Gabrielle, disturbed by the passionate, almost fanatical gleam in her unseeing eyes, when suddenly the woman recalled herself from her reverie and pointed again to the first portrait, an enormous painting of an autocratic-looking man astride a snorting black charger. In the background were stacks of turbaned corpses. "The first Graf von Kleist," she explained matter-of-factly. "He was granted both the title and the estate after the Turks were driven from Vienna by Emperor Leopold I. The painting is probably rather idealized, since it wasn't completed until after the sitter's death."

She proceeded down the line with Megan following her, fascinated in spite of herself. Gabrielle knew the names and histories of each of the subjects, as well as the approximate sitting dates and most of the artists—some of them names even Megan recognized. After a while Megan began to notice a family resemblance among those grim-looking men and women: recurring almost every generation were high cheekbones, a long thin nose and piercing eyes. These features made the woman handsome rather than beautiful, and the men reminded her irresistibly of Kurt. Dominant genes, Megan supposed. Erich had had that look, despite his less-than-aristocratic birth, and Megan wondered irreverently just how many peasant girls over the centuries had produced babies with those betraying features.

Halfway down the hall Gabrielle stopped in front of a portrait of a grim-looking woman with white hair. Beside the picture was a small velvet-lined display case holding a pair of beautiful Italian flintlock dueling pistols, their long walnut stocks ornamented with gold filigree, the mountings elaborately carved and chased. Gabrielle smiled indulgently.

"To look at this portrait you would never believe that Marthe von Kleist was in her youth a great and notorious beauty. Her husband fought two duels over her. He was wounded in the second one, and she was so remorseful that after she had nursed him back to health she became a model wife, and they had eight children. It is said that Marthe and her husband came to regard these pistols as their most treasured memento—" As Megan started to stroke the filigree, Gabrielle warned sharply, "Don't touch them, they're loaded!" Megan jerked her hand away, and Gabrielle added, "Antique firearms were a hobby of my Wilhelm's. There are quite a few throughout the schloss, all in working order."

They went on until at the end of the corridor Gabrielle halted again before a small modern painting that was oddly at variance with the forbidding air of the other portraits in the gallery. It was a charming study of three young people, a boy and girl about seventeen and a second boy several years younger. Megan didn't know the artist, but she appreciated his skill. With deft strokes he had captured the protective air of the older boy toward the girl, while the younger boy fidgeted with obvious embarrassment. Megan stared at the trio. The older boy with his blond curls and soft brown eyes was a stranger to her, but the girl and the other boy looked somehow familiar.

"That's Willi, my husband, and Kurt and me," Gabrielle said wistfully. "So long ago.". She shook her head. "Willi never had his formal portrait painted, so we hung up this one."

"I'm very sorry," Megan said involuntarily. She waited for Gabrielle to lash out at her the way she had done the night before, but the woman was silent. Megan was confused by Gabrielle's presence in the grouping. "You must have married very young?" she asked tentatively.

Gabrielle smiled. "Oh, no, this was painted years before that."

"Then you knew your husband when you were children?"

"We grew up together," Gabrielle said. "I have lived in this house since I was seven years old." Megan stared at her. The older woman explained, "My mother was first cousin to Horst von Kleist, Willi's and Kurt's father. When I was very young our home was in Vienna, a lovely old townhouse on the Ring, nothing like this, of course, but happy and full of light. Then during the war my father died in Poland and our home was destroyed in the bombing raids. As the war began to wind down, my mother said, 'We must go to Cousin Horst.' So we walked here."

"You were seven years old and you *walked* all the way from Vienna?" Megan echoed incredulously.

Gabrielle shrugged. "We had no choice, really. The Russian army was headed our way. We had no food, no transportation, but anything was better than being there when the Russians came." She closed her eyes, and Megan wondered what horrors she was seeing. But Gabrielle blinked and smiled. She reminisced, "When we finally reached the Tirol, spring was just here. Edelweiss and other flowers were breaking through the snow that lingered under the trees, and the breeze was warm. I can still remember how it felt to be warm again after so many months of cold...." She was lost for a second in her memories. When she spoke again her voice was plangent. "My mother and I stood on the hill by the gate, looking down at this magnificent house. My mother was ill, dying, but she said, 'There is your new home, Gaby.' The schloss was so perfect and untouched after all the destruction we had seen that it looked like the entrance to paradise.'' Gabrielle gazed thoughtfully at Megan, and her smile thinned. She added quietly, "And that, little American girl, is why I will not let you or anyone else threaten Schloss von Kleist. Be warned."

KURT PARKED THE STATION WAGON on a hill overlooking a jewellike meadow with a small lake on the far side, and he helped Liesl unload her bay filly from the trailer. The girl leaped onto the horse and galloped across the field like an apprentice Valkyrie, her blond hair streaming behind her. Megan picked her way through the long wet grass, soaking her sandals and the hem of her slacks. The sun was warm and the freshening breeze seemed heavy with the scent of a thousand wild flowers. She bent down to stroke the silky blue petals of a blossom almost hidden by the grass. When she straightened up, Kurt was standing next to her, and she asked him about edelweiss.

"Edelweiss?" he repeated blankly. "It's a pretty little flower, with star-shaped white blossoms that are rather woolly. But you won't find any now; it's much too late in the year. It blooms in the very early spring. Why?"

"Oh, I was just curious," Megan said. "Somehow when I think of Austria I think of edelweiss—

edelweiss and dirndls and the von Trapp family singing 'Climb Every Mountain.'"

Kurt threw back his head and laughed. It was a deep, rich, attractive sound oddly at variance with the clipped cynical tones in which he usually spoke. He said, "I think Liesl has a dirndl somewhere in her closet—the way she is shooting up she has probably outgrown it by now—but not even to please a guest will I sing 'Climb Every Mountain,' and for that you should be grateful! Occasionally in a crowd I will join in the 'Bundeshymne,' the national anthem, but that is the extent of my vocalizing." His blue eyes were bright as he teased her. "So, apart from these disappointments, what do you think of my country?"

Megan surveyed the glistening meadow dotted with wild flowers, the cerulean sky with its one fat white puff of cloud that was reflected like a beauty mark on the shimmering surface of the lake. She sighed, "I thought the ceiling fresco in the music room was a fantasy, but now I'm beginning to believe it must have been painted from real life. Everything here is outrageously beautiful."

"That's an odd choice of words," Kurt observed. "Are you outraged by beauty?"

Megan shook her head. "Not outraged, just surprised. Where I come from, natural beauty is at a premium. Los Angeles is my home and I love many things about it, but the air is unbreathable, and the L.A. River is a concrete ditch where people abandon old cars. One gets used to it. I can't imagine what it would be like to live in a setting such as this. Do you grow accustomed to all this beauty? Does the day come when you can look at all this and not be overwhelmed?"

"Such a day has never come for me," Kurt said. "I love this place. I have known the mountains, the meadow, and lake all my life, and I thank God every day for the privilege of sharing them. Wherever I have gone in the world—my student days in England, and now when I live in Vienna—I have always been comforted by the knowledge that the estate is here, eternal and unchanging. Funny, but I never thought how hard it might be to maintain that placid facade." He made a sweeping gesture with his hand. "Now that my father and brothers are gone, it has fallen to me to be caretaker for all this, and I confess I find the responsibility rather awesome."

Megan said, "Gabrielle told me you were very conscious of your heritage."

"Of course. To be otherwise would be to betray the von Kleists who came before me. My people have been here for centuries. They have struggled, some have even died, to hold on to what is theirs. Sometimes I question the morality of one family having so much in this world we live in today, yet I know I must keep the estate in trust for those von Kleists who will, if it pleases God, follow me." He gazed across the meadow to the shore of the lake, where Liesl and her horse browsed. He smiled ironically. "Will there be more von Kleists? We seem to be dying out rapidly. That lovely innocent child is the last of the race. On her small shoulders rest three hundred years of lusty, not always worthy history. It would be poetic justice if she decided to take the veil."

Megan protested, "But you're still a young man. You should remarry."

Kurt's eyes darkened. "Perhaps," he agreed, and turned away abruptly to light a cigarette. After he had smoked in silence for several minutes he stubbed the butt out in the wet grass and said, "Now, Megan, we come to the reason I asked you to visit Austria. This meadow, down to the lake and around that hill over there, now belongs to you."

Megan stared at him. Her heart seemed to have stopped beating. "You're joking," she croaked.

"I wish I were," Kurt rasped. As Megan flushed he added hastily, "Not because I'm sorry you came—I ought to have invited you long ago—but because we are caught in a morass of legal loopholes and questions of title from which I have been trying vainly to extricate ourselves for more than two years." He reached for his cigarette case yet again. When he saw Megan's eyes drop to the butt still smoldering at their feet, he coughed wryly and pushed the case back into his pocket.

He continued roughly, "In short, the situation is this: during the last years of his life my father apparently regretted his treatment of his youngest son. He realized that nothing he had given Erich—the von Kleist name, the best musical training, the use of the Guarneri—could really make up for those first fourteen years when he ignored the boy's existence. He knew, too, that once he was dead, Wilhelm, who had always considered Erich an interloper, would probably deny his half brother any access to the estate. So father did something that had never been done in all the generations of von Kleists since old Otto himself: instead of bequeathing the estate in its entirety to his oldest surviving son, he left the meadow separately to Erich. No one knew about it except the attorney who drew up the will, and of course no one could foresee that my father and Wilhelm would die at the same time. When I learned of the bequest, I wrote to Erich in America, but he never responded to the letter. I don't know if he even received it."

"Yes, he did," Megan said. "That's how I knew where to write to you after Erich's accident."

"You didn't read it?" Kurt asked suspiciously.

"How could I? I don't read German, remember?"

"Of course." Kurt scratched his ear and watched Megan through hooded eyes. "You do see what I'm leading up to, don't you?"

"I can only assume that you're telling me that since I'm Erich's widow, the property has fallen to me."

Kurt nodded. "More or less, that is the situation. But there are numerous ramifications. Since you are not an Austrian national, you are restricted in what you may inherit. Of course Erich died in the United States, which raises the additional question of whether Austrian or American law should apply." He shrugged. "My lawyers tell me that the best way to handle the problem is for you to sign a document renouncing all right to the property—for a price, of course—and then let them resolve the matter as best they can. It may take years."

Megan studied Kurt's face intently. "I don't know what to say," she concluded helplessly. "Erich never mentioned—I never dreamed—"

Kurt said, "It is no dream, I assure you. The sum we arrived at is a fair one, in keeping with current property values and rates of exchange." He told her.

Megan gasped. Suddenly her legs would not support her, and she sat down abruptly on the wet grass. "My God," she breathed.

Kurt dropped to his haunches beside her, and even in her bemused state Megan noticed how the taut fabric of his black trousers delineated the muscles of his powerful thighs. "I'm sorry," Kurt laughed, "I should have told you while we were still in the car. You're going to ruin your slacks." He held out his hand to help her up.

She waved him away as she stared blindly into the distance. She whispered hoarsely, "No, please, I'll be all right. Just...just give me a minute to take it all in."

"Of course. I'll leave you to think about it." He strode across the meadow to Liesl, his long legs making a trail of darker green through the lush grass.

Megan gazed all around her, oblivious to the damp that was seeping through the thin material of her slacks, unaware of anything but the astounding news Kurt had just told her. This was *her* meadow! The high sweet grass that filled the air with its warm scent when she stepped on it, the wild flowers like tropical butterflies in the light breeze, the fertile black earth beneath—these things belonged to her, Megan Halliday, the city girl who had spent her whole life in apartments or townhouses with handkerchief-sized patches of yellow weeds that passed for yards. The thought was overwhelming. It stirred in her wild atavistic impulses. She wanted to leap into the air and fling herself flat again for the sheer joy of feeling the fragrant verdure crush beneath her. She wanted to yodel with delight.

After glancing across the field to see that Kurt was still talking to Liesl, Megan laughed exuberantly and did a flop backward onto the wet ground. She closed her eyes so that she could concentrate on the feel of the earth beneath her. Blades of grass tickled her neck, and something with a particularly prickly stem scratched her back through the thin shirt, but as she lay there with the sunlight playing on her porcelain skin and vivid hair, for an instant she was one with nature, intimately aware of the life force around and within her.

Lethargic with sensation, she dozed in the somnolent warmth until a shadow came between her and the sun. When she opened her eyes Kurt was standing directly above her, studying her hungrily as he took in every detail of her appearance, the wisps of hair worked loose from her pink scarf and now curled damply against her cheek, her firm breasts pressing against the flimsy cotton of her disheveled shirt, her leg half-bent in unconscious invitation. Megan gazed up at Kurt. The sun glowed in a corona behind the towering length of his body, and when she blinked against the sun, her green eyes met and locked with his blue ones. She thought in wonder, *I want him.* Heat began to pulse through her body like low-voltage electricity, a tingle of indescribable need radiating from low in her abdomen, as basic and elemental as the earth she lay on. While they stared at each other the rest of the world receded, and they were suspended in a throbbing nimbus of golden light.

Slowly, slowly, Kurt extended his hand to Megan. When her fingers curled into his, she trembled. As he shifted his weight to draw her to her feet, she felt his momentary instability; for an endless fraction of a second she could have pulled him down into the inviting grass beside her. Kurt's mouth widened into a grin as he sensed her hesitation.

Then Liesl came trotting up on her horse and the moment was gone.

"*Tante*, your clothes are a mess," Liesl observed as Kurt jerked Megan to her feet and she stood brushing away bits of leaves and dirt. "Your back is all wet, too. Why are you lying on the ground? Did you fall down?"

Kurt explained dryly, "I think Aunt Megan just wanted to get a better look at the sky, *Liebling*."

Liesl craned her neck to peer overhead. "What so special about the sky?"

Wiping her hands on her thighs, Megan stammered, "I—I'm not used to such a—a blue one. Where I come from, Liesl, the sky is usually a dirty brown from the smog."

Liesl wrinkled her nose. "It sounds nasty."

"Sometimes it is." Megan cast a venomous glance at Kurt, who smiled with wry amusement at her discomfiture while he studied the way the damp shirt clung to her arrow-straight spine and her slacks revealed the line of her bikini panties. She turned her back to the hot drying sun and deliberately changed the subject. "That's a beautiful horse, Liesl. What's her name?"

Liesl stroked the filly's graceful neck. "This is Blitzen—Lightning. I call her that because there was a storm the night she was born."

Megan slowly reached up to pat the animal's silky nose, but it nickered softly and she jerked back.

"Don't be afraid, *Tante* Megan," Liesl said kindly, and she leaned over to catch Megan's hand in her own and press her fingers gently against the horse. "See, she won't hurt you."

Timidly Megan glided her hand over the smooth warm brown coat, marveling that such a powerful animal could be so docile. She looked up at Liesl. "Were you there when Blitzen was born?"

"No, I missed that. *Vati* said if we came at

Easter the timing should be just right, but Blitzen arrived ahead of schedule.''

"No one is perfect, Liesl," Kurt murmured patiently just behind Megan.

The little girl shrugged. "I know, *Vati*. Anyway, the Webers' grandson told me all about it."

"The Webers?"

"Our chauffeur's family," Kurt explained. "They board the horses while Liesl and I are in Vienna."

"Do you have many horses?"

"Oh, no, not any longer. Just Blitzen and her dam. Once, of course, the von Kleists maintained a full stable of really fine horses specially bred in Carinthia, not far from where the Lipizzaners are raised. However, that ended long ago, in my grandfather's time." He patted the filly's nose and she nuzzled his shoulder. "If Liesl weren't so crazy about horses, I doubt we would keep even the two we still own, since Gabrielle dislikes riding and I rarely have time for it. From your reaction I gather you don't ride?"

Megan shrugged. "I had my picture taken on a pony once at Griffith Park. I think I was about six. That's the only time in my life I've ever been on a horse."

"And you've never had any inclination to learn?"

"Not really. It's always seemed such a long way to fall."

Kurt smiled warmly. "Yes, you are rather a little thing, aren't you?" He reached toward

Megan's face, and Megan, acutely aware of Liesl's presence, flinched from that caressing gesture. Kurt's smile vanished. "You had a blade of grass in your hair," he said coldly, flicking the offending sprig away from her temple. Megan blushed. Kurt turned abruptly to Liesl and told her to take her horse back to the trailer.

"Oh, *Vati*," Liesl protested, "do we have to go now? I've hardly had any time at all!"

"When we get back to the Webers', you may stay there awhile," Kurt snapped. "I have work to do at the schloss."

Grudgingly the girl complied. When they were ready, Megan reluctantly left the beckoning panorama of the meadow. "It's so incredibly beautiful," she sighed. "I don't suppose there's any way I could keep it?"

"No," Kurt said flatly, "no way at all. If you're wise you'll take the money." He held open the door of the station wagon for her.

As she slid in she said, "Well, with that much capital I ought to be able to go back to school, get my teaching credential and still have some money left over to open a music school of my own."

"All part of your quest for independence, I suppose?"

Megan was puzzled by his snide tone. "I hope so. I'd like to think that I'm capable of supporting myself."

"Isn't that what husbands are for?" he persisted.

Megan stared at Kurt. "I doubt that I'll ever remarry," she said quietly.

Kurt's voice was clipped as he shifted the car into gear. "Very well. I have to return to Vienna for a few days. I'll have the papers drawn up while I'm there."

AT DINNER Megan wore a short sleeveless dress of soft bone white jersey that was very cool and that she hoped would not emphasize the triangular patches of sunburn at her throat and on her nose. She had realized too late that the high altitude made her creamy skin even more susceptible to the sun than it usually was. She pulled her fiery hair back into a heavy chignon, revealing the graceful line of her throat and the dainty ears that seemed almost too small for the faceted gold hoops she wore as her only ornament.

Kurt met Megan at the foot of the stairs and led her into the salon, where Liesl and the other two women were already waiting. This time, Megan noted, Adelaide was clad in a long green dress that was eminently suitable, if a little old for her nineteen years. The girl had effected rather dramatic eye makeup, but the pale pistachio color of the dress brought out the bronze highlights in her smooth chestnut hair, and Megan decided that if Adelaide ever did pursue her ambition to become an actress, her looks would be a definite asset.

Gabrielle glanced up from her drink, her hazel eyes intent as she asked quietly, "Is everything arranged, Kurt?"

"Yes," he answered equally quietly. "Megan was most understanding." He left the women and crossed the room to the bar.

Gabrielle studied Megan for a moment, and then, to Megan's utter amazement, smiled at her. Her thin mouth widened, revealing meticulously perfect teeth, and Megan was reminded once again that Gabrielle must have been a beauty when she was younger, before personal tragedy and nervous strain had ravaged her face. The older woman said, "I am delighted that you are being so cooperative."

Megan shrugged. "Why shouldn't I be? As beautiful as the meadow is, I can understand why you wouldn't want to lose it, and obviously I can't afford to keep it."

At Gabrielle's side Adelaide perked up suddenly. "Meadow?" she asked. "*The* meadow?" She frowned thoughtfully at Megan. "You mean that you—"

Returning with Megan's cocktail, Kurt laughed dryly, "Let's not talk business now. Last night I went to a great deal of trouble to convince our guest that Austrians never speak of anything but literature and fine art at mealtimes." His blue eyes teased Megan, and she blushed uncomfortably.

Adelaide giggled, "What, we can't discuss sports or the cinema?"

Kurt patted her shoulder. "Well, for you, little one, I suppose we could stretch a point and mention a movie or two." He pushed open the door to the dining room and directed the women through.

As Adelaide passed him she paused and said, "Oh, Kurt, mentioning the meadow reminds me: I had to go that way yesterday when I drove to St. Johann, and I noticed that someone has parked a small trailer at the far end, near the highway."

Kurt peered down at her. "Tourists?"

She shook her head. "No, I don't think so. I didn't stop but it looked to me as if there was some kind of equipment inside."

Kurt frowned. "I see," he muttered absently.

Gabrielle turned back to him. She touched his arm and asked urgently, "Kurt, do you suppose—"

He put his hand over hers and squeezed her fingers reassuringly. "Don't worry, Gaby, I'll deal with it."

Although they ate in the huge dining hall again, this time the meal was served with less pomp, and Megan enjoyed it more. Conversation was desultory. Megan, exhausted by emotional shocks, politely remarked on the beauty of the estate but said little else. Adelaide seemed to be mulling something over in her mind. Were it not for Liesl, the table would have been uncomfortably silent, but the little girl chattered about the prizes she and Blitzen were going to win as soon as the pair of them were old enough to study dressage, the highest form of horsemanship. Gabrielle gently indulged Liesl's fantasies, and watching them it occurred to Megan that the older woman might have made a surprisingly good mother. Her relationship with her foster daughter seemed to be rather abrasive, but perhaps that was because Adelaide had been almost grown before she came to live at the schloss. Certainly Gabrielle might have been less neurotic if she had been able to expend her family feelings on a child rather than on the house. During the meal Kurt was withdrawn, almost sullen, and afterward when Liesl went to bed and Gabrielle excused herself and Adelaide to return to the apparently endless party preparations, Megan muttered a polite good-night and retired to her own room.

She kicked off her bone-colored pumps and flung herself into an armchair where, for what seemed hours, she considered her windfall inheritance and what she ought to do with it. Her mind wandered off on delightful tangents as she debated quitting her job and getting a larger apartment. The idea of going back to school was less appealing, but necessary if she wanted to become an accredited music teacher. She contemplated transcripts, examinations, honors recitals, the academic miscellany she had put behind her when she went on the concert trail with Erich. She weighed the merits of various schools. Halstead seemed the obvious choice, except that she did not think she could bear to walk into the rooms where she first met and was courted by her husband.

For a while she amused herself by toying with names for the school she would found. She envisioned Megan Halliday Conservatory of Music in flowing italic script over stained-glass doors; then she decided that a plain Halliday Studios on a discreet brass plate would lend an air of elegant simplicity. She built her castles in the air until she finally rebounded to earth with the wry thought that once Austrian and American tax agencies got hold of her inheritance, she would be lucky if there was enough money left over to fly her back to Los Angeles.

Megan rose from her armchair and stretched her cramped muscles. She wandered restlessly around her suite, far too keyed up to think of sleep. The paperbacks she had brought with her held little appeal. At home she usually assuaged her nerves with music, but here there was no record player or even a radio readily available. She had seen an elaborate stereo console in the music room, but knew she didn't dare touch it. She considered the piano. Would the others mind if she went down to the music room and played away some of her tension? After all, she was supposed to be a guest, although so far the von Kleists had been less than effusive in their welcome.

Megan was halfway down the grand staircase before she realized she had left her shoes in her room. Even in the warm air the cold of the glossy steps seeped through the soles of her nylons as she paused, debating whether or not she should go back for them. While she argued with herself she heard a sound coming from the music room that made her forget all about her shoes. Someone was playing the piano. She recognized the piece instantly, the allegro of the *Facile* Sonata by Mozart, and whoever was playing was doing so with considerable skill, running up and down the scales deftly, with precise trills.

But the person was playing only the part for the right hand.

She crept silently to the door and peeked in. Kurt sat with his back to her. His dinner jacket was slung down on the love seat, and his snowy shirt fitted loosely across his broad shoulders as if he had unbuttoned it. She could see his thin graceful fingers move lightly over the keys, and every few measures his left arm twitched convulsively as the stiff scarred hand lifted to the keyboard and then dropped away.

The door creaked when Megan leaned against it, and Kurt jerked around on the piano bench. "What do you want?" he demanded.

"I'm sorry," Megan flushed. "I couldn't sleep. I—I thought I'd play for a while, if no one minded. That always relaxes me. I—I didn't realize you would—would be—"

"Indulging old fantasies best forgotten," Kurt finished dryly. "Come in, Megan. There's no point in hanging back now that my guilty secret is out." He picked up his coat and tossed it onto the top of the piano, waving her to the short couch on which it had lain. Megan noticed that his ruffled shirt was unbuttoned almost to the waist, and through the gap she could see the tangle of dark hair on his chest, a sight she found strangely disturbing. When she sat back on the love seat her feet stuck out in front of her, and Kurt grinned, "No shoes?"

"I left them in my room," she explained grumpily, tucking her toes beneath her, "I didn't plan to meet anyone."

"I thought you seemed tinier than usual." He shook his head in wonder. "In a year or two Liesl will be as tall as you are."

"Taller, probably," Megan agreed, refusing to react to his teasing. She said, "I didn't know you play the piano."

Kurt arched one eyebrow. "Obviously I don't."

Megan blushed until her sunburned nose looked pale against her hot cheeks. She stammered lamely, "No, but—but once you . . . must have."

Kurt took pity on her. "Poor Megan. You needn't pretend you haven't noticed my injury. I'm much more likely to be offended by someone who very carefully—and obviously—looks everywhere except at my left hand. After twenty-five years I assure you I have accepted the fact that my fingers are not going to bend again."

Megan exclaimed, "Twenty-five years? You must have been very young when it happened."

"Thirteen," Kurt sighed. "It was just a silly prank, the kind all boys play, but that particular time it had disastrous results."

"What happened?"

Kurt said, "My father had to go to Dresden on business, and as a special treat he took me with him. Ironically the trip was a reward for all the time I had spent preparing for my last piano recital." He leaned back against the keyboard, and the harsh discord made Megan jump. He noted, "Erich was not the only musical von Kleist. I was quite a child prodigy. There was some talk of my performing professionally. But as I was saying, the man my father visited had a son about my age, and the two of us went out to play. Although the city was rebuilding at a furious pace, there were at that time still areas of great devastation left from the fire-bombing raids of the war. Against all warnings we decided to explore a burned-out building. Inside we found an unexploded artillery shell."

Megan gasped.

Kurt nodded grimly. "The other boy was killed, and my left hand was permanently disabled. After that I had to concentrate on the visual arts." He reached behind him to close the piano, but instead his fingers stroked the keys. "I tell myself," he said slowly, "that the only reason I perform my little one-handed solos is to strengthen my fingers, but deep inside I know better." He sighed. "I hope you are right about Liesl showing promise as a musician. It would be a comfort to me." Absently he began picking out the main theme of the Mozart sonata.

Megan watched him as he pressed the keys—half a song, less than nothing. As she looked at him she tried to imagine the suffering of a sensitive thirteen-year-old boy maimed for life, a carefree child suddenly crippled in one inconceivably agonizing moment. He had lost the use of his hand, a brutal blow for anyone, but perhaps even more cruelly, he had lost his music. People could learn to cope without a limb, but to the born artist, Megan knew, life wihout music was no life at all.

Without conscious thought Megan rose from the love seat and slipped onto the piano bench at Kurt's left. "Keep playing at that speed," she suggested lightly as she began the bass line of the sonata. Kurt stared at her. After a moment's hesitation he resumed his part, and they performed a clumsy uncoordinated duet for several measures. "No, don't go faster," Megan protested, laughing. "This is a lot harder than it looks." She was still laughing when Kurt's right hand slid down the keyboard and grasped hers.

They were so close together on the piano bench that when she tried to twist away from him her breast brushed his upper arm. Her smoky green eyes were wide and startled when his other arm circled her waist to pull her even closer, and his fingers climbed up caressingly to stroke the line of her jaw and curve around her neck under the heavy chignon. "Kurt?" she asked in alarm.

"Hush, Megan, don't talk," he whispered as his mouth met hers.

His lips were warm and coaxing when they moved over hers, and the kiss was flavored with the tang of the cigarettes he chain-smoked. Phantoms from the last time Megan had been kissed rose up to haunt her, and she held back, turning her face away, afraid of pain or rejection. His long fingers caught her chin with velvet strength and guided her mouth back to his, parting her lips with his thumb. He was surprisingly gentle, demanding no more than she was ready to give. When at last she relaxed against him, she could feel his hair-roughened chest rubbing with intimate discomfort against the sensitive sunburned skin of her throat. His left arm tightened around her, the disabled hand pressing firmly into her back, as the kiss deepened. His mouth burned hers with sweet fire, and at last she dared to respond. She was being swept into a dizzying vortex of sensation, memory and frustrated longing, spinning ever faster as she approached the one reality, the one name that had ever had meaning in her life—

"Erich," she breathed.

Kurt flung her away from him and jumped up to stalk across the room. She staggered back against the piano, cutting her arm on the sharp chipped edge of an ivory key. At first she did not know what she had done to anger him. Her eyes were still murky with passion as she shook her head in bewilderment. When she realized the enormity of her offense, she whispered huskily, "I'm sorry, Kurt."

He was breathing raggedly as he fished through his discarded jacket for his cigarette case. After lighting one, he puffed spasmodically and rasped, "You are obsessed with him."

Megan looked at him helplessly. "Yes," she said.

He stared at her with contempt. "He has been dead well over a year. Have you taken vows of perpetual widowhood? Are you going to worship his memory forever?"

"I do not worship his memory!" she cried.

"What else do you call it when a young, beautiful woman cannot look at another man without seeing the image of her dead husband?"

"You don't understand," Megan protested weakly as she slumped against the piano, rubbing the scratch on her forearm. She spoke quietly, but her voice was harsh and strained. "Erich was the only man in my life," she said, glaring up at Kurt, who towered over her. "Not just my only lover—if you can call it that—but the only man I ever knew as more than a passing acquaintance. I didn't even have a father for a guide, because he left my mother when I was just a child. For good or for bad, all I know about men I learned from my husband." She gasped for air as if she had been running. "So tell me," she continued hoarsely, "how am I supposed to look at a man without thinking of Erich, when every line of a masculine body, every movement, reminds me of him and the evil thing he did to me?"

Kurt's face was drawn. "What do you mean?"

She stared up at him. "Don't you know? Must I spell it out for you?" Suddenly her voice rose hysterically. She jumped to her feet and confronted Kurt, green eyes glowing in her bloodless face as she spat out the words. "I did the unforgivable—I dared to say I was leaving him. But *no one* left Erich, not Erich who could play the violin like one of God's favorite angels. He was the greatest, he was a genius, he was a von Kleist! So to punish me for my insolence, he raped me. Brutally. And the whole time I could hear his mistress giggling in the next room!"

CHAPTER FIVE

IN THE SILENCE THAT FOLLOWED HER OUTBURST Megan thought wretchedly, *oh, God, why did I tell him that?* She had never told anyone, not even Dorothy, her closest friend, who nursed her through her illness when she lost the baby that resulted from Erich's savage attack. She had vowed she would carry that dark shameful secret to her grave, and here she was blurting it out to Kurt, Erich's brother, the very last person in the world who should ever know.

Kurt stared down at her, his blue eyes wide and dark with horror. He opened his mouth to speak, but he seemed to have trouble finding his voice. When he did, the words came out raw and harsh with disbelief as he demanded, "Sweet Lord, what are you saying?"

Megan glowered, then she lowered her eyes, the brief spasm of defiance spent. She felt weak and bereft. She noted numbly that Kurt's cigarette smoldered unheeded in his hand, and she watched the circle of fire creep along the white paper toward his fingers. She shook her head slowly and murmured, "Forget it, Kurt. It doesn't matter." She slipped from the piano bench and turned toward the door.

Before she could take one step Kurt gave a yelp of pain and flung the butt down impatiently. He grabbed Megan and jerked her around to face him, his fingertips bruising the soft flesh of her upper arm. When she tried to pull away from him, his grip was relentless, unyielding. "Let me go, Kurt," she pleaded. "Forget I ever said anything. It's none of your business anyway."

He retorted grimly, "By mentioning it you have made it my business. Now explain yourself, Megan. You can't just make a statement like that and then calmly walk away."

Her thin shoulders slumped. "Oh, Kurt," she sighed, "how can I tell you? I've never told anyone, and you—you're his brother."

"I'm also a man wondering why anyone with a young, beautiful wife should be forced to resort to violence."

Megan glared at him. "How very chauvinistic of you," she gritted. "You don't believe me—or else you think that if it did happen, it was somehow my fault." She paused and then she shrugged, the indignant light fading from her eyes. "Well, maybe you're right. If I'd had the guts to leave in the beginning, none of this would have happened."

Kurt nudged her toward the love seat, and she curled up at one end, tucking her feet beneath her spread skirt. When she was settled, Kurt peered down at her drawn face, colorless except for the pink nose, and he muttered, "I'll be back in a minute." He strode out of the room.

While was he gone Megan stared blindly at the

rosewood piano, remembering, remembering. She was only minimally aware of Kurt's return until he pressed a frosty glass into her hand. She looked blankly at it. He had used too much ice, and the moisture beaded at the lip and ran down the sides. "This must be my night for lushing it up," she murmured as she took a sip.

He explained, "I thought a drink might relax you."

She raised the glass of amber liquid to her lips again, but then instead of drinking she balanced it on her knee, where the damp made wet circles that bled into the soft fabric of her dress. "I'd really prefer music, if you don't mind," she said. Once again Kurt left her, this time to switch on the stereo console inside one of the gilt cabinets, and after a moment the salon was filled with the stately but solemn strains of Ravel's *Pavane for a Dead Princess*. "Cheery," Megan noted ironically, but Kurt did not answer. He sat beside her on the small couch, his thighs just brushing her bent legs, as he waited for her to speak.

She studied her drink, not tasting it again, idly scratching at the designs in the frost with her thumbnail. At last she said baldly, "Erich and I didn't sleep together, not after that disaster of a honeymoon. He didn't need me; he had Lavinia. I was just... around." She sighed. "I should have guessed what was going on before we got married—there were so many signs—but I was very young and naive and I didn't see them until... until it was too late."

Haltingly at first and then with greater facility Megan recounted her life with her husband. Her voice was low and toneless against the mournful background music as she told about the curious way Erich had proposed to her, how he had taken her virginity with callous disregard for her fear and inexperience, how after only a few weeks he had abandoned her bed in favor of his mistress's. With eloquence born out of the long months of silence Megan admitted the humiliation she had endured as the despised wife of Kurt's brother. Only when she came to the final night did she hesitate.

Kurt's brow was furrowed with an emotion as intense as her own as he urged, "Go on, Megan, finish it."

She took a deep breath before she said, "That day I spent all afternoon running errands for Erich—trips to the cleaners, the printers, his arranger—and I was exhausted. I had told him that I was going to eat out and then see the new Dustin Hoffman film that night, but when I saw the long line of people waiting in the rain at the cinema, I changed my mind. Instead I went back to our apartment, and—and I found Erich there with Lavinia." Megan shuddered, and her voice thickened with pain. "They were together on the sofa, already half-drunk, and I looked at the two of them and knew I just couldn't take it anymore. I hated them both, but mostly I hated myself, what I had let them make of me. So I went to the hall closet and dragged out my suitcase and told Erich I was leaving him." Her face was pursed and ashen as she visualized the scene. "They laughed at me," she said. "Erich said that wives were a bore, and Lavinia snuggled up against him, stroking his thigh, and she tittered something like, 'Only if it's your own wife, darling.' Then she giggled and added, 'Herschel thinks Megan ought to have a baby.'"

Megan looked helplessly at Kurt. His face was unreadable. She whispered hoarsely, "I don't know why Lavinia said that, because I honestly don't think she meant for Erich to do what he did. She didn't like it at all when he locked her out of the bedroom. But first he just looked at her, and then he looked at me, and he got this really strange expression on his face. He stood up and muttered, 'What a charming idea, Lavinia.' And then he came after me."

The melting ice cubes clinked in Megan's glass as, trembling weakly, she leaned over the arm of the love seat and set her drink on the floor. She sat up again and smoothed the damp fabric sticking to her slim nylon-clad legs. Kurt lounged back, seemingly relaxed, his long legs extended before him; but his face was hidden behind his left hand, and the scar showed jagged and chalky. When he glanced up at Megan his deep-set eyes were shadowed. Lightly she touched his arm and said, "I'm sorry, Kurt. Erich was your brother, and you loved him. I shouldn't have told you." She grimaced. "I've never told anyone before, not even the doctor when I had the—"

He stared at her, sickened. "My God, is that how you got pregnant?"

She nodded mutely and glanced away, shivering as she remembered with anguish the night she had collapsed with severe abdominal pains and been rushed by Dorothy to the hospital. She had at first been stunned and then, womanlike, overjoyed by the news that she carried Erich's child. Instantly forgetting what had preceded, she had envisioned a tiny gray-eyed infant she could nurture and cherish in a way her husband had always denied her; a new life to give meaning to the chaos that had come before. But her body, wiser than her heart, had recognized that she was at that point barely capable of caring for herself, much less a child, and by morning the baby was only a poignant memory.

Megan laughed brittlely as she looked at Kurt again, but her eyes were tortured. "Funny, isn't it?" she quavered. "The one time he came near me in more than eighteen months, and I got—I got...." Her voice died out in a strangled sob, and to her horror she suddenly began to cry. The scalding tears that she had held back for longer than she could remember welled up in her tormented green eyes and overflowed, burning her skin like acid as they ran down her cheeks. She huddled against the arm of the love seat, burrowing her face into the scratchy velvet in a futile attempt to escape her shame.

Then strong hands gripped her quaking shoulders and she was dragged back across Kurt's knees and turned so that it was not musty worn upholstery that tickled her nose, but the coarse vibrant hair on his chest. With one hand cupping her nape he cradled her against him, rocking her and crooning to her as if she were a frightened child, while she sniffed into the ruffled linen of his open shirt. "Let the tears come," he urged soothingly. "Get it all out of your system. Secrets like this should never be kept bottled up." His voice was gentle as he held her shaking body and whispered snatches of husky German to comfort her.

Comfort. Slowly the tears subsided and Megan relaxed against him. She was increasingly aware of the warm hardness of his musky skin under her cheek, the thud of his heart, and she realized with wistful surprise that this was the first time since her mother died that anyone had comforted her, possibly the first time ever that a man had shown tenderness to her. She snuggled closer, sighing with the sheer luxury of touching him and when his hands smoothed back her shining hair and he bent his mouth to hers once more, she did not pull away.

The kiss was warm, friendly, without passion; a kiss of reassurance, of consolation. He seemed to assess her mood and react accordingly, gentling her as if she were a skittish filly. Megan recognized his restraint and was grateful for it. Only when her own needs made her hand slip up the strong column of his neck to entwine in the dark hair at his nape did the embrace change. Slowly his lips left her mouth and feathered over her cheekbone, pausing at the heavy gold hoop in her earlobe and then working down to her sunburned throat. When his mouth brushed across the reddened skin, she shivered with a sensation somewhere between pain and delight, and she shuddered convulsively when one hand slipped into the low neckline of her bone-white dress and curved possessively around a full breast. As his fingers brought the nipple to hard, pulsing life, she moaned, "Oh, Kurt, I've needed this for so long—"

She did not realize she had spoken aloud until his lips crushed the words back into her mouth and she was lost once more in his kiss. Their eager mouths searched each other, biting, probing, and when she felt his hands fumble at the zipper of her dress, she twisted closer into his arms, as close as the awkward length of the short sofa would permit.

Thus she was shocked and bewildered when suddenly his arms tightened painfully around her and he lifted his head and demanded harshly, "*Was willst du jetzt*, Adelaide?"

Like someone jerked too abruptly from a dream, Megan slowly swiveled in Kurt's arms and blinked in confusion at the tall girl in red bathrobe and fuzzy mules who peeked around the corner of the doorway. Megan was not really certain of what was happening until she felt Kurt discreetly pull her dress back up over her shoulders. His breathing was ragged as he repeated, "What do you want, Adelaide? What are you doing up at this hour?"

The girl slowly stepped into the room. She said, "I'm sorry, Kurt. It's just that I saw the light and I thought—I thought perhaps someone forgot to...."

He swore under his breath. "No," he rasped, "as you can see, the light was left burning on purpose. Now please go back to bed!"

She hesitated, but when Kurt growled, "*Verdammt*, Adelaide, get out of here!" she pivoted and fled. A moment later they heard her mules clattering up the staircase.

Flushed and panting with embarrassment, Megan kept her head bent as she sat up and began to repair her dishabille. She brushed her hair from her eyes and strained to reach her half-open zipper. Calmly Kurt pushed her hands aside and fastened the dress. Then he caught her chin in his fingers and held her head immobile as his blue eyes studied her rosy features. Running his thumb lightly over her lips, he said huskily, "Forgive me, Megan. I forget sometimes that this house has everything but privacy." His mouth brushed across hers in a fleeting caress, then he pulled back and looked at her assessingly. He said, "I have to leave early in the morning to return to Vienna for a few days. Will you come with me?"

"Vienna?" she echoed blankly, puzzled by his matter-of-fact tone.

He smiled engagingly. "I'll be busy at the gallery part of the time, of course, but there will still be plenty of opportunity for us to spend time together, to see the sights. There's so much I want to show you. You do intend to visit Vienna before you go home to the United States, don't you?"

Megan stared at him. His eyes, she noticed, were as vividly blue as the background of the ceiling fresco framing his dark head. His mouth—his mouth was still wet with her kisses, but already it was forming the hateful words, "before you go home—" Why did she suddenly feel so desolate? Of course she was going home. A few minutes in Kurt's arms, even a few nights in his bed, would not change her plans. Once their business was completed she would fly back to Los Angeles, with a large check and a small store of memories to remind her of her European holiday.

Why shouldn't some of those memories be of Kurt's lovemaking? She had already concluded she needed a lover, and he would be a good one, she could tell, skilled and considerate. But could she share his bed for the duration of her trip and then bid goodbye to him without regret once it was all over? She didn't know. He was a von Kleist, and she was peculiarly susceptible where they were concerned. No, it was better not to risk it. She said aloud, "Thank you, Kurt, but I believe I'll stay here, if you don't mind. Perhaps Liesl and I could do some sightseeing. I'd love to see more of Salzburg. I think Mozart's birthplace would be very special to me."

He frowned at her, and she wondered if he was going to argue. But he just shrugged and said wryly, "I think Vienna could be very special to us, Megan."

"Maybe," she admitted, hating the reluctant quaver in her voice, "but—but, Kurt, it's happening too fast. We met only yesterday."

"Sometimes that's all it takes," he said softly.

MEGAN WAVED OVER HER SHOULDER to Liesl as the station wagon pulled away from the split-rail fence that marked the boundary of the Webers' property. The little girl was already scampering across the yard to the stable where Blitzen was kept, and Megan wasn't sure if she had seen her salute. She turned and settled into her seat, adjusting her safety belt, as Adelaide accelerated the car toward Kleisthof-im-Tirol. The narrow highway that snaked through the rolling hills seemed alarmingly rough to Megan, used to the wide smooth grades of the California freeways, but Adelaide handled the car with aplomb, as skilled at the wheel as the chauffeur had been. Megan experienced a momentary panic when she noticed the speedometer creeping toward one hundred—until she realized with relief that the dial was marked in kilometers, not miles. She relaxed again and they drove on in silence, gliding through dark, thickly wooded areas, passing occasional farmhouses where sleek red-and-white cattle grazed on the lush grass.

Adelaide scowled pensively as she guided the car, her severe expression and short smooth hair combining with the wide collar of her demure white smock top to give her the look of a young Puritan—an effect belied by the skintight green jeans encasing her long legs. She didn't seem in the mood for conversation, a fact for which Megan was grateful. She needed time to think. She had fallen into a deep, mercifully dreamless sleep the moment her head touched the embroidered pillow slip the night before, and had awoken so late that she had to scramble to get downstairs to breakfast on time. When she'd heard Adelaide say she was going to town, she'd impulsively asked if she might hitch a ride. She knew she risked being quizzed about the scene the girl had blundered into, but she was determined to escape the cloistered, suffocating atmosphere of the von Kleist home for a while. She had to escape Kurt. He had left very early, laden with the carefully crated Pollock abstract Megan had admired in his study the first day, but even in his absence the schloss was full of him. Every one of those grim portraits was a reflection of him, of his piercing blue eyes that so disturbed her, his hard mouth that could be sensual and coaxing....

The silence stretched on. Megan wondered if Adelaide was uneasy in her presence, embarrassed because she had found Megan in Kurt's arms. When the girl expertly swerved the station wagon around a limb that had fallen into the roadway, Megan commented politely, "You drive very well, Adelaide."

"Danke," the girl said, her hazel eyes still trained on the road. "My father taught me when I was very young. He used to take me out on the country lanes and teach me about cornering and

downshifting. However, after I came to live with Gabrielle she would not permit me to drive at all until last year, when I finally turned eighteen and could get my license."

"Cornering? Downshifting? It sounds as if your father was a race driver."

Adelaide turned her chestnut head and beamed eagerly at Megan. "Yes, he was. You have heard of Arnold Steuben?"

Megan shook her head. "No. I'm sorry."

The warm light faded from Adelaide's face. She gazed intently down the highway again as she said with a shrug, "Well, you would have—everyone would have heard of him—if his tire hadn't blown out during the time trials at Le Mans three years ago." She sighed, and her voice took on a wistful note that made her sound very young. "Life was so happy and exciting when my father was alive. There were just the two of us, and we used to laugh about how we were going to make the Steuben name known throughout the world, he as the premier Grand Prix driver, I as a famous actress. But after he died everything changed."

"I'm sorry," Megan said again.

They traveled awhile farther in silence, and Megan realized that they must be nearing the town. The forest was thinning and the houses seemed to be closer together. As if there had been no pause, Adelaide continued, "I was in the last year of my course at the *Gymnasium*, the higher secondary school, when my father's accident occurred. I had already taken the examination to enter the dramatic academy in Baden, but I—I was in shock, confused. I did not know what to do. Then Gabrielle and Wilhelm, her husband, came to me. Gabrielle was my father's cousin, and when they asked me to live with them, it seemed a kind offer. Horst von Kleist was alive then, too, and I thought it would be good to be part of a family. I didn't realize then that von Kleists never do anything from kindness."

Megan stared at the girl, disturbed by the cynicism and bitterness in her young voice. "Really, Adelaide," she said reasonably, "don't you think you're being rather unfair, melodramatic?"

The car jerked forward as Adelaide gritted, "No!" She glanced sidelong at Megan. "You think you know them after two days, but you don't. Von Kleists use people. They think it is their right, and they will do anything to get their own way. Gabrielle took me in only because I could be of service to her. She pays for my education, but she insists that I go to university, not drama school as my father and I had planned. She provides my clothes and my spending money, but she monitors my friends and demands that I spend every spare moment with her, working on that house." Adelaide breathed deeply and lifted her foot from the accelerator. "You heard how it is, that first evening. All I asked was a few weeks in Rome, to gain some movie experience. They could afford it; they could afford to send me all the way to Hollywood if they chose. But no, every schilling must be poured into the schloss, for the greater glory of the von Kleists!"

Megan frowned. "I gather, then, that you are not interested in the restoration of the house?"

"No, I'm not!" Adelaide spat. "Why should I be? I'm a Steuben. Gabrielle was a Steuben herself before she married, although you would never guess it now. She lets no one forget that her mother was a von Kleist—as if her father's family meant nothing at all."

"I realize that Gabrielle is a little. . .neurotic on the subject, but surely—"

"It is not just Gabrielle, it is all of them! Horst von Kleist borrowed a fortune to renovate the building with all that air conditioning and fancy plumbing—the amount he spent was practically legendary—and his children were almost as bad. Wilhelm died, of course, but now Kurt—" The girl eyed Megan insinuatingly as she murmured, "Kurt is very charming, *nicht wahr*?" Megan's color rose, and Adelaide laughed harshly. "Oh, I don't blame you for falling for him. Women always do. I might myself, were he not twice my age, with that crippled hand. I prefer my men young and whole."

She smiled knowingly, and suddenly her mobile features looked far older than her years. She said, "Kurt knows the effect he has on women, and he knows how to use it. Once or twice I have stayed a few days in Vienna with him and his daughter, and always I have seen the way he charms the ladies who come into his gallery, especially those with a painting he wants that they are reluctant to sell. A little wine, soft music, seduction—with those blue eyes of his, an irresistible combination, am I not right?"

Megan felt sick. "Are you suggesting that he tried something with you?"

"Oh, no, of course not. I am only telling you what I have seen. Kurt regards me as a child, and besides, I have nothing he wants—unlike you." Adelaide slowed the car as it approached an intersection. "We are at the outskirts of town now," she said matter-of-factly. "You must tell me where you want me to let you off."

Megan had been so intent on what Adelaide was saying that she was bewildered to find herself on the fringe of the village. She said blankly, "Anywhere will do. Perhaps I'll walk a little." She pointed to a daisy-covered knoll. There. I'll start from there."

"Sehr gut," Adelaide agreed with a nod. She eased the car onto the shoulder and stopped the engine. She turned to Megan. "I must run a couple of errands here, then I shall be going on to the next town. So when you are ready to return to the schloss you will have to telephone for the limousine. You have the number?"

"Yes, of course."

"Good," Adelaide said. As Megan reached for the door lever, the girl touched her forearm. "Please, Megan," she pleaded urgently, "consider what I have told you. I don't mean about me—I shall work out my own solution, the way my father used to plan his strategy before a race—but you must be careful for yourself. Kurt and Gabrielle can be the most amiable people in the world as long as they get their own way, but if you have something they want, such as the meadow, they will stop at nothing to get it."

Megan shook her head. "I can't believe you mean that, Adelaide. I know they've upset your plans to go to Hollywood, but—"

The girl smiled almost pityingly, then shrugged. "Well, if I cannot convince you, think of—think of your husband. He was a von Kleist, wasn't he?" As soon as Megan stepped out of the car, Adelaide revved the engine and sped away in a spray of gravel.

Megan watched the station wagon disappear into the distance. She was stunned by the girl's spiteful crack about Erich. How did Adelaide know about Erich in the first place? Megan had certainly not discussed her marriage in the teenager's hearing—unless Adelaide had been listening at the door of the music room for quite a while the previous night before Kurt had spotted her. Megan shivered. What kind of game was the girl playing? She was obviously eager for independence and resented anything she considered to be an impediment to her freedom. Like most adolescents she chafed at the thought of adult authority and overdramatized the smallest grievance. But why was she trying to make Megan distrust Kurt?

Whatever Adelaide's purpose, Megan did not

believe the girl's insinuation that Kurt would seduce her to insure that she sign over her rights to the meadow. On reconsideration, Adelaide's studied glances and snide comments sounded like lines from a second-rate soap opera, and they didn't stand up to logic at all. After all, if Kurt had not sought out Megan in the first place, she would never have known about the meadow. He could have used it as he willed, without cost or risk. And as for their lovemaking the night before, it had been abundantly clear to Megan when she touched Kurt that he was as eager a participant as she was....

Megan strolled slowly along the roadside a short distance before she mounted the knoll to admire the beauty of the scene spread before her. The little hill was apparently a favorite vantage point for residents of the peaceful village, for a paved walk with a sturdy handrail ran back and forth in easy ascents to the crest, where a bench was located. Megan ignored the bench in favor of the flower-strewn grass. Although trees and housetops blocked her view of the Kleisthof streets, she could hear cars and other sounds of human activity rising from the neat three- and four-story houses, with sharply slanting roofs, that clustered around the square where the bus had dropped her. Was it really only the day before yesterday? It seemed a lifetime ago!

The spire of a church towered above the other buildings, its onion-shaped dome green with age; Megan thought it might be Byzantine. She remembered from the travel books she had studied superficially just prior to leaving Los Angeles that Austria was a country that showed traces of many cultures, remnants of its turbulent past. Beyond the village lay the floor of the valley, almost iridescent in the bright early light, as flat and green as a giant's billiard table, dotted with prosperous-looking farmhouses. A truck trundled along the road toward town, the same route, she now recognized, that the bus had taken once it left the autobahn from Salzburg. On the other side of the valley she could see densely forested foothills; and above the foothills—majestic, awesome, eternal—loomed the dark craggy peaks of the first range of the Alps.

Megan rose reluctantly from her grassy perch and debated what she should do with her day. She had left the schloss not so much to tour the town as to have a few hours alone, to pause and consider the significance of what had transpired between her and Kurt the night before. It was funny the way she had blurted out everything to him, after all the months of silence. During her illness she had accepted Dorothy's ministrations with gratitude but no explanations, leaving the older woman to draw the obvious conclusion that Megan had been seduced and abandoned. In a very real sense that was exactly what had happened. Erich had seduced her ruthlessly with his devasting charm, and then, once their marriage had put up the smoke screen that prevented Herschel Evans from seeing what was going on between his protégé and his wife, he had callously abandoned any attempt to satisfy Megan's physical or emotional needs. He had used her as arrogantly as his aristocratic forebears had once exercised the *droit du seigneur* on reluctant peasant girls, and by doing so had branded her for life.

Only on the final, horrible night had Megan revolted. When she staggered to the bathroom to scrub away the marks of Erich's violent possession, she had stared at the blurred reflection in the steamy mirror. She knew the ashen, bruised face with its glazed expression must be her own because the hair and the eyes were the correct colors. She had muttered tonelessly, still numb from shock, "Well, Megan Halliday, you can die—or you can finish packing and catch the midnight flight to Los Angeles." In speaking the words her choice had been made. She had carried her suitcases through the living room where Erich and Lavinia roistered, the feudal lord and his lady celebrating victory over an unruly vassal.

"Where the hell do you think you're going?" Erich had demanded in astonishment as she passed him, her thin shoulders resolutely straight. His usually carefully articulated voice was thick and slurred with alcohol, the accent pronounced. But Megan had walked out without speaking.

The air on the hillside was sultry and still, and already Megan's gray Calcutta-cloth pantsuit, which had reappeared in her wardrobe perfectly laundered, felt uncomfortably warm. She had twisted her hair into a thick knot at her crown and tied it with a long thin scarf of gray and green, the tails streaming down her back. Now the morning sun prickled the sensitive skin of her bare nape. As she meandered down the curving walk she decided that the first thing she ought to do was to purchase some sort of hat to protect her delicate skin while she toured the town. The prospect of entering a store was not nearly as daunting as it had seemed that first afternoon when she waited in the square, alone and weak with fatigue. Already her chats with Liesl had convinced her that she could ask such basic questions as "Where is such-and-such?" or "How much does that cost?" without too much fear of being misunderstood. She was going to buy a hat, maybe a few postcards for Dorothy, then she would act the typical tourist, wandering around, asking questions in her fractured German, absorbing all she could of the atmosphere of this lovely Tirolean town.

What she was *not* going to do was think anymore of Erich. Kurt was right: she was obsessed with him. It had been a mistake to keep those memories bottled up inside her all those long painful months. Many people had disastrous marriages, and yet they went on to build new lives for themselves. If she had talked to someone—Dorothy, a psychologist, even the bartender at the Polynesian Paradise—she might have been able to see those two years in perspective. Now that she had told Kurt, she felt—relieved, somehow, as if a burden had been lifted from her. She knew she would never forget her life with Erich, but now she hoped that someday she would understand it.

In a little shop just off the square Megan found a simple straw sun hat that would suit her needs. The storekeeper, a smiling woman in her late forties, knew a few words of English, and together they completed the transaction with much good humor and many grammatical errors. Megan studied her reflection in a hand mirror and decided that the hat lacked a certain pizzazz. To relieve the unadorned plainness she tied her gray-and-green scarf around the crown, and the other woman assured her that the result was *"sehr charmant, sehr moidsch."* When Megan finally left the shop she was grinning happily, and it wasn't until much later that she realized she was genuinely smiling for the first time in days.

As she explored the town she bought a bunch of red-streaked white carnations from a flower vendor, and she carried them in her hand, sniffing the delicious clovelike fragrance from time to time. She passed many other shops but resisted the urge to go inside, content for the moment to admire the quaint buildings, the immaculate tree-lined streets. She knew that logically the town was probably older than the schloss, with construction sporadic over the centuries, but somehow all the architecture blended together. Over everything there lay a curious timeless quality that was not disturbed by the occasional car rattling over the cobbled streets, or by the sight of teenagers utterly contemporary in their Levi's and T-shirts.

Megan walked past an inn with a fascinating painted facade. Tables were set outside in the shade on a terrace, and she promised herself she would return there later for lunch. As she meandered in the general direction of the church, on a side street she suddenly came upon a brick- and-glass structure that seemed raw, almost shockingly new after the mellow, patined buildings she had seen earlier. The design had a very functional look to it, and she guessed even before she found the small sign that read Heilige Elisabeths Krankenhaus that it was a hospital. In the back of her mind a faint memory stirred, something someone had mentioned just recently about a hospital, but she couldn't remember. She shrugged and went on.

The church with its intriguing bell tower was on the outskirts of town, a small but imposing edifice of dark stone with the cemetery spreading out beyond it. Over the arched door was an elaborate stained-glass window, but in the bright sunlight she could not make out the design. Megan glanced at her watch and saw that the last Mass of the day was now being celebrated, and she debated slipping silently inside, but then recalled that the worshipers might consider her trousers inappropriate. Instead she pushed open an ivy-covered gate and entered the cemetery.

The graveyard was cool and shady, utterly tranquil, surprisingly large, the last resting place for more than ten generations of villagers. The stones nearest the church, rising from the moss that grew around the trunks of ancient trees, were so old and weathered that Megan could barely make out the inscriptions. She was drawn to a tiny marker almost lost between two larger ones, and she knelt reverently to trace the carving with her fingers: 1706. Just a date, as if the parents of that infant lost centuries before had hoped to deny their grief by refusing to name it. Megan stood up, repelled and disturbed by her morbidity. Why should her eyes sting with unshed tears for a baby who had died the year Benjamin Franklin was born?

She forced herself to move along the rows of graves, all still scrupulously maintained although some were only sunken hollows in the ground, with rough rectangular holes at the head that had once held wooden markers long since rotted away. She noticed the dates impersonally, observing that the women died young, and the men not much older. When she discovered a large cluster of children's graves with the same year marking their pathetically early ends, she decided there must have been some kind of epidemic. Even when her footsteps brought her to what might be considered the modern section of the cemetery, she noted that many people did not live out their normal span of years—probably because despite its charm and almost unbearable beauty, the Tirol was really a very isolated region, and before the advent of modern transportation life must have been extremely harsh for the average family, especially in the winter. Kurt himself had made some comment about the lack of emergency medical care, that very first night, when he spoke of Erich's mother.

Erich's mother. It occurred to Megan that Eva Müller probably lay somewhere close by, resting eternally oblivious to the violent passions she unleashed when she fell in love with an Austrian nobleman, happily unaware that by an intricate chain of events her affair would ultimately alter the destiny of a California girl not yet born when she died. Megan began walking as fast as decorum permitted, searching the peaceful rows for that thirty-one-year-old grave. The church bell was just sounding the end of the final Mass when she found it.

The grave was located in the shade of a willow tree, next to two much more recent graves that Megan knew without comparing dates must belong to Eva's parents, the grandparents who raised Erich from birth. Eva Müller, Geliebte Tochter. Megan sniffed inelegantly as she translated the inscription. The girl had hurt her parents, caused them what would have been shocking humiliation in a small town thirty years ago, but in death and eternity she was their "beloved daughter," taken from them when she was only nineteen.

Nineteen! Somehow Megan had got the impression that Erich's mother was older than that, a conniving adventuress out to ensnare a wealthy married man. Horst von Kleist must have been at least in his mid-thirties at the time, far too old to be seducing teenagers. Nineteen, a very vulnerable age... the same age Megan had been when she met

Erich. She tried to visualize the dead girl, but all she knew was that Eva Müller had been beautiful and had silver white hair. Megan could not shape her features by remembering Erich's, for Erich, like Kurt, took his looks from his father, the classic von Kleist face that Megan personally found irresistible.

"Eva, was that how it was with you?" she whispered softly. "Tell me, did you take one look at that aristocractic face and know you were his forever, no matter how much unhappiness he caused you?" She felt a sudden poignant kinship with the doomed girl. Impulsively she knelt and arranged the bunch of carnations in front of the headstone.

Above Megan's head a feminine voice asked in German, "Why are you putting flowers on that grave?" Megan craned her neck. A stocky blond woman in an unbecoming orange dress was staring down at her.

"Bitte?" Megan murmured as she straightened to get a better look at her interrogator. The woman appeared to be about ten years older than Megan, of medium height, heavyset, with pale blue eyes and lackluster hair scraped back into a functional chignon. When she tucked a head scarf into her handbag, Megan realized she must have just left the church. The woman repeated her question.

Megan debated how to answer. Her German vocabulary didn't stretch to the word for mother-in-law, which didn't seem to fit the situation anyway, so she said carefully, "She was the mother of my husband."

The blue eyes widened as the woman peered intently under the brim of Megan's hat and demanded, still in German, "Who are you? What is your name?"

Megan sighed as once again she began the inevitable and rather embarrassing explanation. *"Ich heisse Megan Hal—von Kleist. Ich spreche—"*

"Von Kleist?" the woman echoed hollowly. *"Erich?"* Megan nodded. *"Mein Gott!"* the woman exclaimed. She shook her head in wonder as she studied Megan's face. After an interminable inspection she asked, *"Sie sind Engländerin?"*

"American," Megan said.

The woman switched to English, her heavy Teutonic accent almost incomprehensible after the clipped, rather British pronunciation of the von Kleists. "Erich—von Kleist is dead," she observed unnecessarily. "You are his widow?"

"Yes."

"Kurt von Kleist informed us of Erich's death in the United States, but he did not say he left a wife."

"I was married to Erich for two years," Megan said tersely, ignoring the obvious hint for further explanations. "Now tell me, please, who are you?"

The woman said, "I am Dr. Ulrike Müller. Although I never knew her, this woman whose grave you just decorated was my aunt, my father's younger sister. Erich von Kleist was my cousin."

CHAPTER SIX

IN ULRIKE'S OFFICE in the brick-and-glass hospital, Megan observed her newfound cousin-in-law curiously, impressed by what she saw. The woman was only in her early thirties, but her responsibilities made her appear older. When she slipped into her white coat, covering up the orange dress that made her look sallow, she seemed to don a mantle of authority, and her light eyes glowed with intelligence and confidence. She told an orderly to bring coffee, and he responded smartly, *"Jawohl, Fräulein Doktor!"* Megan almost expected him to click his heels.

After the door snapped shut behind him, Ulrike smiled warmly at her, and Megan was stunned at the difference a smile made in the doctor's plain face. Ulrike had good skin and really beautiful teeth, and Megan thought that with judicious use of cosmetics and a less severe hairstyle, the older woman could be quite pretty.

Ulrike marveled, "Erich's wife. Who would have thought we should meet after so many years!"

"Were you and Erich very close?" Megan asked.

Ulrike smiled ironically. "Oh, no, I hardly knew him. No one really knew him, I think. My family lived in Salzburg, but in the summertime I would come to visit my grandparents. Erich was still living with them then. He was only slightly younger than I, but he was a very...difficult child to know. He was quite reserved, always going off into the hills by himself, taking *Opa*'s—that is, my grandfather's—old fiddle with him. Once I followed. I found him standing on a rock playing what even then I recognized must be a very difficult piece. Whe he finished he bowed deeply, as if responding to the applause of an invisible audience." Ulrike sighed. "I'm afraid I reacted as any child would: I laughed. He cornered me in my hiding place and hit me very hard. I remember him shouting, 'Someday my father will come for me, and then nobody will laugh!' I was only about nine. I didn't understand."

"It must have been hard for him," Megan murmured.

"*Ja.* I think it was hard for everyone. He was so obviously a—a changeling." Ulrike clucked sympathetically. "When Erich was in his early teens and his father at long last did come for him, my grandparents relinquished him reluctantly, for they loved him. But they hoped he would be happy in his father's world. Yet even in the schloss Erich was still an outsider...." She looked sharply at Megan. "Tell me, did he find happiness in America?"

Megan frowned, uncertain of her answer. She

realized with shame that, intent on her own misery, she had never actually wondered whether or not Erich was happy. At length she said, choosing her words with care, "I'm not sure any person had the power to make Erich happy. I didn't, at any rate."

"But you were his wife."

Megan grimaced. "Not even a wife could compete with an Ives sonata or a Bach fugue. Erich loved his music. In the States his career blossomed. Perhaps that was enough."

Ulrike nodded, apparently understanding much that Megan was unwilling to put into words. At that moment the orderly returned with a tray of coffee and flaky nut-filled pastries. The doctor poured out two cups of dark aromatic coffee and spooned a mound of whipped cream onto her own, smiling when Megan indicated she preferred hers black. She offered a pastry to the younger woman before she chose two for herself.

"Forgive me my greed," she said. "An emergency appendectomy this morning prevented me from going to Mass at my usual time, so I have not yet eaten today." She grinned wryly. "Not that it hurts me to skip a meal. If I were my own patient, I would order myself to go on a diet. It seems unbelievable that anyone could get fat on hospital food, but alas, our chef here is really excellent. Kurt von Kleist found him for us, and like all good Viennese cooks he is unsurpassed in these delightful but very fattening temptations."

Megan said, "I gather, then, that Kurt is interested in the hospital?"

"Natürlich," Ulrike responded with a faintly puzzled air. "I would have thought you knew."

"I don't really know Kurt at all," Megan said faintly, thinking with a blush that that was an odd statement to make about the man who had kissed and caressed her so passionately just the night before. "I met him only two days ago."

Ulrike watched Megan's rising color with a certain clinical interest. She said slyly, "It takes no more than a second to notice that he is a very handsome man."

Megan nodded mutely. She remembered the awareness that had stirred inside her the first instant Kurt had looked up from his auction catalogs and his dark blue eyes had met hers. Oh, yes, she had noticed right away that Kurt was a very handsome man. Like his brother and his father before him he had the kind of cruel, arrogant, irresistible masculine beauty that could ensnare an unsuspecting girl's heart mercilessly and make her his forever.

"Kurt von Kleist is a kind man," Ulrike stated, unaware that she was contradicting all of Megan's deepest impressions. Despite Adelaide's insinuations to the contrary, Megan was willing to admit that Kurt might be basically a good man, moral in most of the usual applications of that word—but *kind*? Never! Ignorant of Megan's doubts, Ulrike continued, "He has had far more than his share of personal tragedies—the injury to his hand, the loss of his family, his wife—but he is still mindful of the needs of others. He founded this hospital."

Megan stared. "I didn't know that."

"Oh, yes. Were it not for him, the residents of Kleisthof-im-Tirol would probably still have to travel halfway to Salzburg for anything more than the most basic medical care. After the death of his wife he went to great lengths to establish this facility. It is named for Elisabeth von Kleist."

"Oh," Megan murmured, wondering why she felt a pang at the mention of Liesl's mother, the unknown Englishwoman whose picture still adorned Kurt's bedroom in Vienna. "I noticed that this is St. Elisabeth's Hospital, but I didn't realize—"

"Every year on St. Elisabeth's Day the von Kleists open their home for a big charity ball, and the proceeds help support the hospital. This year's fete is in just a few days. Will you still be here?"

"I don't really know," Megan said. "My visit was rather spur-of-the-moment, a business trip. Nothing has been mentioned about my attending—"

"Oh, but you must," Ulrike insisted. "The von Kleist ball is not an event anyone should miss if it can be helped. They open up the grand ballroom, and the clothes and the jewels the women wear—*Gott im Himmel*! Were I a communist I expect I would find it most decadent, but since I'm only a humble doctor I think it's rather enchanting. As director of the hospital I always attend, always in my old black evening gown with the simple string of pearls my parents gave me when I graduated from medical school. Because my position more or less makes me the guest of honor—and also, I think, because it helps him avoid offending other persistent ladies—Kurt von Kleist always dances the first dance with me. After that I retire to the sidelines and weave fantasies about the days when the schloss was still new and the young Mozart came once to entertain." Ulrike smiled reminiscently, but then her expression changed. "It is very easy," she said grimly, "to forget that we owe the ball—and the hospital—to a young woman's tragic and needless death."

"What happened?" Megan asked.

"You don't know at all?" Ulrike questioned. When Megan shook her head, the other woman scowled, peering into the distance. "Unfortunately, I remember it all too well. It was more than seven years ago, at *Weihnachtzeit*—Christmastime. I was newly qualified as a doctor, and I came to visit my grandparents for the holidays. I had made arrangements to join the practice of one of my former instructors in Linz, and I feared I might not have a chance to spend another Christmas with my grandparents, for they were both getting very old. The weather was wild, fierce, all that week, snowing so hard that the plows could not keep the roads clear, and the town was virtually cut off from the rest of the world. Late one night just as we were preparing for bed I heard sleigh bells, and then there was a pounding on the door."

Ulrike paused, and Megan waited impatiently while she poured herself another cup of coffee.

After stirring in more whipped cream, she continued, "It was Karl Weber, who had crossed the fields in an old horse-drawn sledge. There had been an accident at the schloss, he said, and since I was the only physician within reach, would I please come at once.

"I still remember that ride back through the snow. I had never been to the schloss before, although Erich had bragged about it to me, and I was nervous and cold, clutching my medical bag. When they took me to Elisabeth von Kleist, I could see right away that she needed to be in a hospital. She required transfusions and X rays, everything I did not have."

"But what happened?" Megan asked again. "How did she get hurt?"

Ulrike sighed. "She had fashioned an elaborate kissing ball of evergreens and mistletoe as a special treat for her daughter, and she was trying to hang it from a light fixture at the top of the grand staircase. She slipped off the stepladder and rolled all the way to the foot of the stairs."

Suddenly Megan recalled the unease she had felt the first time she descended the steps. "Oh, God," she cried.

Ulrike continued, "Amazingly, she had not broken her neck. She was badly hurt, but she was still alive, and if we could have transported her to the nearest hospital.... It was only fifteen kilometers, no distance at all in a car, but the roads were impassable. I did all I could, but I have never felt so helpless in my life as I did while I watched that lovely young woman die. She was unconscious, so at least she was spared the pain." Ulrike's eyes were bleak as she recalled the scene. "Her husband knelt by her bedside the whole time, clutching her hand, praying, weeping. The rest of the family and the servants stood around the edge of the room, waiting silently for the end. Horst von Kleist himself went out into the blizzard to fetch the priest to administer the last rites. At one point the child wandered in half-asleep. She was only a toddler, and the commotion had frightened her. Her father picked her up and held her in his arms until finally, near dawn, it was all over."

Ulrike's sturdy face was twisted, the light eyes dark with anguish. Megan watched as she visibly got control of herself. She continued firmly, "After the funeral Kurt came to me and asked if I would consider remaining in Kleisthof to help him establish a hospital, so that such tragedies might not have to happen again. I was astounded, for I had almost expected him to blame me for negligence in his wife's death. Although of course it was not true, it would have been a very human reaction, very common. I did not as yet realize what an uncommon man Kurt von Kleist is....

"When I agreed, he persuaded his father to allow him to auction some of the paintings from the family collection, and with the help of his older brother and Gabrielle he organized the first of the charity balls. And now Kleisthof-im-Tirol has a small but superbly equipped hospital, with two other doctors in addition to myself, and a full complement of staff." The admiration rang in her voice. "When you recall that Kurt makes his home in Vienna and runs a thriving art dealership there, the amount of work he has put into this hospital is phenomenal."

Megan said, "I'm sure you've worked as hard as he has."

"It has required tremendous effort," Ulrike conceded after a pause. "There are those occasions when I find myself yearning for the husband and family I had hoped to have in addition to my career."

"Thirty-two isn't old," Megan suggested gently. "You still have time."

Instead of responding, Ulrike glanced at her wristwatch. "Goodness," she exclaimed, "lunchtime already. Come—I will take you to the restaurant with the best *Wiener Backhuhn* in this part of Austria."

WIENER BACKHUHN, Megan discovered, was a dish very similar to Southern-fried chicken, and she ate with relish as she and Ulrike sat on the terrace of the Gasthof zum Goldenen Bären, the inn she had noticed earlier. An enormous beech tree shaded the terrace from the midday sun, and Megan shed her hat. A light breeze ruffled the flaming tendrils that had worked loose from her topknot and curled wispily at her nape. The tree's smooth gray bark was a complement to the glowing colors of the potted geraniums that lined the low wall.

Megan's eyes were drawn continually to the facade of the inn, three stories adorned with elaborate frescoes of the golden bear of the inn's name and larger-than-life figures performing heroic deeds. Ulrike explained that they were characters from local folk legends. "You will see many buildings decorated in this fashion," she said, "in the Tirol and also Vorarlberg, which is the western province bordering on Liechtenstein."

Megan sighed as she finished her last bite of salad. "There's so much to see, and I'm afraid I'll have to return home before I've gone to half the places I want to visit."

"Then your trip is only a short one?"

"Yes. As I said before, I'm here on business. Once Kurt comes back from Vienna with the papers I have to sign, I suppose I'll be free to go my own way. I want to spend some time in Salzburg. All I saw the other day was the inside of the airport and then the bus. It will be almost a holy pilgrimage for me, as a musician, to visit Mozart's birthplace. Then I hope to go to Vienna and hear a couple of operas."

Ulrike frowned. "I think you have already missed the opera season in Vienna, but the Salzburg Festival is going on right now. The city is overrun with tourists, of course, but the performances are superb. And if you can get tickets to Professor Aicher's Marionette Theater, you will find it delightful, as well." Ulrike paused to order *Apfelstrudel* for two from the hovering waitress and smiled ironically as she tucked into the flaky fruit-filled pastry. "Don't you ever have to worry about calories?" she asked Megan enviously, eyeing the girl's too slender figure.

"How much I eat depends on my mood," Megan explained. "If I'm depressed or upset, I just can't face food." When she realized the obvious conclusions Ulrike could draw from that revealing statement, she added quickly, "Today I am very happy. I can't tell you how much it means to me to have met you."

Ulrike nodded sagely. Her physician's eyes, all-seeing, were benign, compassionate, as she patted Megan's hand maternally. "Yes, sometimes it does help to know a little of a person's background, *nicht wahr*?" Megan wondered whether Ulrike was speaking of Erich or of Kurt.

A white sports car pulled up in front of the inn, and Megan heard a man's voice call, "Ulrike, *mein Herzenfreund, wie geht's*?"

Ulrike's face lighted up as she stared over Megan's sholder.

"Peter!" she cried in obvious delight, half rising from her chair. "Come join us, please."

She subsided as a young man in a summer-weight business suit the same light brown as his hair approached their table. He looked about thirty, of average height and build, with a pleasantly homely face and intelligent brown eyes hidden behind heavy-rimmed glasses. As he pulled up a chair he murmured absently, *"Gnädiges Fräulein,"* nodding in Megan's direction.

"Speak English," Ulrike said. "Megan is an American."

"Really? Hey, that's great!" He spoke in unmistakably midwestern tones. He turned to Megan, surveying her intently as he asked, "Where are you from?"

"Los Angeles," Megan said, smiling with the inexplicable relief one feels when encountering a compatriot in a foreign land. "And you?"

"Chicago." He turned to Ulrike. "Aren't you going to introduce us?"

"Of course, how rude of me. Megan," Ulrike intoned formally, her lovely smile at odds with her serious manner, "I would like to introduce you to Peter Swanson, a very pleasant but rather brash American engineer. Peter, this is Megan von Kleist, who, I have just discovered, is my cousin by marriage."

"You're married?" Peter asked in surprise, glancing at her naked left hand. "And to a von Kleist?"

"Widowed," Megan responded tersely.

Peter's brown eyes were speculative as he studied her from her coppery topknot to as far down as the table permitted him to see. He seemed to be trying to place her. At length he snapped his fingers. "Of course! I watched you get into the limousine a couple of days ago. You were down in the square looking rather lost until the Mercedes showed up. I didn't recognize you at first because then you were wearing sunglasses—not that there's any hiding that glorious hair of yours."

He turned back to Ulrike. "Riki, you didn't tell me you had relatives in the castle on the hill."

"I don't," she replied repressively. "It's a long story, Peter, not something I care to explain."

He shrugged it off. "Okay, okay, I only thought...." He smiled charmingly at Megan. "Forgive me, it's just that I've been trying for days to talk to Kurt von Kleist again, and he refuses to see me."

Suddenly Megan remembered Kurt's telephone conversation that first day in his study, when he seethed with irritation while he argued in German and English. Swanson—that was the name of the person on the other end of the line. Megan said carefully, her green eyes darting between the other two, "Kurt's in Vienna now."

Peter made a face. "Well, that's one way of avoiding me," he commented waspishly.

With the air of one determined to avoid unpleasantness, Ulrike said brightly, "You look very nice today, Peter. Very...clean."

Megan's eyes widened, but Peter just laughed. He explained, "Riki's never let me forget that the first time we met I was covered top to tail with mud."

The doctor nodded. "When he staggered into the hospital, we thought we had been invaded by a creature from another world. You can't imagine what he looked like, limping down my immaculate corridor, oozing slime—and all the time with one bright pink flower dangling over his ear." She started to giggle.

"What on earth happened?" Megan exclaimed.

Peter said, "I was working in the field—"

"Picking flowers," Ulrike interjected.

He gave her a teasing sidelong wink. "As I was saying," he continued mock-sternly, "I was out in the field conducting geobotanical explorations—that means I was looking for abnormalities in the plant life that could indicate the presence of certain mineral deposits—and I stepped into a rabbit hole and sprained my ankle. I was working alone, which was stupid, except that we've been trying to keep a low profile on this project. The field was muddy, and by the time I dragged myself back to my car I looked like a character out of a Japanese monster movie."

"Yet you managed to get to the hospital all right?" Megan asked.

"Oh, yeah. I could still drive, albeit slowly. It was just a sprain. Riki was really indignant about that. I think she felt that to justify the mess I'd made, I should have had at least a compound fracture."

Ulrike blushed girlishly. "You know that's not true," she said.

Through lowered lashes Megan studied Peter and Ulrike. She was suddenly certain that the very efficient doctor had a crush on the young American. After a moment she asked, "Geo—what kind of exploration?"

"Geobotanical. It's a fairly new field. The Russians did the early studies, but now the techniques are used all over the world. Uranium strikes were made in Colorado by studying locoweed, and in Sweden they discovered some major copper deposits by checking certain mosses. In my case I'm looking for copper, as well, so I analyze the moss and also pinks and some kinds of mint."

"I've never heard of that before," Megan said. "You're a geologist?"

"Actually I'm a mining engineer. I work for my Uncle Max's company—or rather I would be working, if Kurt von Kleist weren't so damned—"

"Peter," Ulrike said quietly, "before you go any further, you should remember that Megan is herself a von Kleist, and you are speaking about her relatives."

Peter had the good grace to look embarrassed, his abashed expression making him seem very boyish. "I guess I did forget. I'm sorry if I offended you, Megan. I didn't mean to be rude. It's just that this whole deal has been so frustrating, and von Kleist's lord-of-the-manor attitude sends me right up the wall." He glanced toward Ulrike, who was frowning sternly. "Yes, Riki, I know you consider the man just one step short of sainthood, but I think he's obstructive and unreasonable." He took a deep breath. "Before I have to apologize again, let's talk about you, Megan. What brings you to Austria—a vacation?"

Megan shrugged. "Sort of. I have a little family business to attend to, then I hope to do some sightseeing. I'm really looking forward to Salzburg, although I'm not sure when I'll get there."

"I have to go down to Salzburg in a couple of

days," Peter said. "I'd love to have you come." He turned to Ulrike. "What about you, Riki? Do you think you could tear yourself away from the hospital for a few hours?"

Ulrike hesitated, then she smiled brightly. "Yes, of course; I would like that very much. It's been a while since I took a day off."

"You work too hard," Peter grumbled.

"Someone must," Ulrike said. She gave a cursory look at her wristwatch. "As delightful as this has been," she sighed, "I'm afraid that now I must return to work." She signaled for the waitress. "Peter, my friend, do you think you could entertain Megan for the remainder of the afternoon?"

"For you, Riki, anything," he answered gallantly.

The waitress strolled over to the table, and Ulrike said, *"Zahlen, bitte."* The woman took out her note pad and bag of change. Megan watched curiously as Ulrike listed everything they had eaten and the waitress carefully wrote it down. After the total had been agreed upon, Ulrike paid the bill and added a small tip. Then she took her leave.

Megan and Peter stepped over to the stone wall where red geraniums, almost iridescent in the bright sunlight, grew in trim pots. They waved to Ulrike as she departed, and watched from the terrace until she had disappeared down a side street. Megan picked up her sun hat and put it on.

Peter took a deep breath of the warm scented

air. "I love Austria," he declared. "Six years ago I came for a visit, and I've been here ever since. I was fresh out of college, unemployed, and my wife—we were high-school sweethearts—had just filed for divorce. The world was looking pretty bleak to me right then. But Uncle Max took me under his wing, and soon I lost my heart to the beauty of the country, the charm of its people." He glanced at Megan. "But I don't have to tell you all this; you know it already. After all, you were married to an Austrian."

"Yes," Megan said ironically, "I was."

For the rest of the day Peter played guide to Megan's avid tourist, and by the time he drove her back to the Schloss von Kleist she was pleasantly exhausted but utterly relaxed. She had not realized how wearing the constant presence of Kurt and his family could be. As Peter's white Audi pulled up in front of the wide stone steps, Megan said sincerely, "Thank you, Peter. I've had a lovely day, and I'm looking forward to Salzburg."

"Good. You'll really like it, I'm sure. It'll do Riki good to get away from her work for a while, too," he added. He turned in his seat, and his eyes ran up the elaborate facade of the mansion. "Quite a place, this," he noted dryly. "Like something on a postcard."

"Yes, it is. Have you been here before?"

He shook his head. "Nope. The couple of times I've met with von Kleist it's been down in town." He frowned. "Riki wants me to come to the charity ball. I haven't made up my mind yet. That sort of thing isn't really my scene."

"It's as much yours as it is Ulrike's—or mine, for that matter." Megan looked at Peter thoughtfully. She considered the courage it must have taken for the rather retiring doctor to ask a man to the dance. She said, "If Ulrike wants you to come, then of course you must. Besides, you'll be another friendly face for me among all those—foreigners."

After a moment Peter laughed. "Okay," he said. "I'm not sure von Kleist is going to appreciate my turning up on his doorstep, but anything for a fellow American! *Auf wiedersehen*, honey." With a wave he swung his little car around the gushing fountain and sped up the hill toward the gate.

MEGAN WAS PLAYING THE PIANO for Liesl and Adelaide that evening when a maid came into the music room and told her that she was wanted on the telephone. Puzzled, she excused herself and followed the servant through the corridors, trying to imagine who could be calling. When she reached Gabrielle's white-and-gold office, the older woman was seated behind her Louis Quinze escritoire, scowling as she listened to whoever was on the line. As soon as Megan was within reach, Gabrielle held out the receiver to her impatiently.

"Kurt," she said. "He wishes to assure himself that you are comfortable." She picked up a sheet of ivory deckle-edged notepaper and ran a pencil down what appeared to be a detailed checklist.

Recognizing that she had been dismissed, Megan turned her back to the desk and murmured timidly, "Hello?"

The connection was poor, but even the distortion of the crackling line did not take away the low, sensual quality of Kurt's gravelly voice. "Hello, Megan, how are you today?"

"I'm fine, Kurt."

"I missed seeing you this morning," he said. He paused before he added, "In fact, I miss having you here with me right now, alone, with no one to barge in on us...." In the engraved mirror on the opposite wall Megan could see color rise in her pale cheeks, but before she could reply Kurt chuckled, "Poor Megan, it's cruel to tease you, especially since I realize Gabrielle must be right there beside you." He continued briskly, "I'm calling because I wanted to make sure you are enjoying your vacation. Have you had a pleasant day?"

"Oh, yes," she answered truthfully. "I spent the day in Kleisthof. It's a beautiful town, and I had a wonderful time playing tourist."

"Did Liesl go with you?"

"No, I went by myself. But, Kurt, the most amazing thing happened. I met a woman who turned out to be Erich's cousin."

"You mean Ulrike Müller?" he asked in surprise.

"Yes." Megan debated whether she should also mention Peter, then decided against it. There seemed to be some friction between the two men and she had no desire to be drawn into someone else's argument. She said, "Ulrike was very friendly, and I liked her a lot. She's asked me to go to Salzburg with her later this week."

"Oh," Kurt commented, "you really did strike up a friendship quickly, didn't you? I'm glad. Dr. Müller is a fine, very dedicated woman, and I'm delighted that you met her. I should have thought to introduce you myself, but...." He hesitated, sounding uncertain for the first time. "I didn't know if you would want to meet any of Erich's other family—under the circumstances."

"Don't be silly, Kurt. Of course I wanted to meet her." Deliberately Megan changed the subject. "How has your day gone? Did you get the Pollock safely delivered?"

"Oh, yes, that all went as scheduled. However, some other problems have developed—a personality clash between my manager and a promising young painter I've been sponsoring—and I don't think I shall be able to return to the schloss before the day of the ball. Will you be able to keep yourself amused?"

"Certainly. There's the trip with Ulrike, and Liesl and I have discussed having your chauffeur drive us to Innsbruck. And if all else fails I can always fall back on my music. I love your piano, Kurt. It's the sort of instrument every musician dreams of playing."

"Yes," Kurt said quietly, "I know." There was an uncomfortable silence, then suddenly he rasped, "Damn it, Megan, I've had enough of your maidenly qualms. I want you to come to Vienna. You can catch a plane in Salzburg in the morning and be here before lunch."

"But, Kurt—"

"Don't argue with me, Megan. Touring with my daughter or visiting Erich's long-lost cousin is all very good, but you know as well as I do that you would really rather be here with me."

Gasping at his arrogance, she stammered, "Kurt, you have no—"

"Wouldn't you, Megan?" he insisted forcefully.

Megan closed her eyes and held her breath, trying without success to fight back the wave of longing that threatened to engulf her. To be in Vienna with Kurt.... She knew what it would mean. The pair of them would sit in a *gemütlich* little café somewhere, holding hands while they ate Sacher torte and listened to a Gypsy violin playing something delightfully schmaltzy, such as "Fascination." They would watch the sun set over the steeple of St. Stephen's Cathedral, and then in the gathering darkness Kurt's strong arms would pull her close in an ardent, irresistible embrace—

Kurt repeated, "Megan, will you come to Vienna?"

"Yes," she whispered hoarsely.

"Sehr gut," he said. He seemed very calm, very cool. He sounded pleased but not overwhelmed, as if it were nothing unusual for a woman to agree in effect to begin an affair with him. But probably, Megan realized with a sickening jolt, to him it

wasn't anything unusual. Her fingers tightened around the slim handle of the receiver. His wife had been dead for seven years, and he was certainly no monk. While no one had said anything to indicate that Kurt had a particular girl friend, there must be women in his life, perhaps quite a few. Adelaide had hinted that Kurt was something of a playboy, but Megan was sure that the girl was merely conjecturing. Kurt was the type of man who would conduct his affairs discreetly, never letting them intrude on his life with his daughter in that apartment where Elisabeth von Kleist's photograph still graced the dressing table in his bedroom—

Kurt's deep voice penetrated her fugue. "Megan, are you still there?"

"Yes, of—of course," she choked, swallowing hard. "Was there anything else you wanted?"

"I need to speak to Gabrielle again, so that she can make arrangements for your flight."

"Yes, of course," Megan repeated lamely. "I— I'll say good-night, then, Kurt."

"Good night, my dear. I'll see you in the morning. Now let me talk to Gabrielle."

Silently Megan handed the telephone back to Gabrielle, who scowled down at her notes as she listened, until her hazel eyes widened and she cast a startled glance at Megan. Suppressing a blush, Megan fled back to the music room.

Liesl sat at the grand piano, struggling with "The Harmonious Blacksmith," while Adelaide lounged on the velvet love seat, engrossed in

Pauline Kael's latest book. Megan listened to Liesl for a moment before interrupting gently, "No, dear, that's not quite right. You have the notes down almost perfectly, but the phrasing is wrong. Here, let me show you."

Liesl scooted to one end of the piano bench, and Megan perched beside her. "This passage is supposed to be syncopated," she explained, resting her white fingers on the golden keys. "It goes: three-and, four-and, one-and, two, *three*, four-and— There, do you hear the difference?"

Liesl's fair brows came together in an expression remarkably reminiscent of her father. "I think so, Tante Megan. May I try again?" She picked out the offending passage once more, a little more accurately, but still less than perfect.

Megan said, "No, no, Liesl, don't think about me; think about the music. Don't just imitate what I did. You must try to *feel* what Handel was doing here."

Liesl stared at Megan, then shifted her blue glance to the sheet music. "Feel it..." she muttered thoughtfully, as if the idea were totally new to her. "Fräulein Brecht never said anything like that." She began playing the piece once more, hesitantly at first and then suddenly faster, as if some long-sought goal had just come into sight and she was rushing toward it. In her enthusiasm her fingers tripped over each other, striking many more wrong notes than she had before, but despite all the errors Megan could hear in Liesl's performance the first stirrings of that indefinable extra sense that distinguishes the musician from the person who merely plays.

When the child had finished, Megan let out her breath with a sigh and whispered, "Very good, dear."

Liesl's dark blue eyes glowed. "Yes, it was, wasn't it?" She grinned with satisfaction and said, "I like the way you teach, Tante Megan. May we have another lesson tomorrow?"

Megan's face became shuttered. Pushing a stray curl back from her forehead, she said with elaborate casualness, "I'm sorry, Liesl, but I won't be here tomorrow. I'm going to Vienna for a few days."

"What?" Liesl cried. "Why are you going to Vienna? Did *Vati* ask you? What about the drive we were going to take? May I come with you?"

Megan stammered, "N-no, dear, not—not this time." She noticed that Adelaide had raised her chestnut head from behind the barricade of her book and was now gazing at Megan intently. Flushing, Megan continued with an air of calm authority she was far from feeling, "Yes, Liesl, your father did ask me to join him there. I've never been to Vienna, you know. And no, you may not come with me. But if there is anything you need from your apartment, I'll be happy to get it for you."

Adelaide regarded Megan quizzically and asked, "How long will you be gone?"

Megan shrugged. "I really have no idea. Kurt was going to have Gabrielle make the arrangements."

"I see," the girl said. She unfolded her coltish legs from underneath her and stood up, her lanky body graceful in the long dress she had donned for dinner. "I think I'll bid you good-night, then," she muttered as she left the room, turning in the hallway in the direction of Gabrielle's office.

Liesl gazed at Megan with wide accusing eyes. "You're going away," she said.

Megan protested, "But I'll be back. I'm just going to—to spend some time with your father. He wants to make sure I'm entertained while he's away."

"Can't I entertain you? Don't you want to go on that drive with me? If you'd rather go to Vienna, why can't I go with you? I know lots of places to show you. After all, Vienna is my home, too."

"Yes, of course, but—"

"Tante Megan," Liesl pleaded, "don't you like being with me? I thought—"

Exasperated, Megan snapped, "For heaven's sake, Liesl, don't whine!"

The little girl recoiled as if she had been slapped. Suddenly her sapphire eyes shimmered wetly, and with an incoherent sob she leaped from the piano bench and fled from the room. Megan took a step after her, then halted, one hand half-raised in supplication. No, she wouldn't go after Liesl. She was becoming far too involved with the child. She owed her no explanations; she had no responsibility to her. Dear as Liesl was, she still exhibited some of those possessive, autocratic traits that made the adult von Kleists so overbearing. It would do her good to learn early that she couldn't always have things her own way.

So why did Megan feel so guilty for having inadvertently hurt the child?

Resolutely pushing the memory of Liesl's pale tear-marked face to the back of her mind, Megan went to her room and took the smaller of her two suitcases from her wardrobe. Since she wasn't sure how long she would be in Vienna or what she would do there—Megan bit her lip in silent laughter at the unconscious irony of that thought—she packed a skirt-and-slacks suit that could be coordinated several ways, as well as some scarves and chunky jewelry. For the flight she would be wearing a very simple blue dress that could be dressed up or down, so with a couple of pairs of shoes and some lingerie she ought to be prepared for most contingencies. If Kurt should want to take her someplace really elegant, she could always treat herself to a new dress.

Just as she was snapping the chrome lock on her suitcase, Megan remembered that she had not packed a nightgown. With fingers that suddenly trembled she pulled from the dresser the gown she had purchased just prior to leaving Los Angeles and had worn only to try on. Megan had a passion for beautiful nightwear, a ridiculous extravagance for someone who slept alone, she acknowledged, but she loved the cool slide of silky fabrics against her bare skin, the sensual caress of soft lace to make up in part for the lack of other caresses. This gown was a froth of mint-green nylon as delicate as cobwebs, with a wispy lace bodice held precariously by spaghetti straps, and a skirt that began just beneath her bust and flowed like mist to a lacy hem tickling her toes. Megan brushed the gown gently against her cheek, noting that the fabric was so sheer she could read her palm through it. For a moment she puzzled over the pattern of converging lines on her hand, trying to remember which one signified love. Then she shrugged. It didn't matter. She wasn't in love; she wanted nothing to do with love. Love hurt. What she and Kurt were about to embark on was basically nothing more than a satisfaction of mutual needs, and yet—and yet—she knew it was going to be glorious....

In the big canopy bed Megan drifted into a sleep sweetened with vague tantalizing dreams, and when the maid's hushed knock woke her early the next morning, her face glowed with anticipation. She ate her continental breakfast and dressed quickly, her mouth curved into a secret smile as she thought of the days—and nights—to come. Megan's smile did not fade until the chauffeur held open the door of the limousine for her and she slid smoothly onto the gray suede upholstery—only to find that the Mercedes already had an occupant.

"Surprise!" Adelaide grinned. "Gaby told me that since you're going to Vienna for the day, I might as well tag along, too. I need a new dress for the dance."

The blue Danube, Megan noted glumly as the small jet banked to begin its approach to Schwechat Airport, was in reality a nasty yellowish brown, just like every other river she'd ever seen passing through a large city. Somehow the disappointment seemed appropriate to her mood, the depression that had settled over her at the schloss as she handed her suitcase back to the maid with the stammered, embarrassed explanation that she had misunderstood the travel arrangements and would not be needing her bag after all.

The short flight from Salzburg to Vienna had passed quickly and quietly, with Adelaide still engrossed in her book and Megan staring morosely out the window. She ought to be thrilled that she was on her way to the city whose very name was synonymous with great music throughout the world; she ought to faint with an almost religious ecstasy at the prospect of standing in the same streets where once walked composers like Haydn and Mahler and Beethoven. But instead of excitement she was filled with bewildered frustration, mortified that she could so misinterpret Kurt's request to join him. At least Kurt would never know of her mistake; she ought to be grateful for that. What on earth would he have thought if she had arrived obviously prepared to spend the night with him?

She tried to push aside her mood by concentrating on the scenery. Unfortunately, for most of the journey the jet had skimmed just above a layer of white haze, obscuring Megan's view of all but an occasional mountaintop. Then, just before the plane started its descent, the cloud cover finally dissipated, and Megan caught her breath as she glimpsed a huge baroque castle like something from a fairy tale—a Benedictine monastery, she learned later—poised on a crag overlooking the river. Then the seat-belt light blinked on in the cabin and her attention was diverted.

As Megan and Adelaide disembarked from the airplane, the girl gave a mild yelp and stumbled out of the line of traffic to adjust one of her sandal straps, and Megan mounted the covered ramp into the terminal alone. She paused at the gate, unconsciously alluring in a Wedgwood-blue shirtwaist dress that emphasized her figure and contrasted strikingly with her burnished hair, restrained as usual in a heavy chignon at her nape. She glanced around in confusion, perplexed by the milling crowd and the babel of tongues foreign to her. Her green eyes searched the throng, hungry for the sight of Kurt, and then suddenly there he was, towering above everyone else, moving toward her with an air of latent authority that made other people give way to him automatically. He was wearing a dark business suit that set off his lean good looks to perfection, and Megan noticed with a certain smugness the way envious feminine eyes followed his progress toward her.

When he reached her he did not speak at first, but his blue eyes glowed their welcome. His hands rested lightly on her shoulders, and she quivered at his touch, lips parting slightly as she smiled up at him. "Hello," she murmured.

His voice was as husky as her own as he said, "Hello, Megan. I'm very glad you've come." He bent his dark head to brush his mouth fleetingly across hers. Lost in a microcosm of awareness, they were oblivious to the people pushing past them. Megan tilted her head back, exposing the graceful line of her throat, as she reached up to stroke his hard cheekbone. She could feel him inhale sharply. "Not here," he sighed reluctantly, caressing her fingertips before he tucked her hand under his arm and they turned to leave.

Behind them Adelaide called, "Kurt, Megan—don't go! Wait for me!"

Megan could feel Kurt tense with anger as he glanced back over his shoulder and then down at her again, his face stiff with disbelief. He gritted harshly, "Were you so uncertain you could handle me that you had to bring along a chaperon?"

She stared at him, bewildered. "Kurt, I—I—" she stammered, but before she could force the words out Adelaide joined them, bouncy and vivacious—almost too vivacious, Megan thought, as if the girl was trying to hide her doubts about her welcome.

"Hi, Kurt!" Adelaide said brightly, grazing his cheek with her own. "I hope you don't mind my inviting myself along for the day. Gaby thought it would be a good time for me to buy a gown for the St. Elisabeth's gala. I've been so busy that I haven't had time to—"

Kurt interrupted sharply, "Then you are here only for the day?"

"Of course," she responded defensively. "Our return flight is at nine tonight."

Kurt's eyes narrowed at the pronoun. "Our?" he echoed grimly. "I see." He peered down at Megan, and she could only shrug helplessly. After a pause he continued, "Since obviously time is at a premium, I suggest we get on our way." He turned to stride emphatically down the concourse. Megan, still clinging to his arm, struggled to keep pace with him, but Adelaide, she noticed enviously, had no such trouble. As they passed the luggage carousel Kurt glanced at Megan again. "Have you any baggage to claim?"

Megan thought wistfully of the suitcase she had left behind. "No," she muttered, shaking her head, "I didn't bring anything. It's—it's only for the day, after all."

At the entrance to the terminal Kurt halted abruptly. Turning to Adelaide, he asked, "Do you have enough money?"

She laughed. "Does anyone ever have enough?" Then, at the expression on Kurt's face, she amended quickly, "I have some. Gaby told me to charge my dress, and I'm supposed to take Megan to—"

"I shall attend to Megan's entertainment," Kurt said. He took a slim pigskin wallet from inside his jacket and handed a wad of hundred-schilling notes to the gaping Adelaide. "Here," he said, "you've done your duty by escorting Megan to me, and now I'm relieving you of further obligations. You can have a day in the city unencumbered by relatives. After you've found your dress, you may go to the Prater or one of your beloved movies or wherever you wish, as along as you get to my apartment in time for me to drive you back here. About seven-thirty, I should think."

Adelaide, still slightly bemused by Kurt's largesse, asked, "But how do I get downtown? May I come with you?"

"No," Kurt said coldy. "I must get back to the gallery at once, and I won't have time to drop you off. I suggest you catch the airport shuttle bus. It will take you to the city air terminal at Landstrasser Hauptstrasse, next to the Hilton. Since, as you constantly insist, you are a responsible adult, I am sure you can manage on your own. *Auf Wiedersehen,* Adelaide!"

Before the girl could protest further, Kurt whisked Megan through the door, one hand pressed firmly into her back. He headed for the parking lot with an air of silent, inexorable purpose, and as he guided her through the throngs of travelers milling around on the wide walkways, brushing past harassed porters laden with luggage, skirting family groups where strident parents shouted irritably at tired wailing children, the ironic thought suddenly flashed into Megan's mind that now, in the midst of all these people, she was for the first time truly alone with Kurt.

CHAPTER SEVEN

As they crossed the parking lot Megan asked anxiously, "Are you sure you don't want Adelaide to come with us?"

"Of course not," Kurt snorted. "Do you?"

"But a young girl, alone in a big city—"

"This is Vienna, Megan," he said dryly, "not New York or London. She'll be perfectly all right."

"Oh. I just thought—"

In the center of the roadway Kurt suddenly stopped and stared down at her, searching her face intently. "Did you really think I had just asked you here for the day?"

Megan's cheeks colored as she bit her lip. "I—I didn't know what to think. You told Gabrielle to make the arrangements, and she—"

Behind them a car honked its horn impatiently, and Kurt drew Megan out of the lane of traffic. "We'll continue this as we drive," he said, leading her to a stall where a midnight-blue Mercedes 450SL waited with sleek impatience. Glancing at Kurt, Megan realized with pleasure that he wasn't trying to impress her with the car. He seemed to regard the elegant vehicle as impersonally as she did her old Ford in Los Angeles.

When she had settled herself into the caressing cushions of the bucket seat, he tersely ordered her to fasten her seat belt. One end of the belt had fallen into the space between the seat and the door and was tangled with something. As she fumbled for it, her probing fingers touched paper, a book. Curiously she fished out her treasure. She grinned wryly as she smoothed the creased pages and found herself staring at a *Fledermausmann* comic book. There was something rather surreal about the familiar black-and-purple-garbed Caped Crusader sputtering umlauts.

Kurt took the book from her and tossed it into the back. "Sorry. I don't imagine Batman is to your taste. I suppose no one has ridden with me since I took Liesl to the Tirol for the summer." He looked at Megan impatiently. "Do you have that belt fastened yet? It's the law here in Austria." He reached across her lap for the strap, and then suddenly his long fingers were around her throat, holding her head immobile as he pressed her into the cushions and ravaged her mouth hotly. Stunned by the violence of his attack, Megan could not respond, but lay passive in his arms while his lips crushed hers back against her teeth. When at last he lifted his head, his blue eyes were dark and stormy.

"Damn you," he muttered thickly, "why did you let them mess up our plans? Why didn't you tell them you didn't want to return tonight?"

Megan blinked helplessly as she wondered, *just what was I supposed to say? "Sorry, Gabrielle and Adelaide, I won't be back tonight because I plan to sleep with Kurt"*? Aloud she said, shrugging, "But I didn't know until the last minute that this was to be just a day trip, and then I—I supposed I must have misunderstood what you wanted."

Kurt laughed sardonically, "Oh, I think you've known all along just what I wanted." Releasing her, he settled into his own seat and switched on the engine. "We do have to go back to the gallery, I'm afraid," he sighed. "Had I realized just how short your visit was to be, I might have—arranged it differently."

As the blue car hummed along the motorway, Kurt pointed out a turn leading to the Wienerwald, the fabled Vienna Woods, and Megan could see the dark edge of the forest in the distance. "I had hoped to have time to take you to the *Heurigen,*" he said regretfully. Noting her puzzled expression, he explained, "It's one of Vienna's most delightful institutions. When you drive through the vineyards, if you find one with a pine branch hanging over the door, then you know that they are serving the *Heuriger*, the new wine. Everyone sits at long scrubbed tables, drinking wine, eating cheese and cold meats—you may bring your own if you wish—chatting and listening to music. It is all very friendly, very comfortable, very—*gemütlich.*"

"Everything in Vienna is ge-*gemütlich*, isn't it, Kurt?" Megan said, her sore lips stumbling over the word.

He shrugged teasingly. "Everything but the wind, they say—and the wind only comes because it's so *gemütlich* here."

Megan laughed at the old joke. "I haven't noticed any wind today."

"It calmed in your honor." He smiled down at her with heart-stopping charm before he returned his attention to the worsening traffic.

They skimmed across the Danube canal—where the water really was blue, Megan noted with surprise—then headed into the heart of the city. By the time they reached Kurt's gallery on the Bäckerstrasse, a few meters down the road from the Old University, where Franz Schubert lived when he sang in the Vienna Boys' Choir, Megan was totally bewildered. Narrow streets and courts twisted and wound back on themselves, and each turn revealed architecture that varied from Renaissance to contemporary. Shops rubbed against palaces, cafés touched cathedrals. The people all seemed beautifully dressed and attractive—perhaps because they smiled so much—and as Megan and Kurt crossed the sidewalk she could have sworn she heard a passerby humming a phrase from *The Magic Flute*.

The interior of the von Kleist gallery was a symphony of neutral colors and indirect lighting, subdued without being bland, a perfect foil for the bright surrealistic paintings hanging on the walls. Kurt introduced Megan to his staff, and she watched with interest as he dealt with the problems they presented him. He was respectful but firm, listening carefully to what they had to say, then making decisions they accepted without demur. He was very obviously the man in charge. After a few moments Megan turned to puzzle over the paintings displayed, apparently a one-man show. Each canvas was a meticulous, sumptuously colored recreation of some bizarre and ominous fantasy world she could not quite grasp, and was not sure she wanted to.

"Don't you like them?" Kurt asked quietly when she looked at him again. She could hear an undertone of laughter in his deep voice.

"I...I don't know," she said helplessly. "As I told you once before, I know very little about art."

"You need someone to explain them to you, then." He glanced around. "Perhaps I can find the artist. He's usually here at this time of day."

Kurt disappeared into a back room and soon returned with a young man about Megan's age, whose ragged beard and scruffy appearance were belied by the old-world charm with which he bent over her wrist and murmured, *"Küss die Hand, gnädige Frau."* Megan's green eyes widened as she suppressed a gasp of surprise. No one had ever kissed her hand before. As she tried to think of a suitable reply, the artist waved paint-stained fingers toward his creations and proceeded to interpret them for Megan—in intense, rapid German totally incomprehensible to her. Unable to interrupt his monologue, she searched surreptitiously for Kurt, but he had moved to an alcove on the far side of the gallery, where he conferred quietly with his manager and two women who Megan assumed were customers.

Sighing, she returned her attention to the young man, who rambled on and on. Megan gleaned enough to know he thought a lot of himself—"*ich*," she noticed, seemed to be his favorite word. She smiled sweetly and mumbled "*Ja*" or "*sehr gut*" occasionally while she plotted ways to murder Kurt slowly and painfully....

When at last Kurt rescued her and they stood on the sidewalk outside once more, Megan accused, "You did that on purpose, didn't you, knowing I wouldn't be able to understand a word he said?"

"Of course," Kurt grinned, utterly unrepentant. "It kept you occupied while I conducted my business. As for the German—once he gets going on the school of Fantastic Realism and his prominent place in it, I doubt you could understand him any better were he speaking English." At Megan's indignant expression, Kurt laughed openly. "Calm down, *mein Schatz*. I am free for the rest of the day, and I intend to devote it to showing you as much of my city as possible. No, not by car," he added when she turned automatically toward the parked Mercedes. "I have in mind for us something more...special."

Taking Megan's hand, Kurt headed for the Stephansplatz, where the mosaic roof of the cathedral, with its interlocking diamond patterns of black, white and gold, and the double-headed eagle crest of the Hapsburgs, gleamed like some incredible piece of jewelry in the midday light. Overwhelmed by the beauty of the building, Megan did not notice Kurt's destination until he tapped her cheek lightly and she looked around just as a small black hackney coach, lacquer-bright with red pinstriping and drawn by a matched pair of dappled gray horses, pulled to a halt in front of them. A young driver resplendent in velvet jacket, black-and-white-checked trousers and a jaunty bowler hat jumped down to bow them aboard.

Megan gaped at Kurt with astonished delight. "For us?" she whispered breathlessly.

"For us," Kurt said as he handed her into the carriage. "The *Fiaker* have been part of Vienna since the seventeenth century, and they're still the best way to tour the inner city." As he settled into the leather seat, he flung one arm around Megan's shoulders and pulled her close against him, and she was at once acutely aware of the hard strength of his body, the dry subtle fragrance of his cologne. His long fingers fondled her upper arm absently through the thin fabric of her dress, and she shivered at his touch. Kurt felt her tremble, and he studied her face, his eyes dark and unreadable. He took a deep rasping breath. "Shall we forget the tour and go on to my apartment?" he murmured.

Megan lowered her lashes, unable to look at him as her heart began to pound. So this was it; at last the moment had come. She need only say yes, and within the hour she would be in Kurt's bed, quivering under his skilled caress as he taught her what it meant to be fulfilled as a woman. She peeked up at him again, eyes shining with anticipation. But surprisingly, just as she opened her mouth to whisper the word, he laid a finger lightly across her lips and shook his head.

"No," he said. "I withdraw the question. This is not our day." He sighed wryly. "It could have been, but other people's interference has changed all that. When the time comes for us, it will not be when Adelaide may barge in on us at any moment or when you must get up and leave after only a few hours." An ironic smile twisted his thin mouth as disappointment flashed in Megan's eyes. "I know," he said, bending to kiss her gently. "I dislike frustration as much as the next man, but you and I are not so desperate that we must grab at any available moment, however fleeting and uncomfortable, like teenagers in the back seat of a car. We will wait until the time is right—I suppose sometime after I return to the schloss...." He dropped a kiss on the end of her nose and said briskly, "You should have brought a hat; you will be sunburned again."

Kurt signaled to the coachman, and the carriage pulled away from the curb. The slight sway of the well-sprung *Fiaker* and the hollow clop-clop of the horses' hooves on the cobbled pavement imparted an otherworldly air to the ride. After a moment the young driver began his narration in heavily accented English, pointing out sights with his whip. "On the south side of the cathedral you will see the Riesentor, or Giant's Gate," he intoned, "so-called because in the thirteenth century a huge bone was found there, thought by the townspeople to be the leg bone of a giant drowned in Noah's flood. For centuries this bone hung on the door, until scientists concluded that it was in fact the tibia of a mammoth—"

A CLOCK SOMEWHERE was just striking six as Kurt and Megan stepped out of the elevator into the hushed corridor just outside his apartment in a high-rise complex in the twentieth district. Kurt told Megan that the only other apartment on that level belonged to the elderly widow of a South African diamond merchant, who spent the winters in Durban, and thus he and Liesl had the floor to themselves six months of the year.

Disoriented with fatigue, Megan somehow found the idea of occupying an entire floor unaccountably funny, and she began to giggle. Kurt eyed her curiously. When he held the door open for her, she flew into the entryway, twirling on tiptoe as she hummed a snatch of something by Strauss and laughed, "Oh, Kurt, I've had such a lovely day! And this is such a lovely apartment...." The living room was wide and open, with a thick silver gray carpet and low clean-lined furniture dividing the space into smaller areas. Twin sofas formed a conversation pit beneath a picture window, and in the corner gleamed an ebony baby grand. After the florid opulence of the schloss, the apartment seemed almost stark. "It looks as if it was decorated by an American," she said.

"Wrong," Kurt said. "I decorated it. But the architect was American. I find that the simplicity of the furnishings makes a good background for my collection of abstracts."

"Lovely," Megan said again.

Kurt watched her with an indulgent smile. He asked lightly, "My dear, are you drunk?"

"No, I'm not," she protested indignantly. "You know I haven't had a thing to drink all day except the wine with lunch. I'm just—I'm just giddy with the beauty of everything: Schloss Schönbrunn, the concert in the gardens at Belvedere, the Spanish Riding School...." She yawned impressively. "I'm surprised I can still walk."

"Then why don't you sit down?" Kurt suggested, leading her to one of the couches. Glancing out the picture window, Megan could see in the distance the *Riesenrad*, the giant ferris wheel Orson Welles and Joseph Cotten rode in *The Third Man*. She began to hum the theme from the movie. Kurt chuckled, "Now I know you're exhausted," and settled her onto the plump cushions. He slipped off her sandals and began to massage her small feet.

"Mmm, that feels good," she sighed contentedly. Her gold lashes drooped like a sleepy child's as she lay back and gave herself up to his soothing fingers. She giggled deep in her throat when he touched her sensitive insteps. There was something almost unbearably erotic in the feel of his hands on her feet and ankles. If only she weren't so tired....

Kurt said, "Poor baby, I made you do too much this afternoon. I should have known there was no way you could see all of Vienna in a day. You relax now, and I'll make some coffee."

"That sounds good," she said politely as her eyes closed. "But please, not *mit—mit Schlag*. I don't like whipped cream in my...." Her voice trailed off, and she drifted into a dream of melting sweetness, somewhere where she was safe and warm, and somebody kissed her....

She awoke with a start, green eyes wide and troubled. "What time is it?" she cried as she jerked her head back and forth, confused by her surroundings until her sleep-blurred vision cleared and she was able to focus on Kurt sitting on the sofa opposite, studying her inscrutably.

"Calm down," he said. "You've been asleep only about half an hour. Your coffee hasn't even had time to cool off yet."

Megan blinked and shook her head violently as she reached for the cup that still steamed on the table in front of her. "I'm sorry. I was afraid I would be late for the plane back to Salzburg." She sipped the black coffee and smiled her approval. "Is Adelaide here yet?" she asked.

"No," Kurt said. "I don't really expect her until the very last minute. She knows better than to miss her flight, but she will probably cut it as close as she can."

"Adelaide's a funny girl," Megan said, mostly for something to say.

Kurt grimaced. "You mean she's a spoiled brat. Gabrielle indulges her endlessly."

Megan frowned, thinking of the girl's frustrated dealings with her guardian. "I—I'm not sure I agree with that."

Kurt cocked one eyebrow. "You mean because Gaby refuses to let her pursue this idiotic obsession with becoming a movie star?"

"Well, it's—it's none of my business, but...." She shrugged helplessly.

Kurt said, "Personally I think Gabrielle's insistence on making Adelaide study something useful is entirely reasonable, just as I think she has every right to expect the girl to help her with her work on the estate. Of course, Adelaide doesn't see it like that, but then, I suppose that's to be expected, after the way she was raised."

"What do you mean?"

Kurt poured more coffee. "I suppose Adelaide has told you her sad story about her father, the brilliant racing driver cut down before he reached the pinnacle of success? No, don't look at me that way, Megan; I assure you I'm not implying it wasn't tragic that the girl was orphaned at fifteen, for of course it was. But her father was not the paragon she would have you believe. In fact, the man was almost criminally irresponsible, jeopardizing his life and his child's future to pursue a dream he obviously was incapable of achieving."

Megan said, "Then Arnold Steuben was not a—a promising Grand Prix driver?"

Kurt snorted, "Promising? He was never more than second-rate. He was a brilliant mechanic, but as a driver he took too many chances and neglected the routine precautions that can mean the difference between life and death. In the end he died because of a worn tire he should have spotted in time." Kurt scowled. "Steuben couldn't even get a sponsor for his last two seasons, so he had to finance his own racing crew, using up all his capital and going deeply into debt. Adelaide doesn't know it, but Gabrielle and Willi were paying for her education long before her father died."

Megan said, "In that case, for heaven's sake, why doesn't someone tell Adelaide? Wouldn't she be more...amenable to Gabrielle's plans if she realized how much she owes her?"

"I don't know. She might. However, Gabrielle is her guardian, and she refuses to tell her. I think—I think because Gaby lost her own parents when she was so very young, she does not want anything to blemish Adelaide's memories of her father. In this case I fear she is making a bad mistake, for obviously the girl resents Gabrielle's demands on her. But it is Gaby's decision, and I must abide by it. As much as possible I try not to interfere in her life, nor she in mine." He grinned ironically. "The change she made in your travel plans was—most unusual. I can see I shall have to speak to her about that."

Megan's cheeks washed with pink. "I—I don't understand why Gabrielle did it."

"Don't you?" Kurt asked. "Well, perhaps in twenty years you will." Across the coffee table their eyes met and locked, and once more Megan could feel the awareness tingling through her body as she responded to Kurt's tacit desire. For just a second she thought he was going to reach for her, then his glance flickered toward his wristwatch and a shuttered look came over him. He took a deep breath and said lightly, "Would you play the piano for me, Megan? I have never heard you."

Megan nodded and stood up, padding across the lush carpet in her stocking feet. She seated herself at the baby grand and fingered a few chords experimentally to get the feel of the instrument. The piano was a modern one of excellent quality, the tone true, the action smooth and quiet—but, she realized with a sigh, it could not compare with the antique piano in the music room at the schloss.

"I bought this one for Liesl," Kurt said, seeming to read Megan's thoughts as he moved to her side. "Briefly I contemplated removing the other one from the schloss, since no one there plays now; then I realized that to do so would be senseless and almost criminal, rather like ripping a Rubens from its frame and tacking it up over a bar somewhere."

"I'm glad you changed your mind," Megan said. "The piano belongs in the music room, with the gilt cherubs smiling down on it." She chuckled at her fanciful imagery, then became serious again. "Kurt, may I say something about Liesl? I think it's important." He nodded and she proceeded rapidly, "I've listened to Liesl play the piano, and I really believe she shows promise as a musician, but—but I don't think she has the right teacher. I admit I know nothing about this Fräulein Brecht. I'm sure she's very competent, but she doesn't seem to stimulate Liesl. If the child is to aspire to the best of her ability, she needs someone who can excite her and make her understand that the basics she is learning now are not tedious stumbling blocks but are in fact the first very important steps toward the—the musical heights."

Kurt frowned thoughtfully. "And you don't think Liesl's current teacher can do this?"

Megan shrugged. "I don't know. I'm not suggesting you fire her. Perhaps if you talked to her, made her understand Liesl's special needs better, that would be enough. Or...." Megan bit her lip, debating whether she should voice the thought that had come to her suddenly. After a moment's hesitation she plunged on, "Or you could teach Liesl yourself."

She wondered if she had angered him. He did not speak as he stared at her with dark unfathomable eyes. Inevitably his gaze shifted to the rigid fingers of his scarred left hand. The jagged line shone very white against his tan skin, as if he were trying to clench his fist. Megan explained warily, "You'd be a good teacher, Kurt, I know you would. Don't you see? The music is in you, in your von Kleist blood. That's how Erich got it; that's how you passed it on to your daughter. It's part of you, and it always will be. The fact that you can no longer play the piano doesn't change anything."

Kurt's silence stretched on until Megan thought her nerves would snap. Then suddenly he rasped, "No!" He stalked away from the piano and crossed to the window, where he gazed blindly at the panorama of the great city. His voice was low and harsh as he said evenly, "I know you mean well, Megan, and I appreciate your interest. I shall indeed look into finding a more suitable instructor for Liesl. But I must ask you not to concern yourself with dreams and ambitions I gave up before you were even born."

Stung by his coldness, Megan winced. Oh, no, she'd ruined everything now! With a few well-intentioned but rash words she had destroyed the growing rapport between them; she had made him, if not an enemy, then certainly no longer a friend. She should have realized that a man with his very tetchy pride would not tolerate a near stranger mentioning his handicap. And despite the sensual attraction she and Kurt shared, they were still very much strangers....

She wondered if she ought to try to apologize. No, to do so would probably only make matters worse. She would be better off quiet, resigning herself to his distant courtesy until such time as he felt more charitable toward her. She glanced at him, stiff and unyielding, silhouetted against the sunlit window. With a sigh she quietly lowered the piano cover over the bright keys and went to search for her shoes. It was probably just as well that Adelaide chose that moment to burst into the apartment, full of news about the movie she had seen and the absolutely gorgeous dress she'd found in a boutique on the Kohlmarkt.

MEGAN RETURNED TO THE SCHLOSS quiet and thoughtful, still trying to understand the significance of the day that had begun so well and ended so awkwardly. Kurt had remained terse and unapproachable during the long drive back to the airport, acknowledging Adelaide's chatter with brusque nods, seemingly unaware of Megan's silence. Not until they were inside the terminal and the two women waited in line to go through the security checkpoint did his manner soften. When Megan extended a tentative hand and stammered, "Th-thank you for a lovely day, Kurt," he caught her wrist and suddenly pulled her into his arms. Her green eyes widened with surprise as he lowered his mouth to hers.

"Forgive me for being so—*verdriesslich*, my dear," he murmured. "I'm afraid that men, like little boys, frequently become sulky and peevish when they don't get what they want."

Megan's lips were still moist with that kiss when she settled herself into her seat on the commuter jet. Beside her Adelaide regarded her narrowly and muttered, "You aren't falling for Kurt, are you?"

"What?" Megan blinked. Then, "Oh, no, of course not."

"That's good," Adelaide said briskly, with a supercilious air reminiscent of her guardian, "because it simply wouldn't do, you know."

In the morning Megan telephoned Ulrike at her home to ask if they might meet for lunch. She was still resentful about the way Gabrielle had interfered with her plans, and she did not want to face the older woman again until her temper cooled. When Ulrike invited her to come to her house, Megan accepted gladly. It was not until the chauffeur dropped her in front of the trim whitewashed cottage with red shutters and a narrow flower-bedecked balcony across the second story that Megan realized Ulrike now occupied her grandparents' home, the house in which Erich had lived as a young child.

Her hostess welcomed her warmly, again dazzling Megan with her lovely smile, and Megan followed her slowly inside, trying not to stare. A greater contrast to the opulent glory of Schloss von Kleist was hard to imagine, and yet this was clearly a house in which love had dwelt. Megan wondered if Erich had ever regretted leaving it.

When she stepped into the parlor, she knew at once that the room was still furnished as it had been when the elder Müllers were alive. The matched suite of furniture was dark and old-fashioned, worn without being shabby, obviously the pride and joy of a meticulous housekeeper. In one corner of the room resided a porcelain stove—

cool, of course, for the summer—as delicate and fragile as an old teapot. High on the wall hung a large olive-wood crucifix, crackled with age, its yellowed paint and gilt flaking away from a Christ who writhed in eternal penitence. Beneath it were displayed rows of photographs, from faded sepia prints in oval frames to bright Polaroid snapshots, four generations of Müllers.

"I have twelve nieces and nephews," Ulrike said, indicating the newest pictures. "I am a doting aunt, which is nice, since I may never be a...." She hesitated before continuing. "Here, these are the ones I thought you would like to see. I thought they might make you—understand better." She pointed to a dim old-fashioned wedding picture of a young couple standing unnaturally rigid and uncomfortable, their expressions faintly frightened. Under her lace veil the young woman's blond hair was plaited and wound tightly around her small head, and the stiff fabric of her skirt reached to the floor. The man wore a military uniform complete with puttees, and under one arm he carried a spiked helmet of a kind Megan had only ever seen in the movies.

"My grandparents," Ulrike said fondly. "They had been married fifty-seven years when my grandmother died, and then *Opa* followed her three months later. I did not grieve for him, for I knew he had only been waiting to join her again." Her hands moved lightly along the pictures. "Here they are later in the shop they ran together—and here is my father.... He and my mother are still alive," she explained in response to Megan's querying look. "Their home is in Styria now. And here—do you know who this young woman is?"

Megan stared at the young girl who smiled shyly back at her from a full-length black-and-white photograph in a bisque frame. Her silvery hair was styled in the pageboy of the late forties, but she was dressed for some festival in the timeless traditional dirndl costume of the Tirol, full skirt with an embroidered apron tied at the waist, billowy white blouse under a laced vest. Megan's fingers stretched up to touch that smiling face, then fell away.

"It's—it's Eva, isn't it?" she stammered. "Erich's mother?"

"Yes," Ulrike said. "I believe she was seventeen or eighteen when that was taken."

Megan gazed at the picture. The girl was truly lovely, glowing with the radiant pure beauty of a butterfly unfolding its wings for the first time.

And less than a year after that photograph had been taken, she was seduced by Horst von Kleist.

Ulrike watched the angry expressions playing over Megan's pale features, and she touched her arm lightly. "Don't judge them," she said urgently. "We don't know what happened. They are all gone now and cannot defend themselves. We have no right to stand in judgment on the dead. We can—we can only try to live our own lives with honor." She quickly pointed at the next snapshot. "Look here, Megan. Would you believe that this skinny little girl with the missing front teeth is me? Ah, to be so thin again...."

Later in the day, as Megan drove with Ulrike to the hospital, she puzzled over what she had seen. There had been pictures of Erich, many pictures, and yet somehow those candid shots of her husband as an infant and a little boy had affected her much less profoundly than had that one photograph of his mother. Perhaps she could view Erich's early past impersonally because it seemed completely divorced from the man she had known. But that girl, so innocent, so utterly vulnerable... as Megan herself had been. Damn the von Kleists with their seductive, destructive charm! Was no one safe from them?

Ulrike left Megan in the small dining room of the hospital with a cup of coffee and the promise that she would return as soon as she had glanced over the charts of her patients. While Ulrike was gone, Megan surveyed her surroundings. At the moment she was alone, although she could hear the clatter of dishes in the kitchen. The room had the stark utilitarian furnishings usually found in hospitals, but its windows overlooked an enclosed rose garden, and Megan noticed an elderly woman in a wheelchair sunning herself there. The interior walls were decorated with beautiful muted watercolors of alpine scenes, which Megan suspected Kurt had furnished; and pushed into one corner was an upright piano of uncertain vintage.

Megan stared pensively at the piano as she sipped her coffee. When she had finished, she put the empty cup in the pass-through to the kitchen and approached the instrument resolutely. She needed to play. Not only did she dislike missing several days of practice, but she also needed the emotional release that only music could give her. Without it she became as jumpy as a chain smoker suddenly deprived of his cigarettes. Since coming to Austria she had touched a piano only for Liesl's music lessons—except for the night before, in Vienna, which had come to nothing—and now she seated herself at the old upright and began to play quietly but intensely, as if her sanity depended on it.

The piano was out of tune, with mushy, slow-to-respond keys, and the notes sounded with the peculiar twang that betrayed a cracked sounding board. But Megan closed her sensitive ears to the dissonance and heard only clear pure tones inside her. She warmed up with one of the arrangements she frequently played at the Polynesian Paradise, a medley of recent popular songs done in her most florid "cocktail piano" style, all arpeggios and minor-eleventh chords, which sounded challenging but wasn't. Just for fun she whipped through a couple of Scott Joplin's classic ragtime numbers, then she hesitated, her mind a blank, as she waited for her spirit to tell her fingers what to begin next.

A frail liver-spotted hand touched her arm.

Startled, Megan jerked around to find the old woman in the wheelchair whom she had noticed in the garden. *"Bitte,"* the woman said timidly, her voice hoarse and croaky, "please don't stop. I was enjoying the music so much."

Megan smiled gently. "Of course I'd be delighted to keep playing," she reassured the old woman in her weak German. The woman's surprise at her poor accent necessitated the explanation that she was an American friend of Dr. Müller's. "And what would you like to hear?" she added dubiously, since the closest thing to popular Austrian tunes that she knew was the score from *The Sound of Music*.

To her immense relief, the woman said with a shrug, "Oh, anything," and settled back into her wheelchair, a spasm of pain twisting her wrinkled face as she moved an arthritic shoulder.

Megan noticed that fleeting expression with pity, and she turned back to the keyboard determined somehow to soothe the woman's discomfort. She began again with a lilting little waltz by Brahms, then Mozart's sprightlier "Turkish Rondo." As she segued from one light classical piece to the next, pretty, undemanding compositions guaranteed to please and relax the listener, she watched the woman out of the corner of her eye, observing how she seemed to respond best to the dance music, slipping off into some wistful reverie, perhaps of a time when her hair was dark and she waltzed all night with a lover.... *What a pig I am,* Megan berated herself mentally, *to feel so sorry for myself when I am young and have my health and my whole life before me.*

She continued with renewed vigor, digging deep

in her memory for waltzes by Strauss and Lehár and the ever sentimental Waldteufel, playing by ear when her memory failed her. After a while she noticed that other people were drifting into the room, ambulatory patients, a nurse or two, a man in a dark suit whose clerical collar identified him as a priest. They slipped in quietly to drink coffee and listen with respect and evident enjoyment while she performed some of the dozens of pieces that made up her repertoire. She did not mind: she liked giving pleasure with her music, and heaven knew, they were better behaved than her usual audience at the cocktail lounge! But as her fingers tripped lightly over the keyboard she kept wondering, *do any of them know that I am only secondrate?*

When at last her hands stilled, the audience rewarded her with a round of applause and comments of *"Schön!"* and *"Sehr gut,"* and at her side Peter Swanson declared admiringly, "Hey, you're really good!"

Megan pivoted on the piano bench, surprised and delighted. "Peter," she laughed, "what are you doing here?"

He held up a small plate with some kind of cake on it. "Would you believe I came here for the pastry? Here, have some. This hospital has the most incredible chef!" He sat at one end of a long table, grinning, and went on, "Actually, I dropped by to confirm that it's still on about going to Salzburg tomorrow. I figured I'd better remind Riki, or she's liable to schedule an operation or something." He regarded Megan quizzically as she pulled up a chair beside him. "Imagine my surprise when I found myself walking into the middle of a concert! I had no idea you could play that well, Megan."

Megan busied herself with the concoction of cherries, whipped cream and puff pastry that he set before her, noting, "It's just as well this is a hospital: a person could die from an overdose of butterfat!" After a moment she said, "I thank you for the compliments, Peter. Didn't you know I'm a professional musician?"

He frowned. "I guess the subject never came up. As I said, though, you are very good."

Megan shrugged. "I used to be a lot better."

"I find that hard to believe."

She smiled remotely. "Well, believe it or not, once upon a time I performed on the concert circuit. We were—that was when I was first married. But I haven't studied seriously in years, and nowadays all I play is popular junk in a bar—and unfortunately, as in any other skill, if you don't keep up the hard work, you lose it."

"You could probably get it back if you tried."

"Maybe. I think about it sometimes, and I wonder if I could. But then I realize that even if I trained under the best teachers in the world, I would never be good enough."

Peter tilted his head, licking a crumb from the corner of his mouth. "Is any real musician ever 'good enough'? You know what Beethoven wrote about the true artist: 'He feels dimly how far he is from his goal, and while perhaps he is admired by others, he realizes with sorrow that he has not yet reached the place to which the better spirit lights the way before him like a distant sun.'"

Megan stared. "Where did you get a quote like that?"

Peter's brown eyes danced behind his thick glasses as he mocked gently, "Honey, just because I'm an engineer doesn't mean I'm a complete philistine."

Megan blushed. When she regained her composure she moaned, "Oh, damn, I get so frustrated sometimes! Inside me I have this—this *need*, and yet I know I'll never be as good a musician as I want to be." Her voice stumbled over the words as she struggled to articulate something she had never dared express before: her disappointment with her own capabilities. "Have you ever heard the Richter recording of Mussorgsky's *Pictures at an Exhibition*? The grandeur, the passion of that performance! When I listen to it I think I'd sell my very soul to be able to play that way. But—but I never will. I don't have the—the sheer genius or the training, and even if I did, I'm not physically equipped for it. My hands are wrong."

Peter reached across the table and grasped Megan's hands in his own. "What's wrong with them? They look like very nice hands to me."

Megan sighed, "Yeah, but they're too small. I don't have the reach necessary to play very advanced music. Rachmaninoff could stretch a *twelfth*!"

Peter examined her small hands, adjusting his glasses to squint at the knuckles and short unpolished nails. "Personally I think you would look extremely peculiar with fingers long enough to stretch over twelve notes of the keyboard. Although I suppose with plastic surgery...." He glanced up, smiling devilishly. "Ah, here's just the person to tell us whether it can be done. Riki, can you make Megan's fingers about two inches longer?"

Ulrike, looking tired and pallid in her white coat, was carrying her own coffee and cake to the table, murmuring apologies for her long absence. But the words died out as she stopped short and stared at Peter and Megan's joined hands. An unusual expression of pain flickered across her stolid features before she carefully schooled them into an impassive mask of polite interest. "What on earth are you talking about, Peter?"

Carefully Megan disengaged her fingers from Peter's. He gallantly pulled out a chair for Ulrike, who sat down tensely, relaxing only after he had explained the joke. Then he said, "Riki, I came by because I wanted to confirm the time I'm supposed to pick you up in the morning. You are still coming to Salzburg with us tomorrow, aren't you?"

Ulrike hesitated, frowning. "Of course I would like very much to go with you, but I am not sure I ought to leave town. Frau Grünwald is due to deliver at any time, and it may be twins—"

Peter snapped irritably, "Damn it, Riki, you

may be head of the hospital, but there are two other doctors here who are just as capable of delivering Frau Grünwald's wretched twins as you are! And if you don't take a day off soon for some rest and recreation, you're not going to be good for anything!"

"Yes, Peter," Ulrike said submissively. Her pale lashes fluttered down over her light blue eyes, and she smiled at him in a way Megan might have called flirtatious, were not the doctor completely devoid of feminine wiles. Ulrike asked softly, "Then you really do want me to go to Salzburg?"

"Yes, Riki," Peter said, reaching for her hand, stroking the blunt life-giving fingers gently. "Oh, yes."

EVER AFTERWARD Megan's memories of Salzburg were a jumble of mountains and crowds and glorious baroque architecture. The setting of the city was perfect, she thought as they approached on the autobahn and she glimpsed spires and bell towers rising above blue green copper roofs, a view she had overlooked when Kurt's chauffeur had skirted the city to take her and Adelaide to the airport.

Salzburg straddled the Salzach River, nestled in a valley between two mountains, the Kapuzinerberg and the Mönchsberg, with rolling forested peaks all around. Ulrike told her that the site had been occupied continuously since at least five hundred years before Christ. The city swarmed with people, a stunning contrast to her two previous trips through the city. Now tourists laden with cameras trooped dutifully down the Getreidegasse to number nine, the small house where Mozart was born. They wandered through the catacombs to view the tomb of Saint Virgilius, an eighth-century bishop whose real name was O'Farrell. They lined up behind St. Peter's Cemetery to ride the cogwheel railway up Castle Hill to Festung Hohensalzburg, the fortress dominating the skyline. Ulrike pointed out the sights while Peter hunted impatiently for a parking space, and after he had squeezed the Audi into an opening uncomfortably close to a fire hydrant, the three of them crossed Kapitelplatz on foot, past the Neptune Fountain, until they entered the Dom Platz, Cathedral Square.

Megan gaped in awe at the great church, and Ulrike said, "The cathedral of Salzburg was the first baroque building constructed north of the Alps, and it's still one of the finest."

"It's magnificent," Megan murmured as she stared at the superb marble facade and the towers that rose over two hundred feet to gleam in the sunlight. "When I used to see pictures of European cathedrals, I never really conceived how very *big* they are."

"It can hold ten thousand people," Ulrike said. "Would you like to go inside? Peter?"

He shook his head uncomfortably. "Not this time, Riki. Thanks, anyhow."

"Megan?"

Ruefully Megan glanced down at her pantsuit. "I'm afraid I'm wearing slacks again."

Ulrike sighed. She pulled her scarf from her handbag and asked, "Would the two of you mind if I leave you for a few minutes?"

"No, of course not, go right ahead. We'll wait."

They watched Ulrike disappear through the center of three great bronze doors. Coming closer, Megan saw with surprise that the massive doors with their unusual shrouded figures were modern in design. Peter explained, "That door is Faith, that's Hope, and of course the one in the middle is Charity. They're really an outstanding blend of the old and the new."

Megan gazed in silence at the huge church. She noticed that Peter was frowning intently at the door through which their friend had entered. She ventured timidly, "I gather Ulrike is very devout?"

"Yes," Peter said, snapping off the word. "And I'm not. And I'm divorced, to boot. Sometimes I've thought—if only...." He clenched his fists. "Oh, hell," he gritted, "what difference does it make? Between her work and her church, she doesn't need me."

Megan thought it wise to change the subject. "Didn't you say you had business here today?"

He grinned wryly, acknowledging her tactic. "Yeah. I have to drop by to see my Uncle Max, to find out if there's been any progress in the stalemate we have with von Kleist."

"What kind of business does your uncle do? Besides mining, I mean."

Peter shrugged. "Oh, a little bit of everything nowadays. Have you ever heard of Bachmann und Steiner Aktiengesellschaft?"

"No," Megan laughed, "and it's probably just as well, because I'm sure I couldn't pronounce it if I had to! What on earth does that mouthful mean?"

"It translates roughly as Bachmann, Steiner and Company. Most people just call it Bachmann Steiner, although actually you could forget about Steiner, because he was bought out twenty-five years ago. Bachmann—my uncle, Max Bachmann—is still going strong, however." Peter's voice was warm with affection as he spoke. "My Uncle Max is a remarkable man," he said. "At the end of the war Austria was in a state of chaos, about to be partitioned. Max was discharged from the army, penniless and homeless like most everybody those days. His last surviving relative—his sister, my mother—had just married an American G.I. and was preparing to emigrate. She and dad invited him to go to the States with them, but instead he decided to remain in Austria and help rebuild his country. He and a friend, Emil Steiner, formed a construction business, just the two of them breaking their backs repairing war-damaged buildings. There was a lot of work to be done, and they prospered. After a few years Uncle Max wanted to diversify, take a fling at manufacturing. Emil didn't like the idea, so that's when Max bought him out—which was too bad for Steiner, because my uncle has proved to be a man of talent and vision, and today he's one of the top industrialists in the country."

"Did he ever marry?"

Peter shook his head. "No. Like most wealthy men he never needed to." Peter's face hardened, losing that boyish look. "Once or twice lady friends of his have tried to cozy up to me, I suppose because I'm younger and presumably the heir apparent. What they don't realize is that Uncle Max would never leave me a dime if he didn't think I had earned it, and anyway, I don't want anything. I love the old man and I hope he lives forever." He chuckled self-consciously. "Sorry to go on like that, Megan. It's just that I get a little touchy on—"

Suddenly the square resounded with music as a great carillon somewhere began pealing out selections from Haydn and Mozart, the notes as sharp as crystal on the mountain air. Megan jerked around in confusion, trying to locate which of the baroque towers hid the bells. Peter pointed out the correct one. "The Glockenspiel Tower, over there by the Bishops' Palace. It plays a concert three times a day." He looked at his watch. "Eleven o'clock. Riki should be back anytime now."

Soon Ulrike did rejoin them, apologizing for her absence, and the three continued their walking tour of the city. When they reached the Festspielhaus, the grandiose modern building that was headquarters for the Mozart Festival, Peter observed, "Quite a tribute to the town's favorite son!"

As Megan gazed at the immense concert hall she thought of all the shops with their trinkets and plaster busts, and was suddenly filled with a smoldering sense of injustice. She accused, "Mozart wasn't a particularly favorite son during his lifetime! He played before kings and emperors, burned himself out for them, but died a pauper. No one even knows exactly where he's buried, because the only people who showed up for the funeral were the gravediggers!"

Peter stared at her. "Hey, now who's being touchy? The man's been dead two hundred years."

"Sorry." Megan shrugged. "Artistic temperament, I guess."

Ulrike suggested mildly, "It might be a good idea to begin looking for a place to eat, otherwise we'll never get served."

"Right you are, Riki," Peter said lightly, taking each woman by the arm as he directed them toward a likely-looking restaurant.

After lunch they crossed the river on an old stone footbridge and Peter told the others that he had to drop by his uncle's office. "I'll only be a few minutes," he said. "Riki, why don't you take Megan to the Mirabell Garden, and I'll meet you there as soon as I can."

Dutifully Ulrike guided Megan through the large park that had once been the private garden of Schloss Mirabell. She frowned as she explained that a seventeenth-century bishop had built the mansion for his mistress.

Megan said, "Well, I guess love is no respecter of religion."

"No," Ulrike agreed forlornly, and from the expression on her face Megan knew she must be thinking of Peter. Megan repressed a strong desire to shake the doctor. Damn it, she'd like to shake both of them! Didn't they realize that the regard they had for each other was something rare and precious, not to be wasted? Didn't they understand that when two people cared enough, they could work out any problem?

Megan gritted her teeth and told herself to mind her own business. She was the last person in the world qualified to give advice on romantic problems....

The women toured the garden for more than two hours before Peter finally reappeared. His step was light and he looked elated. He almost crowed as he said, "Pardon the delay, but I didn't get in to see Uncle Max for over an hour. He was talking to some woman, and he didn't want to be disturbed." Peter laughed slyly. "I'd about decided that his interview was of a more...personal nature than the receptionist had indicated, but when I saw his visitor I figured I must be wrong. The last time I looked, he wasn't picking his girl friends out of the schoolroom."

Ulrike smiled, "You seem very cheerful, Peter. Did your uncle have good news for you?"

"Yes! All of a sudden it looks as if there may be a break in the deadlock with von Kleist. Uncle Max thinks he has discovered a way to breech that aristocratic brick wall, and at long last I'll be able to start some real work! In fact, on the way back to Kleisthof I need to stop by the site and take care of a couple of things, so if you two don't mind...."

"Megan?" Ulrike asked, rising from the bench where they were sitting. "Would you be upset if we curtailed our visit now?"

"No, of course not. I've had a lovely day, and I'm grateful to the two of you for bringing me. But I think I've had all the walking I can take for a while. I'm not really used to the altitude, and besides, you know us Californians: we never walk anywhere if we can drive."

Megan relaxed half-asleep in the back seat of the Audi as the little car ate up the miles between Salzburg and Kleisthof. Peter and Ulrike conversed quietly in German while she dozed. She felt pleasantly exhausted, replete with memories she would treasure for a lifetime. She hadn't seen everything she wanted to see in Mozart's city, hadn't heard nearly enough music, but in a few days after Kurt came back from Vienna and they completed their business, she would be free to leave the schloss, to continue her travels alone. She could go where she wished, spend all the time she wanted at concerts and operas and recitals....

Why didn't the idea appeal anymore? She had come to Austria to experience all she could of the country's fabled culture. Why did she find herself thinking less about music and more about the moody, enigmatic lord of Schloss von Kleist?

Megan was unaware that the car had left the autobahn and now wound through lushly forested foothills until Peter maneuvered it skillfully off the pavement and onto a faint wagon track that disappeared into a meadow rich with wild flowers. Under an ancient oak tree was parked a rather Spartan aluminum-sided travel trailer, utterly alien against the unspoiled landscape. Peter switched off the engine and said, "I'll only be a minute, if you two want to walk around a bit."

Megan and Ulrike got out of the car and wandered aimlessly while Peter busied himself inside the trailer, which, Megan could see through the open door, was full of surveying and other equipment. She looked around her appreciatively. The old wagon track wound across the field until it died out in fragrant knee-high grass under a massive oak even older than the one under which the trailer was parked. The breeze was warm and scented, and butterflies danced like sparkles in the air. "What a lovely place," Megan sighed. "Los Angeles certainly doesn't have anything like this."

"Yes, it is," Ulrike agreed at her side. "It will be a shame to have to dig it all up—"

"Now, Riki, let's not get started on that," Peter chided, coming up behind them. "I get enough of that kind of flak from von Kleist. I admit the scenery is gorgeous, but hell, there's a lot of beautiful country around here, and it's not as if you will be able to see the mine from the estate. That's one reason I've never been able to understand the man's reluctance to let us go ahead with the excavation." He gestured widely. "After all, the meadow makes a big L around that hill there, and it's hundreds of meters before you reach the little lake, and then the schloss is even farther up the—"

Megan scowled at Peter. "The schloss...little lake? What are you talking about?"

He said, "Surely you've noticed the lake at the foot of the slope that the schloss is built on? I guess you're all turned around now because we approached from a different direction, but actually we're just on the side of the lake opposite the house."

Megan stared around in bewilderment, trying to get her bearings. She said finally, "Then—then this must be my meadow."

"*Your* meadow?" Peter exclaimed. "What do you mean?"

Megan shrugged uncertainly. "I inherited it from Erich, my late husband. That's why I'm here. Kurt wants to buy my interest in it. The land itself is of little use to me, and he wants to keep the estate intact...." Her voice trailed off as she stared at the other two people. Peter was swearing softly but violently, and Ulrike shook her head, her light eyes shadowed with remorse.

Peter looked at Ulrike out of the corner of his eye. "Well, Riki," he muttered crossly, "what do you think of your hero now?"

Ulrike admitted with a sigh, "I don't know what to think."

Megan demanded, "What are you two talking about? What's going on?"

Peter said angrily, "Damn it, Megan, haven't you been listening to anything we've said? My Uncle Max has an option on the mineral rights for this property; he's had it for years. He's sure there is a substantial copper deposit under the meadow, and now that ore prices have skyrocketed he wants to exercise the option. It could mean a great deal of money for everyone concerned."

Megan, breathless with shock, could only stare. Ulrike asked gently, "You did not know about the Bachmann offer?"

Megan shook her head mutely. Peter studied her shadowed face, bleached colorless except for the vivid red hair and green eyes. He asked, "Would you mind telling me how much von Kleist has offered you for the property?"

Ulrike touched Peter's arm. "Peter, I'm not sure we have the right—"

"Damn it, Riki," he swore grimly, "this is my business! If he's trying to cheat her I want to know about it."

Megan regained her voice sufficiently to protest, "Actually, the amount Kurt mentioned seemed very generous to me. I'm sure it's a fair one, especially since there seems to be some legal question about my right to inherit."

Peter snorted, "Legal question, ha! Von Kleist is no fool. If he's willing to pay anything at all, he must be pretty certain your claim is valid. How much?"

Megan told him.

Peter looked sick. He pushed his glasses aside and rubbed his brown eyes wearily. When he'd resettled his glasses on his nose he said quietly, "Megan, if we find what we expect to find, von Kleist could make three times that much in just the first year."

Megan turned away abruptly. She held herself stiffly, unnaturally, as if she were bleeding inside. She shuffled across the wagon track into the high grass, heedless of where she was going, intent only on the short duologue that played over and over in her mind, as insistent and irritating as a stuck record: "I don't suppose there's anyway I can keep it?"

"No, no way at all. If you're wise you'll take the money."

She tripped on a root and fell softly to her knees, automatically breaking her fall with her hands. When she sat back on her heels to brush the grass from her slacks, her fingers wrapped around some kind of flower with crimson petals and thick pulpy leaves. She stared at the flower. Slowly she stroked a leaf. It was warm and slightly resistant to her moving fingers, like the texture of a man's skin.... When she clenched her fist so tightly that a fingernail sliced into her palm, she watched dispassionately as a bead of blood formed and dropped, no redder than the flower.

Looming over her, Peter caught her by the wrists and yanked her to her feet. "Here, Riki," he called to the other woman, who was watching anxiously, "your services are needed for a little first aid. I'll get the kit out of the trailer."

Ulrike was all cool professionalism as she cleaned the scratch with alcohol. The sting on the raw cut finally brought Megan out of her trance. She blinked and blushed, embarrassed by the fuss. "It's nothing," she protested.

"And by treating it so quickly, it will remain nothing," Ulrike said calmly, watching the girl for further signs of shock.

Peter said, "I'm truly sorry I upset you, Megan, but you need to know what's going on. Bachmann Steiner has been trying to negotiate with von Kleist for months and only now does it look as if he's going to sell. We've had to go slowly, since he has a lot of clout in this part of the country. We had no idea anyone else had a claim on the property. We knew it had been willed to a brother named Erich, but when he died we assumed it reverted to Kurt. We didn't know of your existence."

Megan said numbly, "Kurt searched for months before he found me."

Peter shook his head in disgust. "All this time he has sworn up and down that he didn't want the land developed, that he was attempting to raise money to buy back the option, when in fact what he was doing was trying to eliminate you as a claimant."

Megan asked, "But why should he contact me at all? I didn't even know about the property. He could have done anything he wanted and no one would have been the wiser."

Ulrike said, "But, Megan, there would always have been the possibility that you might someday show up, and then the truth would have to come out." She sighed. "No, although I hate to admit it, I'm afraid Peter must be right. If Kurt can coerce you into selling him your rights to the meadow, he in turn can make a very substantial profit when the mine begins producing." She glanced at her wristwatch and clicked her tongue. "What an end to a lovely day! Peter, do you think you could run me by the hospital? It's still fairly early and there are a couple of patients I would like to check on before I go home."

"Of course, Riki. Megan and I need to discuss a few things anyway."

When they stopped in front of St. Elisabeth's, the doctor gave Peter her hand. "Take care of Megan for me," she said gently. "She seems so— bereft right now." Peter squeezed her fingers and nodded.

Ulrike waved as she disappeared inside the brick-and-glass building, but Megan didn't see her. She was gazing at the bell tower of the church, rosy in the westering sunlight, which stood high and proud above the rooftops. She asked suddenly, "Peter, where are the von Kleists buried?"

He gaped at her, his glasses glinting. "What?"

"Where are the von Kleists buried? Erich's in New York, but I expected the rest of them to be here. When I was poking around the cemetery I didn't see a single von Kleist grave. Where are they?"

Peter shook his head in bewilderment. "How should I know? Since they're the local artistocracy, I suppose there may be some kind of crypt under the church, just for members of their family."

Megan nodded grimly as she settled back into her seat. "Good," she said. "I'm glad they don't mix with other people, decent people. The von Kleists are liars and cheats, every last one of them."

CHAPTER EIGHT

MEGAN PADDED RESTLESSLY around her suite. Fresh from a scalding lilac-scented bath, her naked skin glowed delicately pink above the sheer black tights and long lacy black half slip that were all she wore at the moment. When someone tapped at her door, she frantically grabbed up her new shawl that still lay in its bundle of tissue paper on the dresser, and enveloped herself in its warm concealing folds before she called breathlessly in German, "Who's there?"

"It's Greta, Frau Megan," the maid announced as she pushed open the door with her hip and carried a laden dinner tray into the room. The girl in her smart navy blue evening uniform spoke slowly to help Megan understand her. "Frau von Kleist—" no servant would dare call Gabrielle by her first name, even to avoid confusion, Megan thought wryly "—hopes you will not mind eating supper in your room tonight, because the dining room is already being set for the buffet that will be served later after the ball."

"Of course it's no trouble," Megan said as she sat at the table and watched Greta uncover the dishes with a flourish.

The maid looked at Megan anxiously. "Everything is satisfactory?"

"Certainly. Please tell the cook for me that it all looks delicious." When the maid left, only partly reassured, Megan stared glumly at her dinner. As usual the food was perfectly cooked, cunningly garnished—and she was sure she would choke on even the smallest morsel. She had eaten almost nothing for days now, since that traumatic afternoon when Peter and Ulrike had told her the truth about her inheritance. She had returned from Salzburg in a mood that fluctuated between dejection and fury, indignation and despair. What a fool she had been, what a blind fool! Everyone else must have known—even Adelaide, who was only a teenager. The girl had tried to warn her, but out of loyalty to her family she had not dared to be too specific, and Megan had dismissed her hints as adolescent melodrama. Oh, if only she had listened, she could have spared herself this heartbreak....

Megan caught herself. No, not heartbreak, never that. She was immune to von Kleists now; they no longer had the power to touch her heart. The pain she felt inside was only the burning throb of righteous indignation.

But what should she do now? The night she returned from Salzburg she had gone downstairs ready to confront Gabrielle with what she had learned; but when Megan had faced the austere woman across the dinner table with the two girls beside her, she realized she could not say anything. The one person she must accuse was momentarily out of her reach, in Vienna. Until she saw Kurt she must pretend she knew nothing.

In her room Megan regarded the dinner tray. She made a pretense of cutting her schnitzel, disarranging the salad. Gabrielle and Adelaide had been too preoccupied these past few days with preparations for the gala to notice Megan's lack of appetite. But the servants had observed that their guest's plates went back to the kitchen untouched. The cook, a rotund, good-humored woman whom Liesl had introduced to Megan during one of the language lessons, had begun preparing special delicacies to tempt her flagging appetite. On the third day, when Megan was presented with a creditable imitation of an American hamburger, she had nibbled at it vaguely, realizing she must make an effort to eat.

In Los Angeles Dorothy had monitored most of Megan's meals, occasionally threatening to force-feed her if necessary. Dorothy's warnings had been softened by her mellifluous Southern drawl, yet Megan always suspected that her friend was quite capable of carrying them out if defied. But Dorothy was six thousand miles away now, and daily the persistent violet shadows under Megan's rose-leaf eyes were becoming more pronounced as she waited for the opportunity to face Kurt.

She had not talked to him since she'd returned from Salzburg. He had called twice more, but both times she'd found excuses not to come to the phone. She couldn't bear to hear his deceitful seductive voice inquiring innocently after her well-being. She would have choked when she answered him. She knew she must face him to reveal what she had learned, but she dreaded the moment. In town she had discussed the situation with Peter. He had seemed to think he ought to be with her for the confrontation, but she'd refused his offer of support. For once, she insisted, she was going to stand up to a von Kleist on her own.

Megan had deliberately avoided contact with Gabrielle and Adelaide by spending more of her time with Liesl. She found the child a delightful and undemanding companion, and the little girl seemed grateful for her company. With her aunt's permission Liesl had arranged for Karl to drive her and Megan on an excursion to Heilegenblut, one of the most enchanting of the Alpine villages, located on a rise at the end of the Möll Valley, in the shadow of the eternally snowcapped Grossglockner, Austria's highest peak. They had toured the fifteenth-century Gothic church, its tall graceful spire rising like a reflection of the mountains surrounding it, and Liesl had informed Megan that the town took its name from the medieval legend of Saint Briccius, who was supposed to have died carrying a vial of holy blood from Constantinople. Liesl had admitted privately that she thought the idea of hauling around a vessel of blood was *schmutzig*—apparently the German equivalent of "icky"—but she agreed with Megan that the church was very beautiful.

After Megan had abandoned her dinner tray,

she slipped her shawl from her shoulders and folded it neatly. She wadded the tissue paper into a ball and tossed it into the wastebasket beside the dressing table next to her canopy bed. With her fingertips she caressed the deeply fringed wool triangle, marveling at its silky texture. The shawl was heavily embroidered with Tirolean hearts and flowers in the same off-white as the background, giving the primitive design a surprisingly sophisticated look. In her suitcase was another shawl, identical except that it was dark blue, that she had purchased as a gift for Dorothy. She had found the two stoles in a shop in Kleisthof the day before, when she went to purchase a name-day present for Liesl.

As Megan crossed the room to the wardrobe, she glimpsed her half-naked reflection in the cheval glass, and she paused. Against the dusky-rose decor of the room she reminded herself of a poster by Toulouse-Lautrec—flaming hair piled high, slim legs in stark black stockings, and between, impossibly white skin. Growing up in California, where a deep tan was the norm, Megan had never really valued her ivory complexion, although she accepted it, having learned very early that any attempt at sunbathing resulted only in a serious and painful burn. It was probably just as well, she'd concluded long ago, that her music required her to spend hours indoors at the piano and permitted her the luxury of swimming in the warm and inviting Pacific only in the late afternoons when the sun was no longer a threat. Thus her lovely torso with its high full breasts remained one color, the soft cream of a half-opened rosebud, touched with pink only at her nipples.

She had a good body, Megan decided dispassionately, gazing at herself in the mirror. Not for her the golden, sun-bleached California-girl look she had been raised to prize—but still, she had a good body, with unique coloring. Even Erich had noticed it. On that last fateful night, when he was intent only on humiliating her and she was too exhausted to struggle any longer, he had glanced down at her breasts, exposed by his powerful seeking hands, and murmured almost in wonder, "You have the whitest skin—" It was, she realized later, perhaps the one moment in the two years of their relationship when Erich was truly aware of her as a woman.

Megan tossed off her mood and took her long black dress from the wardrobe. At the moment the only thing significant about her skin was that it bore no disconcerting bikini outlines to spoil the effect of the nearly backless halter top of the gown. As Megan slithered into it, she decided that Dorothy must be clairvoyant, for it was only at her friend's urging that she had packed the dress in the first place. "It never hurts to be prepared," Dorothy had insisted, ignoring Megan's protests about airline weight limits as she folded the length of inky jersey with masses of tissue paper to prevent its creasing. "You might go out to dinner or dancing with some of these relatives of yours, and this is the best dress you have."

For "best" read "sexiest," Megan thought dryly as she smoothed the fluid skirt over her thighs: she knew Dorothy was concerned about the absence of men in her young friend's life. Megan had purchased the gown to wear at the Polynesian Paradise, where her boss expected her to dress well and fairly provocatively, but the dress had proved to be an unqualified mistake. The draped halter bodice was alluring, outlining her taut breasts and hinting at far more than it actually showed, but she had not counted on the fact that when she was seated at the piano, from behind she appeared almost nude. The one time Megan had worn the gown at work, she was no more than halfway through her first set before the bartender had to forcibly discourage two importunate customers. At break time she had changed back into her street clothes, much to the relief of the staff.

But tonight—tonight the dress was ammunition. She was waging a battle against the lord of the manor who had seduced her with his charm, lied with his kisses. Megan had neither clothes nor jewels that could compare with those of the moneyed guests at the ball, but for once she was confident in her power. She knew she glowed with youth and beauty and a burning determination to make Kurt von Kleist regret that he had ever attempted to cheat her.

She was just fitting jet dangles into her ears when she heard a knock at her door, and a light voice asked shyly, "Tante Megan, may I come in?"

Megan smiled. The one von Kleist she trusted. "Of course, dear, come on in."

Liesl bounded into the room. She was wearing the shell-pink voile dress she had worn the first night of Megan's visit, and she held out her right arm, shaking the wrist to jingle the charms on her shiny new bracelet.

"Tante Megan, see what my father brought me from Vienna!"

"What a lovely bracelet," Megan exclaimed admiringly, warmed by the child's delight.

"Look," Liesl said, "it has a horse's head, and a tiny piano, and an *E*—because of course my name is really Elisabeth—and there's an ice skate and—"

As Megan listened to the little girl's raptures, some of the resentment she had been feeling all day on Liesl's behalf ebbed away. Megan had been shocked and saddened when she went down to breakfast that morning and found Liesl alone in the salon with a bunch of white roses on her lap, waiting somberly for Karl to drive her into the village for early Mass. It was St. Elisabeth's Day, Liesl's name day and that of her mother before her, and apparently nobody—certainly not Gabrielle with her everlasting party preparations, nor Kurt, still absent in Vienna on business—could be bothered to accompany the child to church.

When Megan had asked Liesl if she might go with her, her heart had ached at the pathetic eagerness with which the little girl accepted the invitation. Adelaide, Liesl had said forlornly, was supposed to go, but she didn't know where she was. Later, as Megan had watched a solitary tear inch its way down the girl's pale cheek while she arranged the roses in a vase at the entrance to the von Kleist crypt, she'd had to turn away, bowing her head so that the brim of her sun hat hid the intense anger that twisted her face.

After church Megan had given Liesl her present, a rock album the child had mentioned—not a very imaginative gift, but all that she could find at such short notice. She had promised that once she returned to Southern California she would send Liesl some souvenirs from Disneyland.

At lunchtime only Gabrielle had joined them. "Have you seen Adelaide?" she'd asked. When Megan said no, Gabrielle scowled. "But where can she be? She knows there are a hundred things to be done before the guests begin arriving tonight."

"Sorry," Megan had said helplessly. After Gabrielle had left them again, Megan and Liesl spent the rest of the day with lighthearted German and piano lessons. Much later Megan heard feminine voices raised in violent argument, and she knew Adelaide had finally wandered home.

Toward dusk, when the shadows of the mountains had begun to creep across the sweeping lawn of the schloss, a flurry of activity at the front entrance heralded Kurt's return. Suddenly reluctant to face him, Megan had murmured hasty excuses and fled upstairs, with Liesl staring after her in bewilderment.

After Liesl finished naming off the charms on her new bracelet she said, "*Vati* told me he was very sorry he couldn't be back in time to go to Mass with us this morning. He said to thank you for taking me, and he hopes I've been good company for you while he was away."

"You've been wonderful company," Megan said truthfully.

"He also said he was sorry he missed you when he got back this afternoon. Why did you run off like that?"

Megan improvised, "I had to get ready for the party. I needed to wash my hair and do my nails and dress and all sorts of things."

Liesl studied her judiciously. "I wish you were wearing that dress you wore the other night," she said, "the one that's all green and purple and blue. I liked it."

"I liked it, too," Megan agreed, "but it's not nearly fancy enough for a dance."

Liesl wrinkled her nose. "Well, I still think it's prettier than this black dress," she insisted. "This dress doesn't have any back, and it makes you look all—all bouncy in front!"

"I *am* all bouncy in front," Megan said dryly.

Liesl glanced down at her own flat chest. "*Vati* says I should begin dev—dev—"

"Developing," Megan supplied.

"He says I should start developing in a couple of years. He says when that happens he'll have to use one of Onkel Willi's old dueling pistols to fight the boys off."

"More than likely," Megan agreed. She peered at her reflection and spiraled a long curl around her forefinger, pulling it so that it hung saucily in front of her ear.

Liesl sighed. "Are you ready yet? I want to go upstairs and see what the ballroom looks like. Tante Gaby wouldn't let me in there earlier. She said that with Adelaide not there to supervise things I'd just get in the way, but now that everything is all set up I want to see it before the people arrive. *Vati* says I may stay up until midnight tonight—just imagine—and he says if I'm very, very good he'll let me have a little glass of champagne. Tante Megan, please, are you ready? I don't want to go by myself." She tugged at Megan's hand.

"All right, Liesl," Megan laughed, allowing herself to be dragged to the door. "I suppose I'm as ready as I'll ever be."

WHEN MEGAN AND LIESL ventured timidly through the massive double doors that opened at the top of the staircase on the third floor, Megan's first impression of the ballroom was that it shimmered with light. Through the heavily leaded panes of the high arched windows she could see that the sun had gone down behind the mountains in a glory of silver and orange; but inside, five Venetian crystal chandeliers glittered and were reflected on the gleaming hardwood dance floor that stretched the entire length of the mansion, and huge mirrors on the white-and-gold molded walls picked up the light and sent it back and forth between them into dazzling infinity.

Liesl clutched Megan's hand. "Isn't it beautiful?" she whispered almost reverently.

"Incredible," Megan breathed.

Uniformed servants scurried about, arranging long tables spaced strategically around the room laden with cut-glass goblets and champagne in silver ice buckets. Megan did not recognize any of the people. Liesl volunteered, "Every year Tante Gaby has to hire extra workers. It took four women almost a week to clean all the glass in here, but she said she wanted everything perfect. I heard her and *Vati* arguing about the cost."

Megan glanced down at Liesl. "You shouldn't be telling me things like that," she said sternly. "That's between your father and your aunt." The child looked rebuffed.

They continued their stroll around the perimeter of the room, oddly reluctant to violate the glossy polish of the dance floor. When they reached the flower-decked dais where musicians were already setting up, Megan observed, "What lovely roses. Do they come from your garden here?" She stroked the velvety petals of a pale yellow bud.

Liesl said, "Tante Gaby orders them from Salzburg because our roses mostly don't have long enough stems. The musicians come from Salzburg, too. I heard *Tante* mention something about hiring an orchestra from Munich, but my father said no, he wanted some money left over for the hospital."

"Liesl—" Megan reproved her.

The little girl looked up at Megan. She sulked, "I can't help it if I hear them arguing. Sometimes they yell." Her eyes widened. "Did you hear Tante Gaby yell at Adelaide when she finally came home today? When Adelaide told her she had gone to a movie in Salzburg, *Tante* called her an ungrateful little...*something*—I didn't know the word—and said she didn't deserve to come to the von Kleist ball and had to stay in her room. Adelaide was furious! She had the prettiest blue dress all ready, too." Liesl wrinkled her nose in concentration. "I don't think Tante Gaby used to argue so much when her husband was alive. I liked Onkel Willi, but I don't remember him very well. Of course, I was just a child then."

Before Megan, disturbed by these revelations, could think of a suitable reply, Liesl sighed and underwent one of the lightning changes of mood that can be so disconcerting to an adult. "Isn't the floor pretty and shiny?" she exclaimed. "It looks as if you could skate on it!" She released Megan's hand and began gliding and pirouetting across the dance floor. In her long pink dress, her pale hair swirling around her as she twirled, her slender body was vibrant with childish grace. As Megan watched, her hand at her throat, a few words of benediction drifted into her mind, flotsam from some forgotten high-school study of Shakespeare: "Thou shalt like an airy spirit go—"

She had not realized she spoke aloud until behind her a quiet baritone voice mused, "*A Mid-*

summer Night's Dream, right? And which of the fairies is my daughter? Peasblossom, Cobweb, Moth, or Mustardseed?"

Megan tensed, refusing to turn around. After a moment she said lightly, "Oh, Liesl is Cobweb, of course. She moves so delicately, as if she were weightless, wafting on the breeze—" She gasped as a long finger traced her naked spine. Angrily she spun on her heel and glared.

"Forgive me," Kurt grinned, utterly unrepentant. His blue eyes glowed devilishly. "The temptation was too great. If you must insist on wearing a gown like that...." His glance raked her slowly, as intimate as a caress, before returning to her intent face. "You are stunning," he said. "That's an outstanding dress."

Megan shrugged. "It's just something I bought off the rack." She looked down the length of the room, where a rainbow of richly dressed people, mostly middle-aged or older, were beginning to drift in. "It's nothing like what they're wearing," she said.

Kurt observed dryly, "But there won't be a woman here tonight who wouldn't gladly change places with you, despite her jewels and designer gown." He quickly surveyed the bank of flowers on the dais and plucked a half-opened rose with rich golden petals toning to apricot. "Something more beautiful than any jewel," he said with a smile, "and it matches the highlights in your hair." He tucked the flower into the deeply draped neckline of her dress, his fingers lingering for just a second. Megan stared down at the rose, which seemed to glow against the mat black jersey. Its sweet perfume wafted headily from between her breasts. Kurt let out his breath in a long shuddering sigh. He said, "God, I missed you."

Megan gazed up at him. He seemed to have grown taller in the few days he had been away, and she was struck again by how impossibly attractive he was, as all the von Kleist men were. He looked utterly devastating in the elegant formal dress suit that would have defeated a man of less aristocratic bearing. A thousand words raced through Megan's mind as she stared breathlessly into Kurt's ultramarine eyes, shadowed by the sharp planes of his face. She had rehearsed the words repeatedly through the endless nights while she struggled to sleep: harsh words, accusing words...silent words. Eager with righteous indignation, she had waited impatiently to confront him, and now when at last he stood before her, almost as close as in an embrace, she was silent. Her green eyes were wide, filled with anguish, while she thought despairingly, *oh, my Lord, I've gone and done it again.*

Kurt frowned. "Megan, what's wrong?"

She shook her head helplessly, aware of the crowd of people flowing toward them. "I need to talk to you about...about things. But not here."

He smiled warmly. "Yes, there are things I want to discuss with you, also—but as you say, not here."

He looked past Megan and his expression altered, the smile still cordial but infinitely cooler. A short plump man in ill-fitting but obviously expensive dress clothes hurried up, dragging behind him a woman in a teal-blue gown that would have looked exquisite on someone twenty years younger and thirty pounds lighter. Her diamonds rivaled the chandelier for glitter. The man rattled off an introduction in French far too rapid for Megan's schoolgirl comprehension, but she didn't need an interpreter when the old woman simpered and curtsied, giggling, *"Monsieur le comte."*

One of Kurt's dark eyebrows rose just fractionally as he bent over the woman's hand and murmured suavely, *"Enchanté, madame."* He introduced Megan as his *belle-soeur* but did not elaborate. When the French couple finally moved away, eyeing Megan speculatively, Kurt turned to her. "What's wrong?" he demanded. "You've gone very pale."

She stammered, "I—I'm sorry, it's just that I— when that women called you *comte*.... I know I've heard people refer to *Graf* von Kleist, but I honestly didn't connect—"

Kurt silenced her impatiently. "Forget it. The title has been meaningless since my grandfather's day. I certainly never use it."

"But that couple—"

"The man is a one-time truck driver from Lyons who now owns a freight company with branches throughout the Common Market. It pleases him to be able to introduce his wife to a real live 'aristocrat,' completely disregarding the fact that he could buy and sell the von Kleists several times over." Kurt shrugged. "But I must not disparage the nouveau riche. In these days of rising inflation and dwindling family fortunes, they're the only ones who keep events like this ball going—although who knows for how much longer? You'll notice that only the elderly now seem interested or able to afford the tickets."

He gazed bleakly down the length of the vast room, blind to its splendor, lost in thought. After a few seconds he roused himself. "Forgive me, Megan, I didn't mean to depress you. You'll have to excuse me now. Gabrielle is signaling frantically to me, and I see that the guest of honor has arrived."

"Ulrike?"

Kurt looked surprised, then he murmured, "Of course, you did mention that you had met her. I'm glad. Ulrike Müller is an admirable woman." He regarded the stocky blond in her plain black dress and pearls, and Megan saw his eyes widen fiercely when he spotted the man at Ulrike's side. He swore quietly in German. "*Mein Gott*, whom does she have with her?"

Megan followed his gaze. When she recognized the brown-haired man with glasses, her back stiffened, as she reminded herself of all she had momentarily forgotten. She said coolly, "It looks to me like Peter Swanson. I met him in Kleisthof, too."

After that Megan's memories of the ball were hazy. She tore herself away from Kurt's side and made her way through the burgeoning crowd to where Peter and Ulrike stood talking to Gabrielle, who was resplendent in yellow. Megan greeted her friends effusively, and then she remained at their side, resolutely ignoring Gabrielle's barbed glance and Kurt's pallor. When Kurt led Ulrike out onto the gleaming floor for the first dance, Megan gaily accepted Peter's invitation, and she flirted outrageously the whole time she was in his arms. As soon as Kurt had returned a nervous Ulrike to Peter, he stepped toward Megan, his face grim, but before he could ask her to dance she almost flew into the arms of a diffident gray-haired man who could not believe his luck in finding himself partnering the youngest, most attractive woman in the room.

After that Megan lost count of the men she danced with, flirted with. She probably could not have described any of them. The music, she noted, was quite good, if a little repetitious. The small string orchestra seemed to concentrate, perhaps inevitably, on waltzes by Strauss and Lehár. Megan wondered what the more expensive group from Munich would have played. Liesl, she observed, had appointed herself page turner for the pianist.

More than one of Megan's partners seemed fascinated by the feel of his hand on her naked back, and as she twirled around the room, giggling manically, she parried a number of dubious suggestions, usually by the simple ploy of pretending her German was even more limited than it was.

She knew she was acting wildly, making a spectacle of herself in her attempt to avoid Kurt, and once when she waltzed past Ulrike she saw that although the doctor was dancing quite skillfully her pale eyes were intent on Megan with professional concern. But Megan couldn't stop. She couldn't permit herself to relax long enough for the unacceptable realization to form in her mind: that now, as before, she was a victim of devastating, utterly fraudulent charm; that once again she had fallen in love with a von Kleist.

When the orchestra took its break at midnight, Megan finally paused. She was flushed and overheated, sipping a glass of champagne pressed upon her by a man who gazed hungrily at the crushed rose at her breast and asked in faltering English if she would like to visit his villa in Gastein, when Kurt suddenly intruded on the conversation. He was supporting a very sleepy Liesl at his side. "Forgive me," he said smoothly to the man, "but my daughter wishes to say good-night to her aunt." Before Megan could protest, Kurt hustled her and Liesl out of the ballroom and down to the second floor, where he turned the child over to Greta, who led her away to her bedroom.

Kurt's powerful fingers gripped Megan's wrist bruisingly as he forced her down the stairs to the first floor. Guests were drifting toward the dining room where the sumptuous buffet was now being served, and he smiled affably at everyone he passed, greeting each one with easy charm, but Megan thought her bones would crack under the pressure of his hand. She had to scurry to keep up with him as he strode implacably through the hall toward his study, and she was sure that if she stumbled and fell, he would not pause but would just continue to drag her across the polished floor. By the time he shoved her into the study and turned the key in the lock behind him, she was gasping for breath.

Megan stood in the center of the Oriental carpet in the room where she had first met Kurt; and he stared down at her, his blue eyes cold and scornful. His contemptuous inspection made her acutely aware of how she must look at the moment, with her hair working loose from its elaborate style, wisps like tongues of flame plastered against her sweaty forehead, and the apricot rose at her breast crushed by a succession of masculine chests. Kurt gazed at her silently, intently, before he turned abruptly toward the portable bar against the far wall and said tersely, "I need a drink. I expect you do, too. What do you want?"

"Oh, anything as long as it's not—"

"Not rum," Kurt finished for her. "Yes, I remember." He gave her bourbon on the rocks, and when she indicated her surprise he noted, "I don't care what the Scots say, nobody makes whiskey like Americans." He lounged against the side of the desk and motioned irritably to the leather armchair. "For God's sake, Megan, stop hovering and sit down! You haven't been off your feet all evening."

"You noticed?" she asked slyly.

His jaw was tense as he said grimly, "Of course I noticed. Everyone did." He finished his drink and banged the empty glass down on the desk, then flipped open a cloisonné box and fished out cigarettes and a lighter. "I can only assume that your extraordinary behavior tonight was your not-very-subtle way of telling me you've found out about the Bachmann interest."

Megan settled into the plump cushions of the chair and nursed her drink, relishing the smooth warmth of the whiskey. She was beginning to feel very tired, and her feet in their high-heeled sandals ached. She said, "Peter told me all about it days ago, when we went to Salzburg."

Kurt frowned. "And all this time you've never mentioned it to Gabrielle?"

"I decided it was between you and me," Megan said. "I didn't want to discuss it with anyone else."

"Obviously you've discussed it with Max Bachmann's nephew!" Kurt snapped. "And after hearing his distinctly biased version of the story, you've concluded that I am an avaricious feudal landowner out to rob a poor starving widow of her inheritance."

Megan lifted her eyebrows delicately. "Don't you think you're being rather melodramatic?"

"My God," he exclaimed, crushing his cigarette into the ashtray, "what could be more melodramatic than the way you've acted tonight, flaunting yourself, cavorting like some drug-crazed bacchante at an orgy—"

Megan jumped up, her green eyes flashing. "Oh, come off it, Kurt!" she snorted. "Just who do you think you're talking to? In case you've forgotten, let me remind you that *I'm* the injured party in this shabby swindle!"

He stared at her for a long minute before he shrugged in resignation. "Shabby swindle," he repeated hollowly. "Of course, it must appear that way to you. I've handled everything badly from the very beginning—which is unusual for me. Anyone I work with in Vienna will tell you that I am normally rather astute in my business dealings. I suppose that this time there have been too many emotional issues clouding my judgment." He massaged the bridge of his nose with his fingertips as he sighed, "I had hoped that once you got to know me— Will it help if I tell you that I never meant to cheat you? That not once have I considered making a profit on your property by allowing Bachmann Steiner to mine it? Will you believe me when I say my only concern is to buy back the option and keep the estate intact and inviolate?"

Megan asked, "If you feel that way, why did you sell an option in the first place?"

"I didn't," Kurt said. "It was my father. He needed the money." He leaned back in his chair and gestured with his scarred hand. "The schloss has not always looked the way it does now," he said tiredly. "When I was a boy it was quite different. Beautiful, of course, but distinctly shabby. My father wanted to change all that. The honor of the von Kleists demanded it, he said. He wanted the decay of the centuries repaired on the outside of the building, and the interior restored and modernized. Do you have any idea what a project like that costs?"

Megan shook her head.

Kurt said dryly, "Neither did my father. After he had liquidated what stocks he held and sold my mother's jewelry—some of which had survived the French Revolution—there still wasn't enough. So he let Max Bachmann buy an option on the mineral rights for the meadow. He never really expected it to be exercised. In his eyes it was an acceptable way for an aristocrat to borrow money, rather like those Regency bucks who never paid their tailors."

Megan did not speak. She relaxed in the armchair and looked at Kurt, whose formal gear with white tie and ruffled shirt was completely incongruous behind the massive walnut desk. It was the first time she had seen him less than perfectly in tune with his surroundings. When he bent to pull a manila folder out of the attaché case on the floor beside his swivel chair, a lock of his dark hair strayed across his forehead, and he brushed it back impatiently. He looked weary, vulnerable, his face creased with lines she did not remember. Her heart ached with love for him. She longed to go to him, put her arms around him and rest that tired face against her breast, stroke away his fatigue....

Kurt was holding out the folder to her. "Here," he said. "This is the contract my lawyers drew up. I wish you would at least read it before you make your decision. It's in German, of course, but there's an English translation, and I think you'll find it self-explanatory. The sum offered is reasonable for unimproved property in this region. There is no way I can pay you what Bachmann would offer. As it is, I've already had to dispose of some family assets just to raise this much." He pressed the folder into her hands. "Please, Megan," he cajoled with an urgent smile, "do it for me."

Megan stiffened. Her eyes went blank for a fraction of a second, and when she stood on her aching legs her expression was noticeably cooler than it had been only seconds before.

Kurt asked, puzzled, "What's wrong? What did I say?"

She laughed humorlessly. "'Please, Megan, do it for me.' I can still hear Erich saying just those words, with that same smile, when he asked me to marry him."

Kurt rose to his full height, towering over her, his face grim. Slowly he said, "You would do well to remember that I am not Erich."

"Aren't you?" she asked.

They stared at each other. The atmosphere in the room was heavy, electric with tension. Someone knocked on the door. Kurt gestured for Megan to ignore it. The signal was repeated. Muttering under his breath, Kurt stalked across the room and unlocked the door, sweeping it open.

Gabrielle stood there in her yellow gown, poised to knock again. Her hazel eyes darted between Kurt and Megan, and her flawlessly made-up face registered surprise when she saw the manila folder in Megan's hand. But she said only, "Kurt, your guests are asking for you."

He nodded. "Of course. I'll be there at once." He turned to Megan. "Are you coming?"

She said, "No, I think I've had enough—dancing for one evening. I'll go to my room."

"Very well." He waited until she stood in the hallway, then he locked the study door. "Will you consider my offer?"

Megan was silent. She glanced at Gabrielle, at the Givenchy gown of daffodil-colored silk clinging to the older woman's willowy body, the exquisite topaz-and-diamond pendant dangling on her mannequin-flat chest. Gabrielle laid her hand lightly, possessively, on Kurt's arm and said with subtle emphasis, "Come, Kurt, we must return to our guests."

Kurt shrugged her off. He repeated, "Megan, will you consider my offer?"

She looked at Kurt and Gabrielle, the man she hopelessly loved and the woman she sometimes feared, two arrogant wealthy aristocrats aligned in all their power and glory against her. Her resolve firmed. She said softly, "Oh, I'll look at your contract, Kurt, if that's what you really want, but if I were you I wouldn't get my hopes up. You can't really expect me to see the need to keep this estate intact. After all, I'm only an American fortune hunter."

MEGAN THREW HER SHAWL over her sheer mint-green nightgown and slipped out into the dark. The air was soft and warm, but the marble balcony connecting all the suites in the guest wing was cool beneath her bare feet, slick with the damp of approaching dawn, as she padded silently toward the stairs at the far end. The great house was quiet at last. Two hours had passed since she had heard the final guests come down from the grand ballroom, followed presently by servants grumbling with fatigue. From her dark room she had watched the glowing patches of grass, etched with the patterns of the panes in the leaded windows, dim as one by one the lights on the third floor were turned off. Only the lamp in a room exactly opposite her own still burned. Now the grounds were dark, and she was alone.

As she picked her way across the lawn, she could feel dew-soaked grass between her toes, wetting the lacy hem of her gown. She paused to slide her hand under her heavy fall of hair, to lift it away from her nape so that it could stream unconfined down her back, over the shawl. As her eyes adjusted to the gloom she noticed that the full moon, now low over the mountains, was bright enough to make the damp lawn before her gleam with the sheen of antique satin, and at the foot of the gently sloping hillside she could see moonlight reflected on the surface of the little lake.

What was there about moonlight on water that made the sight so soothing? A critic had once written that the rippling arpeggios of the adagio of

Beethoven's Sonata in C-sharp Minor reminded him of moonlight on Lake Lucerne, and ever after the piece was known by that name. Megan had always loved it. She had played it for her first recital, when she was ten, and she could still remember the exultation she had experienced when that final chord—pianissimo—died away and the audience began to applaud. Her mother had had tears in her eyes....

She heard a rustle just behind her. "Megan," Kurt said.

She jumped. "I...I didn't think anyone else was still up," she gasped, pulling her shawl tightly around her.

"The master of the house must check to see that all is secure," Kurt said dryly. "What's wrong? Can't you sleep?"

Megan shrugged. "I tried. Finally I just gave up."

"I feel restless, too," he said.

She stared at him, unable to read his expression in the dim light. He was still dressed, smoking his inevitable cigarette, but his jacket and tie were missing, and the ruffled shirt hung loose, fastened carelessly as if he had removed it and then pulled it back on again without bothering to button it. Through the gap she could see his chest shadowed with dark hair. He swayed slightly, and she wondered if he was exhausted or if he had been drinking.

Neither spoke. Finally, just to break the silence, Megan asked, "Was the ball successful?"

Kurt said, "If you mean, did the guests enjoy themselves, then I suppose the answer is yes. But if you mean, did we make a lot of money for the hospital, then I must say no. Once all the bills are in, we'll have done well just to break even."

"That's a shame, after all the trouble you went to."

"Gabrielle did most of the work," Kurt said, "she and Adelaide. That's part of the problem. I haven't been able to make her understand that inflation affects the von Kleists as much as everyone else; that even we must cut back." He inhaled deeply, and when he blew out the smoke in a long plume, the acrid tang of tobacco tickled Megan's nose. Kurt said, "Gabrielle doesn't know it yet, but this was the last of the von Kleist charity balls. Not only is the event no longer profitable, but Ulrike Müller and I have begun the steps necessary to turn control of the hospital over to the national health service."

Megan protested, "But won't it bother you to give up the hospital that memorializes your wife?"

Kurt smiled at her intensity. He said gently, "Elisabeth's memory will live on in her daughter, and in my heart, as long as I have breath."

A fierce twinge of jealousy ripped through Megan, and she shivered, despising herself. It was hateful and stupid to resent Kurt's feelings for a woman who was long dead. She forced herself to comment, "You must have loved her very much."

"I did," he said simply. "Elisabeth was the love of my youth. We met while we were both students at Cambridge, and we could have been happy forever—but we didn't have forever. Seven years ago I built the hospital as penance for still being alive while she lay dead and cold in the crypt beneath the church, but now I think it is time for me to go on to other things." He looked toward the lake that bordered Megan's meadow. "Did you read the contract?" he asked abruptly. "Did you understand it?"

Megan said, "I looked it over."

"Do you understand why I want the land?"

She shook her head helplessly. "No, I don't. If you let Bachmann Steiner go ahead with their project, it could mean a lot of money for you, money you've hinted you could use. Besides, you've told me yourself that your family is dying out. What's so important about keeping the meadow—what did you say—inviolate?"

Kurt said, "Listen to me, Megan, and try to understand." He made a sweeping gesture, and the cigarette cut a glowing streak in the air. "All this land has been in my family for more than three hundred years. My people have died for it. It is a part of a history that is often proud, often...less than admirable. It is my heritage. How can I deny it? I know better than most that the times that created families like mine and holdings like these are over—and well and good, many will say. I realize also that soon all this will inevitably be gone—lost to taxes or inflation, who knows? Soon the von Kleists and their vast estate will be history like the Hapsburgs and the Hohenzollerns, something bored schoolchildren must memorize for examinations and then forget.

"I see all this coming, and I accept it. But I do not want it to happen yet! I want the children who come after me to look at this land and know their heritage. Perhaps I am being illogical and a little vain, but I don't want my descendants to be able to say that Kurt Rainer Friedrich, the fourteenth Graf von Kleist, turned the family estate into an industrial wasteland."

Megan said, "It doesn't have to be a wasteland, Kurt. With careful planning a mine could provide jobs for many families, a better standard of living—"

Kurt shook his head. "No! If I let them sink their mine shafts, soon the lake will be polluted and the air fouled. I will not allow that, never! Megan, you complain about the smog in Los Angeles, but you accept it, just as you accept that in your country buildings are torn down after thirty years, and plots of land too small for a cottage are subdivided even further. No, obviously you cannot possibly comprehend what it means to me to try to maintain my heritage."

Megan snapped indignantly, "I have a heritage, too, Kurt! Maybe it's not as well documented as yours, but it's just as proud. If you think because I've never had anything much—"

"You could have all this," Kurt said quietly.

Megan gaped. "What do you mean?"

He said, "I've given the matter a great deal of thought, and I've reached the obvious solution.

You must become a von Kleist once more, this time without any shadows attached to the name. Bear children and fight to hold this for them." He took a deep breath. "Megan," he said, "I want you to marry me."

CHAPTER NINE

MEGAN STARED UP AT HIM. In the moonlight her eyes were wide shadowed pools in a face as colorless as the white shawl she wore, her mouth a dark gash of disillusion. At last she choked, "That's not funny, Kurt."

"I wasn't joking," he said evenly.

She was slowly shaking her head, trying to deny the bitter irony of the situation. She loved him, and he had just proposed—and instead of rejoicing all she wanted to do was run away and hide. "Do you really expect an answer?" she quavered, her voice thick with pain. "First you speak so tenderly of your late wife, and then in the next breath you ask me to marry you so that you can acquire a piece of land! Am I supposed to be flattered?"

Kurt shrugged lightly as he took a final puff on his cigarette and threw the butt to the ground, crushing it under his foot. He stood for a moment with his legs apart, his arms akimbo, gazing arrogantly over the dark familiar landscape. Megan thought he looked like a buccaneer who had just taken a rich treasure ship and was surveying the seas for new booty. No, she corrected herself;

pirates were coarse and brutal. The tall suave man standing before her was something much more dangerous. No matter how often he denied it, Kurt was the embodiment of all his ancestors, the fourteenth Graf von Kleist, scion of aristocrats who could kill with elegance and impunity because it was their God-given-right. Megan shuddered.

Kurt saw her tremble. "Are you chilly?" he asked, transformed instantly from brooding overlord to concerned host. "You're scarcely dressed for running around outside."

Suddenly she was aware of her sheer gown, how below the long fringe of her shawl her thighs and legs must be outlined against the moonlight. She bent her head, sure her face was glowing with the heat of her blush. She heard Kurt chuckle dryly, then he pulled her into his arms. "Don't be shy, Megan," he whispered insinuatingly. "I like looking at you." Startled, she squirmed, but his grip tightened. His lips brushed her hair as he repeated, "I like looking at you. I like touching you. Think how good it would be if you married me."

Already her senses were betraying her. She longed to relax in his arms, to press her body against the hard length of him, but from somewhere deep in her mind she summoned the strength to moan "No!" and she pulled away.

Kurt loosened his hold but did not release her. As he peered down at her bent head, his thumb caressed her soft shoulder through the silky fabric of the shawl, and he could feel her tremble. He scoffed, "What a little romantic you are, Megan!

I'm offering you my name and my fortune, even—if you're interested—a title, but what you want are tender declarations. *Sehr gut*. Will you marry me if I tell you I love you?"

Megan winced. His scorn was like a dull knife shredding the already tattered fabric of her self-respect, exposing her naked soul to the humiliation of his snide endearments. He was hurting her, stabbing her with words she would have given her life to hear spoken sincerely. In her agony she lashed out at him the only way she could. She smiled at him, fluttered her lashes and said sweetly, "To get back that land you'd say anything, do anything, wouldn't you, Kurt? You'd even sell yourself to me like a gigolo—"

For a moment there was deadly stillness, and Megan knew she had gone too far. When at last Kurt spoke, his voice was hoarse with fury. "You may question my motives," he declared in his husky baritone, "but you will never, ever deny my honor." His arms tightened around her as, ripping the shawl from her shoulders and flinging it onto the grass, he molded her body in its thin nightgown against him. The buttons of his open shirt dug into her left breast, and his long fingers laced into her hair, forcing her head back. "And you will never deny," he gritted, "that from the very beginning there has been something between you and me that transcends all your silly schoolgirl notions of love and romance." And his mouth came down fiercely on hers.

She meant to defy him. She had already tensed

herself to reject the brutal demands he would make of her—but Kurt was the man she loved, and she was almost sick with hunger for him. For fleeting seconds she kept her lips resolutely shut under the bruising assault of his, then her own frustration defeated her, and with a whimper she opened her mouth to him. After that she was lost in the intimacies of tongue and teeth and lips, the lingering taste of whiskey and cigarettes. She was dizzy with the heady male scent of him, the dry citrus of his cologne. Her arms slid inside his unbuttoned shirt, and she clung to him. When he nuzzled her face in the hair on his chest, his pounding heart was absurdly loud under her ear, and when he swung her into his arms and carried her with easy power across the lawn to the balcony stairs opposite those she had come down, she relaxed and gave herself up to his embrace.

He took her to that room where the lone lamp burned, his room, a vast chamber with a huge tent bed draped in brown velvet. After the dark outside, the light hurt her eyes, and as Kurt lowered her onto the ocher coverlet richly quilted with gold threads, she whispered for him to turn off the lamp.

"No," he murmured cruelly, "I want to watch you. I want you to watch me." He was already pulling his ruffled shirt loose from his trousers, dropping it in an untidy heap next to his shoes on the floor beside the bed. Megan gazed hungrily at his lean torso, the broad shoulders with muscles rippling under his smooth skin as he lowered himself onto the bed beside her. She was sure she could not look at him without betraying herself, exposing her love to his ridicule, so she closed her eyes tightly and turned away. Almost instantly his left arm pinioned both her wrists in the tangle of her hair on the pillow over her head, while his other hand gripped her chin painfully, forcing her face back toward his. "Open your eyes, Megan," he commanded, his voice silk over steel, "open your eyes and look at me." When slowly she blinked, her jade eyes wide, he smiled grimly and said, "Now tell me my name."

"W-what?" she stammered, half-strangled by his punishing grip.

"Tell me my name," he repeated. His face was dark and threatening. "Damn you, tell me who I am!"

She stared up at him, bewildered, not understanding at first. Then from deep inside her the name rose, pushing its way through her constricted throat, a throbbing benediction. "You're Kurt," she gasped, "Dear God, your name is Kurt!"

He breathed a sigh of deep satisfaction and released her chin. "Yes, I'm Kurt," he echoed smugly. "Don't ever confuse me with anyone else."

After that he was gentle. He teased her with his kisses, light butterfly caresses that tantalized her eyes, her cheeks, never quite reaching her lips, until with a groan of frustration she dug her fingers into the crisp dark hair at his nape and forced his mouth back to hers. When her lips were red and swollen from his kisses, he raised his head and looked at her thick hair fanning like a corona of flame over the dark bedspread. "I've never seen your hair loose before," he observed quietly. "You always seem to wear it pulled back or piled on top of your head."

"It makes me look taller that way."

He shook his head slowly. "Don't put it up anymore. Leave it down—for me." He twisted one hand through her hair until the long curls were wrapped in a burnished coil around his wrist. He rubbed his face sensually against the gleaming mass. "You smell of wild flowers," he murmured, "such a soft gentle scent. But when I touch your hair I almost expect it to burn me."

His fingers unwound from her hair and began a delicate exploration of her body. He cupped the tender weight of her full breasts through the sheer fabric of the gown, teasing the nipples with his thumbs until they rose hard and eager beneath his avid gaze. He tugged at the nightgown, and she arched her hips away from the bed while he pulled it up, the lace hem stroking over sleek thighs, flat belly, firm breasts and graceful throat. Soon she lay on top of the gown, Venus adrift on the sinuous green foam. She was mindless, afloat in a sea of sensation, pulled out far beyond her depth by the tremulous tides Kurt's seeking hands and mouth were arousing. Under his expert tuition she was becoming aware of her own body as never before, and she responded eagerly when he began to show her how to caress him in return, her tentative fingers searching out the hard raptures of his body. Lost somewhere far back in her subconscious was the knowledge that he touched her in anger, that he was deliberately stimulating her to prove his mastery over her.

Then, just when Kurt's lips and tongue left off savoring her breasts and marked a scorching trail toward her navel, his stubbled chin rasping against her soft flesh, he whispered, "I've never seen anyone with skin as white as yours."

Megan stiffened. In her mind she heard another voice, not unlike Kurt's but cruel, and with a more pronounced accent, saying, "You have the whitest skin—" Erich—and that one fleeting moment of awareness had been followed by pain and humiliation and death. Not again, she had vowed, never again!

She gasped, "Kurt, please stop!"

He looked up, his dark blue eyes glazed with passion. "I'm sorry, darling," he said huskily. "Did I hurt you somehow?"

She shook her head. "No, I—I—just want you to stop. I've ch-changed my mind." She tugged at the gown rumpled beneath them, trying ineffectively to cover her nakedness.

His eyes were clear now, but he was breathing hard. "You must be joking."

"I'm not. Please just go away."

Kurt scowled as he stared closely into her face, his eyes filling the universe. She trembled under the weight of his body, which was tense with indecision. Then silently he pushed himself off of her and sat up on the edge of the bed, zipping his trousers, reaching for his shirt. Only a slight fumbling as he buttoned it revealed his emotional turmoil. When he stood up, Megan clutched her nightgown to her breast. There was a hard edge to Kurt's voice as he asked, "Why Megan? I know some women get their thrills this way, but I would never have suspected it of you."

She bowed her head as if awaiting a blow. Inside she was dying with the agony of rejecting him. "You were just using me," she accused. "You don't care anything about me; it was all part of your nasty game to get my property."

Kurt's eyes narrowed. "Yes, I do want the property, and I'll do what I must to get it. I thought you understood that." After a pause when she would not look at him but huddled shaking on the bed, Kurt added, "Megan, *mein Schatz*, you know a few things about nasty games yourself. My God, if you did something like this to Erich, it's no wonder he raped you."

Megan gasped in horror, her cheeks afire. With a wild cry she flung herself flat on the bed and buried her face in the brown velvet. "Get out!" she sobbed hoarsely. "Get out, go away and don't ever touch me again!" For endless minutes the room was silent except for her muffled sniffling. She waited for Kurt to leave, but he did not move. He towered over her, stern and implacable like some avenging god. She lifted her head and peered up at him through the thick curtain of her hair. "Why won't you go?" she begged. "Please!"

One corner of his hard mouth quirked, but his eyes were cold as he calmly pointed out, "Megan, this is my room."

She knew then that nothing Erich had ever done to her compared with the humiliation she felt as she slowly raised herself up from the bed and dressed under Kurt's merciless gaze. Her fingers trembled as she held the nightgown against her. Her sensitive skin was crisscrossed with the marks of his desire, desire she had welcomed, but now she was ashamed for him to look at her. She turned away while she slithered the sheer gown over her head, and he gritted impatiently, "For God's sake, you needn't fear your nakedness is going to drive me wild with lust! I don't think I could bear to touch you now. I loathe and despise teases."

After the gown was smoothed into place, she stood for a moment with her head drooping as she marshaled her courage. Then she brushed her hair away from her cheeks with both hands and straightened her shoulders. Like a defeated soldier being reviewed by the enemy general, she pivoted smartly on her bare heel and faced him squarely, vanquished but unbowed. Something—respect, perhaps, or admiration—flickered in Kurt's hooded eyes as she asked coolly, "Do you have a robe I might borrow while I return to my room? My shawl seems to have disappeared."

Silently he nodded, and he strode across the

long bedroom, passing the open French windows as he went into his dressing room. When he emerged a second later with a green angora bathrobe in his hands, he glanced casually out the window. He halted in mid-stride.

Megan watched in wonder as Kurt stared into the dark. For the space of a heartbeat he was motionless. His face was a graven mask, the lingering passion and contempt wiped from his features as if they had never been, while he gaped at some horror lurking in the night. Suddenly he was galvanized into action. He dropped the wool robe and barked something to Megan, reverting to German in his shock. Before she could question him he'd sprinted out into the corridor, and the door crashed shut behind him, leaving Megan stunned with apprehension as slowly one word worked its way into her bewildered mind: *Feuer*—fire!

She ran to the window and gasped.

In the gray light of dawn the schloss loomed obscure and forbidding, the banks of windows dark, amorphous—all except one. One window in the guest wing glowed with flickering ruddy light as flames devoured the room.

Megan's room.

Realizing that Kurt must have taken the longer route through the house to get help, Megan ran outside then, her bare feet skittering along the balcony and down the marble steps, flying across the damp grass. She did not notice that she had remembered to pick up Kurt's dressing gown as protection against the cool air until she found herself almost tripping on the hem as she sped up the stairs to the guest wing. The long soft sleeves kept slipping down over her fingers as she fumbled with the tie belt.

Before she reached the double doors opening out from her suite, she could smell the peculiarly acrid tang of charring silk and wood, and the heat struck her like a blow. When she burst into the room it was filled with pungent yellowish smoke. She choked as she jerked her head back and forth. One end of the bedroom was completely engulfed. The mahogany dressing table was aflame, its deep lustrous finish bubbling and blackening, and while she watched, the mirror cracked from the heat. On the floor next to the dresser the satin cover of the wastebasket had burned away, leaving a glowing metal shell full of smoldering paper ash that floated toward the ceiling in chunks, caught by the updraft. Worms of fire ate at the pink silk drapery of her canopy bed, the bed where earlier she had tossed restlessly until her agitation drove her out onto the lawn. Even now in the uncertain light the tumbled blankets looked as if someone still lay there, mindless of the encroaching horror, and Megan suddenly shook with nausea as she realized what she had so narrowly escaped.

Then she heard a feminine voice coughing, "Megan! *Mein Gott*, I thought—I thought—" Megan spun on her heel. At the inside door Adelaide cowered, rigid with terror, her tall slim form pressed against the wood as if she wanted to melt into it. When Megan had first run into the room, she'd been too intent on the fire to notice Adelaide's presence. The girl sobbed, "God in heaven, Megan, where were you? I thought—I was sure you would be—"

Before Adelaide could choke out the words, the door flew open behind her and she went sprawling to her knees. Kurt lunged into the room with a large fire extinguisher. He ignored the girl while he swiftly summed up the situation, his breath hissing between his teeth at the sight of the burning bed. When he tried to turn on the extinguisher, his stiff hand fumbled with the valve, and he swore viciously. Megan pushed his fingers aside and jerked open the valve herself. For a fraction of a second they stared at one another, faces almost touching. Then as white foam began to spew from the nozzle, Kurt shoved Megan behind him and attacked the flames.

A few minutes later he said wearily, "Well, that seems to be it." He dropped the discharged canister to the floor with a noisy clatter and moved stiffly around the room, throwing open windows to let out the smoke. He rubbed a grimy hand across his reddened eyes, leaving behind a black smudge like a mask. His face looked sallow, the skin pulled tight across his high cheekbones, as he regarded the damage, and Megan saw with a spasm of hysteria that the ruffled shirt and dress slacks in which he had graced the ball only hours before were now scorched rags.

Kurt turned to Megan and sighed, "I don't think it's quite as bad as it looks. The fire seems to have been limited to that end of the room." Suddenly he shuddered, "But oh, sweet Lord, if you had been—"

"But I wasn't," Megan interrupted quickly, "so forget it. It's all over." She nudged him toward the armchair, and he sank into it gratefully. "That's better," she said. "Relax for a while. Don't get too worked up."

He smiled tiredly, his bloodshot blue eyes momentarily bright in his sooty face. *"Liebling,"* he chuckled wryly, "I've been—worked up since the first moment I met you."

A hoarse cough made him look in the direction of the door. He blinked as he noticed the teenager for the first time. "Adelaide?" he said in wonder. *"Was machst du hier?"*

The girl stepped forward tentatively, her face very pale under her tan. "I—I got here first," she stammered. "I was looking out my window and I s-saw fire. I ran to—to make sure Megan was all right." She twisted her hands together nervously and moaned with pain.

"Are you hurt?" Kurt and Megan demanded in almost the same breath.

She shook her head violently, but she kept her hands hidden against the front of her T-shirt.

"Adelaide!" Kurt snapped harshly, but Megan waved him to silence.

"Here, let me see," she said gently, reaching for the girl's wrists, and reluctantly Adelaide extended her hands. Megan recoiled, sickened. The palm of

Adelaide's right hand was a mass of puffy livid blisters.

"I—I thought you were still in the bed," she sniffed, tears of pain welling in her hazel eyes. "I didn't want you to get hurt—"

"Hush," Megan cooed. "Don't think about it now." She examined the burn and turned to Kurt. "Do you have some salve and bandages? This looks pretty superficial, although I know it must hurt like hell."

Kurt nodded. "I think I have something to help the pain. I'll be back in a moment."

After he strode out of the room, Megan made Adelaide sit down, and she got her a glass of water. Once off her feet the girl seemed to recover swiftly, and her breathing became more normal. She frowned glumly at her injured hand and muttered, "This is all Kurt's fault."

Megan stared at her. "What on earth do you mean?"

Adelaide shrugged. "Oh, forget it."

"No," Megan said. "You've made an accusation and I expect you to explain it."

Adelaide pursed her lips as she glanced sidelong at Megan. Finally she said, "I think Kurt started the fire."

Megan gasped, "My God, what are you saying?"

The girl continued, "Think how easy it would be. He comes in here, finds you asleep, and then all he has to do is toss one of his cigarettes into a wastebasket full of paper. Poof! No more problem with the meadow."

Megan shivered with exasperation. "That's a stupid and hateful thing to say, Adelaide," she gritted, "and I hope you won't go around repeating it to other people. Good Lord, it sounds like the plot from one of your movies!"

Adelaide insisted, "Well, it could have happened that way. I told you he would do anything to save his precious property."

"Hardly murder," Megan said dryly.

"Well, maybe the fire wasn't supposed to harm you. Maybe he just wanted to scare you a little—"

Megan snapped, "Oh, for heaven's sake, Adelaide, I don't know how the fire started, but I know Kurt didn't do it, so just shut up, will you! You're being childish!"

Adelaide bridled as she demanded, "How? How can you know? Why won't you listen to me? Why won't anyone take me seriously?"

Megan regarded her pityingly. At the moment she felt decades older than the teenager. She took a deep breath and said softly, "I know Kurt didn't start the fire because when it started I was with him, in his bedroom."

Adelaide's eyes widened, and for the first time she noticed the oversized bathrobe Megan wore; but before she could reply, Kurt returned, bearing bandages and medications. Swiftly he examined the girl's hand, and he agreed with Megan that the burns were not as bad as they had first appeared. With a minimum of fuss he dressed the injury and made Adelaide gulp down a couple of codeine tablets. She sat silent throughout the operation, regarding Kurt and Megan balefully.

When Kurt gathered up the gauze and ointments, he pulled Adelaide to her feet and escorted her to the door. There he paused. He said to Megan, "I'll have someone come and move your things into another room."

Megan shook her head. "No, not now, Kurt. Everybody must be dead tired after the ball, and amazingly we don't seem to have wakened anyone. So just let them rest a while longer. I'll be all right. I doubt that I could sleep now, anyway." She regarded the lines of exhaustion on Kurt's pale smoke-marked face. His eyes drooped wearily and he swayed slightly. She touched his arm and said urgently, "Please, Kurt, you go get some sleep. You'll make yourself sick if you don't."

"What touching concern," Adelaide muttered acidly.

The adults ignored her as their eyes met and locked. At that moment Megan was too tired and vulnerable to hide what she was feeling, and Kurt caught his breath sharply. Nodding, he said, "We will talk later."

"Yes," Megan said.

When the door closed behind Kurt and Adelaide, Megan sank into the armchair, prostrated, lolling her head back against the top of the cushion. She turned her face slowly to the right and noticed that from that angle her suite looked as pristine and perfect as always, with only the pervasive smell of smoke to betray what had happened. Luckily, the wardrobe with all her clothes was on that side. But when she looked to the left, the devastation was sickening. The lovely mahogany dressing table was a smoldering ruin, its oval mirror a spiderweb of cracks, and the rose silk canopy of her bed hung in charred tatters, edged with ash like a black ball fringe. Everything was coated with a muddy combination of smoke and extinguisher foam.

Who could have done such a thing, she asked herself. Who could so wantonly attack her and thereby destroy a suite of graceful, valuable antiques? And why? Megan knew Kurt was not the culprit, of course. He had more subtle methods of getting his way; he lighted a different kind of fire. Gabrielle? Well, Megan was willing to concede that Gabrielle resented her presence enough to resort to violence, but she also knew that the woman would never, ever do anything that might damage the schloss. She would resort to self-immolation before she would set a match to the house.

That left only Adelaide. The girl *must* have done it. She had acted suspiciously throughout the incident. But why? What did she hope to accomplish? Adelaide was a self-indulgent, slightly neurotic teenager who liked to envisage herself as the heroine in melodramas of her own devising; but did she really think that if she rescued Megan from a fire, Kurt and Gabrielle would be so overwhelmed with gratitude that they would withdraw their objections and finance her trip to Hollywood?

Slowly Megan stood up. She knew what she had to do. It had been a mistake to come to Schloss von Kleist, thereby becoming embroiled in long-established personal conflicts that had nothing to do with her. She should have stayed in the village; she should have conducted her business with Kurt on neutral ground—if anywhere in the same country as Kurt could be said to be neutral. As long as she remained on the estate she was in danger, both emotional and physical, and if she hoped to return to Los Angeles unscathed she had better get out of the schloss as quickly as possible.

Megan pulled her suitcases out of the wardrobe and began to pack.

THE VOICE on the other end of the telephone said testily in German, "I don't understand. Please speak more clearly."

But I'm speaking as clearly as I can, Megan thought wildly, almost sobbing with frustration. Everything she had learned from Liesl in the past few days regarding German pronunciation seemed to have flown from her mind, and her accent was as Californian as the Beach Boys when she said slowly, desperately, "*Bitte*, I would like to speak to Peter Swanson. I know he is staying there. Peter Swanson!" she repeated forcefully, thinking the clerk at the inn might understand the name if nothing else.

She held her breath. After an interminable

pause the clerk grumbled, *"Jawohl, ein Moment,"* and plodded away from the telephone.

Megan shuddered with relief and slumped against the desk. She glanced at her reflection in the ornate mirror on the opposite wall. Her rose pink slacks and shirt and her vibrant hair made startling splashes of color in Gabrielle's charming gold-and-white morning room, but her face was pallid and drawn. She had had no sleep at all.

As she had crammed the last of her clothes into her suitcase, the great house had just been beginning to stir. A maid had rapped at her door, but she'd told her to go away. She'd shoved the lid of the case down over the untidy heap of clothes and snapped the catches. The only thing still lying out was the manila folder Kurt had given her the night before, the contract by which she was to sign away her inheritance. Megan had stuffed it into her large travel handbag next to her passport and the return half of her plane ticket.

Megan knew then that she would probably sign Kurt's papers. No, not "probably"—of course she would sign them. Why not? She had thought about the situation a great deal while she packed. The money, she'd realized with surprise, wasn't all that important to her. She had been delighted with the sum Kurt offered her, and she wouldn't know what to do with more if she had it. What had hurt was the thought of Kurt's cheating her, using his sensual attraction to seduce her into signing. She supposed she was a coward to succumb to his deceptive blandishments, that she ought to fight him, but she was tired of fighting and she didn't want to be vulnerable anymore. She didn't want anyone to have a reason to attack her.

Besides, a little voice had whispered in the back of her mind, conjuring up fantasies as absurd as Adelaide's dreams of stardom, if she gave Kurt the meadow and he still pursued her, wouldn't that prove he loved her as she loved him?

But if he didn't come after her? Well, at least then she would know.

Megan had sighed wearily. Before she could do anything about the papers, she had to flee the schloss. Once away, she told herself, she ought to be able to find someone, if not in Kleisthof-im-Tirol then certainly in Salzburg, who had authority to notarize her signature. She had no idea how such matters were handled in Austria, and at the moment she didn't really care, as long as the transaction could be completed quickly. After the traumatic episodes in Kurt's room and then in her own, just before dawn, she didn't think she could endure much more.

Megan had stared at her devastated bed, and instead of it she saw another bed, with brown velvet hangings, where she had trembled on the brink of ecstasy and then plunged headlong into deepest humiliation. Oh, God, why couldn't she hate him? Why didn't the taunts and insults he had spat at her wipe out the memory of his feverish lovemaking? Why did she still quiver at the thought of his lean hard body crushing her into the ocher spread on that yielding mattress, his lips at her breast, his long graceful fingers stroking, probing, caressing....

Megan had still been shaking in a torment of unfulfilled desire when she set her luggage in the corridor, locking the bedroom door behind her. So far no one was aware of the damage, and she preferred to let Kurt explain it to the servants. A maid had approached her with her morning coffee on a tray, and Megan had shaken her head, indicating her suitcases. The woman was a stranger to her. Greta presumably still rested from her duties at the ball, and Megan had realized with a pang that she would not see the girl again. She had liked Greta, who was bright and outgoing, and the two of them had conversed remarkably well with a mixture of sign language and pidgin German, punctuated by friendly tolerant laughter.

The new maid had been sullen, betraying no interest in Megan's sudden departure, and she had stared blankly as Megan asked in German how to call for a taxi. It had occurred to Megan then that so far almost everyone she had spoken to either had a nodding acquaintance with the English language or else was at least patient enough to try to unravel her more glaring grammatical errors. She had wondered whether she dared attempt to make her way through Austria on her own, when the slightest mishap could leave her stranded among people with whom she was unable to communicate. The thought was daunting. What Megan needed was someone bilingual but unconnected with the von Kleist family, someone she could trust to help her catch the correct buses and flights. It was then that she had brightened. Of course, who better than a fellow American?

"Ich brauche ein Fernsprecher," Megan had said, and the maid had frowned at her. "I need a telephone!" she'd repeated, louder. The servant had shrugged sulkily and signaled for Megan to follow her.

On the way to the morning room Megan had seen none of the family members, but a cleaning crew was already hard at work wiping out all traces of the previous night's festivities. Several women bustled around sweeping, dusting, picking up discarded champagne glasses and dirty plates. Two men passed her laden with the music stands and folding chairs of the orchestra, which they carried out a side door to a waiting van. Someone brushed by her with a wastebasket of golden roses, not yet fully opened but already destined for the garbage. They left in their wake a swath of air redolent with heavy perfume, and Megan had cringed at the wanton waste of such beauty. "Gather ye rosebuds while ye may," she had muttered ironically before she hurried to catch up with the maid.

Megan had dreaded meeting Gabrielle—or worse, Adelaide—in the morning room, but apparently both were still upstairs. The little office was empty, as perfect and cold as an exhibit in a museum. Megan had wondered why some of the discarded roses weren't placed in there to bring a touch of life to all the dead splendor. Certainly

Gabrielle couldn't object to the color! She'd thanked the maid and gone to the telephone, which was on the desk next to a pristine blotter. Reluctantly she had looked through the desk drawers until she found one holding bulky directories for Salzburg and Vienna, and a much thinner one for Kleisthof-im-Tirol. She'd thumbed through the last book until she found the telephone number for the Gasthof zum Goldenen Bären.

Now Megan almost sobbed with relief when at last she heard Peter's sleepy announcement, "Swanson *hier. Wer ist das, bitte?*" His midwestern twang was discernible even through his excellent German.

"Peter, it's Megan."

Instantly Peter was wide awake, concern evident in his voice. "Megan, are you all right? I've been worried about you ever since last night."

"Of course I'm all right," she said, causing every truthful bone in her body to quiver with outrage. "Why should anything be wrong?"

"After I saw von Kleist drag you away, and then when you didn't come back—"

Megan laughed lightly. The dance seemed aeons ago now. "For heaven's sake, Peter, what do you think he did, lock me in a dungeon? I was tired and I had drunk too much champagne, so after Kurt and I finished...talking, I just went to bed."

Peter's voice lost its boyish note when he spoke again. The change in tone forcibly reminded Megan that the American was, after all, thirty years old and a successful businessman, something she was prone to forget, perhaps because he seemed so callow compared to Kurt, as did all men. But there was nothing immature about Peter when he snapped, "Listen Megan, I know something happened when you disappeared with von Kleist. I saw the expression on the man's face when he saw us dancing together. He looked almost desperate. So don't try to feed me cute stories about being tipsy on champagne. There had to have been some kind of scene when he discovered you knew about Uncle Max's option."

"All right, yes, there was," Megan admitted grudgingly. "But truly, it was nothing I couldn't handle."

"Are you sure? I wanted to confront the man myself, but Ulrike was adamant that we stay out of it. You know what she thinks of Kurt von Kleist; that he's a gentleman and chivalrous to his fingertips, no matter how deformed they are—"

Megan recoiled. "That's an ugly crack, Peter."

After a pause Peter conceded gravely, "Yes, it is, and I apologize, Megan. I don't like the man, but I keep forgetting that he's a relative of yours. But I really was worried about you. I never should have let you face him alone. I should have helped you."

"You can help me right now," she said. "Will you please come pick me up in your car? I want to leave the schloss as soon as possible."

"Is it really that bad, Megan? Are they giving you a rough time?"

"No, I haven't seen any of them this morning." She took a deep breath. "It's just that everything has—has been settled, and I don't want to hang around here any longer than necessary. Please, Peter? We can discuss it in town."

Peter said firmly, "Of course, honey. I'll be up there inside half an hour. Bye."

"Bye, Peter." Megan replaced the receiver in its cradle and sighed. It was all over. In a few minutes Peter would arrive to carry her away, and she would leave Schloss von Kleist forever. If she had any further contact with the family, it would be through attorneys handling the transfer of the property to Kurt. Unless he came for her.... She hugged that thought to her heart for a few seconds, then reluctantly discarded it. No, Kurt would not follow her when she left. He had what he wanted.

Megan wondered if she was being unfair to Peter, asking for his help when he probably assumed, erroneously, that she was going to sell the land to Bachmann Steiner. Once he took her back to the village she would try to explain why she would not be doing so—a difficult task, since she was uncertain of her motives herself. Perhaps in the past few days she had come around to Kurt's passionate conviction that his heritage had to be preserved at all costs, even if nowadays a private estate the size of that of the von Kleists was anachronistic and fiscally untenable. Or perhaps, she thought wistfully, her motives were much simpler: she loved Kurt, and she could not bring herself to hurt him deliberately.

Megan turned to leave the office. She wanted to be waiting with her luggage at the entrance so that Peter, brash, lovable Peter, would not be tempted to storm the castle to liberate her.

Adelaide stood transfixed in the doorway, her hazel eyes glowing. "You're leaving?" she asked with ill-concealed eagerness.

Megan regarded her coldly. Except for the bandaged hand, Adelaide looked about the same. Apparently jeans and T-shirts were the customary uniform for a teenage arsonist. Megan said, "Yes. I don't know if that's what you hoped to accomplish by setting the fire last night, but I am definitely going. Don't worry, though," she continued when Adelaide tried to interrupt her, "I'll sign Kurt's contract before I leave the country."

Adelaide stared at Megan. Suddenly her mobile features twisted with fury and she shouted, "You fool! You can't do that; you'll ruin everything!"

Stunned, Megan gaped. "What are you talking about?"

Adelaide shook her chestnut head wildly. "You can't, you can't!" she sobbed. "I've worked so hard, and you're spoiling it all."

Behind her Gabrielle suddenly appeared in the doorway. "What's going on?" she demanded harshly. With a strangled cry Adelaide elbowed her aside and fled from the room. Gabrielle watched her go, then she turned to scowl at Megan with unfathomable eyes.

Megan wondered just how much of that bewildering conversation Gabrielle had heard. She ventured nervously, "Good morning, Gabrielle. Are you rested after your hard work? The ball was lovely." She noted that even at this early hour the older woman looked as if she had just stepped out of the French *Vogue*, in a deceptively simple coral linen sheath with a matching jacket. Oddly, she carried an untidy bundle of something in her hands.

Megan was unnerved by Gabrielle's unswerving gaze. She added, "I'm sorry I had to trespass here in your office, but I'm leaving, and I needed to make a phone call."

Hazel eyes darted to the telephone and then to Megan's colorless face. "I suppose Dr. Müller is coming for you?"

"No. Peter Swanson."

Gabrielle squinted. "The American," she muttered. "I see."

Megan said, "I'm sorry to leave so abruptly, but I—I think it's best."

"Yes," Gabrielle agreed coolly. "You should never have come here. Does Kurt know you are going?"

"No. But under the circumstances I hardly think he'll be surprised."

Gabrielle glanced down at the wad of grass-stained white wool in her hands. "Here," she said, "I believe this belongs to you. One of the gardeners found it on the grounds, and I could not think of anyone else who would wear such a thing."

Megan blushed. In her haste to pack she had completely forgotten her new shawl, which Kurt had flung savagely to the ground before he carried her upstairs. "Thank you," she said lamely, taking the shawl, "I guess I...I dropped it outside last night." Automatically she began refolding the wool triangle, smoothing the silky fabric, untangling the long fringe. The shawl was no longer a pure eggshell color but was filthy with dirt and grass stains, and in one corner there was the unmistakable imprint of a man's shoe. Gabrielle's eyes seemed riveted to that mark.

Megan said hastily, "It's such a shame for the shawl to be ruined like this. I'll have it cleaned just as soon as I get back to L.A., but I don't know if it will ever be wearable again." She waited for Gabrielle to move out of the doorway. Finally she murmured, "Please, Gabrielle, I must go put this in my suitcase."

Slowly, stiffly, as if in great pain, Gabrielle stepped aside, and Megan hurried upstairs. When she came down a few minutes later, lugging her bags, the older woman was still standing where she had left her.

Outside the bright morning air was already warm with the promise of heat by afternoon. The dolphin fountain danced and sparkled inside the circle of the driveway. Megan waited at the head of the wide stone steps. When a grumbling woman in a denim overall, with a bandana tied around her grizzled hair, pushed a broom vigorously in her direction, Megan quickly perched on the marble balustrade to get her feet out of the way, but the woman still had to shove the two suitcases aside. Megan tried to mollify her with a smiled *"Guten Morgen,"* but the woman just stared at her and went on with her sweeping. At the foot of the steps a gardener muttered fierce Teutonic curses against those guests at the ball who had crushed out cigarettes in the vast urns that held his prize topiaries—an indication, Megan decided wryly, that you could be rich and still be a slob.

She checked her wristwatch again and glanced up toward the arched gate at the top of the hill. Any moment now Peter's little white Audi should be cresting that hill, rocketing down the long curved driveway that slashed the emerald lawn, charging like the cavalry to the rescue, coming to take her away, away....

Megan gulped. She suddenly realized she had not said goodbye to Liesl.

Oh, no, she thought in anguish, how could she forget? Liesl was the one person who had shown her consideration and affection during her stay, the one von Kleist she trusted. And, Megan sensed, in the few days they had known each other, she had filled some need in the little girl's life, some longing for the company of an adult woman. It was going to hurt to leave her, but to go without saying goodbye would be worse than thoughtless, it would be cruel.

Megan went looking for Gabrielle. When she found her descending the stairs, she asked,

"Please, where is Liesl? Is she still in her room? I must speak to her before I go."

Gabrielle's hazel eyes flicked over Megan's tender expression. She said thoughtfully, "No, I believe Kurt took her out riding very early this morning."

Riding, Megan thought in bewilderment. *How could he, exhausted as he was?* Aloud she said, "I don't want to see Kurt."

Gabrielle shrugged. "Oh, I'm sure he went on about his business once he had Liesl situated. If you will excuse me a moment while I—attend to something, I'll take you around to the back lawn. I'm certain we'll see Liesl riding down toward the lake, and we'll walk down to meet her. It's such a lovely morning for a stroll, don't you think?"

Disoriented by Gabrielle's effusiveness, Megan nodded. She had never seen the woman so outgoing before. Probably Gabrielle felt she could afford to be warmer now that Megan was no longer a threat to the von Kleist estate. While she disappeared into the gallery, Megan loitered at the door to the music room, studying the antique piano and conjuring up images of elegant minuets performed by dancers in satin and velvets. No, Megan decided, she was not sorry she had come to Schloss von Kleist. It was an opportunity few people had in the modern world.

When Gabrielle rejoined her, they exited through the back of the house, near the foot of the stairs up which Kurt had carried Megan only a few hours before. Megan gazed out over the lush lawns toward the little lake and protested, "But I don't see Liesl anywhere."

"Don't worry," Gabrielle reassured her, "I'm sure I saw her down this way only a little while ago. Come, we'll find her."

"But Peter will be here—"

Gabrielle's lips thinned at the mention of the American. "I'm sure he'll wait for you," she said. Then she brightened. "Of course he'll wait for a lovely young girl like you! Come now, remember how upset Liesl will be if you don't see her to say goodbye. Hurry, my dear, it's not that far down to the lake. Most likely Liesl is watering her horse. Lucky girl, it's such a beautiful day for a ride...."

And it was a beautiful day, Megan decided as she trudged along behind Gabrielle. By afternoon it would be a scorcher. She was already missing her sun hat, and even Gabrielle had relaxed enough to remove the jacket of her dress, although she did carry it stiffly over her arm.

When they reached the gently lapping water of the lake, Megan glanced around her irritably. "I still don't see her."

Gabrielle insisted, "But I know she was here."

Megan frowned and looked at her watch again. "I'm sorry, but I really must go back up to the house now. I do wish I could see Liesl before I leave, but Peter should be here by now."

Gabrielle grabbed at Megan's arm again. "Look, there in the copse, do you see her? She's playing a game with us!" She called, "Liesl, you silly girl, come out now! We see you!" After a pause during which all Megan could hear was the birds exulting in their summer madness, Gabrielle, still clutching her arm, called again, "Liesl, I said, come out! Your Aunt Megan has to leave!" After another silence she muttered, "I suppose we'll just have to go in and get her. Come along, Megan."

"Really, Gabrielle," Megan protested, trying to free herself from the other woman's punishing grip, "this has gone far enough. If Liesl doesn't want to say goodbye to me, I'll have to forget it." But she could not pry Gabrielle's bony fingers loose from her arm, and in the end she stumbled along after her, trying with difficulty to match Gabrielle's much longer strides, until they were underneath the sheltering oaks and beeches.

Gabrielle released her, and Megan turned away from the older woman to stare around, seething with anger. "She's not here, either," she gritted. "You've dragged me all this way for nothing."

Behind her Gabrielle said in an odd voice, "Oh, I wouldn't say it was for nothing." Out of the corner of her eye Megan saw the coral jacket flutter to the ground, followed by a peculiar metallic snapping noise, and she whirled on her heel to find herself gazing into the ten-inch barrel of the antique flintlock dueling pistol that had once defended the honor of Marthe von Kleist.

Much, much later, Megan wondered why she had not been afraid. She never found a satisfactory answer to that question, but she did know that the situation struck her as more farcical than dangerous. As she stared at Gabrielle, at the two quaking hands that awkwardly clutched the elegantly carved walnut stock of the gun, its gold filigree ornamentation glinting in the dappled sunlight filtering through the trees, she felt a sudden urge to laugh.

One glimpse of Gabrielle's wide eyes stopped Megan's laughter.

Megan asked evenly, "But why, Gabrielle? I'm going. What is the point of this game?"

Gabrielle hissed, "It's not a game, little American girl. I'm not going to let you ruin this family."

"But I'm not—"

Gabrielle continued implacably, "Ever since you arrived I've watched you worm your way into Kurt's affections. My Wilhelm would have seen through you in an instant, but Kurt refuses to believe you are an opportunist, a fortune hunter, just like that upstart husband of yours. And now you plan to sell the meadow, von Kleist land, to Max Bachmann, a man who got his start in the ashes of his country. This house has been the only security I have known for more than thirty years, and I will not let you tear it down! If Kurt will not defeat you, then I must."

Megan shook her head slowly. She was glad now that she had not laughed, for she saw that under Gabrielle's glossy exterior was a pathetic, neurotic woman, deranged with fear. Megan said sincerely, "I have never wanted to harm you,

Gabrielle; you must believe that. I have already decided to sign the property over to Kurt."

"You're lying," Gabrielle said.

"No. The papers are in my handbag up at the schloss. Come with me and I'll show them to you." Megan could see that Gabrielle's hands were trembling violently. "Why don't you put the gun away?" she urged gently, soothingly. "Put it down, Gabrielle, and then we'll go together to find the papers." Megan took a deep breath and reached for the pistol.

"Don't touch that!" Gabrielle shrieked, and she pulled the trigger.

The gun exploded with a deafening boom, with billowing clouds of sparks and pungent black sulfurous smoke. The .55 caliber ball grazed Megan's temple, a claw of flame ripping into her hairline. She was knocked backward by the force of the blow, and her head struck hard against the gnarled root of an ancient oak tree.

As Megan lay on the ground, stunned, nauseated with pain, her colorless face already streaming with blood, she was only vaguely aware of Gabrielle standing over her, rigid and horrified. The woman made a strangled noise deep in her throat, then she began to screech Kurt's name hysterically, her voice as shrill and dissonant as that of an incompetent Brünnhilde sounding the cry of the Valkyries. The nerve-shredding noise offended Megan's sensitive ears, and she wondered tiredly why Gabrielle wouldn't be quiet.

Comforting muffled darkness began to cover

Megan, a seductive promise of peace after so much tumult. She gave herself up willingly to its enveloping clouds. Her last conscious thought was a wistful regret that she had never really had a chance to show Kurt how well she could play the antique piano in the music room.

CHAPTER TEN

PAIN. The world was a red haze, full of pain, and somewhere close by someone was screaming. Where was she? She felt so disoriented, confused, and the bed was hard and lumpy. She ought to shift her head just a little, away from the pillow that felt like a rock, but she was dizzy, queasy, and it was easier not to move. Her temples throbbed as if someone were playing the finale of the *1812 Overture* inside her skull. With difficulty she lifted her lashes so that she could peer overhead, and her mind struggled to interpret the wavering images that swam before her eyes.

Was she in her bedroom? No, her chaste little room in the Manhattan apartment was decorated in soft blue, and all she could see above her was bright dappled green, with splashes of gold like sunlight. Trees? No, how silly of her. It must be the feathery Boston fern in the macrame hanger that she'd fashioned laboriously during the long evenings when Erich went somewhere with Herschel and Lavinia, or just Lavinia. Her vision was blurred; there was something in her eye, something warm and sticky. In a minute she would blink and everything would become clear again. In a minute. But oh, her eyelids were so heavy....

Dear Lord, why wouldn't Lavinia be quiet? She kept shrieking and caterwauling until Megan wanted to slap her, strangle her, anything for a little peace. What was she bellowing about, anyway? She sounded so hoarse that the words came out garbled, almost like a foreign language. Now someone else shouted, too. She liked the new voice, it was deep and attractive, except that it was too loud. And the words, if only she could interpret them. Erich was dead, was that what they said? No, no, no, Erich was right here, bending over her, pulling her into his arms, rocking her like a baby. Erich, Erich, tender as he had never been before. How tan and fit he looked, how impossibly handsome. And wasn't it funny? In this light his gray eyes looked almost blue....

HE CARRIED HER across the threshold, out of the bright sunlight into the succoring coolness of Schloss von Kleist. Servants clustered around him, then retreated quickly, repelled by his face that was a graven mask, adamantine. Liesl elbowed her way through the crowd, but before she could reach him he barked, "No! Don't come any closer!" and half turned so that his body shielded Megan from his daughter's gaze.

Liesl halted abruptly, her pale face marked with tears. "But, *Vati*, I must see—"

He gritted, "No, Liesl, it would only upset you." He scanned the group quickly and spotted

Greta. He called her name and she stepped forward, a neat figure in her light brown uniform, puzzled but ready to do whatever he asked. "Take Fräulein Liesl to her room and keep her there until we have gone."

"But, *Vati*!" Liesl pleaded again.

He stared down at the little girl, and his expression warmed. "Please darling," he said softly, "don't argue with me now. I know you are worried about Aunt Megan, but there's nothing you can do for her except stay out of the way. We are going to take her to the hospital, and I promise I will telephone you just as soon as I have news."

Defiant blue eyes challenged implacable blue eyes, then Liesl nodded reluctantly. "Yes, *Vati*," she sniffed, biting her lip. When Greta caught her gently by the shoulders and urged her in the direction of the staircase, Liesl went silently.

Kurt sighed as he watched his daughter shuffle away. In his arms Megan coughed painfully, and he addressed his staff with a voice only a little less obdurate than his jaw. "Have you telephoned the hospital? Good. Then tell Karl to bring the car around at once. We do not have time to wait for an ambulance. I shall need warm blankets in the salon. *Schnell!*" The people in the hallway knew that voice from generations past, the overlord commanding his vassals, and they jumped to do his bidding. When a maid who had somehow missed the onset of the disturbance blundered into the scene bearing a tray of dirty champagne glasses, he swept past her, oblivious to her choked outcry and the crystal that shattered on the floor like shrapnel.

A few paces behind him stumbled Gabrielle, dazed and defeated. The servants eyed her warily. She was no longer the proud lady of the manor. Her hazel eyes were opaque, and her sallow skin looked ashen except for the spot of red rapidly turning into a bruise on her cheekbone where Kurt had slapped her to stop her hysterics.

Kurt lay Megan down gently on the couch in the salon, straightening the limp limbs that had wound so vibrantly through his only hours before. He sucked in his breath through his teeth as the white linen handkerchief he held against her temple crimsoned under his fingertips. He pressed harder.

She moaned now, her voice a frayed thread of sound, and she hesitated between each word as if she had to remember how to speak. She peered unseeing at him before her violet-shadowed lids slowly drooped shut again. "You're—hurting—me," she whimpered.

"I know," he rasped. Someone handed him a cobweb-soft wool blanket, and he tucked it around her, trying not to jar her. As she began to twist restlessly to escape him, he crooned, "Still, still, *kleine* Megan. Hush now. Help will be here soon." The words seemed to relax her a little.

He turned to survey once more the avid but bewildered faces huddled in the double doorway. His mouth thinned as his eyes raked over Gabrielle, who had slumped into a delicate French

Regency armchair. She seemed lost somewhere very far away. To the servant closest to him he said, "Go fetch Fräulein Steuben and inform her that I want her to take Frau von Kleist to her quarters. She is not to leave until I...."

His voice trailed off as a new sound distracted the waiting group. Indignant shouts emanated from the direction of the front entrance, then noises of a scuffle. Suddenly Peter Swanson burst into the room, shaking off the burly gardener who still clung to his elbow. "What the hell's going on here?" he demanded. "Where's Megan? I found her luggage on the steps, but—" His brown eyes widened as he spotted the still figure lying on the sofa. He gasped. "My God," he choked in an entirely different voice, "what have you done to her?"

He tried to rush to her, but Kurt caught him by the shoulders and growled, "Don't touch her. She mustn't be moved more than necessary."

Peter stared at him, at the long powerful hands gripping him, hands still smeared with Megan's blood. Behind the thick glasses Peter's face twisted with contempt as he hissed, "So I was right about you all along, von Kleist. You'd stop at nothing to get your own way. Not even a lone girl is safe from—"

Kurt snorted wearily, "Oh, shut up, Swanson. Don't make a bigger fool of yourself than is absolutely unavoidable."

On the couch Megan stirred and moaned,

"Kurt. Peter. Please—don't shout. My head aches so—"

"God, where's the car?" Kurt muttered as he dropped to his knees beside her. "Quiet, my love," he soothed, trying to staunch the blood that trickled from underneath the makeshift bandage. "We'll take you to the hospital in just a moment."

He held Megan gently as he would have held Liesl, as he had once held the dying Elisabeth.

Behind him Peter shuffled helplessly, adding in low urgent tones, "That's right, Megan, honey. We'll—we'll take you to Ulrike. Riki will make you feel better."

Once more the people hovering in the doorway parted, and Adelaide rushed into the salon, skidding to a stop at the end of the sofa. She stared at the trio and gasped, "*Gott im Himmel!* What has happened?"

Kurt lifted his head to scowl at her. "Don't ask questions now, Adelaide; just do what I say. I want you to take Gabrielle to her room and keep her there."

Horror distorted the girl's expressive features as her glance darted between her guardian and Megan. "Oh, Gaby," she said sadly, "what have you done?"

Kurt said brutally, "She shot Megan. Now get her out of here, I'll deal with her later."

Peter frowned in obvious puzzlement as he watched Adelaide stride across the room to the chair where Gabrielle sat. "Don't I know you from somewhere?" he asked suddenly.

Adelaide stiffened. After a pause she shook her head. "No, I don't think so." She touched Gabrielle's arm. The older woman looked up at her blankly. "Come on, Gaby," she said. "You're tired. Let's go to your room. You can show me the swatches you got for the new upholstery in the—"

Peter snapped his fingers. "Of course!" he cried. "I remember now. You're the girl I saw talking to my Uncle Max the other day in Salzburg!"

Adelaide paled. "No," she said hoarsely. "No, I haven't been to Salzburg lately except to go to the cinema. You must be thinking of someone else."

Peter surveyed her intently. "No, it was you all right. Young, tall, slim, with chestnut hair. You spent more than an hour with my uncle in his office, and as soon as you left he told me he finally knew the way to get the von Kleist meadow."

Time stopped. Half a dozen pairs of eyes accused the girl in jeans and T-shirt as the people in the salon and at the door formed a *tableau vivant*, utterly motionless, like figures on the frieze of a courthouse. The only sound was Megan's shallow uneven breathing. Abruptly Adelaide jerked to life. She turned to flee, but Gabrielle's long crimson nails dug into her arm, holding her back, and the woman whispered in confusion, "Adelaide, what is this man talking about?"

"Yes, Adelaide," Kurt said coldly, "I think you'd better explain yourself."

Adelaide backed toward the wall, stumbling on the rug, bumping into a small table. Her smooth cap of hair was wild as she flung her head back and forth. She choked, "I never meant for anyone to get *hurt*! How was I supposed to know that Gaby would go off the deep end like that? All I wanted was a little money so that I could go to Hollywood."

"Oh, dear God," Kurt groaned, "that again."

"Yes, that!" Adelaide spat. Her vindictiveness was almost tangible, a dark cloud dimming the gilt splendor of the room. "I've tried time and again to make you understand how I feel about acting, but you never listen to me! You treat me as if I'm a stupid child, incapable of planning my own life, of taking charge of my destiny. But you're wrong, and I've proved it! I went to Max Bachmann and told him about Megan and the papers you wanted her to sign. You never made any secret of them. You talked about them in front of me all the time, as if I were too ignorant to understand—"

"Perhaps," Kurt said heavily, "we credited you with enough loyalty not to betray a family secret."

Adelaide sneered. "What family? Not my family!"

Now Gabrielle spoke, her voice weak and full of pain. "What do you mean, Adelaide? Didn't Willi and I make you welcome into our home? Haven't I always treated you as my daughter? Haven't I done everything in my power to make you one of us?"

"But I'm not one of you!" Adelaide declared fiercely, her voice high and shrill. "I'm a Steuben! My father and I would have made the Steuben name famous, but no, you couldn't allow that; you had to try to make me over into your idea of what I should be. And then you had the gall to expect me to be grateful! You expect me to devote my whole life to preserving this mausoleum of a house; you expect me to forget everything my father and I ever wanted for myself."

"I...I have tried to give you everything you need," Gabrielle protested pitifully.

"Oh, sure," Adelaide said, shrugging, quieter but just as vituperative. "You could be generous enough—as long as it was on your terms. If I dared break one of your rules.... I worked my ass off to help you organize that miserable charity ball, then just because I missed the final preparations you wouldn't even let me come to it!" She smiled humorously. "Well, on second thought, maybe that's only right, because yesterday morning I was down in Salzburg again, making the final arrangements with Max Bachmann to get Megan to sell the meadow to him."

Peter regarded her grimly. "You mean my uncle encouraged you to sell out the von Kleists?"

Adelaide snorted, "Does that bother you, to think a relative would do something not quite pure and upright? Well, don't worry; I assure you he was going to pay me well. And believe me, even if he hadn't been so liberal, I would have done anything—I would have sold my very soul, if that's what it took—to avoid becoming a vestal virgin in the temple of the von Kleists! I would—"

Megan groaned again, and Kurt said, "I think you've said quite enough, Adelaide."

The girl turned on him. "Oh, don't get so holier-than-thou, Kurt von Kleist! Those crippled hands of yours aren't exactly clean. You weren't even going to tell Megan about Bachmann. You were going to swindle her out of—"

"That's *enough*, Adelaide!"

The girl glared at him, then the hot light went out of her eyes and she drooped her head. "Yes," she said wearily, "maybe it is enough. I failed. You bought Megan with something she wanted more than money. I didn't count on that. I didn't count on her becoming so besotted with you that she'd give up everything for the chance to crawl into your bed."

"God!" Kurt gritted, rising to his full menacing height. He flexed his fingers as if he wished they were around Adelaide's throat. She retreated.

But surprisingly, Gabrielle stepped between Kurt and Adelaide. "Please, Kurt," she said in a soft cajoling voice, "she didn't mean it. She's so very young." She touched the girl's arm in a tender pleading gesture. "Tell him, Adelaide, tell him he doesn't understand. We know you would never do anything to harm us. It's the outsiders who cause all the turmoil: that upstart Erich and now his wife, the nouveau riche like Max Bachmann. People of that sort are the real threat to—''

Adelaide shook her arm off viciously and glowered. Between clenched teeth she growled, "Don't touch me! Don't you understand, you crazy old lady? I hate you! I hate all the von Kleists; I hate everything about them—" Her fierce words ended with a strangled cry, and she broke away from Gabrielle and fled from the room, tearing through the crowd of stunned servants who had watched the entire confrontation from the doorway.

Gabrielle sank back into the armchair, her drawn face pallid and haggard. She shook her head as if to clear it. "She doesn't understand," she repeated dully. "It's all a mistake; it's not her fault. Adelaide would never do anything to hurt us or damage the house. She's not a von Kleist, but she has the calling—" She buried her face in her hands and began to sob.

"God," Peter breathed fervently, sickened by the scene he had watched. Just then the chauffeur appeared in the doorway to announce that the car was waiting out front. With a terse nod Kurt swept Megan up into the steel cradle of his arms. He strode grimly from the room, and Peter hurried after.

ULRIKE ASKED, "Well, now, how is my star patient today? Any headache?"

"Not today," Megan grumbled, looking up from the lurid paperback she had been trying fitfully to read. "But I'd feel a lot better if you'd let me get out of bed."

Ulrike shook her head. "Patience, patience," she chided. "I keep telling you, you must rest. You lost a lot of blood—scalp wounds do that, you know—and with that knock on the head you've had quite a shock."

"But I feel so much stronger."

"Ha! If you tried to stand you would find out very quickly how weak you are." Ulrike's pale eyes darkened. "Please, my young friend, listen to me. I know the condition you were in when Kurt and Peter brought you here three days ago. You were slightly concussed, and for a while I thought you might need a transfusion." She smiled dryly. "Your blood completely ruined the suede upholstery in the back seat of Kurt's Mercedes."

Megan grimaced. "Ugh, Ulrike, must you be so vivid? Your bedside manner leaves a lot to be desired." She set aside her book. She knew that Ulrike's levity was assumed to hide the true seriousness of her injury.

Once her mind cleared Megan had been able to recall very little of what happened after Gabrielle pulled the trigger. Images swam before her, obscured by clouds of pain. She could remember the flash of gold as the pistol arced high in the sunlight and plopped with a soft splash into the middle of the lake, flung there by Kurt. When they carried her into the house, one of the maids had squealed with shock and dropped a tray of champagne goblets, scattering shards of crystal all over the parquet floor. She could hear people shouting in German, and then the screech of tires and the blare of the auto horn—strictly forbidden in Austria—as the limousine sped toward the village.

Faces loomed up, too, in her mind, hazy and distorted: Kurt and Peter, two very different men whose features assumed strangely similar scowls of determination in a crisis. Gabrielle, sobbing, haggard far beyond her years. And, oddly, Megan could even remember Adelaide, flushed with resentment, defiance and—and guilt.

By the time they reached the town Megan had been almost completely unconscious, but later one of the nurses gave her a disturbingly graphic account of how Peter had bellowed for people to move out of the way while he cleared a path for Kurt, who strode into the hospital with Megan limp and moaning in his arms....

Ulrike said, "Actually I came in here to tell you I plan to remove the bandage today. The stitches will still be in place, of course, but you won't have that bulky dressing to annoy you whenever you turn your head."

"Thank heaven for that," Megan murmured fervently. She relaxed as Ulrike, assisted by a nurse, swiftly and efficiently tended her wound.

After the nurse had carried away the stained bandages, Ulrike studied Megan's scalp and judged, "Yes, that is healing very nicely. If there is any scarring at all, it will be right at your hairline and no one will ever notice it. You are a lucky girl."

"Yeah," Megan muttered. "I could have bled to death."

The doctor said quietly, "You must not think of that, Megan. You were found almost instantly. With Peter tearing up the schloss looking for you, and Kurt and Liesl riding nearby—"

"Then they really were out for a ride?" Megan asked in surprise. "I thought...." She paused, sickened. "Oh, no, don't tell me Liesl saw me when I was—I was—"

"No. Her father sent her galloping for help at once. She was frightened, of course, but she did not see you."

"What happened to Gabrielle?"

Ulrike made a face. "Poor woman, she broke down completely, I'm afraid. It's no wonder, after the shock of discovering her foster daughter's treachery. How could that wicked girl betray her family like that? To think that the very day you and Peter and I were having such a lovely time in Salzburg, she was there, also, plotting with Peter's uncle.... And she might have got away with it if Peter hadn't recognized her."

Megan sighed. So that was why Adelaide had tried repeatedly to make her distrust Kurt, even to the point of setting a fire and accusing him of it. She wanted the money, of course. The von Kleists wouldn't finance her venture into movies, so she had determined to get the money some other way, and she was clever enough to realize that Max Bachmann would pay well to learn the carefully guarded secret of Megan's inheritance. The girl's snide remarks had never really rung true, but as usual Megan had been too blind to figure out why. She asked, "What will become of Adelaide and Gabrielle now?"

Ulrike hedged, "You'll have to ask Kurt about them."

"How can I? He hasn't been to see me."

"He was at your side constantly until we knew you were out of danger. Peter was, too." Ulrike was silent for a moment, then she noted brightly, "What pretty carnations. Did Peter bring them?"

Megan nodded, regarding the big bouquet of candy-striped flowers with affection. "He's visited me every day."

"Yes, I know," the doctor said. After a pause she added, "Peter was very upset about his uncle's part in this unsavory affair. He told Max Bachmann that if he ever tried to go behind him like that again, he would pack up and return to the United States."

Ulrike's bleak tone made Megan glance at her sharply. Was this the time to meddle, she wondered. "Riki," she asked, using Peter's pet name, "you do like Peter, don't you?"

"I like Peter very much."

Megan hesitated. "Are you in love with him?"

Ulrike laughed sardonically, her pale blue eyes flashing. "You're certainly blunt, aren't you?"

Megan felt rebuffed. She drew back against her pillow. "I'm sorry, Ulrike, I—well, I thought you wouldn't mind my asking because...because I thought we were friends."

Ulrike relaxed and patted Megan's shoulder. "We are friends, my dear. I find it difficult to believe that less than two weeks ago I met you for the first time. As I recall, you had carnations then, too." She smiled ironically. "For such a small thing, you've certainly had a big effect on my life."

Ulrike moved restlessly around the room. She adjusted the chintz window curtains and re-checked the medical chart hanging from the foot of Megan's bed. At last she sighed, "In answer to your question, yes, I am in love with Peter Swanson. I love his impulsiveness and exuberance and the way he sometimes teases me, making me laugh as I have not done in years. If he should return to America, I think I might just die." She shook her head impatiently. "Forget I said that. I am being absurd."

"It's not absurd to care for someone!"

"No," Ulrike said, "but even if Peter remains, there will still be problems."

"You mean the difference in your religion?"

Ulrike nodded. "I had always assumed that if I fell in love, it would be with someone of my own faith. I never dreamed my heart could be so capricious."

Megan frowned. "I know that the rules about intermarriage are not as strict as they used to be. Aren't there ways you can overcome your differences?"

"Yes, there are always ways, assuming two people care enough. But—but Peter does not care enough. He likes me, I know, but he does not see me as a woman. I think he regards me as some sort of favorite aunt."

Megan made a rude noise. "Don't be asinine. You're what—two years older than he is?"

"Something like that," Ulrike murmured. She wandered over to the window and stared out, while Megan studied her broodingly. She was already almost as fond of Ulrike as she was of Dorothy, and she wished she could help in some way. The problem, as Megan saw it, was not Peter's feelings for the doctor, but rather Ulrike's own lack of self-esteem. She was supremely confident as a physician, but when it came to being a woman, she was as unsure of herself as any gangling adolescent.

Megan smiled cynically. She supposed her concern was ironic, since she personally had had lousy luck with the men in her life, but she thought she might be able to help Ulrike. Her life on the fringes of the entertainment world had taught her a little about fashion and makeup. She pondered Ulrike's blond hair, scraped back into a functional chignon, her sturdy, cosmetic-free face, and the shapeless dresses that always seemed to be in unbecoming colors. She ventured timidly, "Ulrike, have you ever considered getting your hair cut?"

The woman turned and smiled. She really had a lovely smile, Megan thought. It was a shame that her duties as director of the hospital left her so little time to smile, to enjoy herself. Ulrike asked, "What are you plotting now, Megan? Some sort of Cinderella transformation to make Peter fall helpless at my feet, stunned by my beauty? I'm afraid nothing will ever make me Miss World."

"And why should you want to be Miss World?" Megan retorted indignantly. "You're an intelligent and capable woman with far more to offer a man that some busty moron in a swimsuit. I'm sure Peter knows that." *I'm sure Peter loves you,* Megan thought silently, *but you'll have to find that out for yourself.* Aloud she continued, "Maybe you just need a few feminine tricks, a new hairdo, some pretty clothes. I think you've devoted so much time to this hospital that you've forgotten you owe yourself something, as well."

Ulrike laughed, "The wisdom of the young! You are very sweet, Megan, but a hopeless romantic, I'm afraid."

"I guess I am," Megan admitted, suddenly somber, remembering a moonlit hour when a gravelly baritone voice had scorned her with almost those very words. "I can't say it's done me much good," she muttered.

Just then an orderly looked into the room and signaled to Ulrike. After a muffled discussion the doctor returned to Megan's bedside. She spoke matter-of-factly, although her eyes were intent. "Kurt von Kleist has telephoned to ask if he may visit you. I said it was all right. He should be here within the hour."

"Ulrike!" Megan cried, almost leaping out of the bed.

Ulrike gently pushed her back against her

pillow. "Calm yourself," she ordered. "You are well enough to see him, and I think you should."

"Like this?" Megan's hands fluttered with dismay over her scarred face and the drab hospital gown. "But Ulrike—"

Ulrike said sternly, "Megan, right now your looks are the least of your concerns."

"What do you mean?"

The doctor continued, "I know there is something between you and Kurt. The night of the ball, the pair of you seemed to strike sparks off each other, even when you were separated by the length of that huge room. I am also observant enough to realize that something is wrong with your relationship, quite apart from this dispute over the property. Although I'm not sure what the trouble is, I do know that as long as you permit it to distress you, your recovery will be impaired."

"So you think I should face him?"

"I think you must resolve your differences somehow. If you do not, when you return to America you will become even more of a nervous wreck than you were when you first arrived in Austria."

"Well, gee, thanks!" Megan retorted childishly.

Ulrike smiled placidly. "My dear, I'm a physician. It's my job to notice symptoms."

After Ulrike left the room, Megan fidgeted with the inadequate mirror that was built into her bedside table, trying to position it so that she could use both hands while she concentrated on her hair. Now that the bulky dressing had been removed, she could see that the wound on her temple was not nearly as large as she had feared; and as Ulrike had reassured her, once it healed, the scar should blend into her hairline. But now the cut was still swollen and discolored, and the ragged line of black sutures reminded her of Frankenstein's monster. What distressed her most, however, was the glaring bald patch on her temple where her fiery curls had been shaved away from the wound. Her hair would grow back, of course, but at that moment only a faint blush hinted at the tendrils that would eventually re-cover the blue white scalp.

Megan did not consider herself a vain woman, but she felt ugly and disfigured—yet another crime to charge against the von Kleists. She picked up a brush and began carefully repairing her hair on the opposite side, trying to cover the offensive bare spot, when she heard a sharp rap at her door. She glanced up, startled, unaware that she looked like a frightened doe, her eyes enormous.

Kurt halted just inside the door and stared at her. She gazed at him hungrily. He looked older in just a few days, she thought, and thinner, too. His high cheekbones seemed ready to burst through the taut skin of his face, and that long aristocratic nose was more prominent, making his features almost a caricature of themselves. His tall frame was beginning to appear less lean than gaunt. He caught his breath with a hiss. "They told me you were better," he rasped, "but you look as if—as if...."

Megan set down her hairbrush and pushed the table away from the bed. It was torture to speak without declaring her love, and frustration made her voice sharp. She said coldly, "I know how I look, but as a matter of fact I do feel better. Haven't you heard? When a woman begins to worry about her appearance, it means she's well on the way to recovery."

"Don't be flippant," Kurt gritted. "If you knew how worried I've been—"

"Not worried enough to come see me!" Megan retorted before she could stop herself.

Kurt looked at her strangely. He said, "I would have come—you could not have kept me away—but I had to...to make arrangements for Gabrielle."

Distressed that she had betrayed herself, Megan snorted nastily, "Oh, Gabrielle. Well, I'm sure that any lawyer you hire will be the best." When she saw a puzzled expression flicker in Kurt's dark blue eyes, she demanded, "She *is* going to be charged with assault, isn't she? I know your family has a lot of influence, but surely even in Austria it's a crime to shoot someone."

Kurt shook his head. He said, "I thought you knew. Gaby has checked into a clinic in Baden. It belongs to a friend of mine, and she will be well cared for there."

Megan gasped, "You're joking."

"No, I'm very serious. Dr. Weiss is a noted psychologist, and under the circumstances—"

"Circumstances! My God, Kurt, she tried to kill me! Doesn't that mean anything to you?"

Kurt gestured helplessly. "Megan, please try to understand. Gabrielle has always been...high-strung, even as a child. She endured much during the war, and it left its mark on her. She has always felt insecure. She loved Willi very much; she felt safe with him. But when he died so suddenly, it was as if her whole world had ended. I have tried to make allowances for that. Perhaps I indulged her too much. But whatever you think of her, Megan, whatever she has done, Gaby has always been like a sister to me, and it is my duty to protect her."

Megan said, "I suppose this protection extends to destroying evidence?"

He stared. "What on earth are you talking about?"

She cried, "The gun, damn you! I saw you throw the gun into the lake!"

He frowned, clearly puzzled. After a moment he said slowly, "Yes, I remember now that I did throw away the gun. But I did so in the heat of the moment. You were lying there looking so pathetic, and the sight of it revolted me. I never even thought about— If it should become necessary to procure the gun for evidence, the lake is not so large that it couldn't be dragged."

"But that's not very likely to happen, is it?" Megan asked quietly.

He shrugged. "No, probably not."

"Of course not!" Megan responded cuttingly.

"No one would dream of prosecuting Gabrielle for her attack on me. After all, she's a von Kleist, a *true* von Kleist, and I am only the—what was it she called me that first night—the unwanted wife of an illegitimate upstart."

Kurt's eyes narrowed. He said, "Yes, that is it exactly."

Megan fell back against her pillow. She murmured, "No wonder Adelaide wanted out."

Kurt flared, "Don't mention that little bitch's name to me. She's the cause of all this!"

"Oh, really, Kurt—"

"If you had heard her," he spat, "you wouldn't argue with me. I wanted to throttle her! After the way poor Gabrielle cared for her.... And she wasn't the least bit sorry! All she was interested in was her own selfish ambitions. All she wanted was some way to get away from her guardian."

"And you don't understand that?" Megan asked incredulously. "Certainly I'm the last person to condone Adelaide's methods, but don't you see? It's not Adelaide who's at fault. She's little more than a child, victimized by a woman you yourself admit is unstable. When she made that deal with Bachmann Steiner she was striking out in the only way she could find. She was wrong, yes, but the real culprit is not Adelaide, but rather this obsession you have with the estate. If only you would—"

Kurt said coldly, "Megan, the way I run my family is none of your business."

She recoiled as if he had slapped her. She stared

up at him, tears of fatigue welling in her wide troubled eyes. She wiped them away impatiently as she began to tremble with reaction.

Instantly he flinched with contrition. "Forgive me," he said quietly. "I keep forgetting how ill you are."

Megan's head drooped, and her girlish voice sounded dull. "So what did you do to Adelaide?"

"Do?" Kurt shrugged. "I suppose you could say I threw her out. I gave her the money to go to Rome to see if she can break into films there. I thought that if she does not succeed, it will be punishment enough."

"Some punishment," Megan said sarcastically.

Kurt replied simply, "Adelaide is family."

"Of course," Megan murmured. "Family, always family." She collapsed again. She could not bear to look at Kurt. She stared at the ceiling, counting the holes in the acoustic tile, and mused aloud, "The night of the ball I had this vision of you and Gabrielle and all the von Kleists as far back as Otto I, a long string of you all lined up against me. I felt so helpless. But now it occurs to me that I'm not helpless at all; I have the perfect weapon against you. I was reluctant to use it, but now I know I must. You have to be stopped before you hurt someone else. Sometime when Gabrielle is rational you might tell her I'm grateful to her, because she finally made up my mind for me. I'm going to sell the meadow to Max Bachmann."

She heard Kurt make a strangled noise, but still she would not look at him. "I never had time to tell Peter I was going to sign the property over to you, and now I'm very glad I didn't. Because when I sell out to Bachmann Steiner, not only will I get all that lovely money, but I'll also have the satisfaction of knowing that at long last you've been defeated. Watching them dig up the meadow will be like having a chunk bitten out of you von Kleists. You won't be able to treat the wound, and in time it will begin to fester—"

Kurt's hands clenched the bed rail. *"Mein Gott!"* he choked, trembling with fury, making the whole bed shake. "How can you be so vindictive?"

"Vindictive?" Megan echoed, her green eyes jewels of rage as she glared up at him. "Have you ever stopped to think what I've suffered at the hands of your precious family, starting with Erich? I've been lied to, cheated, humiliated, raped and almost murdered! Don't you think I have the right to be vindictive?"

Kurt stared at Megan's paper-white face, at her absurd glorious hair and eyes. His anger ebbed away, and Megan saw his shoulders slump in an attitude of defeat. After a long pause he sighed wearily, "I wish—I wish I had been the one to find you in that music school in New York. Sometimes I think everything would have been different if it had been me instead of Erich."

Megan's heart lurched. What would her life have been like if Kurt had burst into her rehearsal room that day, not Erich? She looked up at Kurt, longing naked in her face. Her eyes slid over him, devouring him. He was so good to look at, and she had to send him away, she knew that now. It accomplished nothing to ache for what might have been. Erich had been the one who found her. He had made of her the emotional mess she was today, and perhaps even more to the point, he had precipitated the property dispute that stood between her and Kurt. Because of those unchangeable facts, the two of them had no future together. They were incapable of doing anything but hurting each other—just as she knew she hurt him when she whispered softly, "Nothing would have been different if you had been first. You see, Kurt, in every way that matters, you and Erich are exactly alike."

For a moment Kurt seemed turned to stone. Then he took a deep breath. His eyes wandered over her body, lingering on the curves that the ugly hospital gown could not disguise. He smiled remotely, as if remembering another time when not even a nightgown had come between them. He shook his head, and his eyes were dark with irony. He said, "One thing would have been different, Megan. Believe me, my darling, if I had been your husband, no power on earth could have made me leave your bed." He turned on his heel and walked away.

THE BREEZE FROM THE OPEN WINDOW ruffled Megan's hair as Peter's little white Audi sped across the valley on the road that led from Kleisthof-im-Tirol to the junction with the autobahn. The tails of the yellow-and-brown scarf that she had tied Gypsy fashion over her head whipped into her face, and she brushed them away irritably. Already she was finding the scarf annoying, but it matched the full swinging skirt she had purchased the day before on her shopping trip with Ulrike, and it had the more important virtue of hiding her injury. The doctor had suggested the scarf to Megan.

During their outing Ulrike had followed Megan's lead at first uncertainly and then with self-deprecating humor, as the young woman induced her to buy clothes in flattering colors and in styles more suitable to her age than the matronly, serviceable dresses she usually wore. Ulrike had even admitted that she ought to use more cosmetics, something she rarely bothered to do, busy as she was at the hospital. But when the hairdresser who cut Ulrike's long blond mane offered to restyle Megan's hair to cover the wound, Ulrike had sternly turned professional and ordered Megan to avoid shampoos and lacquers until her own physician in Los Angeles removed the sutures and gave her permission to resume normal care of her hair. Megan's disappointment was forgotten once she saw the astonishing difference new clothes and a different hairstyle made in her friend.

As Peter drove, he said, "Since you're not answering, I guess my suggestion didn't meet with your approval."

Megan started. "I'm sorry, Peter, I wasn't listening. What did you say?"

"I was saying," he repeated carefully, "that instead of going from Salzburg to Munich, you might catch a plane in Vienna. You can get a flight direct to the States from there."

"But I've already been to Vienna, and anyway, it's clear across the country!"

Peter smiled indulgently. "Honey, it's not as if I was suggesting we drive from California to New York. The whole country of Austria is only about the size of Maine. It's just a three-hour drive on the autobahn. We would be passing through some of the most beautiful scenery in the world, and I think you ought to get more than just a glimpse of it before you leave. If you're not in any particular hurry, the two of us might detour to upper Austria and spend a few days in the Traunsee. There's this lovely inn I know of in Traunkirchen, right on the shore of the lake...." He glanced at Megan's expressionless face. "Besides," he added briskly, "Uncle Max will be in Vienna for the next couple of weeks, and I want you to meet him."

Megan turned and stared at him in genuine astonishment. "Why would you want me to meet your uncle?"

Peter shrugged, "Well, for one thing, he's a very nice man and I think you'll like him, and certainly he's intrigued by the woman who finally brought the von Kleists to heel. For another— I guess we'll have to wait and see about that, okay?"

Megan regarded Peter uneasily. "I thought you

were mad at your uncle," she said. "I thought you threatened to go back to the States."

Peter shrugged. "I suppose I did say that, but I didn't really mean it. I was furious with him at the time. I kept thinking about the way you looked, lying there with blood—" He shook his head as if trying to free it of disturbing memories. "You know," he said, "Uncle Max was just as horrified as I was at what happened to you. When that girl came to him and said she knew a way to end the stalemate that had existed for so long between him and Kurt von Kleist, well, he never dreamed it would end with someone getting hurt."

"Forget it," Megan said roughly. "It wasn't an experience I'd care to repeat, but it's over now with no lasting damage. I don't blame anyone."

"That's very tolerant of you," Peter observed. "I don't think I'd be that forgiving."

Megan said, "I'm not being noble, just sort of fatalistic. I've come to accept that people's actions are dictated by influences beyond their control, and we can't expect them to behave differently no matter how much we desire it."

For a while they drove in silence. They left the valley behind, and the Audi began winding along what Megan now recognized was the road to the meadow. "I need to check a few things," Peter explained. He breathed deeply. "Have you ever tasted air like this? God, I love this country! Maybe it's because I'm half-Austrian myself, but when I arrived here six years ago I knew I had come home. With Uncle Max's help I've built a good life for myself, and lately I've been thinking it's time I got married again, settled down, had a few kids...."

He pulled the car onto the shoulder next to his equipment trailer. After parking the Audi under an old oak tree, he switched off the engine and twisted in the bucket seat until he faced Megan. "Megan, darling," he began fervently.

Megan held up her hand to stop him. She cried, "Good Lord, Peter, you aren't getting ready to propose, are you?"

He looked stunned, then laughed as he realized what he had said. "No, honey, I'm not, although I admit it must have sounded that way." When he saw that Megan was not offended, he said with a twinkle, "Actually, I had something a little less... permanent in mind. What would you say to a week or so of touring the country, complete with charming accommodations and congenial company?"

"Sounds delightful. But why me?"

"You're very beautiful," Peter said simply, his brown eyes skimming lightly over her. After a pause he added, "It's a serious offer, if you choose to take it that way. I promise I'd make sure you—weren't disappointed."

Megan smiled faintly. "Thanks, but no thanks, Peter. I can't think of anything guaranteed to ruin our friendship more quickly. Besides, you're just feeling excited because your business is finally working out. We both know I'm not the one you want."

"Don't underestimate yourself," he said. Tilting his head to one side, he asked curiously, "Tell me, though, what would you have answered if it had been the lord of the manor doing the asking?"

Megan lowered her lashes, and despite herself she thought of dark hair curling down into an untidy comma over sea-blue eyes. A delicate wistful expression flitted across her face.

Peter caught his breath, and he muttered, "That stupid bastard, to let you go—"

"What?" Megan asked, not really listening.

"Nothing." Peter stepped out of the car, closing the door gently in order not to disturb her reverie. But she heard the click, and watched him through the open window as he meandered toward the tree, his hands shoved deep in his pockets. After a moment he declared, "I don't know what it is with you and these von Kleists. They're all arrogant prigs with feudal mentalities and they think the earth stays in its orbit only because it suits them to have it that way. I've gathered that your husband was no prize, but now you've gone and fallen for Kurt, the worst of the lot. For God's sake Megan! Oh, I'll grant you the man is attractive, very dashing in an eighteenth-century sort of way. Even Riki, the most sensible woman in the world, is not immune to his charm." After a moment he added, not unkindly, "If the man turns you on that much, why don't you just have an affair with him and get it over with?"

"I almost did," Megan answered, forcing a smile to hide the pain that "almost" cost her.

When Peter looked at her sharply, she said firmly, "I'm not going to answer any more questions."

Peter shook his head. "No, no more questions." He opened her car door and held out his hand to her. Megan took it, and together they wandered down the old wagon track toward a massive oak even older than the one beside the trailer.

Megan looked all around her. The meadow was so beautiful, and it was all hers, at least for a little while. Soon she would sign the property over to Peter's uncle's company, and then she would return to the United States almost a rich woman. That was certainly a heady thought! And yet, how lovely it would be to be able to keep the meadow, to hold it as a place of refuge so that its peace and natural glory could seep into her soul, easing her wounded spirit. . . .

For she was wounded. As she had told Peter, she accepted the inevitability of people's actions, but that acceptance did nothing to ease the pain. She knew now that she was fated to love Kurt. Her need for him grew out of their kindred interests and sexual attraction, and the unresolved conflicts remaining from her life with Erich. Meeting Kurt, she could no more have avoided falling in love with him than she could have stopped the tide. And it was equally inevitable that a man of Kurt's breeding and culture would put the needs of his family before his interest in a young woman of unremarkable background.

But if their love was so obviously doomed from

the beginning, why, dear God, oh, why did it have to hurt so much to leave?

Peter called, "Come admire my artwork!" and Megan turned back toward him. He was carefully carving something into the gnarled bark of the old tree. She peered over his shoulder. He had inscribed an elaborate heart, and inside he was carving P.S. Loves—

"You imbecile," Megan giggled.

"I'm just a boy scout at heart," he said, flourishing his pocketknife. "How do you think I should finish it? M.H. or M. von K.?"

Megan offered lightly, "How about U.M.?"

Peter stared at her. After a moment he croaked, "Riki?"

"Of course."

Peter's cheeks colored. "Am I that obvious, Megan?"

"To me," Megan answered. "But maybe I'm just sensitive to things like that. Anyway, I think you two would make a great couple."

"So do I," Peter said. "Ulrike Müller is one of the finest women I have ever met, and I love her with all my heart. But she's not interested in me. She doesn't have time for anything but that damned hospital of hers."

"I don't know about that. I have the distinct impression that before long she'll be leaving St. Elisabeth's."

"Really? You mean she's going away somewhere?"

"I don't know, Peter. You'll have to ask her that yourself."

He shook his head in wonder. "I can't believe it. That hospital is her whole life."

"Maybe that's the problem," Megan pointed out gently. "Maybe it's time she found a new interest in life—like a husband and family."

Behind his glasses Peter squinted. He was obviously thinking along lines new to him. He muttered, "I meant to tell her this morning how lovely she looked in that pink outfit. Is it new? That color is good on her, and I must admit I liked the way the blouse emphasized her— And her hair. I've always thought it was pretty, but all short and fluffy that way, it makes her look almost girlish."

Peter's voice grew fainter, and from the way his mouth quirked Megan could tell that he was indulging in some very private thoughts. She turned away and ran her fingers lightly over the trunk of the tree, noticing for the first time the numerous carvings.

Suddenly Peter exploded, "Oh, hell, what difference does it make how I feel about Riki? I'm not Catholic, and she'll never forgive me for being divorced!"

Startled, Megan stared at him. "It can't be as bad as that, surely?"

"You have no idea, Megan. The first time I happened to mention my ex-wife, Riki was really shocked. She made me feel like a dirty old man."

"Maybe she was just surprised. If she hadn't suspected—"

Peter puzzled. "I don't know. I suppose it

could have been a shock to her. We'd known each other for a while, and the subject had never come up." He shook his head again. "If only she'd let me explain. Annie and I were just kids playing at being grown-ups. It was nobody's fault, really. She remarried four years ago, and as far as I know, she's perfectly happy. Riki and I could be, too, if only—"

Megan snapped, "Damn it, Peter, I wish you'd quit whining, 'If only!' If you love Ulrike, go and tell her so. While you're at it, tell her that the two of you are going to reconcile your religious differences and get married. Period. I don't think she'll give you much of an argument."

"But—but—"

"Peter," Megan said more softly, "have you ever stopped to think what Ulrike has to put up with? She's a young woman, but for seven years she has been literally in charge of the life and death of the people of Kleisthof-im-Tirol. Don't you think she must get rather tired of making the decisions, that it would be a welcome relief for someone else to call the shots for a while? If you love her, don't you owe it to her to take some of the burden from her?"

Megan went back to inspecting the tree. She had said all she had to say—too much, perhaps. Peter would have to take it from there. If he didn't, then she was mistaken about the man she was sure lived beneath that boyish exterior.

She murmured, "I wonder how old this oak is. It seems to have attracted lots of lovers." Initials and designs were inscribed in the wood, many so old they were difficult to discern from the natural cracking and weathering of the black bark. Stefan und Mina. Wolfgang Liebe Elke. So many sweethearts, now grown old or in the grave, had met under this tree. On a moonlit summer night it would be a very inviting trysting place. Megan couldn't help wondering how many maidens, only a little unwilling, had struggled and submitted to their ardent beaux on the sweet grass in the shadow of those spreading branches. Maybe this was where the young von Kleists in centuries past had brought their peasant girls. . . .

Megan quivered with a feeling that might have been envy. She continued around the massive trunk. "I've found a word I can't read," she said to Peter. She spelled it out to him. "I don't know what that means."

Peter grinned wickedly. "It means, you dear illiterate, that even our ancestors liked to scrawl obscenities in public places!"

Megan colored and looked away. Her eyes were attracted to a graffito somewhat lower than the others, so old that the scarring of the bark disguised it almost completely. She picked away flakes of gray green lichen so that her fingers could trace the faint letters. S. von K.—1763. Megan felt a tremor run through her, as if she had brushed against eternity. 1763. More than two hundred years ago a little von Kleist boy—of course it was a boy; girls didn't do such things in those days—had leaned against this tree and struggled to carve the ornate Germanic script into the bark. From the height of the letters Megan guessed that he couldn't have been much more than nine years old, about the same age as young Mozart, who was already astonishing the world with his prodigy. The boy had carved his initials into the tree and then had gone away, probably forgetting all about it. He went away to an uncertain fate, but the tree remained. The boy could have died young, as children often did then, or he might have grown up to become one of the stern faces peering down from the gallery walls in the schloss—but whatever happened to him, he had been dust for centuries. Only the faint letters in the bark of a tree remained, and would remain for centuries more, if foolish people did not destroy them.

Megan's eyes misted. For the first time she understood what Kurt had meant when he spoke to her that night about the heritage he wanted to preserve for his descendants. It occurred to her all at once that if she sold the property, the person who would lose most would be Kurt's daughter, Liesl, the one von Kleist she had never wanted to hurt.

Megan said huskily, "Peter, what will happen to this tree after you begin putting in the mine?"

Peter quickly surveyed the meadow and wrinkled his brow as he made mental calculations. "It'll depend, of course, on exactly where we sink the first shaft, but unless my measurements are way off, the tree will probably have to go."

Megan said deliberately, "Then why bother to carve your initials?" When Peter had the grace to look embarrassed, she went on, "I can't do it; I can't be the one to destroy all this. It isn't mine, no matter what the law says. I have no right to it. The only ones who can decide what will happen to this tree and this meadow are those people who are a part of these things—Kurt, and especially Liesl."

Peter's jaw dropped. With an incoherent cry of frustration he took the knife still clutched in his hand and drove it into the heart of the tree. "I knew it," he fumed. "I knew this would happen! Everything was going too smoothly!" He shook his fist at the tree. "Why did I have to bring you here? Of all the lamebrain—"

Megan watched in horror. She said, "Then all those charming things you said to me were just to make sure I'd sell?"

He was instantly contrite. "Oh, no, Megan... oh, no. I really did want you to go away with me. Any man would. But I wanted the meadow, too." He put his hands on her shoulders and watched conflicting emotions play across her face. "So after all they've done to you, you're determined to sell the property to the von Kleists for a fraction of what it's worth?"

"I'm not selling it," Megan said flatly. "I've thought it over, and I'm going to give it to Liesl, who probably has more right to it than anyone. After all it's her future we're bargaining for. I'm still carrying the original papers Kurt gave me.

The transfer ought to be fairly easy to arrange."

Peter studied her intently. "And then what?" he asked.

She bowed her head. Her temple hurt, and she began to shiver with reaction. She was weary and defeated at last. "I don't know," she whispered hoarsely, her voice suddenly thick. "I guess—I guess then I just want to go home."

Peter recognized the universal cry of the hurt child. He pulled her into his arms. She drooped her tired face against his shoulder, and he patted her back as he inquired gently, "But where is home, Megan?"

She sniffed, "I don't know. Los Angeles, I guess. But not here. Oh, God, anywhere but here!"

CHAPTER ELEVEN

AT THE FRONT DOOR Megan sighed with relief, "Thanks, Dorothy—I don't know what I'd do without you. My hair dryer *would* break down just when I needed it!" She signaled for her friend to follow her as she padded across her tiny living room to her tinier bedroom and then on into the bathroom.

Dorothy lounged on the patchwork coverlet on the bed and watched through the open door as Megan quickly dried her hair into a glowing aureole of short coppery curls. Over the roar of the hand-held dryer Dorothy yelled, "So who's this guy you're going out with tonight? Anyone I know?"

Megan switched off the dryer and fluffed her hair with her fingertips. In the sudden silence her laughter seemed to reverberate as she explained, "No, he's someone I literally bumped into at the music store yesterday. I was heading for the checkout to pay for all that new sheet music I got for work and I ran right into him. My movie themes and Barry Manilow songs got mixed up with thirty-five copies of Vivaldi's *Gloria*." She added, "He's an instructor at U.C.L.A. and also the choir director for that big church on Wilshire Boulevard—you know, the Gothic-looking one."

Dorothy commented dryly, "A match made in heaven, obviously. How old is he?"

Megan shrugged, "I don't know—twenty-five, twenty-eight. We started talking while I helped him straighten out the mess. I told him I had just signed up for some of the classes I'll need to earn my teaching credential, and he said he was glad I was going back to school. Then he mentioned that he had tried to get tickets for the benefit concert at the Hollywood Bowl tonight, and I said I just happened to have an extra ticket going to waste, and so—"

Dorothy exclaimed, "You mean you asked him out?"

Megan chuckled. "I guess I did."

"Well, what do you know?" Dorothy drawled. "I can see right now that soon the Polynesian Paradise is going to have to find a new pianist. Church choir directors simply do not have wives who work in bars."

Megan stared at her friend. "Wives? Good heavens, Dorothy, I only met him yesterday!"

"Sometimes that's long enough," Dorothy said, but she regretted the remark the instant she saw the spasm of remembered pain flicker across Megan's face. Dorothy gritted, "Don't think about the von Kleists anymore, Megan. Those people aren't good for you! When I think of the way you looked when you stepped off that plane...! I sent you on a vacation, and you came back looking like a war casualty! Forget about Austria and start making yourself a good life here at home in Los Angeles where you belong."

Megan nodded bleakly. "Of course you're right, Dot. That's all behind me now." She concentrated on applying her makeup, dabbing extra foundation on the shadows beneath her eyes. After she had slipped gold hoops into her pierced ears she stepped into the bedroom and twirled for Dorothy's inspection. "Well, how do I look?" she asked brightly. "Am I dressed for sitting on the grass and listening to music?" She was wearing red jeans and white sandals and a gaily embroidered man's shirt that hung loose like a smock.

"Very nice," Dorothy judged, "but aren't those pants supposed to be tighter?"

"They were when I bought them," Megan said. "I've lost a little weight."

Dorothy refrained from commenting. She said, "I like your Mexican wedding shirt. Is it new?"

"Yes, I picked it up on Olvera Street last Saturday. I was feeling depressed after getting my hair cut, so I decided to treat myself. I also got some earrings and a new poncho that will be good for when the evenings turn cool, now that I don't have that mane to keep my shoulders warm anymore." Megan forced a smile.

Dorothy could tell that her young friend was still regretting the loss of her hair, and she said, "You can always let it grow out again if you like, but it really does look better now that you don't have to try to hide the short part." Dorothy's fists clenched tightly. Her mother-tigress instincts were aroused whenever she thought about Megan's injury. She suppressed a shiver of fury as she rose from the bed. She said seriously, "You look lovely, Megan, and I hope you have the time of your life tonight. I can't tell you what it means to me to see you dating again." She kissed the girl tenderly on her cheek and chuckled, "Now I have to get back to my place and get a move on, or I'll be late for work. Not all of us have the night off, you know." She picked up her hair dryer and walked out, and a second later Megan could hear her entering her own apartment next door.

Megan sighed. Dorothy was so obviously delighted she had a date tonight that Megan didn't have the heart to admit she couldn't even remember what the young man looked like. She did recall that he was a sunbleached blonde and that yesterday at the music store he had seemed personable and presentable; but when she tried to conjure up his face she saw only blue eyes and a drooping lock of dark hair, high cheekbones and a long aristocratic nose—

Oh, God, was she never to be free of the von Kleists? First Erich and now Kurt haunted her, and she did not know how to exorcise them. In the weeks since she had last seen Kurt she'd tried every way imaginable to free herself of him. In Salzburg, against Peter's advice and even rejecting a telephoned plea from Max Bachmann himself, she had signed the meadow over to Liesl. A few weeks later, back in Los Angeles, when a strange man had appeared at her door, explained that he was an attorney acting as agent for Kurt von Kleist and tried to present her with a check for the amount of money Kurt had first offered her for the property, she had politely but firmly declined to accept it.

She had even cut her hair, as if by cutting the beautiful tresses that excited Kurt she was cutting him out of her life, severing the ties that stretched halfway around the world and still bound her to him. Like most symbolic actions this one had been pointless. She could shave her head if necessary, but there was no way she could be free of the lips Kurt had kissed so fiercely, the body that still tingled feverishly when she allowed herself to remember those moon-drenched moments on the sweeping lawn of Schloss von Kleist. Peter had told her she ought to go to bed with Kurt and thus get him out of her system. Would that have done it? Would allowing him to ravish her like one of his ancestors taking a peasant maid have made her see him as just a man, one of billions? No, no, of course she was better off the way she was—frustrated, unfulfilled, but at least with her self-respect intact.

She flitted around her apartment straightening pillows and wiping away nonexistent dust. The place was small, furnished with nondescript, rather shabby furniture, but she had personalized it with hanging plants and posters of music festivals. She rearranged the sheet music on her spinet piano, her one extravagance, for at least the fourth time. She was growing more tense by the second, worried not so much by the young instructor whose face she could not remember, as by the prospect of the first genuine date she had had since meeting Erich. This was the beginning of a new era in her life. What would she do? What would the man expect of her? Would he want to kiss her good-night? Would he want to—

The doorbell rang. Right on time, she noted, a good sign. She straightened her shoulders and marched across the room and flung open the door.

The man at the door was Kurt.

She stared at him, framed calmly in her doorway as if it were the most natural thing in the world that he should appear there. He was dressed more casually than she had ever seen him, in black slacks and a pale gray shirt open at the neck. Over his arm he carried a lightweight gray-and-black-checked jacket, and even in casual clothes he looked so suave, so impossibly handsome, that just seeing him made her ache. As she gazed hungrily at the long length of him her body felt stone-cold and empty, incapable of movement... except for her heart, which began to pound in an astonishing manner. She tried to breathe his name, but no sound came out. She was mesmerized by the blue eyes that still dominated her daydreams, and she wondered how she had ever thought she could escape him merely by fleeing halfway around the world.

Kurt peered down at her small face that was rigid with shock, and one corner of his mouth twitched slightly. He said, "Hello, Megan." When she remained mute he asked, "May I come in?"

She moved her dry mouth to speak, but nothing happened. She licked her lips and tried again. "I—I'm just going out," she croaked. "I have a—a date."

Kurt's eyes darkened. He said, "I've flown all the way from Europe just to see you, Megan. Don't you think you could cancel your date just this once?"

As if on cue they heard footsteps bounding up the stairs two at a time, and a young blond man in jeans and a U.C.L.A. sweatshirt appeared at the end of the corridor. "Hey, Megan," he called brightly, his tenor voice that of a trained singer, "I'm sorry I'm a little—" He halted abruptly at the sight of the tall man who stood beside the red-haired girl, regarding her possessively. "Hey," he repeated awkwardly, "did I misunderstand? I thought we were going to that concert tonight."

Before Megan could speak Kurt said flatly, "I'm afraid Megan's plans have been changed. She's going out with me tonight."

"Kurt!" Megan protested indignantly, coming out of her trance, but she didn't have the strength to defy him. She touched the younger man's arm lightly, ignoring Kurt's scowl, as she apologized, "I'm so very sorry. I was looking forward to going to the concert with you. Kurt is—my brother-in-law, and he just arrived in town unexpectedly. I had no idea—"

The younger man frowned petulantly. "Yeah, sure," he snorted, starting to turn away.

Megan pleaded, "Maybe some other time?"

He hesitated, running his eyes suggestively over Megan's body, then he glanced up at Kurt. "I don't think so," he grunted, and he stalked away, his hands deep in his jeans pockets.

As soon as he had disappeared down the stairs Megan turned furiously to Kurt. "How could you?" she demanded. "Who do you think you are to send him away like that?"

Kurt said mildly, "Actually, you are the one who sent him away. But if we are going to argue, I suggest we do it inside with the door closed." He nudged her back into her apartment and pulled the door shut. When the lock clicked behind him Kurt glanced around the tiny room before he looked at Megan again and asked, "How long have you been seeing that...jock—that's the term these days, isn't it?"

"He's not a jock," she said. "He's a music instructor."

"Indeed. Do you sleep with him?"

"No!" Megan blazed.

"No?" Kurt raised one eyebrow in polite disbelief. "He wanted to."

"For heaven's sake, Kurt, I only met the man yesterday."

Kurt laughed unpleasantly. "And already you're going out with him? That's quick work."

"We were going to a concert at the Hollywood Bowl, that's all."

Kurt's eyes narrowed. "No, that's not all, Megan. Haven't you learned by now that every man who looks at you wants to make love to you?"

Megan said, "That's just not true, Kurt, and even if it were, what business is it of yours? Don't you think I'm capable of fending off unwelcome advances?"

Kurt said, "Based on past experience, I'd say no."

She glared at him, then her anger ebbed away and she sank wearily into a chair, murmuring, "What's the use?" She waved a hand toward the sofa. "Sit down, Kurt, and tell me why you're here. Surely you didn't fly all the way from Austria just to insult me?" She watched him fold his long lean frame onto the worn couch. As he brushed his hair back with his scarred hand, she noticed that the lines on his face were more deeply engraved than they had been the last time she saw him. He looked as exhausted as she felt. She asked, "When did you get into town?"

He glanced at his watch. "About three hours ago. I had hoped to be here sooner, but it took some time for me to arrange to rent a car, then I had to leave my luggage at my hotel, and by that time it was rush hour on the freeway. The congestion, the smog—*mein Gott*, Megan, how do you stand it?"

She shrugged. "You learn to live with it. Where are you staying?"

He named a very expensive hotel in Beverly Hills.

"Where else?" Megan snorted. After a pause she continued lightly, "How is Liesl?"

"Very well, thank you. She's staying with friends now. She misses you."

Megan nodded. "I miss her, too." For a moment she couldn't think of anything to say. Then she asked again, "Kurt, why are you here?"

He said, "I had to—I wanted to know why you refused payment for the meadow."

Megan's eyes widened. "You traveled six thousand miles just to ask me that?" she asked incredulously. "Wouldn't a telegram or even a phone call have been quicker and cheaper?"

"I didn't worry about the cost," Kurt said.

"You never do."

He sat forward, his blue eyes aflame. "You really resent the money, don't you, Megan? Right from the beginning it's been the von Kleist fortune—such as it is—that you've hated. It's always prevented you from viewing me or my family objectively."

Megan shook her head. "It's not the money, Kurt, it's the arrogance that derives from it, this belief that you can make anyone do anything you want, whenever you want."

"Generally I can," he said cynically.

She jumped up, blazing with indignation. "Your money couldn't make me marry you," she shouted, "any more than it could keep Gabrielle from having a nervous breakdown! If you must know, I sent back the payment for that land because my pride, my Halliday pride, wouldn't allow me to accept it. There, you have your answer to your question, so get out! Get out!" She flung her door open and gestured melodramatically.

Slowly Kurt rose from the sofa. With a heavy sigh he walked to the door. When he spoke his voice was resigned. He said, "There was one other thing I wanted to tell you before I go, the main reason I wasn't able to come sooner. I've been talking to Max Bachmann. By signing the meadow over to Liesl, you've tied up the estate at least until she comes of age, but Bachmann and I have been discussing some sort of lease arrangement whereby the property could be utilized and still remain under von Kleist control."

"You're going to let them begin the mine?"

"Yes," Kurt said, "if Swanson's explorations indicate it would be worthwhile. It's not the way I would have liked it, but I think it is—inevitable." He paused. "You know, Max Bachmann is quite an interesting man. I've discovered to my surprise that he is as committed as I am to maintaining the historical and environmental integrity of the estate. We're organizing a committee comprised not only of him and me, but also of representatives from the people of Kleisthof, to oversee the operation and make sure the countryside is not adversely affected. The mine is going to mean a lot of new jobs in the area, probably an increase in the population. The revenues will also mean that the schloss can stay in the von Kleist family for a while longer." Kurt shrugged. "I just thought you'd want to know." He turned to leave.

Megan's heart lurched in her breast. Dear God, what was she doing? The man she loved had come halfway around the world to see her, and in a gesture worthy of Adelaide she was screaming like a fishwife and throwing him out! If he walked through that door now she knew she'd never see him again. She had to make him stay, if only for a little while longer. She had to store up a few more memories to cling to at night in her lonely bed.

Megan put her hand on Kurt's arm. When he looked down at her she smiled weakly, and said, "Please don't go, at least not like this. You and I always seem to end up yelling at each other, and then one of us storms out. I'd like, just this once, for us to part friends."

Kurt smiled warmly, and Megan's heart flipped over. He said, "I'd like that, too. What do you suggest?"

Love me, she wanted to cry. *Hold me, kiss me, make me yours!* But aloud she laughed shyly, "Well—I seem to have a pair of tickets to a concert that will go to waste if we don't use them. We could have dinner somewhere, I could show you a little of my city, and then we could go on up to the Hollywood Bowl and relax with some lovely music."

Kurt nodded. "I can't think of a more delightful way to spend an evening." Then he chuckled, "On the other hand.... But no, perhaps it would be best if you show me around Los Angeles."

They went to Little Tokyo and ate at a Japanese *teppan* restaurant where they sat on the floor and watched the chef prepare the meal right at their table. They chatted about impersonal things—weather, politics, music, art. Megan told Kurt about the time her mother had taken her as a child to the Los Angeles County Museum of Art to see Rembrandt's *Portrait of Titus*, which had just made headlines by bringing what was at the time the highest price ever paid for a single painting. "We stood in line for what seemed like hours," Megan reminisced, "and then finally we got to file into the room where the painting was displayed. I remember that the area was roped off and there were two armed guards flanking it. I don't know what I'd expected to see, but I do recall that I was very disappointed. It was just a picture of a little boy."

Kurt nodded sagely. "One of the tragedies of our age is that we equate quality with price. The most expensive painting must therefore be the best painting, when it would surely make more sense to say that the 'best' of any form of artwork is that which inspires the viewer and gives the most pleasure, whether it be a Rembrandt painting or a sculpture by Henry Moore or even an illustration in a magazine." He laughed slyly. "Just don't repeat what I said to any of the customers in my gallery!"

By the time they had reached the Hollywood Bowl, Megan felt relaxed and content in Kurt's presence. She accepted the fact that he would return to Austria and she would probably never see him again, and she knew that she would also regret not being his lover, but for the moment they were warm friends, gentle companions, and she was at peace.

They crossed the gigantic parking lot hand in hand, with Kurt carrying over his left arm the plaid stadium blanket Megan had insisted they would need. After exchanging their tickets for a pair of programs, Megan guided Kurt up the steps away from the whitewashed bleachers and onto the grassy slope at the back of the huge open-air auditorium. They spread their blanket on the grass where other groups of people were also opening up aluminum folding chairs and sleeping bags in preparation for the concert. Megan gestured toward the grandstand in front of the great white bandshell. "I've always preferred it up here on the grass. Those benches get so hard, and you can't move around."

Kurt smiled indulgently as Megan sprawled on the blanket. "That's because you're young," he laughed. "When you get to be my age you'll find that sitting on the ground can be just as cramping." His fingers brushed across Megan's cheek. "You are very young, aren't you, Megan? Much too young for those shadows. Those baby curls make you look about sixteen." He sighed, "I did so love your hair long."

Quivering at his touch, Megan said uneasily, "I really didn't have much choice. My hair was so uneven with that awful patch Ulrike had to shave off."

After a pause Kurt asked, "Did you know that

Ulrike Müller and Peter Swanson are engaged? They strike me as an unlikely couple."

Megan said, "I knew. Ulrike wrote and told me. She said that she's leaving the hospital to go into private practice, so that she can blend her career more smoothly with Peter's. And I think they'll be good for each other. She needs someone to remind her that she's still a young woman, and sometimes Peter could use a more mature, stabilizing influence."

Kurt said, "Oddly enough, I thought Swanson fancied you."

"Me?" Megan echoed innocently. "Oh, no, you're wrong about that."

Kurt shrugged and began looking over the program. The concert was a benefit for certain drought-stricken countries in western Africa, and various vocalists and musicians had donated their time. He noted, "Quite a varied program: a couple of Puccini arias, Debussy's *Engulfed Cathedral*, a sonata by Halstead—"

Megan jerked her head toward him. "What?"

Kurt ran his fingers down the page. "Right here, almost the last number. Sonata in A Minor for Violin and Piano, by Halstead. I'm afraid I don't know that work, although the name seems familiar."

Megan blanched. "I didn't know they were going to play that," she whispered hoarsely. "I don't think I would have come if I'd known."

Kurt stared at her. After a pause he muttered, "I assume this has something to do with Erich?"

She nodded. He said sternly, "Megan, you can't spend the rest of your life avoiding violins."

"I know, but—"

The stadium lights began to lower, and Kurt patted Megan's hand. He whispered, "Hush, darling, everything will be all right." He took off his jacket and settled back to listen with the serious intensity of the true musician.

In the dark Megan huddled rigid on the blanket, staring at the bandshell in front of her. She was deaf to the impassioned plea for donations that was made by the famous actor who was master of ceremonies for the benefit. She did not hear the familiar arias from *La Bohème* and *Madama Butterfly*, and the pianist who performed Debussy's exquisite and evocative tone poem could have played "Chopsticks" for all she knew. Her ears, her whole body, were tense, alert for the dreaded moment when she would have to sit there and listen to the husband-and-wife team of musicians, favorite concert artists in Latin America, play Philip Halstead's haunting sonata.

The opening chords echoed sweetly over the heads of the enrapt audience. The pianist sounded the theme and then with consummate skill softened his part to muted arpeggios as the violinist picked up the melody. Together the two musicians were weaving a tonal fabric that shimmered and rippled—"like satin sheets," Megan had once described it. She stared with open mouth at the stage and waited for the old familiar pain to come.

At this distance the couple in evening dress were

little more than irregular blobs, black baroque pearls in a glowing white shell. They played with great artistry, unaware that to one member of the audience the Halstead sonata symbolized all that had ever gone wrong with her marriage—with her life. The piece was not well-known. It had been composed by Philip Halstead, the man who founded the music school where Megan studied, and Erich had liked it so much that he made it his signature. When he and Megan performed the sonata, to her it had seemed almost as if they made love to music, and in her innocence she had imagined he shared her feelings—until one evening after a recital in a small college town in Pennsylvania, still tingling with that last triumphant chord, she had returned to their dressing room and found Erich and Lavinia wrapped in each other's arms.

She had thought that she would never again be able to hear the piece without remembering the purring sounds Lavinia had made while she kissed Erich, the way her arms had clung to his waist, pulling his thighs tight against hers. She had thought she would see once more the resentment and irritation that had flared in Erich's gray eyes as he looked over his mistress's shoulder at her, his wife, standing ashen faced in the doorway.

But now she realized to her amazement that the music no longer had the power to hurt her. She felt no pain, only—only pity. As she listened to the performance, analyzing it with her trained ear, she thought dispassionately, *they're very good, but we used to play it faster, and Erich always performed that phrase of the second theme pizzicato....*

Scanning the sea of heads between her and the stage, Megan wondered if anyone in the audience remembered or had even heard of Erich von Kleist. Quite possibly not. When he died he had been on the brink of fame, known to the handful of musical connoisseurs who recognize and appreciate real talent, but as yet unfamiliar to the general public. He had never had a chance to become a household word. Poor Erich, so brilliant, so gifted and tormented, dead so young. He had made a whipping boy of the shy young girl who was his wife, and she had hated him for it, but Megan knew now that he had been as much a victim as she was, his personality twisted by the circumstances of his birth. Probably the only thing that ever gave him any peace, any happiness, was his music.

She blinked, and as she watched the musicians hot tears trickled down her cheeks—tears for Erich, for the tragedy of his short unhappy life. She knew him now as she had never known him while he lived, and at last she forgave all.

Then Kurt's arms were around her, pulling her across the plaid blanket. His left hand slid down to the small of her back, pressing her close to him, while with his right he covered her ear, winding his fingers through her hair, holding her head against his chest so that the music was overpowered by the pounding of his heart. Megan clung to him, weeping away the pain and grief that had fermented inside her so long, barriers against love. An amorphous sound grew in her head like the disintegration of high brick walls. When Kurt slowly released her she discovered to her bewilderment that the roar she heard was the thunder of thousands of hands clapping their delight at the couple who had just finished playing.

Megan settled back on the blanket, brushing away the tears with her fingertips. She sniffled and smiled sheepishly at Kurt. "Forgive me. Romantic music affects me that way."

Kurt pulled his cigarette case from his jacket. When the lighter flared, Megan saw that his expression was bleak, but the flame died away, and in the dark his voice sounded neutral, guarded. Only the jerky movements of the glowing tip of the cigarette revealed his emotional state. He rasped, "Are you going to let your whole life be ruined by what Erich did to you, Megan? Are you never to be free of him?"

"But I am free of him," she said simply, smiling because she knew now that it was true.

"Just a second ago you cried because you loved him."

"Yes I did," she agreed, "and it's true, I did love Erich. *Did* love, past tense. Erich is dead now, and I've felt sorry for myself long enough." Kurt did not answer. Megan turned back to watch the stage. She listened to the final numbers, but later she could not have said what was played. She was surprised when she noticed spectators all around them rising and gathering up their blankets and folding chairs. In the lighted area down by the shell, stagehands began to clean up, oblivious to the masses of people streaming toward the exits.

She glanced expectantly at Kurt, but he did not move. He was puffing on another cigarette, and several butts smoldered on the grass beside him. Megan wondered what he was waiting for. In the spill of light from the stage Megan could see that he frowned at her, his hard mouth pursed, and he asked, "What makes you so certain you are over Erich?"

Shrugging, she said, "Well, for one thing, thinking back on those two years, I realize that at least part of what happened, I brought on myself. I was very young and—and very much afraid of being alone." Kurt tilted his head to one side and regarded her curiously. She explained, "When I met Erich, my mother had just died, and I was bewildered and unbearably lonely. Erich's proposal seemed like a gift from heaven, because it meant I would belong to someone again. Later, when I found out about Lavinia, I was still such a coward that I thought living on the fringes of his life would be better than trying to build one of my own. It was two years before I admitted I was wrong." She straightened her shoulders and said firmly, "But that's all behind me now. I'm a big girl, in charge of my own life. If being true to myself means being alone—well, I know I can do it."

There was a silence, and then as if the words were ripped from him Kurt choked, "I can't."

Megan stared. "What?"

He repeated harshly, "I can't. I can't go it alone any longer. I've lived that way for years, and I don't think I could stand it if I had to continue in the same way." He flung the cigarette aside and grasped her shoulders, shaking her lightly to make her understand. His face was tormented. He grated, "Except for my daughter, I've lost everything I ever cared about: Elisabeth, my family, my music—now even part of the estate. I've always prided myself on my self-sufficiency, but I've endured all I can. If anything else goes, it will be the end of me. Please, Megan, I need you to help me."

Megan gaped at him, speechless with shock. Could this be Kurt, Graf von Kleist, the lord of the manor, humbling himself, pleading with her?

When she did not speak, Kurt continued desperately, "Is it that you think I don't love you? Dear God, I've loved you ever since that first afternoon in my office at the schloss, when you almost fainted. I'll never forget how you looked, with your pale face and your long red hair—promise me you'll never cut your hair again, Megan—and those enormous green eyes. You were so obviously nervous and exhausted, but until your legs gave out you stood there defiantly, with such courage, a petite Fury challenging me to prove my absurd accusations. I knew before that interview was over that I was in love with you."

"But—but you certainly didn't act like it," Megan protested.

"I know. I acted like a swine. I was terrified—"

"Terrified?" Megan echoed. "I don't believe that. You've never been afraid of anything in your life."

"I was afraid of you," Kurt said, "afraid of the way you made me feel. It was unlike anything I had ever known before. For Elisabeth and me, love came slowly, a gentle flowering. With you— one look and I was lost. I refused to believe it could happen so fast. I told myself it was sexual attraction, that once I had you the need would go away. I didn't want to admit that anyone could have such power over me." He became aware that he was bruising her arms, and he released her with a sigh. "I've hurt you again," he murmured contritely. "That's all I ever seem to do, lashing out at you from frustration and hurt pride. The old von Kleist arrogance, I suppose."

Quickly Megan put her fingertips to his lips, hushing him. Her green eyes searched his face intently for any sign of the mockery and cynicism she usually saw there. She found none. Instead she found humility, anxiety—and the one emotion she had been sure she would never see. She whispered, "I love you, Kurt."

He stared at her, stiff with tension. She repeated, "I love you. I've loved you almost from the beginning." With a breathy sigh, he relaxed.

They gazed at each other silently, and passion sprang up between them, the feverish hunger they were helpless to deny. Kurt caught her hands in his and kissed the palms. The touch of his lips on her sensitive skin sent needlelike tremors shooting up her arms, and while she quivered he pushed her gently down onto the blanket. His jacket was a makeshift pillow, and she lay there looking up at the stars. She wriggled with delight as his long lean body moved over hers. He touched her more slowly than she had expected, with infinite tenderness, his lips and fingers tracing the curves of her body in a delicate exploration that left her languid, unwilling to resist. Knowing now that his need was as great as her own, her hands began to flutter avidly over his body, impatient with the clothes that came between them. She fumbled with the buttons on his shirt, as her fingers sought the pleasure points she had learned of that night in Austria, and Kurt's mouth trailed fire down her throat toward her breast—

Suddenly a rough voice shouted, "Hey, you kids, the show's over!"

Megan and Kurt both jumped as a shadowy figure grumbling, "Damned teenagers!" shone a flashlight in their faces. Quickly Kurt pulled Megan against him so that her naked breasts were shielded from the view of the usher who stood over them, chuckling ribaldly. "Sorry, folks," he leered, "but it's usually the young ones we have to run off from up here on the grass. You two had better go now; the performance is over and we're closing up. Why don't you just find a nice motel somewhere?" He ambled away, snickering, and Megan could feel Kurt's hand clench in anger.

As she hastily readjusted her shirt, she said, "Don't get upset, Kurt. It was our own stupid fault, letting something like that happen." She stood up, trying to laugh. "God, I was embarrassed. I felt like a teenager at a drive-in movie." When he glanced at her out of the corner of his eye, she added quickly, "Not that I had much experience with drive-ins. I was always too busy practicing the piano."

Kurt was still angry, but after a moment he relented and shrugged. "No, of course you are right. We should have been more—discreet. At least we won't need to worry about that sort of thing after we are married."

Megan stared up at him, her heart in her throat. She swallowed and whispered hoarsely, "Kurt, I never said I'd marry you."

He scowled. "What? What are you saying?"

She repeated, "I can't marry you, Kurt."

Even in the dim light she could see his face go pale. But before he could speak again they heard the usher call, "Hey, you two, get a move on!"

With a muttered curse Kurt handed Megan her purse and folded the blanket; then he strode toward the exit with her stumbling as she tried to keep up with him. When they reached Kurt's rented car, one of only half a dozen left in the gigantic parking lot, he opened her door and tossed the blanket into the back seat. As he leaned forward to switch on the ignition, she timidly touched his arm. "I'm sorry, Kurt, but I—"

"Shut up," he snapped.

Megan sank back into her seat. After a quick glance at a map, Kurt guided the car along the winding road away from the bowl and out of the Hollywood Hills. Even at this late hour traffic was heavy. Without comment he crossed the sleazy district that had once been the glamorous Sunset Strip, then continued southward until he reached posh Wilshire Boulevard. When he turned west toward Beverly Hills Megan was moved to ask, "Where are we going?"

Kurt looked grim. "You heard that man. We're going someplace where we can be alone and undisturbed. We have to talk."

After Kurt had left his car keys with the parking attendant at his hotel, he dragged Megan along the open passageway lined with tropical plants, past the Olympic-sized swimming pool, to his bungalow, where he shoved her inside and locked the door behind them. Megan surveyed the room curiously, absorbing the air of elegant understated luxury that seemed to waft from the hand-rubbed Swedish modern furniture and the ankle-deep wall-to-wall carpeting. "Some motel," she was muttering ironically, trying to interpret a gigantic abstract painting hung over the long low sofa, when suddenly Kurt caught her by the shoulders and turned her around to face him.

"Now," he demanded fiercely, "what is this nonsense about not marrying me?"

Megan bristled at his tone. This was the old arrogant Kurt she knew and resented. She choked, "Of all the unmitigated— Nonsense, is it? You mean the lord of the manor can't imagine anyone turning him down? Don't forget, I said no once before, too!"

He was having difficulty controlling his temper, she could tell. He said, "But you also just told me you loved me."

"Yes," she spat. "And a long time ago I told you I would never marry again. I've been married. I didn't like it."

His fingertips tightened on her arms. She was going to be bruised in the morning. "Damn it, Megan, you know you've never been married in any way that matters. The experience you had with Erich had nothing whatsoever to do with real marriage, the joyful union of two people who love each other." His tender words were so at odds with his irritable tone that she wanted to laugh. He said intensely, "Megan, I love you. You love me."

"Yes, I love you," she admitted reluctantly, "and I want you like hell. But you and I could never sustain a relationship. Look at us now. The only time we don't argue is when we're kissing. Our love is all—sound and fury, signifying nothing." She pulled away from him, and he released her. She went to the picture window, pushing the draperies aside with her hand to peer at the twinkling lights of the city, obscured even in the night by a murky haze. She sighed, "Besides that, Kurt, I don't think you know just what you're asking of me. At the schloss, when you proposed, if you'd gone about it differently I probably would have said yes. That time I spent in Austria seems almost magical, unreal—not the way it ended, of course, but at first, when everything was so beautiful, with music and dancing, like something from a fairy tale. If you had told me you loved me then, I might have believed that Cinderella could marry the prince and live happily ever after. Disillusion would have come later."

Kurt tried to protest, but Megan stopped him. "No, Kurt, let me finish, please." She took a deep breath. "When I came home to dear old smoggy Los Angeles, I got my perspective back. I saw myself as I am, as I was meant to be. I'm Megan Halliday. I was born and raised in this crazy city, and it's where I belong, with the freeways and the beaches. I play the piano in a bar, and at night I go home to my dinky apartment. I was not meant to be a concert pianist, any more than I was meant to live in a mansion and be a—a—what's the word for countess?"

"Gräfin," Kurt supplied.

"Thank you." She let the curtain fall back into place. "That's another thing. Can you imagine me as the Gräfin von Kleist, when I don't even speak German?"

Kurt said impatiently, "You're just making excuses and you know it. Megan, I need you."

She stared up at his dear lined face and wondered how long she could hold out. Why wouldn't he listen to reason? She was sure the only way they could ever get along would be if she gave in to him all the time, became a doormat again. Why couldn't he understand that she was terrified of losing the independence she had struggled so hard to achieve? She argued unconvincingly, "That's all you think about it, isn't it, Kurt? *Your* needs, *your* wants—"

"To hell with this," he gritted. "I know one thing we've both wanted from the very beginning." He pulled her fiercely into his arms.

"No!" she squealed, pushing impotently at his shoulders with fingers that had a distressing tendency to curl instead into the dark hair at his nape. "I don't want you to do this."

"So stop me," he mocked, his mouth scorching her throat.

Her control was slipping away, and she felt herself drowning in her own desire. She whimpered, "But you're not being fair—"

He molded her body to his, and one hand curved possessively around a full breast. Against her mouth he laughed sardonically, "Life is unfair. Now be quiet; you talk too much."

Later she had no memory of him carrying her into the bedroom, yet she knew he must have done, for her knees suddenly felt so weak she could not stand. She could not have said who undressed first, or if they undressed each other, but somehow their clothes were piled in an untidy heap on the floor at the foot of the bed. They lay naked on the cool cream-colored linen sheets, breathless, not touching, devouring each other with their eyes, as they waited for one of them to bridge the last, easiest and yet most difficult gap between them.

"I...I love you, Kurt," Megan said huskily, as his scarred hand reached out to stroke her rose-tipped breast. Quickly she caught his long fingers in her own, holding them so that he could not touch her.

His blue eyes narrowed. "Does it bother you?" he asked quietly.

She shook her head. "Oh, no, of course not!" She kissed the inflexible fingers one by one. "It does hurt me to know that you have been hurt, that you suffered." After another hesitation she whispered shyly, "Let me touch you first. Let me...know that I can touch you."

He searched her face intently, saw the nervousness and uncertainty in her expression, and with a reassuring smile he relaxed against his pillow and allowed her to begin her exploration of him.

Despite her marriage Megan was almost totally inexperienced, and she was curious about this marvelous thing called a man's body. She wanted to know every square inch of him. She nuzzled the palm of the hand she held, then let her sensitive fingertips slide up over his wrist and along his strong arm. He was very tan, except for the paler streak where he wore his wristwatch, and the fine dark hair on his arms was bleached gold at the tips. Her hands moved over his powerful shoulders, feeling not only the warm brown skin but also the hard bones underneath. She shaped the column of his neck with her thumbs, searching out the pulse points. A V of darker skin at the collar line pointed toward the triangle of thick, almost black hair covering his broad chest. She wove her fingers into that hair, delighting at the resiliency of those crisp short curls as she tugged gently. His heart pounded beneath her palms. When her hands slipped over his flat stomach to probe an unsuspected appendectomy scar, she could feel him shudder.

Then she touched him intimately. She gloried in his obvious driving need of her, his gasping response. Her own body was responding wildly to her studied caress. Her breasts grew firm, the nipples taut and inviting, and deep inside her she throbbed with a maddening ache. By the time she ran her fingers over his muscular thighs and down the length of his legs to sinewy feet and square toes, she was breathless and shaking.

She began her exploration again, this time with her lips. His skin was damp and faintly salty. He groaned incoherently and pulled her on top of him.

"My God, you've got a lot of faith in my self-control!" he rasped, burying his face between her breasts as he crushed her body over his. He laced his fingers into her red curls and forced her mouth down. They locked together in a kiss that was fierce, fluid, biting, a total blending, and their mouths still devoured each other when, with a single lithe movement, almost before she realized it, Kurt took control of her. The sheets were cool and silky against her heated back as he possessed her completely.

He was the master now, the explorer, guiding her into realms of sensation she had never dreamed of. Her green eyes stared up into his, wide with astonishment and gratitude until they glazed erotically, and her voice rose with the music of passion, a series of sharp staccato moans like little grace notes of pleasure. Like vibrant instruments playing a duet of desire, they flew on a rising cadenza of love and need and want, until at last they exploded together into the finale.

Later, when the sighing had stopped, and flushed and fevered limbs unwound, Megan lay with her head on his chest, listening to the slow satisfied throb of his heart under her ear. Her drowsy eyes glistened with tears of bemused joy. Kurt's hand absently stroked her spine while he nibbled at her bright curls and whispered endearments in German. After a while he asked quietly, "You see how it is with us, Megan, how it must always be?"

"Yes," she murmured. The slight movement of her bruised lips ruffled the hair on his chest.

He had flipped off the light, and in the dark his deep voice went on, "Knowing what we share, now will you say you'll marry me?"

The room was so still that only the lurch of his heart told her he waited anxiously for her answer. After a moment Megan said softly, "Yes."

He gave a great sigh of relief as if he had been holding his breath. Shifting her weight slightly so that she lay comfortably in the crook of his arm, he brushed his lips across her tousled hair. "Then, go to sleep, *Liebling*," he whispered. "We have all the time in the world now."

THE SUN WAS SINKING INTO THE PACIFIC when from the porthole of the jumbo jet Megan watched the crossed arches of the Visitors' Center of the Los Angeles International Airport disappear beneath a layer of brown smog. She wondered if Dorothy still stood at the window in the terminal, following the lights of the giant plane as it headed out to sea and then banked steeply over Malibu, turning inland to begin its transcontinental flight. When they crossed the Tehachapi Mountains and she lost sight of the city that had been her birthplace but was now no longer home, Megan sank back into her seat with a sigh.

Beside her, her husband asked quietly, "Tired, darling?"

She shrugged. "Oh, a little. The past few days have been so hectic, with all the packing and everything." Glancing sidelong at him, she grinned wickedly. "Not much sleep at night, either."

Kurt chuckled. "I promise that now you may rest—at least until we get to London." He caught her left hand in his long fingers and toyed with her rings. Even in the muted cabin light the square-cut emerald on her gold filigree wedding band flashed green fire. Megan had been genuinely astonished when Kurt told her he wanted them to be married in California, for she had assumed that he would prefer to wait until Liesl could join them. Although Kurt had made the excuse that it would be less complicated if she reentered Austria as his wife, rather than on a tourist visa, he'd admitted to himself that his motive was far simpler: sheer cowardice. He had been deathly afraid that if he did not put his mark of possession on her at once, he would lose her again.

And now at last she was his—for however long God granted them.

He wondered if he was being selfish, asking too much of her by expecting her to leave her homeland and live with him in an alien country. He would do everything in his power to make her new life a happy one. There was so much he wanted to give her. He knew he was going to enjoy spoiling her. But he also knew that his greatest pleasure, as well as his most sacred duty, would be to erase those violet shadows that marred her young face, legacies of a past best forgotten....

Watching her drooping mouth as she stared out the window, Kurt said suddenly, "*Liebling*, I have a present for you."

She turned to look up at him curiously. "Another one?"

"Of course, you won't get it till Christmas, but I think now is the right time to tell you." He paused for tantalizing seconds before he said, "I've arranged for your friend Dorothy to come spend Christmas with us in Vienna."

Megan's green eyes widened joyfully, and with a squeal of delight she tried to fling herself into his arms—only to be restrained by her safety belt.

Kurt pushed her down into her seat, teasing, "Control yourself, Megan. A *Gräfin* must behave more circumspectly. Besides, it's a long, long time until we get to London."

Her pale face glowed, and she blinked back tears of gratitude. "Oh, Kurt," she sighed, "I—I thought I'd never see her again."

"Of course you will," he said roughly, humbled by the magnitude of the sacrifice she had been willing to make for him. He would have to work hard to be worthy of that sacrifice. He must never try to forge her wedding ring into a shackle, demand more of her than she could willingly give. "Someday we'll return to Los Angeles," he said, raising her hand to his lips and kissing the fingertips one by one. His warm breath tickled her skin. "After all," he murmured, his voice low and sensuous, "our children will have to learn about their mother's heritage, too." And despite the seat belts, he bent to her and his mouth came down hard on hers.

HARLEQUIN SUPERROMANCE

GREAT NEW OFFER!

HARLEQUIN SUPERROMANCE 6
MAURA MACKENZIE
SWEET SEDUCTION

HARLEQUIN SUPERROMANCE #5
CLOUD OVER PARADISE
ABRA TAYLOR

Get all the exciting new
HARLEQUIN SUPERROMANCES
the moment they come off the press!

NEVER BEFORE PUBLISHED

HARLEQUIN SUPERROMANCE®

Contemporary Love Stories

NOW! Your chance to receive all the books in this exciting new series the moment they come off the press!

BEST-SELLING SERIES

HARLEQUIN SUPERROMANCES are the newest best-sellers in the North American romance market.

And no wonder.

EXCITING!

Each HARLEQUIN SUPERROMANCE contains so much adventure, romance and conflict that it will hold you spellbound until the tumultuous conclusion.

DRAMATIC!

HARLEQUIN SUPERROMANCE gives you more! More of everything Harlequin is famous for. Spellbinding narratives... captivating heros and heroines... settings that stir the imagination.

1981 brings you...

HARLEQUIN SUPERROMANCES novels every other month, commencing in February with #5 and #6.

Each volume contains more than 380 pages of exciting romance reading.

Don't miss this opportunity!

Complete and mail the Subscription Reservation Coupon on the following page TODAY!

HARLEQUIN SUPEROMANCE
SUBSCRIPTION RESERVATION COUPON

Complete and mail TODAY to

Harlequin Reader Service

In U.S.A.
901 Fuhrmann Blvd.
Buffalo, NY 14203.

In Canada
649 Ontario St.
Stratford, Ont. N5A 6W4

Please reserve my subscription to the 2 NEW HARLEQUIN SUPEROMANCES published every eight weeks (12 a year). Every eight weeks I will receive 2 NEW SUPEROMANCES at the low price of $2.50 each (total—$5). There are no shipping and handling or any other hidden charges, and I am free to cancel at any time after taking as many or as few novels as I wish.

MY PRESENT SUBSCRIPTION NUMBER IS_____

NAME_____
(Please Print)

ADDRESS_____

CITY_____

STATE/PROV._____

ZIP/POSTAL CODE_____

Offer expires July 31, 1981
Prices subject to change without notice.

BPC